Praise for *The Light Behind the Window*

'A fast-paced, suspenseful story flitting between the present day and World War II . . . Riley expertly weaves Emilie's story into a dual narrative . . . A real old-fashioned romance which manages to have a compelling narrative as well as something of a history lesson in the Special Operations Executive. Brilliant escapism'

Red

'A beautifully written book that secures Riley's authorial status and proves that her golden penmanship is no mere fluke . . . This is the perfect literary novel to move those readers who wish for something more fulfilling than chick-lit, yet just as entertaining, witty and heart-stopping. The language is dramatic yet truthful and Riley has such a delicate touch with mystery and intrigue that it's difficult to predict where the plot is going . . . Riley's descriptive nuances are so evocative a TV drama is bound to be imminent. A literal and literary page-turner'

WeLoveThisBook.co.uk

Praise for *The Girl on the Cliff*

'[Lucinda Riley] manipulates the strands
of her plot with skill'
Independent on Sunday

'An emotionally charged saga . . . Riley is a writer to watch'
Sunday Express

'Lucinda Riley knows how to write a captivating
novel . . . it's layered, it's intricate, it's just
brilliant . . . a truly brilliant read'
Chick Lit Reviews

'[A] haunting and engrossing new novel . . . Superb
characterization, atmospheric locations and a well-
paced narrative keep the pages turning and the
imagination in thrall . . . Perceptive, warm and
exquisitely wrought, *The Girl on the Cliff* is
another triumph for a talented author'
Burnley Express

'An enchanting and mysterious story of hope
after loss, populated with warm characters'
Candis

The Midnight Rose

Lucinda Riley was born in Ireland and wrote her first novel at twenty-four. *Hothouse Flower* was a Richard and Judy Book Club choice and became a number one international bestseller. Since then, her novels have gone on to sell over three million copies worldwide and her books are translated into twenty-six languages. She lives in Norfolk and the south of France with her husband and four children.

Also by Lucinda Riley

Hothouse Flower

The Girl on the Cliff

The Light Behind the Window

The Midnight Rose

LUCINDA RILEY

PAN BOOKS

First published 2013 by Macmillan

This edition published 2014 by Pan Books
an imprint of Pan Macmillan, a division of Macmillan Publishers Limited
Pan Macmillan, 20 New Wharf Road, London N1 9RR
Basingstoke and Oxford
Associated companies throughout the world
www.panmacmillan.com

ISBN 978-1-4472-1843-2

A CIP catalogue record for this book is available from the British Library.

Typeset by Ellipsis Digital Limited, Glasgow
Printed and bound by CPI Group (UK) Ltd, Croydon, CR0 4YY

Visit **www.panmacmillan.com** to read more about all our books
and to buy them. You will also find features, author interviews and
news of any author events, and you can sign up for e-newsletters
so that you're always first to hear about our new releases.

For Leonora

Let my thoughts come to you, when I am gone, like the afterglow of sunset at the margin of starry silence.

Rabindranath Tagore

Darjeeling, India,
February 2000

Prologue

Anahita

I am a hundred years old today. Not only have I managed to survive a century, but I've also seen in a new millennium.

As the dawn breaks and the sun begins to rise over Mount Kanchenjunga beyond my window, I lie on my pillows and smile to myself at the utter ridiculousness of the thought. If I were a piece of furniture, an elegant chair for example, I would be labelled an antique. I would be polished, restored and proudly put on show as a thing of beauty. Sadly, that isn't the case with my human frame, which has not mellowed like a fine piece of mahogany over its lifetime. Instead, my body has deteriorated into a sagging hessian sack containing a collection of bones.

Any 'beauty' in me that might be deemed valuable lies hidden deep inside. It is the wisdom of one hundred years lived on this earth, and a heart that has beaten a steady accompaniment to every conceivable human emotion and behaviour.

One hundred years ago, to this very day, my parents, in the manner of all Indians, consulted an astrologer to tell them about the future of their newborn baby girl. I believe I still have

3

the soothsayer's predictions for my life amongst the few possessions of my mother that I've kept. I remember them saying that I was to be long-lived, but in 1900, I realise, my parents assumed this meant that, with the gods' blessing, I would survive into my fifties.

I hear a gentle tap on my door. It is Keva, my faithful maid, armed with a tray of English Breakfast tea and a small jug of cold milk. Tea taken the English way is a habit I've never managed to break, even though I've lived in India – not to mention Darjeeling – for the past seventy-eight years.

I don't answer Keva's knock, preferring on this special morning to be alone with my thoughts a while longer. Undoubtedly Keva will wish to talk through the events of the day, will be eager to get me up, washed and dressed before my family begins to arrive.

As the sun begins to burn off the clouds covering the snow-capped mountains, I search the blue sky for the answer I've pleaded with the heavens to give me every morning of the past seventy-eight years.

Today, please, I beg the gods, for I have known in each hour that has ticked by since I last saw my child that he still breathes somewhere on this planet. If he had died, I would have known the moment it happened, as I have for all those in my life whom I've loved, when they have passed over.

Tears fill my eyes and I turn my head to the nightstand by my bed to study the one photograph I have of him, a cherubic two-year-old sitting smiling on my knee. It was given to me by my friend, Indira, along with his death certificate a few weeks after I'd been informed of my son's death.

A lifetime ago, I think. The truth is, my son is now an old man too. He will celebrate his eighty-first birthday in October of this year. But even with *my* powers of imagination, it's impossible for me to see him as such.

I turn my head determinedly away from my son's image, knowing that today I deserve to enjoy the celebration my family has planned for me. But somehow, on all these occasions, when I see my other child and her children, and her children's children, the absence of my son only feeds the pain in my heart, reminding me he has always been missing.

Of course, they believe, and always have, that my son died seventy-eight years ago.

'Maaji, see, you even have his death certificate! Leave him to his rest,' my daughter, Muna, would say with a sigh. 'Enjoy the family you have living.'

After all these years, I understand Muna becomes frustrated with me. And she is of course right to. She wants to be enough, just her alone. But a lost child is something that can never be replaced in a mother's heart.

And for today, my daughter will have her way. I will sit in my chair and enjoy watching the dynasty I have spawned. I won't bore them with my stories of India's history. When they arrive in their fast Western jeeps, with their children playing on their battery-operated gadgets, I will not remind them how Indira and I climbed the steep hills around Darjeeling on horseback, that electricity and running water in any home were once rare, or of my voracious reading of any tattered book I could get my hands on. The young are irritated by stories of the past; they wish to live only in the present, just as I did when I was their age.

I can imagine that most of my family are not looking forward to flying halfway across India to visit their great-grandmother on her hundredth birthday, but perhaps I'm being

LUCINDA RILEY

hard on them. I've thought a great deal in the past few years about why the young seem to be uncomfortable when they're with the old; they could learn so many things they need to know from us. And I've decided that their discomfort stems from the fact that, in our fragile physical presence, they become aware of what the future holds for them. They can only see, in their full glow of strength and beauty, how eventually they will be diminished one day too. They don't know what they will gain.

How can they begin to see inside us? Understand how their souls will grow, their impetuousness be tamed and their selfish thoughts be dimmed by the experiences of so many years?

But I accept that this is nature, in all its glorious complexity. I have ceased to question it.

When Keva knocks at the door for a second time, I admit her. As she talks at me in fast Hindi, I sip my tea and run over the names of my four grandchildren and eleven great-grandchildren. At a hundred years old, one wants to at least prove that one's mind is still in full working order.

The four grandchildren my daughter gave me have each gone on to become successful and loving parents themselves. They flourished in the new world that independence from the British brought to India, and their children have taken the mantle even further. At least six of them, from what I recall, have started their own businesses or are in a professional trade. Selfishly, I wish that one of my extended offspring had taken an interest in medicine, had followed after me, but I realise that I can't have everything.

As Keva helps me into the bathroom to wash, I consider that my family have had a mixture of luck, brains and family connections on their side. And that my beloved India has probably another century to go before the millions who still starve on her streets gain some modicum of their basic human needs. I have done my best to help over the years, but I realise my efforts are a mere ripple in the ocean against a roaring tide of poverty and deprivation.

Sitting patiently whilst Keva dresses me in my new sari – a birthday present from Muna, my daughter – I decide I won't think these maudlin thoughts today. I've attempted where I can to improve those lives that have brushed against mine, and I must be content with that.

'You look beautiful, Madam Chavan.'

As I look at my reflection in the mirror, I know that she is lying, but I love her for it. My fingers reach for the pearls that have sat around my neck for nearly eighty years. In my will, I have left them to Muna.

'Your daughter arrives at eleven o'clock, and the rest of the family will be here an hour later. Where shall I put you until they come?'

I smile at her, feeling much like a mahogany chair. 'You may put me in the window. I want to look at my mountains,' I say. She helps me up, steers me gently to the armchair and sits me down.

'Can I bring you anything else, Madam?'

'No. You go now to the kitchen and make sure that cook of ours has the lunch menu under control.'

'Yes, Madam.' She moves my bell from the nightstand to the table at my side and quietly leaves the room.

I turn my face into the sunlight, which is starting to stream through the big picture windows of my hilltop bungalow. As I bask in it like a cat, I remember the friends who have already passed over and won't be joining me today for my celebration.

Indira, my most beloved friend, died over fifteen years ago. I confess that was one of the few moments in my life when I have broken down and wept uncontrollably. Even my devoted daughter could not match the love and friendship Indira showed me. Self-absorbed and flighty until the moment she died, Indira was there when I needed her most.

I look across to the writing bureau which sits in the alcove opposite me, and can't help but think about what is concealed inside its locked drawer. It is a letter, and it runs over three hundred pages. It is written to my beloved son and tells the story of my life from the beginning. As the years passed, I began to worry that I would forget the details, that they would become blurred and grainy in my mind, like the reel of a silent black-and-white film. If, as I believe to this day, my son is alive and if he were ever returned to me, I wanted to be able to present him with the story of his mother and her enduring love for her lost child. And the reasons why she had had to leave him behind . . .

I began to write it when I was in middle age, believing then that I might be taken at any time. There it has sat for nearly fifty years, untouched and unread, because he never came to find me, and I still haven't found him.

Not even my daughter knows the story of my life before she arrived on the planet. Sometimes I feel guilty for never revealing the truth to her. But I believe it is enough that she has known my love when her brother was denied it.

I glance at the bureau, viewing in my mind's eye the yellowing pile of paper inside it. And I ask the gods to guide me. When I die, as surely I must soon, I would be horrified for it to fall into the wrong hands. I ponder for a few seconds on whether I should light a fire and ask Keva to place the papers onto it. But no, I shake my head instinctively. I can never bring myself to do that, just in case I do find him. There is still hope. After all, I've lived to a hundred; I may live to a hundred and ten.

But whom to entrust it to, in the meantime, just in case . . . ?

I mentally scan my family members, taking them in generations. At each name, I listen for guidance. And it's on the name of one of my great-grandsons that I pause.

Ari Malik, the eldest child of my eldest grandson, Vivek. I chuckle slightly as the shiver runs up my spine – the signal I've had from those above who understand so much more than I ever can. Ari, the only member of my extended family to be blessed with blue eyes. Other than my beloved lost child.

I concentrate hard to bring to mind his details; with eleven great-grandchildren, I comfort myself, a person half my age would struggle to remember. And besides, they are spread out all over India these days, and I rarely see them.

Vivek, Ari's father, has been the most financially successful of my grandchildren. He was always clever, if a little dull. He is an engineer and has earned enough to provide his wife and three children with a very comfortable life. If my memory serves me, Ari was educated in England. He was always a bright little thing, though quite what he's been doing since he left school escapes me. Today, I decide, I will find out. I will watch him. And I'm sure I'll know whether my current instinct is correct.

With that settled, and feeling calmer now that a solution to my dilemma is perhaps at hand, I close my eyes and allow myself to doze.

*

9

'Where is he?!' Samina Malik whispered to her husband. 'He swore to me that he wouldn't be late for this,' she added, as she surveyed the other, fully present members of Anahita's extended family. They were clustered around the old lady in the elegant drawing room of her bungalow, plying her with presents and compliments.

'Don't panic, Samina,' Vivek comforted his wife, 'our son will be here.'

'Ari said he'd meet us at the station so we could come up the hill together as a family at ten o'clock . . . I swear, Vivek, that boy has no respect for his family, I—'

'Hush, *pyari*, he's a busy young man, and a good boy, too.'

'You think so?' asked Samina. 'I'm not so sure. Every time I call his apartment, a different female voice answers. You know what Mumbai is like; full of Bollywood hussies and sharks,' she whispered, not wishing any other member of the family to overhear their conversation.

'Yes, and our son is twenty-five years old now and running his own business. He can take care of himself,' Vivek replied.

'The staff are waiting for him to arrive so they can bring in the champagne and make the toast. Keva is concerned your grandmother will become too tired if we leave it much longer.' Samina sighed. 'If Ari's not here in the next ten minutes, I'll tell them to continue without him.'

'I told you, there will be no need for you to do that,' Vivek said, smiling broadly as Ari, his favourite son, entered the room. 'Your mother was in a panic, as always,' he told Ari, smiling as he clasped his son in a warm embrace.

'You promised to be there at the station. We waited an hour! Where were you?' Samina frowned at her handsome son but, as always, she knew it was a losing battle against the tide of his charm.

'Ma, forgive me.' Ari gave his mother a winning smile and took her hands in his. 'I was delayed, and I did try to call your cellphone. But, as usual, it was switched off.'

Ari and his father shared a smirk. Samina's inability to use her cellphone was a family joke.

'Anyway, I'm here now,' he said, looking around at the rest of his clan. 'Did I miss anything?'

'No, and your great-grandmother has been so busy greeting the rest of her family, let's hope she hasn't noticed your late arrival,' replied Vivek.

Ari turned and looked through the crowd of his own blood to the matriarch whose genes had spun invisible threads down through the generations. As he did so, he saw her bright, inquisitive eyes pinned on him.

'Ari! You have thought to join us at last.' She smiled. 'Come and kiss your great-grandmother.'

'She may be a hundred today, but your grandmother misses nothing,' Samina whispered to Vivek.

As Anahita opened her frail arms to Ari, the crowd of relations parted and all eyes in the room turned to him. Ari walked towards her and knelt in front of her, showing his respect with a deep *pranaam* and waiting for her blessing.

'Nani,' he greeted her using the affectionate pet name that all her grandchildren and great-grandchildren addressed her by. 'Forgive me for being late. It's a long journey from Mumbai,' he explained.

As he looked up, he could see her eyes boring into him in the peculiar way they always did, as if she were assessing his soul.

'No matter,' she said as her shrunken, childlike fingers touched his cheek with the light brush of a butterfly wing. 'Although –' she lowered her voice to a whisper so only he could hear – 'I always find it useful to check I have set my alarm to the correct time the night before.' She gave him a surreptitious wink, then indicated that he was to stand. 'You and I will speak later. I can see Keva is eager to start the proceedings.'

'Yes, Nani, of course,' said Ari, feeling a blush rising to his cheeks as he stood. 'Happy birthday.'

As he walked back towards his parents, Ari wondered just how his great-grandmother could have known the exact reason why he was late today.

The day progressed as planned, with Vivek, as the eldest of Anahita's grandchildren, making a moving speech about her remarkable life. As the champagne flowed, tongues loosened and the peculiar tension of a family gathered together after too long apart began to ease. The naturally competitive edge of the siblings blurred as they re-established their places in the family hierarchy, and the younger cousins lost their shyness and found common ground.

'Look at your son!' commented Muna, Anahita's daughter, to Vivek. 'His girl cousins are swooning all over him. It will be time for him to think of marriage soon,' she added.

'I doubt that's how he sees it,' grumbled Samina to her mother-in-law. 'These days, young men seem to play the field into their thirties.'

'You will not arrange anything for him, then?' enquired Muna.

'We will, of course, but I doubt he'll agree.' Vivek sighed. 'Ari is of a new generation, the master of his own universe. He has his business and travels the world. Times have changed, Ma, and Samina and I must allow our children some choice in picking their husbands and wives.'

'Really?' Muna raised an eyebrow. 'That's very modern of you, Vivek. After all, you two haven't done so badly together.'

'Yes, Ma,' agreed Vivek, taking his wife's hand. 'You made a good choice for me.' He smiled.

'But we're swimming against an impossible current,' said Samina. 'The young do as they wish these days, and make their own decisions.' Wishing to change the subject, she glanced across to Anahita. 'Your mother seems to be enjoying the day,' she commented to Muna. 'She really is a miracle, a wonder of nature.'

'Yes,' Muna sighed, 'but I do worry about her up here in the hills with only Keva to care for her. It gets so cold in the winter and it can't be good for her old bones. I've asked her many times to come and live with us in Guhagar so that we can watch over her. But, of course, she refuses. She says she feels closer to her spirits up here and, of course, her past too.'

'Her *mysterious* past.' Vivek raised an eyebrow. 'Ma, do you think you'll ever persuade her to tell you who your father was? I know he died before you were born, but the details have always seemed sketchy to me.'

'It mattered when I was growing up, and I remember plaguing her with questions, but now,' Muna shrugged, 'if she wants to keep her secrets, she can. She could not have been a more loving parent to me and I don't wish to upset her.' As Muna glanced over and looked at her mother fondly, Anahita caught her eye and beckoned her daughter towards her.

'Yes, Maaji, what is it?' Muna asked as she joined her mother.

'I'm a little tired now.' Anahita stifled a yawn. 'I wish to rest. And in one hour I want you to bring my great-grandson, Ari, to see me.'

'Of course.' Muna helped her mother to stand, and walked her through her relations. Keva, as ever hovering close by her mistress, stepped forward. 'My mother wishes to have a rest, Keva. Can you take her and settle her?'

'Of course, it has been a long day.'

Muna watched them leave the room and went back to join Vivek and his wife. 'She's taking a rest, but she's asked me if Ari will go and see her in one hour.'

'Really?' Vivek frowned. 'I wonder why.'

'Who knows the workings of my mother's mind?' Muna said, sighing.

'Well, I'd better tell him, I know he was talking about leaving soon. He has some business meeting in Mumbai first thing tomorrow morning.'

'Well, just for once, his family will come first,' said Samina firmly. 'I will go and find him.'

When Ari was told by his mother that his great-grandmother wished an audience with him in an hour's time, he was, as his father had predicted, not happy at all.

'I can't miss that plane,' he explained. 'You must understand, Ma, that I have a business to run.'

'Then I will ask your father to go and tell his grandmother that on her hundredth birthday, her eldest great-grandchild could not spare the time to speak with her as she had requested.'

'But, Ma—' Ari saw his mother's grim expression and sighed. 'Okay,' he nodded. 'I will stay. Excuse me, I must try and find a signal somewhere in this place to make a call and postpone the meeting.'

Samina watched her son as he walked away from her, staring intently at his cellphone. He'd been a determined child from the day he was born, and there was no doubt that she had indulged her firstborn, as any mother did. He'd always been special, from the moment he'd opened his eyes and she'd stared at the blueness of them in shock. Vivek had teased her endlessly about them, questioning his wife's fidelity. Until they'd visited Anahita and she'd announced that Muna's dead father had also been the owner of eyes of a similar colour.

Ari's skin was lighter than that of the rest of his siblings, and his startling looks had always attracted attention. With the amount of it he had received over his twenty-five years, there was no doubt he had an arrogance about him. But his saving grace had always been his sweetness of character. Out of all her children, Ari had always been the most loving towards her, at her side in an instant if there was a problem. Up until the time he'd taken off for Mumbai, announcing he was starting his own business . . .

Nowadays, the Ari who visited his family seemed harder, self-absorbed, and if she were being frank, Samina found she liked him less and less. Walking back towards her husband, she prayed it was a stage that would pass.

'My great-grandson may come in now,' Anahita announced, as Keva sat her up in bed and fluffed the pillows behind her head.

'Yes, Madam. I will get him.'

'And I do not wish for us to be disturbed.'

'No, Madam.'

'Good afternoon, Nani,' said Ari as he walked briskly into the room a few seconds later. 'I hope you are feeling more rested now?'

'Yes.' Anahita indicated the chair. 'Please, Ari, sit down. And I apologise for disrupting your business plans tomorrow.'

'Really,' Ari felt the blood rushing to his cheeks for the second time that day, 'it's no problem at all.' He watched as she gazed at him with her penetrating eyes, and wondered how she seemed to be able to read his mind.

'Your father tells me you're living in Mumbai and that you now run a successful business.'

'Well, I wouldn't describe it as successful right now,' Ari said. 'But I'm working very hard to make it so in the future.'

'I can see that you're an ambitious young man. And I'm sure that one day your business will bear fruit as you hope it will.'

'Thank you, Nani.'

Ari watched as his great-grandmother gave the ghost of a smile. 'Of course, it may not bring you the contentment you believe it will. There's more to life than work and riches. Still, that's for you to discover,' she added. 'Now, Ari, I have something I wish to give you. Please, open the writing bureau with this key, and take out the pile of paper you'll find inside it.'

Ari took the key from his great-grandmother's fingers, twisted it in the lock and removed an ageing manuscript from inside it.

'What is this?' he asked her.

'It is the story of your great-grandmother's life. I wrote it to keep a record for my lost son. Sadly, I've never found him.'

Ari watched as Anahita's eyes became watery. He'd heard some talk from his father years ago about the son who had died in infancy in England when his great-grandmother had been over there during the Great War. If his memory served him right, he thought she'd had to leave him behind when she returned to India. Apparently, Anahita had refused to believe that her son was dead.

'But I thought—'

'Yes, I'm sure you've been told I have his death certificate. And I'm simply a sad and perhaps mad mother who is unable to accept her beloved son's passing.'

Ari shifted uncomfortably in his chair. 'I have heard of the story,' he admitted.

'I know what my family think, and what you almost certainly think too,' Anahita stated firmly. 'But believe me, there are more things in heaven and earth than can be explained in a man-made document. There is a mother's heart, and her soul, which tells her things that cannot be ignored. And I will tell you now that my son is not dead.'

'Nani, I believe you.'

'I understand that you do not.' Anahita shrugged. 'But I don't mind. However, it's partly my fault that my family don't believe me. I've never explained to them what happened all those years ago.'

'Why not?'

'Because . . .' Anahita gazed out of the window to her beloved mountains. She gave a slight shake of her head. 'It isn't right for me to tell you now. It's all in there.' She pointed a finger at the pages in Ari's hands. 'When the moment is right for you – and you will know when that is – perhaps you will read my story. And then, you will decide for yourself whether to investigate it.'

'I see,' said Ari, but he didn't.

'All I ask of you is that you share its contents with no one in our family until I die. It is my life I entrust to you, Ari. As you know –' Anahita paused – 'sadly, my time on this earth is running out.'

Ari stared at her, confused as to what his great-grandmother wished him to do. 'You want me to read this and then make investigations as to the whereabouts of your son?' he clarified.

'Yes.'

'But where would I start?'

'In England, of course.' Anahita stared at him. 'You would retrace my footsteps. Everything you need to know you now hold in the palms of your hands. And besides, your father tells me you run some kind of computer company. You, of all people, have the webbing at your disposal.'

'You mean the "web"?' Ari held back a chuckle.

'Yes, so I'm sure it would only take you a few seconds to find the place where it all began,' Anahita concluded.

Ari followed his great-grandmother's eye-line out to the mountains beyond the window. 'It's a beautiful view,' he said, for want of something better to say.

'Yes, and it's why I stay here, even though my daughter disapproves. One day soon, I'll travel upwards, way beyond those peaks, and I'll be happy for it. I will see many people there whom I've mourned in my life. But of course, as it stands –' Anahita's gaze landed on her great-grandson once more – 'not the one I wish to see most of all.'

'How do you know he's still alive?'

Anahita's eyes reverted to the skyline, then she closed them wearily. 'As I said, it's all in my story.'

'Of course.' Ari knew he was dismissed. 'So, I'll let you rest, Nani.'

Anahita nodded. Ari stood up, made a *pranaam*, then kissed his great-grandmother on each cheek.

'Goodbye, and I'm sure I'll see you soon,' he commented as he walked towards the door.

'Perhaps,' she answered.

As Ari made to leave the room, he turned back suddenly on instinct. 'Nani, why me? Why not give this story to your daughter, or my father?'

Anahita stared at him. 'Because, Ari, the story you hold in your hands might be my past, but it is also your future.'

Ari left the room feeling drained. Walking through the bungalow, he made for the coat rack by the front door, underneath which his briefcase sat. Stowing the yellowing pages inside it, he continued into the drawing room. His grandmother, Muna, approached him immediately.

'Why did she want to see you?' she asked him.

'Oh,' Ari replied airily, 'she doesn't believe her son is dead and wants me to go and investigate in England.' He rolled his eyes for full effect.

'Not again!' Muna rolled her own eyes equally dramatically. 'Listen, I can show you the death certificate. Her son died when he was about three. Please, Ari,' Muna laid a hand on her grandson's shoulder, 'take no notice. She's been going on about this for years. Sadly, it's an old woman's fantasy, and certainly not worth wasting your precious time with. Take my word for it. I've listened to it for much longer than you. Now,' his grandmother smiled, 'come and have a last glass of champagne with your family.'

*

Ari sat on the last plane from Bagdogra back to Mumbai. He tried to concentrate on the figures in front of him, but Anahita's face kept floating into his vision. Surely his grandmother was right when she'd told him Anahita was deluded? And yet, there were things his great-grandmother had said when they were alone – things she couldn't have known about him, which had unsettled him. Perhaps there was something in her story . . . maybe he would take the time to glance through the manuscript when he arrived back home.

At Mumbai airport, even though it was past midnight, Bambi, his current girlfriend, was there at Arrivals to greet him. The rest of the night was spent pleasantly in his apartment overlooking the Arabian Sea, enjoying her slim young body.

The following morning, he was already late for his meeting, and as he packed his briefcase with the documents he needed, he removed the papers Anahita had given him.

One day I will have time to read it, he thought, as he shoved the manuscript into the bottom drawer of his desk and hurriedly left his apartment.

One year later

. . . I remember. In the still of the night, the merest hint of a breeze was a blessed relief from the interminable dry heat of Jaipur. Often, the other ladies and children of the zenana and I climb up to the rooftops of the Moon Palace, and make our beds there.

And as I lie there gazing up at the stars, I hear the sweet, pure sound of the singing. And I know then that someone I love is being taken from the earth and gently cradled upwards . . .

I awake with a start, and find myself in my bedroom in Darjeeling, not on the palace rooftops in Jaipur. It was a dream, I try to comfort myself, disoriented, for the singing still continues in my ears. Yet I know for certain I am conscious.

I try to recover my senses and realise what this means: if I'm in the present, someone I love is dying at this moment. As my heart-rate increases, I close my eyes and scan my family, knowing that my second sight will tell me who it is.

For once, I come up with a blank. It is strange, I think, as the gods have never been wrong before.

*

But who . . . ?

I close my eyes and breathe deeply, calmly, listening intently.

And then I know. I know for certain what I'm being told.

My son . . . my beloved son. I know it is he who is finally being taken upwards.

My eyes fill with tears and I gaze out of my window, looking up to the heavens for comfort. But it's night and beyond my window is only blackness.

There's a gentle knock at my door and Keva enters, concern on her face.

'Madam. I heard you weeping. Are you ill?' she asks as she crosses the room and stares down at me, taking my pulse at the same time.

I shake my head silently, while she reaches for a handkerchief to dry the tears that have fallen down my face. 'No,' I comfort her, 'I'm not ill.'

'Then what is it? Did you have a nightmare?'

'No.' I look up at her, knowing she won't understand. 'My child has just died.'

Keva stares at me in horror. 'But how did you discover that Madam Muna is dead?'

'It is not my daughter, Keva, but my son. The one I left behind in England many years ago. He was eighty-one,' I murmur. 'At least he enjoyed a long life.'

Again, Keva looks at me in confusion, and puts a hand to my forehead to see if I have a fever. 'But, Madam, your son died many years ago. I think that perhaps you were dreaming,' she says, as much to convince herself as me.

'Perhaps,' I say kindly, not wishing to alarm her. 'But nonetheless, I would like you to make a note of the time and the date. It's a moment I don't wish to forget. For, you see, my waiting is over.' I smile weakly at her.

She does as I request, noting the time alongside the day and date on a piece of paper and handing it to me.

'I'll be fine now, you may leave me.'

'Yes, Madam,' Keva replies, uncertainly. 'Are you sure you're not ill?'

'I'm sure. Goodnight, Keva.'

When she leaves the room, I take a pen from my bedside table and write a short letter to accompany the time and date of my son's death. I also pull out his tattered death certificate from my bedside drawer. Tomorrow, I will ask Keva to put them in an envelope and address it to the solicitor who is charged with handling my affairs once I pass over. I will ask him to telephone me so I can give him instructions as to whom to send the envelope when I die.

Closing my eyes, I wish for sleep to come now, for I suddenly feel desperately alone here on earth. I realise that I've been waiting for this moment. Now that my son has left me, it is finally my turn to follow him . . .

Three days later, at the usual time in the morning, Keva knocked on her mistress's door. Getting no initial response was normal; Madam Chavan often dozed late into the morning these days. Keva busied herself with the housekeeping for another half an hour. She returned to knock again, eliciting further silence from inside the room. Now, this *was* unusual, so Keva opened the door quietly and found that her mistress was still fast asleep. It was only after she had opened the curtains, chatting to her about nothing, as was her habit, that she realised Madam Chavan was not responding.

*

Ari's cellphone rang as he was driving in the chaotic Mumbai traffic. Seeing it was his father, to whom he hadn't spoken in weeks, he pressed the button on his phone to take the call on speaker.

'Papa!' he said brightly. 'How are you?'

'Hello, Ari, I am well, but . . .'

Ari could hear the sombre note in his father's voice.

'Yes?' he asked. 'What is it?'

'It is your great-grandmother, Anahita. I have to tell you that she died in the early hours of this morning.'

'Oh, Papa. I'm very sorry to hear that.'

'We all are. She was a wonderful woman and will be greatly missed.'

'Yes. At least she lived a long life,' Ari said in a consoling tone, as he steered quickly round a taxi that had drawn to a sudden halt right in front of him.

'She did. We're holding the funeral in four days' time, to allow the family to gather for it. Your brother and sister are attending and everyone will be there. Including you, I hope,' Vivek added.

'Do you mean this Friday?' enquired Ari, his heart sinking.

'Yes, at midday. She'll be cremated at the *ghaat* in Darjeeling with just her family in attendance. We'll arrange a memorial service for her later, as there are many people who'll wish to attend and celebrate her life.'

'Papa,' Ari groaned, 'really, Friday's impossible for me. I have a prospective client flying over from the States to talk to me about my taking over his software contract. It would take the company from loss to profit overnight. With the best will in the world, I can't be in Darjeeling on Friday.'

There was silence on the other end of the line. 'Ari,' his

father said eventually, 'even *I* know there are moments when business must take second place to one's family. Your mother would never forgive you, especially as Anahita made it obvious at her birthday celebrations last year that you were special to her.'

'I'm sorry, Papa,' Ari said firmly, 'but there's simply nothing I can do.'

'And that is your final word?'

'That is my final word.'

Ari heard the sound of the receiver at the other end slamming down.

Ari was in a euphoric mood when he arrived home the following Friday night. The meeting with the Americans had gone so well that they'd shaken on the deal then and there. He was taking Bambi out tonight to celebrate and had popped home to his apartment to shower and change first. He picked up a letter from his pigeon hole in the lobby and took the elevator to the sixteenth floor. Inside his apartment, he tore open the envelope as he walked into his bedroom, and read the contents of it.

Khan & Chauhan Solicitors
Chowrasta Square
Darjeeling
West Bengal
India

2 March 2001

Dear Sir,

On the instructions of my client, Anahita Chavan,
I have forwarded this envelope to you. As you may

already know, Madam Chavan passed away a few
days ago.

With my deepest sympathy,
Devak Khan
Partner

Ari sat down on the bed, realising that, due to his excitement about the meeting and preparing his team for it, his great-grandmother's funeral that day had completely slipped his mind. He sighed heavily as he opened the envelope the solicitor had enclosed, doubting that his parents would ever forgive him for not even contacting them today.

'Well, so be it,' Ari told himself grimly, as he unfolded the piece of paper inside the envelope and read the letter attached to it.

My dearest Ari,

When you read this, I will have passed over. Enclosed
are the details of my son Moh's death. The exact date
and the time of his passing. And also, his original death
certificate. As you will see, the dates do not correspond.
This may not mean anything to you now, my dear boy,
but in the future, if you do decide you wish to investigate
what happened to him, both may be of relevance.

Meanwhile, until we meet again in another place, I
send you my love. Always remember that we are never
truly the masters of our destiny. Use your ears to listen,
your eyes to see, and I know you will find guidance.

Your loving great-grandmother,
Anahita

Ari sighed. He really wasn't in the mood either for his great-grandmother's hocus-pocus, or to think about how angry his parents currently were with him. He didn't want anything to dampen his good mood tonight.

Running the water in the shower, he flicked on the CD player by his bed and stood under the shower-head listening to the thumping music.

Dressing in one of his hand-tailored suits and a shirt, he turned off the music and was about to leave the bedroom when Anahita's letter caught his eye. On instinct, he refolded the pages back into the envelope and put it in the drawer with the yellowing manuscript. Then he switched off the lights and left the apartment.

London,

July 2011

1

Rebecca Bradley pressed her face to the window as the plane descended towards London. The patchwork quilt of different hues of green shimmered as if with early-morning dew on this beautiful summer's day. As the city began to appear beneath her, the sight of Big Ben and the Houses of Parliament reminded her of Toy Town in comparison with the soaring skyscrapers of New York.

'Miss Bradley, we'll be taking you off the aircraft first,' the stewardess informed her.

'Thank you.' Rebecca managed a smile in return. She reached into her shoulder bag for the large pair of black sunglasses which she hoped would mask her exhaustion, although it was unlikely there would be photographers waiting to greet her. She'd needed to get out of New York fast, so she'd called up the airline and changed her original flight for an earlier one.

She felt a certain satisfaction that no one, not even her agent or Jack, knew where she was. Jack had left her apartment that afternoon to catch his flight back to Los Angeles. She'd been unable to give him the answer he wanted, had told him she needed time to think.

Rebecca rifled further through her bag for the red velvet

box and opened it. The ring he had given her was certainly substantial, if too ostentatious for her taste. But Jack liked doing things big, as befitted his status as one of the world's most famous and highest-paid film stars. And he could hardly present her with anything less, given that, if she said yes to his proposal, the ring would be pictured in newspapers and magazines around the world. Jack Heyward and Rebecca Bradley were Hollywood's hottest couple and the media couldn't get enough of them.

Rebecca closed the velvet box and numbly stared out of the window as the plane prepared to touch down. Since she and Jack had met a year ago on the set of a rom-com, she'd felt as if her life had been taken hostage by those who wanted to live vicariously through not only the films she starred in, but also her private life. The truth was – Rebecca bit her lip as the plane continued its descent – that the 'dream' relationship the world imagined the two of them had was just as much make-believe as her films.

Even Victor, her agent, was encouraging her in her relationship with Jack. He had told her countless times that it could only benefit the trajectory of her rising global star.

'There's nothing the public like better than a real Hollywood couple, honey,' he had said. 'Even if your film career takes a dive, they still want to take photos of your kids playing in the park.'

Rebecca thought back to the amount of time she and Jack had actually spent together in the past year. He was based in Hollywood, she in New York, and often their hectic schedules had meant that they wouldn't see each other for weeks on end. And when they *were* together, they were hounded wherever they went. Even yesterday lunchtime, they had eaten in a tiny hole-in-the-wall Italian restaurant and had been besieged by customers wanting pictures and autographs. Jack had ended up taking her for a walk in Central Park to propose in peace and quiet. She only hoped no one had spotted them there . . .

The overwhelming claustrophobia she'd felt as they had taken a cab back to her SoHo apartment and Jack had pressed her for an answer had resulted in her sudden decision to take an earlier flight to England. Having the world scrutinise your every move, to be hounded on a daily basis by strangers who all felt that somehow they owned a part of you, was, Rebecca felt, currently unsustainable. The lack of privacy which came with conducting a high-profile relationship, let alone not being able to grab a bagel and latte from the local coffee shop without being mobbed, was slowly taking its toll.

Her doctor had prescribed Valium a few weeks ago, when she'd been door-stepped at her apartment block and had ended up locking herself in her bathroom, crouching on the floor and crying hysterically. The Valium had helped, but Rebecca knew it was a road to nowhere. The slippery path to dependency to enable her to cope with the pressure she lived under loomed before her. Just as Jack knew all too well.

He'd assured her in the first heady days of their romance that the cocaine he used was not a regular habit. He could take it or leave it. It simply helped him unwind. But as she'd come to know him better, Rebecca had discovered this wasn't an accurate assessment. He had become defensive and quarrelsome when she questioned his continual heavy usage and the amount of alcohol he was drinking. As someone who didn't take drugs and very rarely drank, Rebecca loathed it when Jack was high.

At the beginning of their relationship she had thought that

her life could not be any more perfect: a hugely successful career and a handsome, talented life-partner to share it with. But between the drugs, the absences and the slow unveiling of Jack's insecurity – which had culminated in a show of rage towards her when she'd been nominated for a Golden Globe seven months before and he hadn't – the rose-tinted glasses had begun to turn grey.

The offer of a great part in a British film, *The Still of the Night*, set in the 1920s and focusing on an aristocratic English family, could not have come at a more opportune moment. Not only was it a move away from the lightweight parts she'd played so far, but it was also a huge honour to be chosen by Robert Hope, the acclaimed British director. Jack had even managed to put a damper on that, citing the fact that they needed her to be the Hollywood 'name' in the film to satisfy the money men. He had then proceeded to tell her that her biggest attribute would be looking great in the array of period costumes she'd wear, and that she shouldn't really get any ideas about her talent having won her the part.

'You're far too beautiful to be taken seriously, sweetheart,' he'd added as he'd slopped more vodka into his glass.

After the plane touched down at Heathrow and taxied to a halt, Rebecca undid her seatbelt as the lights came on in the aircraft.

'Are you ready, Miss Bradley?' asked the stewardess.

'Yes, thank you.'

'They should be no longer than a couple of minutes.'

Rebecca ran an urgent comb through her mane of long, dark hair and fixed it into a coil at the nape of her neck. Her 'Audrey Hepburn' look, Jack called it, and indeed the media constantly likened Rebecca to the iconic star. There was even some talk of remaking *Breakfast at Tiffany's* next year.

She mustn't listen to him, mustn't let her self-confidence as an actress be broken any further. Jack's last two films had been flops and his star was not shining as brightly as it used to. The dreadful truth was that he was jealous of her success. She took a deep breath to calm herself. Whatever Jack had said to her, she was determined to prove that she was far more than a pretty face, and the meaty script gave her a real chance to do just that.

And at least, tucked away on location in a rural part of the English countryside, Rebecca hoped she'd have some peace and space to think. Underneath all his problems, she knew there was a Jack she loved. But unless he was prepared to do something about his growing dependency, she knew she couldn't say yes to his proposal.

'We're taking you off the aircraft now, Miss Bradley,' said the dark-suited airline security officer who'd appeared at her side.

Rebecca donned her sunglasses and left the First Class cabin. Sitting in the VIP lounge waiting for her luggage to be collected, she reflected that it was a road to nowhere with Jack unless he admitted his problems. And perhaps, she mused, taking her cellphone from her bag and staring at the screen, that was exactly what she should tell him.

'Miss Bradley, your luggage is being taken to your car,' said the security guard. 'But I'm afraid there's a barrage of photographers waiting for you outside.'

'No!' She looked up at him in dismay. 'How many?'

'*Many*,' he confirmed. 'Don't worry, I'll see you safely through.'

He indicated that they should make a move and Rebecca stood up.

'I wasn't expecting this,' she commented as she walked with him towards Arrivals. 'I took a different flight to the one I'd originally planned.'

'Well, you've hit London on the morning your big news has broken. May I offer my congratulations?'

Rebecca stopped dead. 'What "news"?' she asked him bluntly.

'Your . . . engagement to Jack Heyward, Miss Bradley.'

'I— oh, Jesus,' she muttered.

'There's a lovely photo of you in Central Park with Mr Heyward putting a ring on your finger. It's on the front pages of most of our newspapers this morning. Right –' he paused in front of the sliding doors – 'are you ready?'

Behind her sunglasses, tears pricked Rebecca's eyes and she nodded angrily.

'Good, we'll get you through as quickly as we can.'

Fifteen minutes later, as the car nosed its way out of Heathrow, Rebecca gazed helplessly at the photograph of her and Jack taking pride of place on the front of the *Daily Mail* and the headline:

JACK AND BECKS – IT'S OFFICIAL!

The grainy image was of Jack placing the ring on her finger in Central Park. She was gazing up at him with what *she* knew was an expression of panic, but what the journalist had described as one of delighted surprise. Worst of all, there was a comment from Jack, obviously given after he'd left her apartment yesterday afternoon. He had apparently confirmed that he'd asked Rebecca to marry him, but they were yet to name the date.

She reached with shaking hands into her bag and drew out her cellphone again. Seeing there were numerous messages from Jack, her agent, and members of the press, she switched it off and returned it to her handbag. She couldn't cope with responding to any of them at present. She felt furious with Jack for making *any* comment on what had taken place in the park.

By tomorrow, the world's media would be speculating on who would design her wedding dress, where they would hold the ceremony and, probably, whether she was pregnant.

Rebecca closed her eyes and took a deep breath. She was twenty-nine years of age and, up until last night, the idea of marriage and kids had been but a fleeting thought, something that might happen in the future.

But Jack was pushing forty, had bedded most of his co-stars and, as he had told her, felt it was time to settle down. Whereas for her, this was only her second serious relationship, after many years of being with her childhood sweetheart. Her burgeoning career and eventual fame had destroyed that love story too.

'I'm afraid it's going to take a good few hours to get down to Devon, Miss Bradley,' said her friendly driver. 'My name is Graham, by the way, and you let me know if you need to stop for any reason on the way.'

'I will,' said Rebecca, feeling at this moment that she'd rather he drove her to a vast desert somewhere in Africa, someplace where there were no photographers, newspapers or cellphone signals.

'Pretty isolated where you're going, Miss Bradley,'

commented Graham, mirroring her thoughts. 'Not a lot of bright lights and shops on Dartmoor,' he added. 'Magnificent old place you're filming in, mind you. Like going back to a totally different era. I didn't think anyone still lived in grand places like that any more. Anyway, the countryside makes a pleasant change for me, I can tell you. Normally I'm ferrying actors to the studios through the London traffic.'

His words comforted Rebecca somewhat. Perhaps the media would leave her alone if she was out in the middle of nowhere.

'Looks like we've got a bike on our tail, Miss Bradley,' said Graham, looking in his rear mirror and abruptly destroying her hopes of privacy. 'Don't worry, we'll lose him as soon as we're on the motorway.'

'Thank you,' said Rebecca, trying to calm her fraught nerves. She sank back into her seat, closed her eyes and did her best to try to sleep.

'We're nearly there, Miss Bradley.'

After four and a half hours in the car, dozing intermittently, Rebecca was feeling the disorientation of jet lag. She looked blearily out of the window. 'Where are we?' she asked as she gazed out at the rugged, empty moorland surrounding them.

'On Dartmoor. It looks pleasant today with the sun shining, but I bet it's pretty bleak in the winter. Excuse me,' Graham said as his phone rang, 'it's the production manager. I'll just pull over to take the call.'

As the driver answered his cellphone, Rebecca opened the door and stepped out onto the rough grass at the side of the narrow road. She breathed in deeply and smelt the sweet freshness of the air. There was a slight breeze blowing across the moorland, and in the distance she could see clumps of jagged rocks silhouetted against the skyline. There was not a single human being to be seen for miles. 'Heaven!' she breathed, as Graham started up the engine and she climbed back in. 'It's so peaceful here,' she commented.

'Yes,' he agreed, 'but unfortunately, Miss Bradley, the production manager was phoning to say there's already a collection of photographers gathered outside the hotel the cast are staying in. They're waiting for you to arrive. So he suggests I take you straight to Astbury Hall, where you're filming.'

'Okay.' Rebecca bit her lip in further despair as they drove off.

'Sorry, Miss Bradley,' he offered sympathetically. 'I'm always telling my kids that being a rich and famous movie star isn't quite what it's made out to be. It must be hard for you, especially at moments like this.'

His sympathy prompted a lump in Rebecca's throat. 'It is, sometimes,' she agreed.

'The good news is that whilst you're filming, no one can get near you. The private land surrounding the house is a good few hundred acres, and it's about half a mile or so from this entrance to the house itself.'

Rebecca saw that they had arrived at a pair of vast wrought-iron gates with a security guard on duty beside them. Graham signalled to him and the guard opened the gates. Rebecca looked in wonder as they drove through parkland dotted with ancient oak, horse chestnut and beech trees on either side of the road.

Up ahead was a vast house, more of a palace, really, the kind she had only seen in books or on historical programmes on the television. A baroque confection of carved stone and fluted columns.

'Wow,' she breathed.

'It's pretty spectacular, isn't it? Although I'd hate to think what the heating bills are like,' Graham joked.

As they drove closer and Rebecca saw the vast marble fountain at the front of the house, she wished she knew enough correct architectural terms to describe the beauty in front of her. The graceful symmetry of the building, with two elegant wings on either side of a crowning central dome, made her catch her breath. Sunlight was glinting from the perfectly pro-portioned panelled windows set like jewels along the entire front, the stonework between them interspersed with carved cherubs and urns. Under the massive central portico, sup-ported by four enormous columns, she glimpsed a magnificent double-fronted oak door.

'Fit for a queen, eh?' said Graham as he skirted around the house to a courtyard at the side, which was filled with vans and lorries. A hubbub of people were carrying cameras, lights and cables inside through a door. 'They're hoping to be ready to start shooting tomorrow, so I'm told,' Graham added, park-ing the car.

'Thank you,' said Rebecca as she climbed out and Graham walked round to the boot to retrieve her case.

'This all you brought with you, Miss Bradley? Film stars like you normally have a container full of luggage,' he teased her good-naturedly.

'I packed in a hurry,' Rebecca admitted as she followed him across the courtyard towards the house.

'Well, just remember, Miss Bradley, I'm on call for the

whole of the shoot, so if there's anywhere you need to go, you just tell me, okay? It's been a pleasure to meet you.'

'Ah, you made it!' A lean young man strode towards them. He held out his hand to Rebecca. 'Welcome to England, Miss Bradley. I'm Steve Campion, the production manager. I'm sorry to hear you've had to run the gauntlet of our appalling gutter press this morning. You're safe from them here, at least.'

'Thank you. Do you know when I'll be able to go to my hotel? I could use a shower and some sleep,' said Rebecca, who was feeling bedraggled and travel-weary.

'Of course. We didn't want to put you through another ordeal at the hotel after the airport this morning,' said Steve. 'So, for now, Lord Astbury has very kindly offered you a room here in the house to use until we find you alternative accommodation. As you may have noticed –' Steve indicated the huge building and grinned – 'he has a few going spare. Robert, the director, is very keen to start shooting tomorrow and didn't want your concentration, or that of the other actors staying at the hotel, to be disturbed.'

'I'm sorry to be the cause of all this fuss,' Rebecca ventured, blushing with a sudden wave of guilt.

'Well, never mind, that's what we get for having such a famous young actress in the film. Right, the housekeeper said to find her when you arrived and she'll take you upstairs to your room. There's a full cast call in the drawing room at five p.m. tonight, so that gives you a few hours to sleep.'

'Thank you,' Rebecca repeated, not missing the timbre in Steve's voice. She knew she'd already been labelled 'trouble' and was sure that the cast of talented British actors – none of whose fame or box-office power could currently match her own – would agree with him.

'Wait there and I'll go and find Mrs Trevathan,' Steve said, leaving Rebecca to stand uncomfortably in the courtyard, watching the camera crew heave their equipment past her.

A minute later, a plump, middle-aged woman with greying curly hair and a rosy complexion bustled out of the door towards her.

'Miss Rebecca Bradley?'

'Yes.'

'Well, of course it is, dear.' The woman smiled broadly. 'I recognised you immediately. And let me tell you, you're even more beautiful in real life. I've seen all your films and it's a pleasure to meet you. I'm Mrs Trevathan, the housekeeper. Follow me, and I'll take you up to your bedroom. It's a long walk, I'm afraid. Graham will bring up your case later,' she commented as Rebecca made to pick it up. 'You can't imagine how many miles I cover each day.'

'I probably can't,' agreed Rebecca, struggling to understand the woman's thick Devon accent. 'This house is totally amazing.'

'Less amazing now there's just me and some daily help here to care for it. I'm run ragged. Of course, many years ago, there were thirty of us working here full-time, but things are different now.'

'Yes, I suppose they are,' Rebecca said as Mrs Trevathan led her through a series of doors into a huge kitchen, where a woman in a nurse's uniform was sitting drinking coffee at the table.

'The servants' stairs are the fastest way to the bedrooms from the kitchen,' Mrs Trevathan said, as Rebecca followed her up a steep and narrow flight of steps. 'I've put you in a nice room at the back of the house. It's got a lovely view of the gardens and the moor beyond. You're very lucky Lord Astbury agreed for you to use a room here. He doesn't like houseguests. Sad really, this house could once sleep forty comfortably, but those days are long gone.'

Finally, they emerged through another door onto a wide mezzanine landing. Rebecca gazed up in wonder at the magnificent domed cupola above her, then followed Mrs Trevathan along a wide, shadowy corridor.

'You're in here,' she said, opening the door to a spacious, high-ceilinged room dominated by a large double bed. 'I opened the windows to air it a while ago, so it's a little chilly. But better than the smell of damp. There's an electric fire you can use if you're cold.'

'Thank you. Where is the restroom?' she asked.

'You mean the bathroom, dear?' said Mrs Trevathan with a smile. 'It's two doors down to the left, on the other side of the corridor. I'm afraid we haven't quite run to en-suite facilities just yet. Now, I'll leave you to rest.'

'Would it be possible for me to have a glass of water?' asked Rebecca timidly.

Mrs Trevathan paused on her way to the door, then turned round, her face full of sympathy. 'Of course, you must be all in. Have you eaten anything?'

'No, I couldn't face breakfast on the plane.'

'Then how about I get you a nice pot of tea and some toast? You really are looking quite peaky.'

'That would be wonderful,' Rebecca thanked her, feeling suddenly dizzy and sitting down abruptly in an armchair placed by the empty fire grate.

'Right then, I'll be off to get it.' Mrs Trevathan gazed at her thoughtfully. 'You're only a slip of a thing underneath all that glamour, aren't you, dear? Now, you sort yourself out and I'll see you in a bit.' She smiled kindly and left the room.

Shortly afterwards, Rebecca made her way along the corridor and after a number of false starts into a linen cupboard and another bedroom, found a large bathroom with an old-fashioned cast-iron tub sitting in the centre of it. A rusting metal chain dangled from the cistern above the toilet and, having drunk some water from the tap, she returned to her room. Walking over to the long windows, she gazed out over the view below. The garden beyond the wide terrace that flanked the rear of the house was obviously well tended. Flowering plants and shrubs grew along the borders in immaculate abundance, their multi-coloured blooms softening the green of the central lawns. Beyond the tall yew hedge which encircled the formal garden lay the moors, their ruggedness in direct contrast to the flat, manicured lawns below her. Kicking off her shoes, she climbed onto the bed, the mattress comfortably softened by years of wear.

When Mrs Trevathan knocked quietly on the door ten minutes later and entered the room, she saw Rebecca was fast asleep. Putting the tray down on the table by the fireplace, she covered her gently with the bedspread and quietly left.

2

'My lords, ladies and gentlemen, may I welcome you all to Astbury Hall, which I'm sure you'll all agree is the perfect setting in which to shoot *The Still of the Night*. I certainly feel honoured to be allowed to film in one of England's most beautiful stately homes, and I hope our time here together will be happy and productive.'

Robert Hope, the director, smiled benignly at his assembled cast. 'I should think these old walls are positively quaking with the vast array of talent and experience they currently contain. Many of you will know each other already, but I'd like to extend a special welcome to Rebecca Bradley, who joins us from America to put a touch of Hollywood sparkle on us fusty old Brits.'

All eyes in the room turned to Rebecca, who was hiding in a corner, overwhelmed by the sight of so many iconic British actors. 'Hi,' she said, blushing and offering the room a smile.

'I'll be handing you over now to Hugo Manners, whose wonderful screenplay is going to bring out the best in all of you,' continued Robert. 'We'll be issuing you all later with the final script, hot off the press. Steve, the production manager, will also be handing out your schedules. So all that remains for me to say is: here's to a successful shoot of *The Still of the Night*. Now, here's Hugo.'

There was a round of applause as Hugo Manners, Oscar-winning screenplay writer, took to the floor. Rebecca half-listened to what he had to say, feeling suddenly overwhelmed at what she'd taken on. What worried her most was her English accent; she'd been taking lessons in New York in diction and pronunciation and had done her best in the past two months to speak like an Englishwoman in her daily life. But she knew only too well that by accepting this part, she'd put her head above the parapet and might very well be shot down. There was nothing the British media liked better than to annihilate the performance of an American actress playing an English role. Especially an actress who had seen as much commercial success as she had.

It didn't seem to matter that she had attended the Juilliard drama school in New York on a scholarship and had won her year's award of Best Actress for the role of Beatrice in a production of Shakespeare's *Much Ado About Nothing*. Every actress in Hollywood considered herself 'serious', even if she had come down the model route, which Rebecca most definitely hadn't. She knew that this was her chance to prove herself as a classically trained actress, to make the leap to critical acclaim.

There was another round of applause as Hugo finished speaking and Steve, the production manager, began to hand round the new script and a personal schedule for each of them.

'You'll be glad to know you're not needed on set tomorrow, Rebecca. You have a morning in Wardrobe with the costume designer and her team for dress fittings, and after that, Hair and Make-up want to see you. Robert has suggested you also have an hour with the voice coach to go over your lines for your first day's shoot.'

'Fine. Have you any idea when I'll be moved to my hotel? I'd like to unpack and get settled.'

'Apparently the photographers are still hovering outside. So, for tonight, Lord Astbury has agreed with Robert that you can have a room here whilst we try and find somewhere discreet for you to stay. Lucky old you,' Steve added, smiling, 'a little more luxurious than the box room above the local pub I've been billeted to. And it means you'll really have a chance to soak up the atmosphere here.'

A strikingly handsome man with chiselled features wandered over and held out his hand to her. 'Miss Bradley, I presume? I'm James Waugh. I'm playing Lawrence, and I think we have a number of, how shall I put it, intimate scenes together.' He winked at her, and Rebecca took in his immediate charm and expressive blue eyes, which had undoubtedly helped to propel him to the forefront of young British screen actors.

'I'm delighted to meet you, James,' she said, standing to take his hand.

'Poor thing,' he said sympathetically, 'you must be feeling rather shell-shocked, newly arrived from the States and having to face the furore over your engagement to Jack Heyward.'

'I . . .' Rebecca was unsure how to reply. 'I suppose I am,' she finished lamely.

'Congratulations, by the way.' James was still holding her hand. 'He's a very lucky man.'

'Thank you,' she replied stiffly.

'And if at any point you'd appreciate a run-through of our scenes together before we film, please don't hesitate to let me know. Personally, I'm terrified,' he confided. 'Working with all these luminaries of film and theatre is rather daunting.'

'I know,' agreed Rebecca, warming to him somewhat.

'Well, I'm sure you're going to be wonderful, *and*, if you fancy some company whilst we're stuck down here in the middle of nowhere, just give me a shout.'

'I will, and thank you.'

James gave her one last meaningful glance, then let go of her hand and walked away.

Too shy to go and mingle with the other actors, Rebecca sat back down and studied her schedule, contemplating how, in one breath, James had congratulated her on her engagement and then in the next made it quite clear that he would like to see more of her.

'Rebecca, the cast and crew are going back to the hotel for dinner in a few minutes,' Steve said, appearing suddenly at her side. 'The location caterers are arriving first thing tomorrow morning, but I'm going to ask your new best friend, Mrs Trevathan, to put something together for you from the kitchen for tonight. She was very taken with you, said you needed feeding up.'

'That's sweet of her. I want to read through the new script anyway,' she replied.

'Are you all right, Rebecca?' Steve's eyes were concerned.

'Yes, maybe just a little jet-lagged and, to be honest, overwhelmed by meeting so many incredible actors. I'm nervous I won't make the grade,' she confessed.

'I understand, and if it's any help, I've worked with Robert for many years and he never makes mistakes when he's casting his films. I know he thinks very highly of your skills as an actress. If he didn't, no matter how famous you are, you simply wouldn't be here. Okay?'

'Yes, thanks for that, Steve,' she replied gratefully.

'Well then, I'll see you tomorrow. And enjoy the night in your palace. No one can get to you here, that's for sure.'

Steve moved away and began to shepherd the actors out of the drawing room. When everyone had left, Rebecca stood up and had her first chance to truly take in her surroundings. The July sun was sending a glow through the enormous windows, softening the austere mahogany furniture which filled the room. Sofas and easy chairs were dotted around it and a huge marble fireplace formed the centrepiece. Rebecca shivered, feeling the sudden chill of evening and rather wishing it was lit.

'There you are, dear.' Mrs Trevathan appeared through the door and walked across the room towards her. 'Steve tells me you need some supper. I have a slice of homemade steak-and-kidney pie and some spuds left over from His Lordship's lunch.'

'"Spuds"?' questioned Rebecca.

'Potatoes to you, dear.' Mrs Trevathan smiled.

'I'm not very hungry, so maybe just a salad?'

'I see.' Mrs Trevathan surveyed her with a beady eye. 'From the look of you, I'd say you're on a permanent diet. If you don't mind me saying so, Miss Rebecca, a puff of wind would blow you sideways.'

'I have to be careful, yes,' Rebecca answered, embarrassed by the woman's well-meaning scrutiny.

'As you wish, but you'd be doing a lot better with a proper square meal inside of you. Shall I bring supper up to your room?'

'That would be very kind, thank you.'

As the housekeeper left, Rebecca grimaced at Mrs Trevathan's instinctive knowledge of her eating habits. There was no denying that she watched everything she ate, but what could she do? Her career depended on her slim figure.

She left the drawing room and walked into the grand hall to mount the wide staircase up to her room. Pausing, she looked up at the magnificent dome above her, the small panes of glass set into the edges of it sending shards of light onto the marble floor beneath her feet.

'Good evening.'

Rebecca jumped at the sound of a deep male voice and turned round. She stared at the man standing by the front door, dressed in an ancient tweed jacket and threadbare cords tucked into a pair of wellingtons. His wiry, unkempt hair was greying and needed a decent cut. She guessed he was in his mid-fifties.

'Hello,' she replied uncertainly.

'I'm Anthony, and you are . . . ?'

'Rebecca, Rebecca Bradley.'

'Oh.' His eyes registered a flicker of recognition. 'The American film star. They tell me you're very famous, but I'm afraid I've never heard of you. Films really aren't my thing. Sorry.' He shrugged.

'Please don't apologise, there's no reason why you should have heard of me.'

'No. Anyway, I must be off now.' The man shifted from foot to foot, obviously uncomfortable. 'I've got work to do outside before the light fades.' He nodded at her briefly before disappearing out of the front door.

Rebecca crossed the hall and made her way up the stairs,

admiring the oil paintings of the generations of Astburys which covered the wall. Mrs Trevathan appeared on the top landing with a tray and followed Rebecca into her room.

'There we are, dear; I've found you some soup and some fresh bread and butter. Oh, and I gave you a slice of my Bakewell tart too, with custard,' she added, removing the bowl shielding the pudding with a flourish.

'Thank you.'

'Now, anything else you need?'

'No. Thank you. This really is the most beautiful house, isn't it?'

'It is, dear, it is. And you don't know the sacrifices that have been made to keep it, either.' Mrs Trevathan sighed softly.

'I can only imagine. By the way, I met the gardener downstairs,' Rebecca added.

'Gardener?' Mrs Trevathan raised an eyebrow. 'Downstairs, *inside* the house?'

'Yes.'

'Well, we have a chap who comes in once a week to mow the lawns. Maybe he was looking for His Lordship. Right, I'll let you eat your supper in peace. What time would you like your breakfast tomorrow morning?'

'I don't really eat breakfast, but fruit juice and yoghurt would be great.'

'Well, I'll see what I can do.' Mrs Trevathan sniffed with obvious disapproval as she walked towards the door, but turned to smile comfortingly at the younger woman as she made her exit. 'Goodnight, my love. Sleep well.'

'Goodnight.'

Rebecca ate the flavoursome leek and potato soup and all

of the crusty bread smothered thickly with butter. Despite herself, she was still hungry, so she tried a small spoonful of the strange pudding Mrs Trevathan had left for her. Finding it delicious, she finished that as well, then threw herself guiltily on the bed, knowing she mustn't make a habit of devouring stodgy English food, however tasty.

When her stomach had settled, she rolled off the bed and reached for her handbag. Tentatively pulling out her cellphone, she switched it on. She pressed the button to retrieve her messages and put the phone to her ear. It could not connect, and when she checked the screen, she saw there was no signal. Taking out her iPad, she saw that there were no available networks on that either.

A glimmer of a smile appeared on her lips. This morning she had wished to be someplace where no one could find her or make contact with her, and it seemed that for tonight, at least, this was the case. She lay back and looked out of the window at the approaching dusk, the sun slowly disappearing below the horizon on the moors beyond the garden. And realised then that all she could hear was silence.

Picking up her script from the side table, Rebecca began to read through it. She was playing Lady Elizabeth Sayers, the beautiful young daughter of the house. The year was 1922 and the Jazz Age was in full swing. Her father was determined to marry her off to a neighbouring landowner, but Elizabeth had very different ideas. The film focused on the British aristocracy in a changing world, as women took tentative steps towards emancipation and the working classes no longer accepted their subordination to the aristocracy. Elizabeth fell in love with an unsuitable poet, Lawrence, whom she had met through a fast bohemian set in London. The choice she faced between disgracing her parents and following her heart was an old story. Yet, with Hugo Manners's witty but moving script, it was a gem of a part.

As always, the filming schedule did not start at the beginning of the story and Rebecca was to shoot her first scene the day after tomorrow with James Waugh, who was playing her improper poet. It was to be filmed out in the garden and included a passionate kiss. Rebecca sighed. No matter how professional she was as an actress, or how many times she had been seduced on camera, she always dreaded filming love scenes with co-stars she hardly knew.

Out of the corner of her eye, she saw a flicker of movement in the garden below her. Moving over to the window, she saw the gardener sitting down on a bench. Even from here, she felt there was something lonely about him, something sad. Rebecca watched as he sat, still like a statue, staring ahead into the descending dusk.

After having a bath, Rebecca climbed beneath the scratchy starched white sheets. As she lay there, going over her lines and practising the clipped British accent of the 1920s, she realised how tonight it felt as if she were actually living in the world of the film script. So little seemed to have changed in this house since those times, it was almost unsettling.

Seeing it was past ten o'clock now, but convinced she wouldn't fall asleep due to the jet lag, Rebecca reached to switch off the light. To her surprise, she slept soundly through the night, only waking when Mrs Trevathan appeared at eight the next morning with a breakfast tray.

At ten o'clock, she went downstairs and found her way to Wardrobe for her costume fitting. Jean, the Scottish costume designer, eyed her and said, 'My dear, you were made for this period. You even have an old-fashioned face. And . . . I have a surprise for you.'

'Really?'

'Yes. I was speaking to the housekeeper here yesterday, and she told me that there's a large collection of vintage 1920s gowns upstairs in one of the bedrooms. Apparently they were worn by a long-dead relative of the current Lord Astbury and have remained untouched over the years. I asked if I could take a look, obviously out of pure personal interest, and, of course –' she winked at Rebecca – 'to see if there was anything suitable that would fit you. It would be wonderful to use them in the film.'

'It would,' Rebecca agreed.

'And –' with a flourish, Jean pulled a silk drape from a clothes rail, 'just take a look at these.'

Rebecca gasped as a row of exquisite gowns was revealed. 'Wow,' she breathed. 'They're amazing.'

'And perfectly preserved. You'd never know they were ninety years old. A lot of them are by the top French designers of the day, like Lanvin, Vionnet and Patou. What a treasure trove,' Jean remarked as they both went through the rails, picking out and admiring the fabulous dresses. 'At auction they'd go for a fortune. I just can't wait to try them on you and see if they fit. From your measurements, they definitely should. It seems the original owner of all these was almost identical in shape and size to you.'

'But will I be allowed to wear them, even if they do fit?' asked Rebecca.

'Who knows? The housekeeper sounded very doubtful and said she'd have to ask Lord Astbury. But the first thing to do is to try them on you and take it from there. Now –' Jean pulled a dress off the rail – 'how about this one for your first scene with James Waugh tomorrow?'

Ten minutes later, Rebecca was staring at herself in the mirror. Not since her Juilliard days had she worn period costume; her parts in Hollywood had always been those of young modern women, more often in jeans and T-shirts than not. The Lanvin dress she was standing in was made from silk, overlaid with chiffon and embroidered with delicate hand-sewn beading. The handkerchief hemline floated gently around her ankles as she moved.

'Right, even if I have to go down on my knees and beg, I'm going to persuade Lord Astbury to let me hire some of these from him,' said Jean firmly. 'Let's try the next one on.'

After Rebecca had paraded in a fabulous array of gowns, each one fitting her perfectly, Jean grinned at her. 'Right, I think you're done. I'll speak to the housekeeper as soon as I can. My dear, you're going to look like a dream,' she commented as she helped Rebecca remove the last gown. 'And once Hair and Make-up have sorted you out, you'll be a real 1920s beauty!' She gave Rebecca a conspiratorial wink. 'They're just down the corridor on the right.'

'I think I need a GPS in this house,' Rebecca said, smiling, as she headed to the door. 'I keep getting lost.'

She left Wardrobe and walked down the corridor until she found Hair and Make-up. As she sat down in a chair in front of the mirror, one of the hair stylists took a shiny tendril of Rebecca's thick, dark locks in her hands.

'How are you feeling about having it cut and dyed tomorrow?' she asked.

This had been a bone of contention with her agent, Victor, when the contract had come through; the stipulation was that

Rebecca's long hair needed to be cut into a 1920s bob and dyed blonde to match the colour of the actress playing her mother.

'Okay, I suppose.' Rebecca shrugged. 'It'll grow back, won't it?'

'Of course it will. And when the shoot is over, we can easily dye it back to your original colour. It's good to see you're not being precious about it,' the hair stylist said approvingly. 'So many actresses are. Besides, you might find you like the style; you have the perfect elfin features to go with a bob.'

'And maybe nobody will recognise me any more as a blonde, either,' mused Rebecca.

'Sadly, I don't think that's going to help you,' interjected the make-up artist, coming over to take a seat opposite Rebecca. 'That face of yours will always give you away. So, what is Jack Heyward like in person? He's such a god on the screen. Does he look like that first thing in the morning?' she teased.

Rebecca thought about it. 'He does look kind of cute in the morning.'

'I bet he does.' The make-up girl grinned. 'I'm sure you can't believe you're actually going to marry him.'

'You know what? You're right, I *can't* believe it. I'll see you guys bright and early tomorrow for the chop!' Smiling to cover the irony of her words, Rebecca stood up and gave them both a wave before she left the room. She checked her watch and saw that it was only three o'clock, which meant that she had two hours before her appointment with the voice coach.

One of the dressers had told her earlier that it was apparently possible to get a cellphone signal if you walked in the direction of the moors, so she ran upstairs to get her phone. Shooting had already started in the drawing room, and as she slipped out through the French windows in the dining room that led to the terrace, her stomach turned over at the thought that it would be *her* in front of the cameras tomorrow.

Walking down the crumbling stone steps and into the garden, Rebecca marched at a brisk pace across it. Sitting down on the bench where she'd spied the gardener yesterday, she tried her cellphone, which was oscillating between one bar and none.

'Damn!' she said as yet again her voicemail refused to connect.

'Everything all right?'

Rebecca started at the voice and looked towards the rose beds where she saw the gardener she'd met last night holding a pair of secateurs.

'Yes, I'm okay, thanks. I just can't get a signal on my cellphone.'

'Sorry. Dreadful coverage we have here.'

'Maybe it's not such a bad thing to be cut off. Actually, I'm rather enjoying it,' she confided. 'Do you like working here?' she asked him politely.

He gave her an odd look, then nodded. 'I've never thought about it like that, but I suppose I do. I can't imagine being anywhere else, anyway.'

'It must be a gardener's dream here. Those roses are magnificent. Such beautiful colours – especially the one you're pruning. It's such a deep, velvety purple, it's almost black.'

'Yes,' he agreed, 'it's named the Midnight Rose and it's rather a mysterious plant. It's been here as long as I have and should have died many years ago. Yet every year, without fail, it blooms as though it's just been planted.'

'All I have in my apartment are some indoor pot plants,' Rebecca commented.

'You like gardening, do you?'

'When I was growing up, I used to have my own small patch in my parents' garden. I used to feel it was a comforting place.'

'There's certainly something about exerting control over the land that helps pick away frustrations,' the gardener said, nodding in agreement. 'How are you finding it here after the States?'

'It's completely different from anywhere I've ever been before, but I just had the best night's sleep I've had in years. It's so peaceful here. But they're moving me to a hotel later today. I don't think Lord Astbury wants houseguests. To be honest,' Rebecca confessed, 'I wish I could stay. I feel safe here.'

'Well, you never know, Lord Astbury might change his mind. By the way,' he indicated her cellphone, 'if you ask Mrs Trevathan, you may be able to use the landline in his study.'

'Okay, thanks, I will,' said Rebecca, standing up. 'See you around.'

'Here –' the gardener clipped off a single stem of a perfect Midnight Rose – 'something pretty to look at in your room. The smell is quite beautiful.'

'Thank you,' Rebecca said, touched by the gift. 'I'll put it in water right away.'

Eventually finding Mrs Trevathan in the kitchen, she explained that she needed a vase for her rose and that the gardener had said there was a phone in the study. Mrs Trevathan led her into a small, dark room lined with bookshelves, the desk piled high with unevenly stacked papers.

'There you go, but don't be too long if it's to America. His Lordship has a fit as it is over the telephone bills.'

As Mrs Trevathan left the room, Rebecca thought that 'His Lordship' sounded like an ogre.

Sitting down and finding the number on her cellphone, she picked up the receiver of the ancient telephone, which had a circular dial with numbers written on it. Finally having worked out what to do, she inserted her finger into the holes one-by-one and turned the dial to call Jack. Guiltily, she felt relieved when she heard it go straight to voicemail.

'Hi, it's me, and I'm someplace where there's no Internet or cellphone signal. I'll be moving to a hotel later today, so I'll contact you then. I'm fine, by the way. I –' Rebecca paused as she thought what to say to him, but the subject was so big and complex that no words came neatly to mind to describe it. 'I'll call you soon, bye.'

Picking up the receiver once more, dialling and getting the voicemail of Victor, her agent, she left a similar message.

Leaving the study, she went in search of Steve, determined to pin him down and find out exactly where she was going to stay for the duration of the shoot. She found him by the location catering van, set up in the courtyard to the side of the house.

'I know, I know, Rebecca, you want to know where you're going,' Steve said, obviously harassed. 'As a matter of fact, I was just coming to find you with what I hope is good news. Lord Astbury came to see me five minutes ago and said it was fine if you wanted to stay here for the duration of the shoot. I'm somewhat surprised, given his previous antipathy to the idea,' he remarked. 'We had found you a discreet bed-and-breakfast in one of the nearby villages, but to be frank, the accommodation probably isn't up to your usual standards. And there's no guarantee the paps wouldn't find you there eventually anyway. So, it's up to you.'

'Okay, can I think about it?' Even though she loved the security and tranquillity of her current accommodation, she was uncertain of sharing it with the so far unseen Lord Astbury.

'Yes,' said Steve as his walkie-talkie crackled. 'Excuse me, Rebecca, they need me on set.'

Back in her room, Rebecca ran through her lines in preparation for seeing the voice coach in half an hour. She stood up and gazed out of the windows. She really did feel safe here. More than anything, she needed peace and quiet to concentrate fully on her performance. This role would make or break her future career.

After the session with the voice coach, Rebecca found Steve on the terrace and said she'd be delighted to stay on at Astbury Hall.

'What with your current circumstances, I think it's probably the only sensible thing to do,' Steve replied, relieved that the problem had been solved. 'And Mrs Trevathan said she'd be happy to feed you in the evenings. She seems to have taken you under her wing.' He smiled.

'Oh, I rarely eat much in the evening, so—'

'Hello there,' said a voice from behind them.

Rebecca saw the gardener walking up the terrace steps towards them.

'Good afternoon, Lord Astbury. Rebecca has said she'd like to stay on,' Steve said. 'It really is extremely kind of you to make an exception for her.'

'Anthony, please,' the man clarified.

Shocked, Rebecca looked first at Steve and then at Anthony.

'Maybe in the evenings, Miss Bradley, when everyone has left, you can come and help me with the gardening,' he said, an ironic glint in his eye.

'I – *you're* Lord Astbury?' she managed to splutter.

'Yes, although as I just said to Steve, everyone calls me Anthony.'

Rebecca felt the heat rising to her cheeks. 'I'm so embarrassed, I didn't realise who you were.'

'No, well, perhaps I wasn't quite the image you had in your mind,' Anthony answered calmly. 'Sadly, these days, the poor, penniless gentry have to do their own dirty work. No black tie and tails for us any longer. Now, if you'll excuse me, I have some laburnums to attend to.'

He turned away and headed around the side of the house.

'Oh, Rebecca.' Steve threw back his head and laughed. 'Classic! I'm not sure how it goes in the States, but the modern aristocracy here in England tend to be the scruffiest bunch in society. It's become their badge of honour to wear the oldest clothes and drive clapped-out cars. No self-respecting peer of the realm would think of dressing up at home. It just isn't done.'

'I see,' Rebecca replied, feeling stupid and very foreign.

'Anyway, your ignorance doesn't seem to have done you any harm,' Steve continued in her silence. 'It's solicited an open-ended invitation to stay here with him.'

James Waugh appeared and sauntered over to them. 'Rebecca, I was just going to ask you, are you busy tonight? I thought maybe we could have a bite to eat and get to know each other a little better. We have our first scene tomorrow morning and it's rather – how would one put it – up close and personal.' He gave her a cheeky grin.

'Actually, I was going to have an early night,' she replied.

'I'm sure Graham can come and collect you afterwards, so that you can still do that.'

'I'd . . . rather not. The press . . .'

'All gone, as of this morning,' James confirmed. 'And you really can't let all that celebrity business get in the way of your performance, can you?'

'No. Okay,' Rebecca conceded finally, not wishing to appear aloof.

'Good.' James smiled. 'I'll see you at eight at the hotel. And don't worry, I'll tell them to find us a discreet table.'

As James left, Steve's eyes twinkled at Rebecca. 'Think you've made a hit there too. Watch him, he's got a reputation for being a naughty boy.'

'I will. Thanks, Steve.' She walked off, her head held high.

Back upstairs in her bedroom, there was a knock on the door.

'Come in.'

It was Mrs Trevathan. 'Sorry to bother you, Rebecca, but I hear that you've met His Lordship.'

'Yes, I have,' Rebecca murmured as she continued hanging her few items of clothing in the old mahogany wardrobe.

'Here, let me do that,' said Mrs Trevathan.

'No, it's fine, I—'

'Sit yourself down and we can talk as I sort you out.'

Rebecca acquiesced and perched on the end of the bed as Mrs Trevathan put away the remaining contents of her case.

'You really haven't brought much with you, have you, dear?' she commented. 'Anyway, I came to say that His Lordship has invited you to join him for dinner tonight. He always eats at eight p.m. sharp.'

'Oh no – I'm afraid I can't. I have a prior engagement.'

'I see. Well now, His Lordship will be disappointed. And after him being so kind as to have you here.'

Rebecca could hear the disapproval in the housekeeper's voice. 'Please apologise to him for me, and tell him I'd be delighted to join him any other night,' she said placatingly.

'I will. He really doesn't enjoy people swarming all over his house. His Lordship needs peace, and lots of it. But needs must when the devil drives, I suppose.'

'Pardon me?'

'I mean, dear, he needs the money from the film to keep the house going,' Mrs Trevathan said, clarifying her previous statement.

'I see. Does Lord Anthony have a family?' she enquired tentatively.

'No, he doesn't.'

'So he lives alone here?'

'Yes. Right, then, I'll be seeing you in the morning. Bright and early, I hear. Don't you be getting home too late tonight now, will you, dear? You need to be fresh for tomorrow.'

'I won't, I promise. Thanks, Mrs Trevathan.' Rebecca knew the older woman was mothering her, and it was a comforting feeling.

Her early childhood was not a time Rebecca cared to go back to. Very few people, not even her agent, knew the truth of her past. Although one evening, when Jack and she had taken a short vacation in an autumnal, windswept Nantucket, she had told him the truth.

He had held her as she'd cried, tenderly wiping the tears from her eyes.

Rebecca shook her head and sighed. She had felt truly loved by Jack then. She stood up and paced across the creaking floorboards, the memory so at odds with more recent times when he'd been high, incoherent and aggressive. Not for the first time, she wished with all her heart that they were just Mr and Mrs Average, like they'd been that weekend, wrapped up against the chill and unrecognised. Just a boy and a girl in love.

But that wasn't how it was, and she knew it was pointless wanting it to be.

Brushing those thoughts aside, Rebecca saw she had less than an hour before she joined her co-star for dinner.

'Good evening,' said James as Rebecca entered the small sitting room of his suite, where a table had been set up for dinner. He kissed her on both cheeks and led her towards it. 'Thought you might prefer to eat up here, under the circumstances.'

'Yes, thanks,' agreed Rebecca, grateful for the privacy from beady-eyed diners, but at the same time worrying about gossip amongst the hotel staff. Being spotted entering her attractive co-star's suite at night was in many ways worse than being seen with him in the hotel's public restaurant.

'And don't worry about the staff saying anything.' James seemed to read her mind as he pulled the chair out to sit her down. 'Robert informed me the hotel has signed a privacy clause whilst we're all staying here. If one word leaks out to the press on any of the cast's activities, the production company's lawyers will sue the hide off them.'

'Okay,' said Rebecca.

'It's madness, really, isn't it?' sighed James, sitting down opposite her. 'Anyway, the soup is already here, so tuck in before it gets cold. Wine?' He proffered a bottle.

'No, thanks,' said Rebecca. 'I need to be fresh for tomorrow.'

'So, how did you get "discovered"?' asked James, pouring a healthy slug of wine into his own glass.

Rebecca stirred the bowl of thin, nondescript soup as she considered how to answer, thinking that Mrs Trevathan's offerings were far superior to this. 'I don't actually feel I ever *was* discovered. I just got a small part in a TV series when I was twenty, and from there, the parts just grew and grew.' She shrugged.

'I've yet to make it to Hollywood,' said James. 'The press attention here in the UK is bad enough, but from what I've heard, it sounds like a nightmare in LA.'

'Oh it is,' agreed Rebecca, 'which is why I don't live there. I have an apartment in New York.'

'Good for you. I think you're wise. I have a friend who went across to do a movie in LA a couple of years ago and he says that most film stars literally never go out. They barricade themselves in their homes in the hills behind their high-security walls and banks of cameras. That wouldn't suit me at all,' he added with a grin.

'Your friend is right, and it doesn't suit me either. New York is way more relaxed.'

'Except for times like now, when they even stalk you in deepest Devon.' James raised his eyebrows.

'Yes, it's hell right now.' Rebecca gave up on her soup and placed her spoon on the plate beside it.

'I always find it ironic that every young actor's goal is your kind of fame and fortune,' James mused. 'But the price is high. I'm not in your league, of course, but even *my* antics end up in the papers.'

'I guess you're supposed to get used to it.' Rebecca sighed. 'It becomes normal. But it's the lies they tell that get me.'

'But this engagement isn't a lie, is it, Rebecca?'

Rebecca paused and thought how to answer, whilst James cleared away the soup and produced two dishes from the warmer that room service had provided.

'I'd say the announcement was a little . . . premature. But yes, Jack has asked me to marry him.'

'And you've said yes?'

'Kind of. Anyway, let's talk about the film, shall we?' she said abruptly.

'Of course.' James took the hint. 'So, Miss Bradley, tomorrow morning, I get to kiss one of the most beautiful women in the world. Woe is me.' He raised his eyes heavenward and sighed dramatically. 'Acting really is the most rubbish job. And I have to say, Rebecca, you really are the most gorgeous-looking creature.' James leaned forward to study her features. 'I can't even detect a speck of make-up on that face of yours. Not even lipstick.'

'Then you won't recognise me tomorrow. They'll be plastering it on. I'll resemble a painted doll, for sure.'

'Well, it was the era for that kind of look,' said James equably. 'So, apart from Jack, have you ever fallen for any of your co-stars before?'

'No,' Rebecca answered honestly. 'Have you?'

James took a sip of his wine. 'I wouldn't say that my reputation has been exactly spotless,' he admitted, with a mischievous gleam in his eye. 'I have been a bit like a child in a sweet shop, working with so many gorgeous women. But to be honest, I've been no better or worse than any other red-blooded young man in his twenties; the difference is I've done it in the media spotlight. So, moving swiftly on,' he smiled, 'how are you finding England so far?'

Over the course of the evening, Rebecca found herself warming to James. For a well-known actor, he was self-deprecating and possessed a keen sense of humour. She liked the fact that he didn't take himself or his career too seriously; he saw his acting very much as a job. After Jack and his preciousness about his talent and the lack of chances he'd had to show off his ability in the roles he'd been given, James's attitude was a breath of fresh air.

'Let's face it,' he said over mint tea for her and coffee and brandy for him, 'if you and I both looked like the back end of a bus, it's doubtful we'd be playing Elizabeth and Lawrence. That's just the way it is.'

Rebecca smiled. 'I really have to go,' she said, seeing it was already after ten o'clock.

'Of course, and I shall slink next door to my comparative broom cupboard of a bedroom, as you're taken off to sleep like a princess in your tower. I'll say goodnight here, shall I?' He smiled. 'I don't want any lurking photographers outside getting the wrong idea.'

'Yes, thanks,' Rebecca said as she stood up. 'See you tomorrow on set.'

James kissed her gently on both cheeks. 'And seriously, Rebecca, if you ever need to talk, I'm here.'

'Thanks, goodnight,' she whispered as she left the suite. She took the stairs down, rather than risk being caught coming out of the lift, then hurried through the front door of the hotel. Spying Graham waiting in the Mercedes outside, she climbed swiftly into the back of it.

Fifteen minutes later, Rebecca opened the door to her bedroom and closed it behind her. Mrs Trevathan had switched on the bedside lamp and turned back the bedcovers. Undressing and slipping in between the sheets, Rebecca decided that she did indeed feel like the princess James had described.

Sometime during the night, Rebecca awoke with a start, sure she'd heard a sound in the room. After switching on the light, she saw it was empty. She sniffed the air, which seemed to be filled with a smell of heady floral perfume. It wasn't unpleasant, just oddly strong. Rebecca shrugged, turned off the light and eventually drifted back to sleep.

'You're on set in five minutes, Miss Bradley,' said the runner, entering the make-up room.

'And she's ready to go,' said Chrissie the make-up artist, placing a last dash of powder on Rebecca's forehead. 'There,' she said as she removed the protective apron from around Rebecca's shoulders.

'Wow,' said the runner, as Rebecca stood up and turned round. 'You look amazing, Miss Bradley,' he added admiringly.

'She does, doesn't she?' agreed Chrissie.

'Thank you,' said Rebecca, still trying to get used to her newly blonde, bobbed hair, the heavily painted eyes, the alabaster-white skin and the dark red lipstick. She hardly looked like herself at all. Following the runner along the corridor and emerging into the main hall, she saw Anthony walking down the wide marble staircase towards her.

She looked up at him and smiled. 'Good morning.'

As Anthony caught sight of her, he paused on the stairs, a look of shock on his face.

'My God,' he breathed.

'What is it?'

Anthony didn't reply, he just continued to stare at her.

'We'd better go, Miss Bradley,' urged the runner.

'Goodbye,' Rebecca said uncomfortably to the stationary figure on the stairs, and then followed the runner out of the entrance hall.

James was waiting inside the drawing room as the crew set up camera positions on the terrace.

'Love the hair, darling,' he said with a broad smile, 'and is that you under all that make-up?'

'Somewhere, yes,' she quipped back, as they were called on to the set.

'Well, as I'm sure everyone has told you, you look simply ravishing. But personally, I prefer you naked . . . I mean your face, of course,' James whispered cheekily as he offered her his hand and they stepped outside.

Robert Hope, the director, came over and put an approving arm around her shoulders. 'You look perfect, Rebecca. Ready?'

'As I'll ever be,' she breathed nervously.

'You're going to be wonderful, I promise you,' he reassured her. 'Now, you two, let's take a run through from the top of the scene.'

Two hours later, Rebecca stepped back inside the drawing room with James. She flopped into a chair, exhausted from the tension. 'Boy, am I glad that's over.'

'You were great, really,' James commented, as he lit up a cigarette by the open door and smiled at her. 'Your accent was perfection.'

'Thank you,' Rebecca said appreciatively. 'You really helped me feel comfortable.'

'I think we make a good team, don't we? And I really enjoyed that kiss,' he added with a wink.

Rebecca reddened and stood up. 'I'm going in search of a

cool drink. See you later.' She left the room before he could follow her, not wanting to give him any encouragement that their on-screen relationship had any chance of developing off it. She'd seen that look in a number of her co-stars' eyes before. James was a lovely guy, but she needed him as a friend, not a lover.

'Rebecca.' Steve caught her as she made her way to the location catering van. 'The production office has just had an irate call from your agent, saying that your fiancé has been in touch with him. They both want to know where you are. Can you contact them?'

'I did leave them both a message to tell them I was fine,' Rebecca countered. 'But I have no cell service here.'

'I know. It's causing a real problem for everyone, so we've asked Lord Astbury if we can use his landline. We're picking up the bill, of course, so by all means, go and use it. We don't want any scare stories in the press about how you've been kidnapped, do we?' he added and walked swiftly away.

Sighing, Rebecca began to mount the stairs to her room to retrieve her cellphone for the numbers.

'Rebecca?'

She turned round and looked below her. Anthony was standing in the entrance hall.

'Hello,' she said uncertainly. Again, he was staring at her, and she felt distinctly uncomfortable under his piercing gaze.

'Have you got a few minutes?' he asked. 'I want to show you something.'

'Of course,' she answered. She could hardly say no.

Anthony reached out his hand, signalling that she should make her way back down the stairs towards him. He smiled at her as she arrived next to him, his eyes never leaving her face.

'Follow me.' He led her along the corridor that accessed the formal rooms overlooking the garden at the back of the house. Stopping outside one of them, he turned to her. 'Prepare yourself for a surprise.'

'Okay,' Rebecca replied as he opened the door and they entered a spacious library. Pulling her into the centre of the room, Anthony put his hands on her shoulders and turned her round to face the fireplace.

'Look at the painting above it.'

Rebecca found herself staring at a portrait of a young, blonde woman, dressed similarly to herself, with a jewelled headband across her forehead. But it wasn't just what the woman was wearing that struck her, it was her face.

'She –' Rebecca found her voice. 'She looks like me.'

'I know. The likeness is –' Anthony paused – 'extraordinary. When I saw you this morning, with your hair blonde and dressed as you are, I thought I was seeing a ghost.'

Rebecca was still taking in the huge brown eyes, the heart-shaped face as pale as her own, the small retroussé nose and the full lips. 'Who is she?'

'My grandmother Violet. And, what's even stranger, she was American. She married my grandfather, Donald, in 1920 and came to live with him here at Astbury. She was regarded both in England and America as one of the great beauties of her day. Sadly, she died very young, so I never met her. And my grandfather died only a month after her.' Anthony paused, then sighed heavily. 'You could say it was the beginning of the end for the Astbury family.'

'How did Violet die?' Rebecca asked him gently.

'Hers was the fate of many women in those days; she died in childbirth . . .' Anthony's voice trailed off miserably.

'I'm so sorry,' said Rebecca, at a loss.

Recovering himself, Anthony continued. 'Subsequently my poor, sainted mother, Daisy, grew up an orphan, in the care of her grandmother. That's my mother there.' He indicated another portrait, showing a stern-lipped, middle-aged woman. 'I apologise for sounding maudlin, but it's strange that the Astburys have been blighted, one way or the other, ever since Violet's death.' He turned his attention suddenly from the portrait to Rebecca. 'You're not in any way related to the Drumner family of New York, are you? They were a very rich and powerful clan in the early twentieth century. In fact, it was Violet's dowry that saved this estate from ruin.'

Anthony looked at her, waiting for an answer. Her past was not something Rebecca wished to reveal to anyone, and certainly not to a stranger.

'No. My family hails from Chicago, and I've never heard the Drumner name mentioned. The likeness must be simply coincidence.'

'Still –' Anthony offered her a tight smile – 'odd all the same to have you here at Astbury, playing a character from the era Violet lived in. *And* resembling her so strongly.'

'Yes, it is, but I can assure you there's no family connection,' Rebecca repeated adamantly.

'Well, there we are. As you can imagine, it was rather a shock to see you in the hall this morning. Please do forgive me.'

'Of course.'

'Well, I won't hold you up any longer, but I felt I must show you Violet's portrait. And perhaps you would do me the honour of joining me for dinner tonight?' he added.

'Thank you, I'd be delighted to. And now I really have to go. I'm due back on set in an hour.'

'Of course.' Anthony walked to the door, opened it and let Rebecca pass through ahead of him. They walked in silence back to the entrance hall. Rebecca smiled goodbye and once again mounted the stairs to retrieve her cellphone. When she reached the sanctuary of her bedroom, she closed the door, her legs suddenly feeling weak underneath her. She sat down quickly in the armchair next to the fire, put her head forward to rest on her hands and took some deep breaths.

She had lied to him. The only thing she knew about her parents was her mother's name – Jenny Bradley. And the fact that Jenny had put her daughter into foster care when Rebecca was five years old.

The people she regarded as her parents were Bob and Margaret – a kind couple who had fostered Rebecca when she was six. Over the years, they'd tried to adopt Rebecca, but her mother had always refused to sign the paperwork, assuming that one day she would be well enough to care for her daughter herself.

Emotionally, the situation had been difficult for her to cope with; the permanency and security she so craved were not available to her. When she'd been a young girl, fear had coursed through her on many a night at the thought of her mother coming to claim her, taking her back to the life she dimly remembered before she'd gone into care.

Finally, when Rebecca was nineteen, Bob and Margaret told her gently that her mother had died of an overdose.

She'd never known who her father was. She had no idea whether Jenny had either. She guessed she'd probably been conceived when her mother was turning tricks to buy alcohol and drugs.

Rebecca stared forlornly across the room. Who knew if her

father *had* been related to Violet Drumner? It was as good a possibility as any. But as there was no name for him on her birth certificate, she would never be able to investigate.

Rebecca felt the first pang she'd experienced since her arrival here for the familiar comfort of Jack's arms. She grabbed her cell, which contained his number, and took herself down to Anthony's study to call him on the landline.

Yet again she got his voicemail, but knew that Jack never answered calls from numbers he didn't recognise, for security reasons.

'Hi, honey, it's me. There's no signal here so I'm using the landline again. I'll try again later. I've got an hour until I'm back on set. Hope you're okay. Bye.'

Ending the call, she then dialled Victor's number; this time he answered.

'How are you, sweetie? I was about to send the CIA to hunt you down.'

'I'm good. We're filming in an amazing old house and, because of all the media attention, the guy who owns it, Lord Astbury, has let me stay here. Don't worry at all, Victor, I'm perfectly safe,' she reassured him.

'Good. So, what is all this about you and Jack getting engaged? You might have discussed it with me first before you went ahead and said yes.'

'Really? I kind of think who I want to marry is my decision, Victor, don't you?' Rebecca drummed her fingers on the table, irritated.

'You know I didn't mean it like that, honey,' Victor soothed. 'All I'm saying is that it might just have been easier if you'd told me you were going to announce it and we could have managed it for you.'

'As a matter of fact,' she retorted, 'between you and me, I haven't even said yes to him yet.'

There was a momentary pause at the other end of the line. 'What? Are you kidding me, Rebecca?'

'No, I'm not.' Rebecca could hear the panic in Victor's voice and wanted to laugh. 'I told Jack I needed time to think about it. And I do,' she emphasised. 'It's not my fault he decided to go ahead and confirm it before he got my answer.'

'Jesus, Rebecca. The world has been besieging me for a quote from you. You can't retract now; you'd have an army of Jack's fans sending you hate mail and boycotting your movies.'

Rebecca could feel her blood pressure rising further. 'Victor, I need time to think about it, okay?' she stated firmly.

'Well, this time, can I be the second guy you tell your decision to? And I hope the answer will be in the affirmative. Hey, kiddo,' he added, lowering his voice, 'you can always divorce him if things don't work out. This is a crucial moment in your career and I don't want you to jeopardise it with any negative publicity.' There was another pause on the line before Victor said, 'There isn't anyone else, is there?'

'Jesus, Victor! Of course not.' Rebecca felt herself losing patience with him.

'Well, that's something, I guess. Just don't you be getting nice and cosy with that young British guy playing your lover. His reputation with women stinks.'

'Is the lecture over?' Rebecca asked bluntly. 'Do you want to hear about how filming went today or not?'

'Listen, baby, can we speak another time? I've got to get moving for a breakfast meeting.'

'Sure.'

'Good girl. Call me later, okay?'

'I will. Bye, Victor.'

Rebecca ended the call and stared disconsolately at the pretty satin shoes on her feet. She knew Victor meant well – he was a very good agent and had built her career perfectly. But sometimes his protectiveness went too far. He didn't own her, nor was he her father.

Rebecca stared at the array of old photos in silver frames on Anthony's desk, envying him for having the stability of a proper family he could trace back for generations. They were all taken in black and white, and Rebecca immediately recognised Anthony's mother from her portrait. In the photograph, she was holding the hand of a pretty young girl with blonde ringlets. The resemblance to Anthony was marked, and Rebecca surmised the child must be his sister. Rising from the desk, Rebecca glanced at the old travel alarm and saw that she had only twenty minutes left to eat something before the afternoon shoot.

4

There was a light tap on Rebecca's door at seven forty-five that evening.

'Come in,' Rebecca called, wishing she hadn't accepted Anthony's invitation to dinner. She was exhausted after her first day's filming.

'Are you ready, Rebecca?' Mrs Trevathan said, her bright face peering round the door.

'I'll be down in a few minutes.'

Rebecca climbed out of her bathrobe, donned jeans and a shirt and hand-dried the new and still-strange short bob. Standing in front of the mirror, she surveyed her face. Without make-up, she thought her new hair colour made her look sallow. She hardly felt like herself at all.

As she left her bedroom and walked down the main staircase, she pondered over Mrs Trevathan's obvious devotion to Lord Anthony. Like everything else here, their master-and-servant relationship was from another era. It was as if time had forgotten Astbury Hall and its residents. She paused outside the dining-room door, then knocked.

'Come.'

Rebecca pushed the door open and found Anthony already

seated at the top of a long, graceful mahogany table. The fact that he sat alone in the grand, formal room, at a table meant to accommodate many, only emphasised his solitude.

'Hello.' He smiled at her and indicated the place-setting next to him on his left. As she approached the chair, he stood up and pulled it out for her.

'Thank you,' she murmured as he returned to sit in his own chair.

'Wine?' he asked her, lifting the decanter of ruby-red liquid from a silver salver on the table. 'We're having beef, and this claret is the perfect accompaniment.'

'Just a small glass,' Rebecca said, not wishing to be rude, but she so rarely drank. And if she did, her choice would not be red wine. Nor, in fact, would she have chosen beef to eat.

'Of course, my dear mother had a butler to decant and serve this,' Anthony commented as he poured the wine into her glass. 'Sadly, when he retired, there was no money to replace him.'

'I can't imagine how much it must cost to keep this place going,' commented Rebecca.

'No, and you don't want to either,' Anthony sighed as Mrs Trevathan entered with a tray and placed soup in front of both of them. 'But we struggle on somehow, don't we, Mrs Trevathan?' He looked at his housekeeper with a warm smile.

'We do, My Lord, we do,' Mrs Trevathan nodded as she left the room.

'Mrs Trevathan keeps the place going virtually single-handedly. If she ever decided to leave, I don't know what I'd do. Please –' he indicated her soup – 'let's begin.'

'Has she worked here all her life?'

'Yes, as did her ancestors before her. In fact, Mabel, her mother, cared for me when I was a child.'

'It must be wonderful to have years of family history, to know where you come from,' said Rebecca, sipping her soup.

'In some ways, I suppose.' Anthony sighed. 'Although as I mentioned to you earlier, a pall fell on this house when Violet died. You do know, my dear, that the dress you were wearing when I saw you on the stairs belonged to her?'

Rebecca looked at him and felt a sudden shiver run up her spine. 'Really?'

'Yes. And her daughter Daisy – that is, my mother – kept all her gowns in perfect condition after she died.'

'So I suppose Daisy never knew her mother, if Violet died giving birth to her?'

'No, but she worshipped Violet, or at least the thought of who her mother had been. As I worshipped *her*,' Anthony said sadly.

'How long ago did your mother die?' Rebecca asked softly.

'Twenty-five years ago now. I still miss her, to be truthful. We were very close.'

'Yes, to lose a mother is the worst,' agreed Rebecca.

'It was only us, you see. She was everything to me.'

'What about your father?'

Anthony's craggy face darkened. 'He wasn't a good man. My poor mother suffered terribly at his hands. He never liked Astbury to begin with and spent most of his time in London,' he explained. 'My mother wasn't exactly sorry when he died in some grubby whorehouse in the East End. He'd apparently got so drunk that he fell and broke his neck.'

Rebecca saw Anthony shudder at the memory. She understood completely what he felt. Instinctively, she wanted to tell him that she, too, knew that pain, but she wasn't ready to share her secret with a virtual stranger. 'I'm sorry, that must have been tough on you,' she managed.

'Thankfully, I was barely three at the time, so I hardly remember him. I certainly didn't miss his presence as I grew up. Anyway, let's not talk any more of the past.' Anthony placed his soup spoon by his empty dish. 'Tell me about yourself,' he said, as Mrs Trevathan cleared the soup bowls and set a large slice of beef in front of each of them.

'Oh, I guess I'm just an average American girl from Chicago,' she answered.

'Hardly "average",' Anthony chided her. 'Everyone tells me I'm sitting at dinner with one of the most well-known and beautiful women in the world. Just as my grandmother Violet was described in her heyday.'

Rebecca blushed, embarrassed by the compliment on her looks. 'I've been very lucky and got the breaks. So many young actresses don't.'

'I'm sure talent has got something to do with it,' continued Anthony, 'although, as I said, I haven't ever seen any of your films. However, I would add that many women are beautiful, but very few have that personal magnetism that marks them out. You have it, and from what everyone told me, Violet had it too. She was the toast of London and New York society and entertained the great and the good here at Astbury Hall. Those were the days,' he added wistfully. 'I sometimes feel I had the misfortune of being born in the wrong era. But enough of that.'

Silence ensued as Anthony cleared his plate of the tender beef, while Rebecca merely played with hers. Eventually, Anthony asked, 'Have you had all you'd like to eat, my dear?'

'Yes.' Rebecca looked guiltily at her still half-full plate. 'I apologise, I really don't have a big appetite.'

'So I see. So I couldn't tempt you to a taste of Mrs Trevathan's apple and blackberry crumble?'

'I'm afraid not.' Rebecca stifled a yawn, and Anthony placed a surprisingly soft hand on hers.

'You're tired.'

'Yes, a little. I was up real early this morning for Hair and Make-up.'

'Of course. And I'm sure the last thing you want is to be bored to death by a crusty old man like me. Why don't you go upstairs, and I'll have Mrs Trevathan bring you some hot milk? It might be old-fashioned, but I believe in its somnolent qualities.'

'If you're sure you don't mind.'

'Of course not. Although I might well request the pleasure of your company again. Despite my usual preference for solitude, I've rather enjoyed this evening. Ah, Mrs Trevathan –' Anthony glanced up – 'Rebecca is retiring and I said you'd take her some hot milk.'

'Of course, Your Lordship.'

'Well then, my dear.' Anthony stood up with Rebecca, took her hand in his and kissed it. 'It's been a pleasure. Sleep well.'

'I will. And thank you so much for dinner.'

Tucked up in bed with a glass of warm milk by her side and gazing at a heavy dusk which still seemed reluctant to give itself up completely to the night, Rebecca thought back over her conversation with Anthony. With his perfect manners and quaint way of speaking, he was as much a relic of the past as the house. But living here, amidst the glorious yet empty acres, in a house untouched by the present, it was easy to imagine how life had been a hundred years ago. With the cast and crew gone and the house returned to its usual rhythms, she herself almost felt modern reality was slowly melting away, too.

Rebecca shook herself; tomorrow she must force herself back into the present, the one that existed outside the enchanted world of Astbury, and make a real effort to contact Jack. Switching the light off, she settled down to sleep.

Once more, sometime during the long hours before dawn, Rebecca smelt the strong aroma of flowers, which filled her nostrils and made her dream of exotic places she had longed to visit but never had. Then she was sure she heard singing, a high-pitched sound which drew her from sleep. She climbed out of bed and, disorientated, the noise still in her ears, she walked towards the door and opened it. The corridor outside was in darkness, and the sound stopped abruptly.

It was a dream, Rebecca convinced herself as she made her way back to bed and lay down. There was silence again now, but the sound of the high, sweet voice stayed with her and lulled her back into sleep.

5

Mumbai, India

Ari was glad to be home. It had been a long day at the office, at the end of a difficult week. He opened the door to his duplex and went straight to the kitchen to pour himself a hefty gin and tonic, hoping it would calm his frayed nerves. And equally hoping that Lali wouldn't start complaining that he drank too much. Compared to some of his Western business associates, what he consumed was nothing. He wandered through to the sitting room and, finding it deserted, assumed that Lali must be taking a shower downstairs. Throwing himself lengthwise onto the sofa, he took a gulp of his drink.

He wondered why currently he felt so stressed, given that his company was going from strength to strength. Especially recently, as the global financial crisis had forced America and the European countries to look to India, with its less costly possibilities. They now had more work than they could possibly cope with, and that, Ari sighed, was part of the problem. Trying to find trustworthy and trained managers to help him cope with the influx of business was proving a nightmare. Subsequently, he was doing the jobs of ten employees.

Lali was always at him about taking a holiday, proffering brochures of tranquil beach resorts. She didn't seem to understand that the thought was simply impossible to contemplate at the moment.

'When I find some staff I can trust, we can go, I promise.'

'Ari, sweetheart, you've been saying that now for the past three years,' she would sigh sadly, as she collected the brochures from him and threw them into the wastepaper bin.

Feeling guilty after these outbursts, Ari would arrive home with a piece of jewellery his secretary had picked out, or perhaps a dress from one of her favourite designer stores. He would apologise profusely for neglecting her and make an effort to arrive home on time and take her out to dinner. In the following few days, they would go through the motions of discussing how they could spend more time together, but by the following week Ari would be back to his usual eighteen-hour days.

As he drained the gin and tonic and went to pour himself another, he admitted to himself that, out of frustration, he sometimes shouted at her.

'How else are we meant to get the money to pay the mortgage on this duplex? Or buy you all the lovely things in your wardrobe?'

Her answer was always the same. 'I don't care where I live, or what I wear on my body. Those are the things *you* care about, Ari, not me.'

It wasn't true, of course, he told himself as he stepped out onto the terrace of the duplex and looked out across the beach to the Arabian Sea. She'd like to think she wouldn't miss all this, but of course she would.

His working hours aside, Ari knew a far bigger problem lay between them. Lali was almost thirty now, and eager to get married. He didn't blame her for that; she herself had compromised and gone against the wishes of her family to move in with him four years ago, trusting that he would soon propose. Yet, try as he might, Ari could never bring himself to say the words she needed to hear. He wasn't sure why this was, because there was no doubt that he loved Lali. She was very beautiful and her gentle, sweet nature and calm temperament were a perfect foil to his more volatile personality. As his friends had said many times, she was perfect for him.

So, what was he waiting for? He was thirty-six now, and had played the field with a string of gorgeous women before Lali. But, somehow, there was an instinct inside him that prevented him from taking the final leap.

He had noticed in the past few weeks that she had withdrawn from him, was often not at home to feed and comfort him after his long day. She said she was spending more time at the gym or hanging out with her girlfriends. And who could blame her? Often, if he was working at home, he hardly noticed whether she was there or not.

Ari wandered inside, searching the huge apartment for her. Tonight, he missed her presence, and it seemed she hadn't even left him a note or sent him a text as to her whereabouts. He showered, then walked to the fridge to find something to eat. He heated up last night's leftovers in the microwave, poured himself a glass of wine and went through to the sitting room. He switched on the enormous TV and channel-hopped until he found some English football. He had work to do as always, but felt too exhausted to contemplate it tonight.

The one piece of good news on the horizon was that he had noticed a young salesman he had taken on two years ago was outperforming his colleagues. Ari had re-interviewed him a couple of weeks ago and had offered him a promotion to a position taking care of the Indian side of the operation, which was also growing as the national economy continued to pick up steam. If Dhiren proved himself in the next six months, Ari reckoned he had director potential.

In three weeks' time, Ari was heading off to meet possible new clients in London. He needed someone to steer the ship when he was travelling and this would be a good test.

Perhaps, he mused, he should ask Lali to come with him. Even though he'd have little time to spend with her, she might enjoy seeing the sights. Yes, he thought, he would suggest that when she came in.

At half past eleven, Ari switched off the lights in the sitting room and wandered downstairs to the bedroom. It was extremely unusual for Lali to be out this late, and certainly without telling him where she was. A nerve began to flicker in Ari's temple. He tried her cell, but it went directly to voicemail. Probably sulking, he told himself, remembering the several occasions she had threatened to leave him before. With the help of his considerable powers of persuasion, he always managed to talk her round. And he would again, this time.

At eight o'clock the following morning, as he was downing a coffee before leaving for the office, Ari heard the key turn in the lock. Lali entered the kitchen, looking pale and drawn. Without her usually perfect make-up in place, she resembled a small, weary child. She stood by the entrance to the kitchen and Ari realised that she was nervous.

'And where have you been, may I enquire?' he asked.

'I stayed with my parents last night.'

'Really? I thought you didn't speak to them any more,' he said in surprise.

'I didn't. I knew you didn't like them.'

'Excuse me,' Ari countered, 'if I remember rightly, when you said you were moving in with me, they told you never to darken their doorstep again. I thought you weren't too keen on them either.'

She stared at him, her huge dark eyes filling with tears. 'They're my parents, Ari. I have missed them and felt guilty every day for letting them down.'

'Letting them down?' Ari stared at her. 'What do you mean? You took a decision they didn't like, that's all.'

'I . . .' She sighed and shook her head. 'Ari, I think you are very different to me.'

'What do you mean?'

'It doesn't matter now.' She shrugged sadly. 'I don't want to fight.'

'Lali, what is this all about? Come on, spit it out.'

She paused, then took a deep breath in preparation. 'I'm moving back in with my parents, Ari. I'm only here to collect my things.'

'Right. Is this new arrangement for a night? A month? Or forever?'

'Forever. I'm sorry.'

'So, what you're actually trying to say is that you're leaving me?' Ari confirmed, finally understanding.

'Yes. I don't want an argument or any discussion. I just want to collect my stuff and go.'

Ari could see she was shaking with emotion. He nodded slowly. 'Okay. Are you sure you don't want to talk about it?'

'Yes. There's nothing left to say. I'll go and start packing.'

He watched her as she turned away from him and left the room. He wasn't too concerned; they'd been here before.

However, the idea of her moving back in with her parents – who had never liked him – was not a satisfactory one. He got up from the table and followed her downstairs to the bedroom.

'Lali, *pyari*, I can see you're very upset, but I really think we should talk. As a matter of fact, I was going to suggest that you come with me to Europe. You're right, we do need a break, some time together.'

'There will be no time, Ari, there never is. You'll spend your days in meetings and I will wait for you at the hotel. And when you come in, you'll be too tired to do anything but sleep.' Lali dragged a suitcase from the bottom of the wardrobe, heaved it onto the bed and went to the chest of drawers. She began throwing its contents into the case.

'Lali.' Ari moved towards her to hug her. 'I—'

'Don't touch me!' she cried as she dodged out of his embrace and went back to the wardrobe to remove her clothes from their hangers.

'Lali, what is it you're upset about? Please, tell me. I love you, you know I do, *pyari*, I don't want you to go.'

'No.' She looked up at him then, her expression one of sadness. 'I believe you. But I have to, for me.' Lali lowered her head and her eyes filled with tears.

'But why? I thought we were okay, and things have been good recently. I—'

'I know you think they've been okay,' she said as she zipped up the suitcase, then took a holdall and began putting the toiletries from her dressing table inside it. 'Ari, this is not your fault. It's just the way it is.'

'You're talking in riddles, sweetheart, and I don't get what you're trying to say. If it's not my fault, then whose fault is it?'

Lali paused and gave a long sigh, staring off into the

distance. 'We both want different things from our lives, that's all. I want marriage, children and a husband who can find some time in his day to enjoy being with me.' Her gaze moved towards him and she gave the ghost of a smile. 'All you want is success and money. I hope it brings you the contentment you think it will. Now,' Lali said as she closed the holdall and dragged the suitcase from the bed, 'my father is waiting downstairs for me. I must go.' She fished in the pocket of her jeans and brought out a key ring. 'Here are the keys to the apartment and the car.' Putting them on the dressing table, she looked at him. 'Goodbye, Ari. I will always love you and wish for your happiness.'

Ari stood, mesmerised, as Lali wheeled her bags out of the bedroom and dragged them up the stairs. He heard the front door close behind her before he was prompted into action. He ran out of the apartment and saw the lift doors closing on her.

'Lali!' He slammed his fist on the button to reopen them, but the lift had already begun its descent. Ari slowly walked back inside his apartment, closed the door behind him and leaned against it. Surely she didn't mean it? Perhaps this was merely a ruse to finally get him to marry her. Well, if it was, he thought determinedly, it wouldn't work. He didn't respond to blackmail.

Besides, he thought, it was doubtful that she would last two minutes at her parents' shack. They didn't even have running water, for God's sake, and she'd have to share a room with her four younger siblings. After the life she'd been used to with him, she wasn't going to like it at all.

Anger was replacing shock now, as he thought of what he'd done for her. She had always said she didn't care about material possessions. That if he'd been camping in an illegal shack on the beach selling fenugreek for a few rupees a day, it wouldn't have mattered for it was *him* she loved.

'Well,' he said out loud to the silent apartment, 'once she's been at her parents' for a while, we'll see if that's true.'

With a new defiance, and realising that he was late, Ari picked up his car keys and left for the office.

A week later, Ari wasn't feeling quite so gung-ho. Lali had made no contact since she had left and he, despite having relished the thought of time spent uninterrupted on his computer catching up properly on work, had spent most of it staring out of his huge windows, watching the families on the crowded beach below screaming in delight as they entered the choppy sea.

The truth was, he missed her. He missed her far more than he could ever have imagined. Numerous times he had picked up his cellphone and dialled her number, but then his pride had refused to let the number connect. *She* was the one who had left *him*, it told him. And it was Lali who must make contact first. He wouldn't give her a hard time, he thought. He would listen to her apology, take her back without a word and then, in his own time, ask her to marry him. He'd let her win . . .

But as the days had worn on, Ari's resolve had started to weaken. He wished that night, as he sat alone in his large, empty apartment, that he could talk to someone about his dilemma, ask their advice. But try as he might, he could think of no one he was close enough to who might listen. He had been too busy in the past few years to make an effort to keep in contact with his childhood friends, and since he had refused to attend Anahita's funeral ten years ago, his relationship with his parents and siblings had deteriorated. Nowadays, he would call home once a month at most, and speak to whoever answered, asking after their health and if there was any news. Even his mother, when it was she who picked up the call, sounded cool and distant. And none of his family ever called him spontaneously any more.

They've given up on me, he thought with a sigh as he made his way downstairs to the big lonely bed. He climbed under the sheet and lay there with his hands behind his head, wondering how it was that before Lali had left, there never seemed to be enough time for anything. But now that she was no longer here, the evening hours dragged past like a slowly shifting fog.

The following morning, facing a long, empty weekend, Ari made up his mind. He'd have to swallow his pride and go after her. Girding his loins, he dialled her cellphone number and, for the first time, waited for it to connect without ending the call. But instead of hearing Lali's cheerful voice asking the caller to leave a message, there was a monotonous drone that indicated the number was no longer in use.

For the first time since Lali had walked out, Ari felt a faint tingle of fear clutch at his heart. Up until now, he had been convinced that he was merely involved in a battle of wills which he'd been prepared to lose graciously. It had never struck him for an instant that Lali might actually be serious about ending their relationship.

Ari tried her cellphone again but received the same sound. As panic began to rise within him, he thought of how he might actually find her. He only knew that her parents lived somewhere in the labyrinthine streets of Dharavi – he'd been there once but would have no idea how to retrace his footsteps. Ari then racked his brains for friends of hers whom he knew. Lali had kept her female social life to herself, as many of the girls she had grown up with were from poor families, like herself. She'd understood that they were not the kind of sophisticated women one could make up a four with for dinner at the Indigo Café. Ari had absolutely no idea how to find any of them.

He wondered how it was possible that he could have lived under the same roof as Lali for the past four years yet know almost nothing about her life beyond their front door. *Was I responsible for that?* he asked himself brutally as he paced back and forth on the sun-filled terrace.

Of course he was, he admitted finally. Certainly, as far as her parents were concerned, he'd made it clear that he wasn't interested in forming a relationship with them. And he'd made no effort to try to, even for her sake. They were not bad people . . . poor, yes, but hard-working and devout Hindus who had brought their children up with a strong set of moral values and fought to educate them to the best of their meagre resources.

Ari dropped in exhaustion onto a chair and leaned forward, his head in his hands. He realised that he had patronised not only them, but also what they stood for – the blind faith in their gods, humility and acceptance of their lot, was what he despised. They were the 'old India' – just as his parents were – whose servility had been engendered by over a hundred years of British rule.

The older generation didn't seem to understand that the power had transferred, that there was no longer any need for subservience. The race he had been born into was coming into its own, there was nothing holding them back any longer and the sky was the limit.

He'd wanted to run away from all the old values, which he

felt placed limitations on those who believed in them. Sitting there, staring into space, Ari realised he was angry. But why?

Suddenly, he did something he had forbidden himself to do for years. He put his head in his hands and wept.

Ari knew he wouldn't forget the long dark hours of that weekend in a hurry, as he faced what he had become and why. Whether he was grieving over the loss of Lali, or for himself and the solitary, self-obsessed, angry person he had become, he wasn't sure. As his pain poured out of him, he wondered whether he was having some form of breakdown, perhaps the result of fifteen years of pushing himself, day after day, without respite.

Yes, he realised, he had gained a successful business, and the financial benefits that went with it. But in the process, he'd lost himself.

He tried to work his way through the reasons for his anger and, more frighteningly, his dismissal of any emotion and compassion that had once been inside him. He thought back to his time at his boarding school in England, and the way the boys had looked down on him, simply because he was Indian. Independence may have come to India over sixty years before, but back then, the upper-class British had not surrendered their claim to empirical superiority.

What had made it worse was that his parents had been so proud of him. Despite what *he* saw as the many terrible consequences of British rule for the Indian race, the culture and traditions of their masters had been indelibly imprinted upon them. To them, for an Indian boy to attend a British public school was still the ultimate jewel in the crown.

However, Ari was aware that, even if his five years in

England had contributed to his need to prove that he was as worthy and clever as any of the English boys there, the integral drive to succeed came from within himself. And he also realised that, by eschewing all the qualities that made his race unique, he had become as much an imperialist as those who had once ruled his country. He had lost his Indian soul.

On Sunday evening, Ari walked out of his apartment block and asked the first person he met on Juhu Tara Road for directions to the nearest temple. Out of embarrassment, he explained that he was a stranger to Mumbai.

Once inside the temple, he removed his shoes and went through the rituals of worship and prayer that years ago had been as instinctive to him as breathing but now felt strange and foreign. Ari made *puja* offerings, not as he had done on his rare visits in the past few years to Lakshmi, the goddess of wealth, but to Parvati, the goddess of love and to Vishnu, the all-powerful preserver and protector. He asked them for forgiveness, especially for the way he had exiled himself from his parents. And he pleaded for Lali to return to him.

When he arrived home, calmer now, Ari immediately called his parents. And it was his mother who answered.

'Hello, Ma. I—'

'What is it, *beta*?'

The fact that she had heard immediately that something was wrong brought the tears to his eyes again and he broke down. He begged forgiveness of her, his father and his brothers and sisters. 'I'm so sorry, Ma, really,' he wept.

'My son, it breaks my heart to hear you. Is it Lali who has broken yours?'

Ari paused. 'How did you know, Ma?'

'Did she not tell you that she came to see us two weeks ago?'

'No, she didn't.'

'I see.'

'What did she say, Ma?' he asked.

'She said –' Ari heard Samina sigh – 'that she couldn't wait any longer for you to commit to her. That she was sure now it was because you didn't love her enough and that it was best she set you free. You know how much she wanted a family, *pyara*.'

'Yes. Yes, of course I did. And I still do. Please believe me, Ma, I love her. I miss her . . . I want her to come home. If you know where she is, tell her that from me. I –' Ari could not speak any more.

'Oh, my son, I'm so sorry, but she won't be coming home to you.'

'Why not?' Ari could hear that he sounded like a spoilt three-year-old child, asking why he couldn't have his favourite toy to play with.

'I'm sorry that it's me who has to tell you this, but perhaps it's best that you know. I'm sure you remember that her parents had arranged a marriage for her, which she refused to accept when she met you.'

'Yes.' Ari remembered it vaguely. 'Some cousin near Kolkata, I seem to recall. He was a farmer and much older than she was. Lali said she loathed him on sight.'

'Well, maybe she did and maybe she didn't,' Samina said, equivocating, 'but she married him yesterday.'

Ari was shocked into silence.

'Ari, are you there?'

'Yes.' He managed to find his voice. 'Why? I don't under-stand –'

'I do,' replied his mother quietly. 'Lali is almost thirty years old, Ari. She has no trade or profession by which to earn her own living, and her parents are too poor to provide a dowry. She said that at least she would be safe and secure financially with this older man for the rest of her life.'

'What?!' Ari could hardly believe the words his mother was saying. 'But, Ma, she was safe and secure here, with me! I may not have given her enough time, but I gave her everything I could financially.'

'Yes, but you neglected to give her the one thing she needed. That every woman would like, especially in India.'

'You mean marriage?' Ari groaned.

'Of course. As Lali said herself, if you had tired of her, you could have thrown her onto the streets with nothing. She had no rights as your mistress, no status, no property . . . these are things that are deeply important, you must understand that.'

'If only she'd spoken to me about it.' Ari bit his lip.

'I believe she had, many times, until she gave up.' Samina sighed. 'She said you didn't hear her. All she had on her side was her youth and beauty. And time was running out.'

'I . . . didn't understand. Really, Ma, believe me.'

'And of course, she was too proud to beg you.'

'Ma, what do I do?' he asked despairingly.

'Start again?' Samina suggested. 'And perhaps learn a lesson too. But Lali has gone forever.'

'I . . . need to go now, I have work to do.'

'Keep in touch—' he heard his mother say as, unable to hear any more, he pressed the button to end the call.

For the first time in his life, Ari did not go to the office the following day. He called Dhiren, his new sales manager, and told him he was sick with a fever. For the next few days, he slept as though he was a hibernating animal. He left his bed only to eat, drink and go to the bathroom. His legendary energy seemed to have left him and when he saw his reflection in the mirror, he looked smaller somehow, and pale – as if part of him had been stripped away. Which, in some ways, he thought miserably, it had.

In the rare moments he was awake, he lay staring at the ceiling, wondering how the spark of determination that had driven him on every day for the past fifteen years could have disappeared. When calls came through from the office, he didn't answer them. He simply couldn't face it.

On Tuesday night, as he staggered out into the brightness on the terrace and hung over its railings looking down at the world continuing beneath him, he contemplated his own future. And there it hung ahead of him, gaping like an empty, dark void. He rested his head on his hands. 'Lali, I'm so, so sorry,' he sighed.

From inside, he heard the intercom buzz. Running towards it, praying wildly that it might be her, he grabbed the receiver.

'Hello?'

'*Beta*, it's me, your mother.'

'Come up,' he said, disappointment coursing through him that it wasn't Lali. He was surprised, too; his parents lived a five-hour car journey away from Mumbai.

'My son.' Samina held out her loving arms to her boy as Ari opened the door to let her inside.

In that moment, all the tension and bitterness of the past ten years dissolved and Ari stood, cradled in his mother's embrace, sobbing like a child.

'I'm so sorry, Ma, so very sorry.'

'Ari –' Samina pushed her son's hair back from his eyes and smiled at him – 'you are back with your family and that is all that matters. Now, how about making your old mother some tea? She's had a long drive.'

That evening, Ari talked with his mother, letting out the thoughts that had surrounded him for the past few days and the bleakness he felt for his future.

'Well, at least now you're speaking to me from your heart and not that hard head of yours,' Samina said, trying to comfort him. 'I'd wondered all this time where my son had gone, and if he would ever return to me. So this is a good beginning. You have learned a very important lesson, Ari; that contentment comes from many different things and not just one alone. Money and success can never make you happy if your heart is closed.'

'Anahita said much the same thing to me when I last saw her,' Ari mused. 'And she said that one day I would realise it.'

'Your great-grandmother was a very wise woman.'

'Yes, and I feel ashamed I wasn't there to say goodbye to her.'

'Well, if you believe, as she did, in the spirits, I'm sure she is here with us, accepting your apology. Now –' she yawned – 'I'm tired after my journey and need some sleep.'

'Of course,' Ari replied, and led her downstairs to one of the beautifully furnished bedrooms.

'So much space, just for you,' Samina said as Ari put her overnight bag down. 'And a whole night without your father snoring in my ear. I may never want to leave!'

'Stay as long as you want to, Ma,' said Ari, surprised that he actually meant it and ashamed that he had never invited her to his home before. 'And thank you for coming,' he added as he kissed her goodnight.

'You are my son, I was worried for you. No matter how big your apartment, or how rich you are, you are still my beloved firstborn.' Samina stroked her son's cheek affectionately.

As Ari climbed into bed half an hour later, he felt bizarrely comforted that his mother was sleeping only metres away from him. He was humbled by her lack of recriminations for his past behaviour and the fact that she had flown immediately to his side the minute she had heard he was in trouble. He then thought of Anahita, and the way she'd refused to believe her *own* firstborn was dead for all those years.

Was there an innate sixth sense for a mother when it came to her child?

Ari's eyes were drawn to the chest of drawers. Inside it lay his great-grandmother's story, untouched for eleven years. Even though he was alone, Ari felt a blush rise to his cheeks, just as it had when he had last been in his great-grandmother's presence.

If she *were* with him now, he hoped she would hear how sorry he was for ignoring what she had entrusted to him. Climbing out of bed, he opened the drawer and took out the yellowing pages. Looking at the immaculate handwriting, he saw that it was scripted in small, neat English.

Ari could feel his eyelids were heavy. Now was not the time to try to decipher the words, but he promised himself that he would begin reading it tomorrow.

The following day, Ari took his mother out for breakfast before she began the long journey home.

'Will you be returning to work tomorrow?' Samina asked him. 'You really should, it will help take your mind off everything, rather than mooning around in that soulless apartment of yours by yourself.'

'Honestly, Ma,' Ari said, chuckling, 'one minute you're at me for working too hard, the next, you're pushing me back to the office!'

'There should always be a balance in life, and you must try to find that in yours. Then you might find the happiness you seek. Oh, before I forget –' Samina dug inside her handbag and brought out a tattered copy of Rudyard Kipling's book of poems *Rewards and Fairies* and handed it to Ari – 'your father sent this for you. He said you were to read the poem "If", and to tell you that it's one of his favourites.'

'Yes.' Ari smiled. 'I know it, but I haven't read it since school.'

Once his mother had left, having secured from Ari a promise to visit the family the moment he arrived back from his travels, he drove to the office.

Calling Dhiren in to see him, Ari told him that he was entrusting the business to him whilst he was in London and that he might be away for longer than he had previously thought.

Twenty-four hours later, he boarded the night flight to Heathrow. Ignoring the film selections, Ari reread the poem by Rudyard Kipling that his father had sent him and smiled ironically. He understood its message. Then, ordering a glass of wine, he took his great-grandmother's pile of yellowing pages from his briefcase.

Jaipur, India,

1911

6

Anahita

My child, I remember. In the still of the night, the merest hint of a breeze was a blessed relief from the interminable dry heat of Jaipur. Often, the other ladies and children of the zenana and I would climb up to the rooftops of the Moon Palace, where we would make our beds.

The city of Jaipur lies on a plain, surrounded by brown desert hills. As a child, I used to think that I must live in the most beautiful place on earth, for the city itself had a fairy-tale quality. The buildings were painted the prettiest pink imaginable. Domed houses with exquisitely carved lattice-work and elegantly pillared verandas laced the wide streets. And, of course, the Moon Palace itself occupied the best location – it was a town in itself, surrounded by lush gardens. The inside was a labyrinth, the scalloped arches leading to inner courtyards, which would in turn reveal their own secrets.

And the Jaipur residents themselves were colourful; the men wore vivid turbans of yellow, magenta and ruby-red. I used to gaze down on them sometimes from one of the high terraces which overlooked the city from the palace, and think how they reminded me of hundreds of bright ants, going ceaselessly about their business.

In my palace at the centre of the magical city, living amongst the highest in the land, it was easy to feel as though I was a princess, just like many of my playmates were.

But, of course, I was not.

Up until the age of nine, I had lived amongst the people in the streets below me.

My mother, Tira, was from a long line of *baidh*, the Indian term for a wise woman and healer. From a young age, she would have me sit with her as people from the town came to consult her for help with their problems. Out in our small back garden she grew many sweet-smelling herbs with which to mix her Ayurvedic potions, and I often watched her grinding the *guggulu*, *manjishtha* or *gokhru* on her *shil noda* to prepare a remedy. The customer would seem pacified and go away feeling happier in their heart that their true love would love them back, or that their bad tumour would disappear, or that they would conceive a child within the month.

Sometimes, when a female customer came to the house, my mother would tell our maid to take me out walking for a few hours. I began to notice that, when she asked this, the woman would be sitting on the cushions in our back room, her face drawn and terrified.

Of course, I didn't know then how my mother helped these women, but I do now. She helped them take care of unwanted babies.

My child, you may think that such a deed is a sin against the gods. It was usually because a woman already had half a dozen children or more – there were no forms of stopping babies from arriving in those days in India – and the family was so poor, they simply couldn't afford another mouth to feed. Conversely, she would help mothers when a child wished to come *into* the world too. And as I grew up, she started to take me along to assist her. When I first saw a baby being born, I admit to shielding my eyes, but, as with anything, especially when it's nature, one becomes used to the sight and starts to view it as the miracle it is.

Sometimes, my mother and I would ride out on the pony that my father kept stabled outside the city, and visit the villages outside Jaipur. And that was when I began to understand that everyone did not exist in a pink, fairytale city with loving parents and food on the table every night. I saw terrible things on those visits: poverty, disease, starvation and the agony that human beings can suffer. I learned when I was very young that life was not fair. It was a lesson I was to remember for the rest of my days.

My mother, like all Hindus, was highly superstitious, although my father used to tease her that she took it to new levels. Once, when I was six years old, we were preparing to journey to see relatives two hundred miles away for *Holi*, a joyous festival when each of us throws as much coloured dust as they can at the others. By the end of the day, everyone is covered from head to toe in every hue of the rainbow.

That day, we left our house and began to walk along the road to the railway station to embark on the first part of our journey. Suddenly, a white owl flew right in front of us and my mother came to a sudden halt, her expression aghast.

'We cannot go,' she said to my father and me. 'We must turn back.'

LUCINDA RILEY

My father, used to my mother's superstitions and wanting to visit his relatives for *Holi*, smiled and shook his head.
'No, my *pyari*, it was simply a beautiful creature flying past
us. It means nothing.'

But my mother had already turned tail and was walking
back in the direction of our home. Despite my father's remonstrations, she refused point-blank to change her mind. So,
that weekend, we sat, the three of us, my father and I sulking
as we thought of all our cousins, uncles and aunts having *Holi*
fun together hundreds of miles away.

A day later, however, we heard that there had been floods
in the region. And the very train which we were due to board
had crossed a bridge which had collapsed under the weight
of it. The train and its occupants had crashed into the
swirling, muddy-red waters. One hundred souls from our city
did not return home.

After that, even my father began to take my mother's instincts more seriously. As I grew older, my mother began to
teach me simple remedies for coughs, colds and broken hearts.
I was instructed to watch and learn the lunar calendar – there
were times every month when mixing the remedies would
make them more potent than at others. She told me that the
moon gave women our feminine power. And how nature,
which the gods had created for humans to provide all we
needed, was the most powerful force on the planet.

'One day, Anni, you will hear the spirits singing to you,'
she told me as she tucked me up in bed. 'Then we will know
for certain the gift has been passed down to you.'

At the time, I didn't understand what she was saying, but
I nodded in agreement anyway. 'Yes, Maaji,' I said as she
kissed me goodnight.

I knew that it was thought in my maternal family that she had married beneath her. My mother was born into a high caste. She was a second cousin of the Maharani of Jaipur, although, in truth, it always seemed to me that everyone I knew in India was a cousin of ours or someone we knew. She had been betrothed from the age of two to a wealthy cousin in Bengal, who had inconveniently caught malaria at sixteen and subsequently died. While my mother's parents searched for another suitable match, she met my father at the *Navratri* festival, and they began a secret relationship composed entirely of smuggled letters.

When my grandparents announced to her that they had found a high-born but older husband of fifty who wished for my mother to become his third wife, she threatened to run away unless they allowed her to marry my young and handsome father. I'm not sure what lengths my parents went to in order to see each other – the stories had become a part of their own folklore by the time I was born – but eventually, my grandparents reluctantly agreed to the match.

'I told your grandparents that I could not give their daughter rubies, pearls and a palace to live in, but I could house her in love always,' my father had told me. 'And, my *beti*, you too must remember that to love and be loved is worth all the treasure in a maharaja's kingdom.'

My father, Kamalesh, was the polar opposite to my mother. A philosopher, poet and writer, who took his ideology from Rabindranath Tagore, the famous Brahmin poet and activist. He earned a pittance of a living, producing a monthly pamphlet on his radical thoughts, especially where the British occupation of India was concerned. He had taught himself excellent English and, ironically, given his political views, subsidised his writings by tutoring high-born Indians who wished to learn the language in order to converse with their British counterparts.

He also taught me, his daughter, not just English but a whole host of subjects, ranging from history to science. Whilst other Indian girls were learning the art of embroidery and the necessary prayers to offer Shiva to find a good and kind husband, I was reading *On the Origin of Species* by Charles Darwin and studying mathematics. I could also ride bareback by the age of eight, charging across the flat desert plains outside the city, my father urging me to go faster and catch up with him. I adored my father, as all little girls do, and worked as hard as I could to please him.

So, between my father, the radical, who thought of all things logically, and my mother, who once saw a bat in the bedroom she shared with my father and had an *ojha* come to the house to clear it of evil spirits, I grew up with an uncommonly varied overview of the world. There was much of each of them inside me, but also something that was uniquely myself.

Once, as my father comforted me on his knee after I'd seen a group of young boys beating a half-starved dog in the street, he tipped my chin up to look at him as he wiped my tears away.

'My sweet Anni, you have a bleeding heart that beats louder than one hundred *tabla*. Like your father, you abhor injustice and embrace fairness. But be careful, my Anni, for humans are complex, and their souls are often grey, not black and white. Where you believe you will find goodness, perhaps you may find evil, too. And where you can only see evil, maybe there will also be some good.'

When I was nine, my father died suddenly during a typhoid outbreak that was plaguing our city during monsoon season. Even the potions in my mother's considerable armoury failed to save him.

'It was his time, *pyari*, and I knew it was,' my mother told me.

I struggled to understand her calm acceptance of my father's death. As I yowled like a banshee over his lifeless body, she sat by him, tearless, peaceful and still.

'Anni, when it is your time and you are called on, you must go,' she comforted me. 'There is nothing to be done.'

Her response didn't suit me at all. I kicked and screamed and refused to leave my father as his body was lifted onto the funeral pyre. I remember being forcefully dragged away as the swami began to chant and they lit the straw pallet below him. As acrid smoke plumed into the air, I turned and hid in my mother's skirts.

After my father died, we had little to support us. The Maharani of Jaipur, being a cousin of my mother, offered us a home with her. So we moved, the two of us, from our pretty little house in the city up to the Moon Palace, and into the zenana.

The zenana was where all the ladies of the palace lived together, separated from their male counterparts. Because, of course, back then, from the moment puberty struck, all the ladies adhered to the tradition of purdah. No man, apart from husbands or close male relatives, could gaze upon our faces. Even if one of us was sick, the doctor would have to diagnose our condition through a screen. And if we were out in public, our faces and bodies would be heavily shrouded and veiled. Now, I struggle to believe that this was the way it was, but none of us had ever known anything different and it was simply part of our daily lives.

When I first arrived, the noise and bustle of the zenana took much getting used to. In our own home, we had had a maid and a boy to take care of the garden for us. But after they had left at the end of each day there had only been three of us, with a front door we could shut to keep out the world if we wished. Palace life was very different. We lived, ate and slept communally. Sometimes I yearned for the peace and privacy of my old home, where I could close my bedroom door and lose myself in a book without being disturbed.

However, communal living did have its advantages. I was certainly never short of a playmate, for there were many young girls of my age living in the zenana. There was always someone around to join me in a game of backgammon, or to play the *veena*, a stringed instrument, as I sang.

My playmates were all polite, well-mannered daughters of local nobility. But the one thing that I missed terribly was my lessons. It was only after entering the zenana that I realised just how progressive my father had been by starting to educate me.

It was he who had nicknamed me 'Anni'; my proper name, Anahita, means 'full of grace'. I always felt it didn't suit me. I may have had a scholarly mind (and could outrace any of my contemporaries on a horse) but when it came to girlish 'graces', I felt ill-equipped. I would often watch in the zenana as the other women pampered themselves and preened in front of the mirror, spending hours choosing the right coloured bodice to wear with a skirt – traditional-style saris were not worn in the province of Rajasthan.

All of the princesses and many of their noble cousins were already betrothed to a male whom their parents thought suitable. I, however, came from a high-caste but poor family. My father had left little in the way of material possessions and I was aware my mother had no dowry to offer for me. I was not a 'catch' for any eligible man, and my mother was still searching the family tree to find someone who would want me. I was not disappointed or worried by this; I simply remembered my father's words to my mother's parents when he had asked to marry their daughter.

I wanted to find love.

When I was eleven, and had been in the zenana for over a year, my previous education and skills on horseback began to pay dividends. I was chosen by the Maharani to become companion to her eldest daughter, the Princess Jameera.

Even though being the princess's companion gave me a new set of privileges and an open door to all sorts of new and exciting activities, such as accompanying her on one of the many game shoots or being allowed access to parts of the palace that up until now had been forbidden to me, I don't remember it as a happy time.

Jameera was spoilt and difficult. If we played a game and she lost, she would run to her mother in floods of tears, complaining that I had cheated. When I spoke to her in English, as I had been asked to by her mother, she would put her hands over her ears and refuse to listen. And if I ever dared outrun her on our morning horseback ride, she would howl with rage and ignore me for the rest of the day.

We both knew what the problem was; even though she

was the princess, I was blessed with certain natural talents and skills which she lacked. Even worse, despite the fact that I had no inclination for preening and pampering myself, everyone remarked on my slim figure and good bone structure. Whereas Jameera had been blessed with neither.

'Maaji,' I used to cry in my mother's arms, as she wiped away my tears. 'Jameera hates me!'

'Indeed, she is a difficult girl. Here, *pyari*, there is nothing we can do, is there? We can hardly tell her mother, the Maharani herself, that you dislike her eldest daughter! You must do the best you can,' my mother entreated me. 'You are honoured to have been chosen by her, and I'm sure you will reap the benefits one day.'

As usual, my mother was right. In 1911, there was great excitement in India amongst all the princely states. Edward VII, Emperor of India, had died the previous year. His son, George V, had become king and his formal coronation was to take place in England in June. After that, in December, there was to be a great Coronation Durbar held in Delhi, to which all the princes of India were invited. And as Princess Jameera's companion, I was included in the vast entourage that the Maharaja of Jaipur – her father – would take with him.

My mother was in a flurry of excitement. 'Anni,' she said as she took my face in her hands and looked down at me, 'when you were born, as is the tradition, I consulted an astrologer to prepare your life chart. And do you know what it said?'

I shook my head. 'No, Maaji, what did it say?'

'It said that when you were eleven, something extraordinary would happen to you. You would meet someone who would alter the course of your life.'

'That is indeed incredible,' I replied respectfully.

It is only now, as I write this, that I can look back and see how right the astrologer had been.

7

It would be simply impossible to describe in words the splendour and majesty of the Coronation Durbar. As we approached the plains on which Coronation Park – the tented city just outside Delhi – had been erected, it felt as though the whole of India was on its way to the same destination.

As Jameera, the younger princesses and I sat in our purdah *howdah* atop one of the great elephants in the Maharani's train, we peered through the curtains to snatch a glimpse outside. The dusty highways were thronged with every conceivable form of transport: bicycles, carts loaded high with possessions and pulled by bullocks shining with sweat, automobiles and elephants all jostling for space on the road. Rich and poor alike were all headed to Coronation Park.

Each of the maharajas had his own tented camp, each one a village with water and electricity provided. When we arrived at our camp, I looked with awe at the richly furnished women's quarters.

'There's even a bathtub,' I called to Jameera, wondering at the modern miracles that could produce everything we might need to live here forever if we wished.

Jameera was less impressed. It had been a long journey and she had not taken well to travelling.

'Where's my *puja* box?' she barked at the maids who were unpacking the endless trunks they had brought with them from the palace for the royal women. 'These sheets are rough,' she said sulkily as her fat little fingers felt the linen on her bed. 'Change them for me!'

I was not to be cowed by Jameera's ill temper. Once I had helped her maids unpack and Jameera was safely in the bathing room being tended to, I wandered off to explore. Outside, in the immaculate, beautiful gardens that surrounded our camp, the lights from the enormous park lit up the night sky. In the distance, I saw a sudden explosion of fireworks, whirling dervishes of colour – the acrid smoke mingling with the scent of incense that hung heavy in the air. I heard elephants trumpeting far away and the sweet sound of sitars playing.

I felt a moment of pure, unadulterated joy. Every princely state in India was gathered within these few square miles. Amongst the many thousands of people inhabiting the park were the most revered, powerful and learned in the land. And I, Anahita Chavan, was part of it.

I searched the heavens and spoke to my father.

'I'm here, Father, I'm here,' I told him with glee.

It goes without saying that a gathering of the grandest in the land in such close proximity will bring out a certain spirit of competition. Each maharaja aspired for his camp to be the most sumptuously furnished, or to have a larger retinue or a greater number of elephants than his neighbours. The parties and dinners each prince hosted strove to be more lavish than the last. The rubies, diamonds, emeralds and pearls that adorned the bodies of the great princes and their wives could surely have bought the rest of the world, I thought as I scurried to help Jameera dress for the first banquet her mother and father would hold in our camp. Everyone was in a state of high excitement.

'Eighteen princes and their maharanis are attending tonight!' Jameera commented as she endeavoured to force a gold bracelet over her plump knuckles and onto her wrist. 'Maaji told me that the father of the prince I am betrothed to will be present. You must help me look my best.'

'Of course,' I agreed.

Finally, the Maharaja's four wives and their senior ladies left to sit behind a purdah screen and observe their husbands and their male guests at the great reception before the banquet. The rest of us breathed a sigh of relief that everyone had departed in good spirits and made ready for the imminent arrival in our zenana quarters of the women and children who would dine with us, separate from the men.

Later that evening, the reception area of our tented quarters was swarming with female guests and their offspring. I watched in wonder as wives of the guest maharajas were greeted by our own maharanis. To an eleven-year-old child, these women were the stuff of fairytales; oiled, scented and delicately tattooed with henna, adorned with pearls the size of birds' eggs around their necks, glittering headpieces encrusted with rubies and emeralds, and priceless diamond nose clips. Their children were just as magnificently attired – boys and girls as young as three wearing solid gold, bejewelled anklets and necklaces of intricate design and impeccable craftsmanship.

I remember these sights impressed me, but unsettled me too. I was struck by how all this wealth could be in one room, taken for granted by the wearers, when I had seen so much poverty and starvation in our country.

Yet I could not help but be awed by the spectacle.

And it was to be at this gathering that my birth astrologer's prediction would come true. Perhaps one never sees an auspicious, pivotal moment when it occurs in one's life. It happened, as these things usually do, without fanfare.

I was sitting quietly in a corner of the zenana reception area watching the splendour taking place all around me. By that time, I was bored and hot, so I stood up and walked surreptitiously towards an opening in the tent for some air. I drew back the flap and peered out, feeling a soft breeze brush my face. I remember gazing up to the heavens at the infinite stars, when I heard a voice beside me.

'Are you bored?'

I turned round to see a young girl standing next to me. I knew from the strings of pearls wrapped in layers round her neck, the tiny glittering headpiece adorning her thick, wavy hair, that this was a child of wealth and influence.

'No, of course not,' I said hurriedly.

'Yes you are! I can see it, because I am too.'

I shyly forced my gaze to meet her eyes. We stared at each other for a few seconds, as if we were processing each other's inner blueprint.

'Shall we go outside and explore?' she asked me.

'We can't!' I said in horror.

'Why not? There are so many women in here, no one will notice we have even gone.' Her extraordinary liquid-brown eyes, the irises flecked with amber, challenged me.

I took a deep breath, knowing the trouble that I would get

into if someone discovered I was missing. Against my better judgement, I nodded in assent.

'We must keep in the dark, or we will surely be spotted,' she whispered. 'Come on.'

And then she took my hand.

I still remember the way her long, slim fingers reached out for mine. I looked into her eyes and saw the glint of mischief that sparkled there. My fingers closed round hers and our palms joined.

Outside, my new friend pointed across the camp. 'See? That's where all the maharajas are having dinner.'

The surrounds of the central durbar tent were lit with a thousand candles in glass holders, illuminating the dark shapes of the trees and plants in the exotic gardens.

I found myself being pulled towards it, the soft grass tickling the soles of my bare feet. She seemed to know exactly where to go, and soon enough we'd arrived at the enormous tent. She darted along one side of it, back into the shadows where no one could see us. Then she knelt down on the ground and prised the heavy canvas upwards. She leaned forward and put her eye to the tiny gap.

'Please, be careful, someone might see,' I entreated her.

'No one is going to be looking at the ground,' giggled the girl as she pushed the canvas higher. 'Come, I will show you my father. I think he's the most handsome of all the maharajas.'

The girl made way for me to kneel down in the same spot and I took the thick canvas in my fingers and looked through the peephole.

Inside, I could see a lot of big, bejewelled male feet and nothing else. But I didn't want to disappoint my new friend.

'Yes!' I said. 'It is indeed an impressive spectacle.'

'If you look just to the left, you'll see my father.'

'Yes, yes,' I said, eyeing the row of ankles, 'I can see him.'

'I think he is better looking than your father!' Her eyes twinkled at me.

I realised then that this girl thought I too was a princess, and that the Maharaja of Jaipur was my father. Sadly, I shook my head.

'My father is dead, he is not here.'

A warm brown hand was again placed on mine. 'I am sorry.'

'Thank you.'

'What is your name?' she asked me.

'My name is Anahita, but everyone calls me Anni.'

'And mine is Indira, but my family calls me Indy.' She smiled. At that point, Indira lay down full-length on her stomach and propped up her head with her hands. 'Who are you, then?' she asked. Her glittering eyes, like an inquisitive tigress's, surveyed me carefully. 'You're far prettier than the other Jaipur princesses.'

'Oh no, I'm not one of the princesses,' I corrected her. 'My mother is a second cousin to the Maharani of Jaipur. My father died two years ago, so we live at the Moon Palace in the zenana.'

'Sadly for me –' she raised her eyebrows – 'I *am* a princess. The youngest daughter of the Maharaja of Cooch Behar.'

'Don't you like being a princess?' I queried.

'Not really, no.' Suddenly Indira rolled gracefully onto her back, put her hands under her head and gazed up at the stars. 'I'd prefer to be a tiger tamer in a circus, I think.'

I giggled.

'Don't laugh,' she cautioned me, 'I'm serious. Ma says that

I'm a very bad princess. I'm always getting dirty and finding myself in trouble. She's thinking of packing me off to an English boarding school to teach me some manners. I said that if she did, I'd run away.'

'Why? I'd love to see England. I've never travelled anywhere,' I said wistfully.

'Lucky you. We're always on the move. Ma is very sociable, you see, and she drags us all with her for the seasons here and in Europe. I wish I could stay at home in our lovely palace all the time and look after our animals. If I can't become a tiger tamer, then I'd like to become a mahout and live with an elephant instead. Anyway, you'd hate England. It's grey, cold and foggy and everyone in our family always ends up with terrible colds, especially Pa.' Indira sighed. 'I worry about his health, really I do. Do you speak English?' she asked me.

I began to realise her brain continually flitted like a butterfly from one subject to the next. 'Yes, I do.'

Indira immediately sat up on her knees and held out her hand to me. 'How do you do?' she said, in a perfect parody of a clipped English accent. 'I'm awfully pleased to meet you.'

I reached out my hand to her and our palms joined again. 'The pleasure is all mine,' I replied as we looked into each other's eyes, still shaking hands. Then we both lay down on the grass, convulsed in giggles. When we had calmed ourselves, I realised that we should get back to the zenana before someone missed us. I stood up.

'Where are you going?' she asked me.

'Back to our tent. We'll both be in trouble if they discover we've escaped.'

'Oh,' replied Indira airily, 'I'm used to being in trouble. In fact, I think they expect it from me.'

I wanted to say that, since I was not a princess, but in fact earned my board and lodging being a companion to one, I was not likely to be forgiven as easily.

'Just five more minutes?' she begged. 'It's so hot and boring in the tent. So,' she continued, 'who are you to be married to?'

'It's not been arranged yet,' I answered stoically.

'Lucky you again. I met my future husband only a few days ago here and he's old and ugly.'

'Will you marry him? Even if he is old and ugly?'

'Never! I want to find a handsome prince who will love me *and* will let me keep tigers,' she said with a grin.

'I, too, want to find my prince,' I agreed softly.

So there we were, two little girls staring up at the stars, dreaming of our handsome princes. Some people say they wish they could see into their future. But thinking back to that moment of pure childish innocence, as Indira and I lay on the grass with our entire lives before us, I am glad we could not.

8

For the following three weeks, as the festivities at Coronation Park continued, leading up to the grand presentation of all the princes to King George, Indira and I became inseparable. How she managed to escape as often as she did, I'm not sure, but she would arrive at our prearranged meeting place on time and we would go off to explore. The camp became our playground, a garden of delights for two inquisitive little girls. Stalls sold a multitude of delicious-smelling foods such as *panipuris* and samosas stuffed with spicy vegetables and deep-fried to a golden brown. There were trinket shops containing all manner of clay and wooden figurines. Indira, who always seemed to have plenty of rupees, bought me a clay tiger I had particularly admired and gave it to me. 'When we are not together,' she said, 'then you will just look into this tiger's eyes and know I am thinking of you.'

Luckily enough, Princess Jameera was often otherwise engaged, usually on formal visits to the camps of the various maharajas with her parents, and my presence was not required in such cases. I asked Indira why she rarely seemed to be needed by her family at these functions.

'Oh,' she explained airily, 'that is because I am the youngest child. No one is interested in me.'

I knew this wasn't quite true, and there were some occasions when Indira was unable to meet me and complained afterwards about having had to sit around for hours in hot tents whilst her parents socialised. But, for the most part, we managed to see each other every day.

One morning, when our time together was drawing to a close and I was dreading returning to the restrictive environment of the Moon Palace in Jaipur, she arrived with her eyes alight.

'Come on,' she said, starting to pull me along, expertly weaving her way through the tents.

'Where are we going?' I asked.

'You'll see,' she replied mysteriously.

A few minutes later, we arrived at what I knew was the Maharaja of Cooch Behar's camp, as Indira had pointed it out to me before.

'First and most importantly,' Indira said, 'I'm taking you to meet my favourite elephant. She's only a baby, born two years ago. She shouldn't be here at all, as she's not yet trained to walk in the procession, but I insisted she came anyway. She would have pined away without me and her mother.'

As we entered the *pilkhana*, my nostrils stung from the noxious smell of dung. There must be at least forty elephants in the hall, I thought, as Indira led me along the stalls saying good morning to them all by name as she passed. We headed directly towards the end of the stalls and in the very last one was the baby elephant. As we approached, the young animal heard our footsteps and trumpeted at Indira in recognition.

'How are you, my pretty Preema?' Indira said as she

nuzzled her face against the elephant. 'I was there when you were born, wasn't I, my darling?' The elephant wound her trunk around my friend's waist. Indira turned to me as she picked two bunches of bananas off a heap.

'Ditti, your mahout, let me name you, didn't he?' she said as she fed the baby elephant. 'I decided to call her Preema, which, of course, in Latin is spelt *P-R-I-M-A*, meaning "first". Because she was the first elephant I'd ever seen being born.' Indira's eyes sparkled at me. 'Now I just call her "Pretty", because she is, don't you think?'

I stared into the soft, trusting eyes of the elephant and felt a ridiculous pang of jealousy at how much Indira loved her.

'Yes, she's very beautiful,' I replied.

A tiny, nut-brown Indian man appeared out of nowhere.

'Ditti, is my Pretty behaving herself?'

'Yes, Your Royal Highness, although I know she will be happy to return home.'

'As will we all,' agreed Indira.

The elderly mahout bowed his head in respect as we left the stall. I realised it was the first time I'd ever seen my friend treated like the princess she really was. A sudden wave of despair passed over me as I followed Indira out of the *pilkhana*. The girl I had laughed and played and talked with as though she was my sister belonged to a different world, somewhere far away across India. And soon she would be taken from me and returned to it.

The feeling of tears beginning to well made me blink as fast as I could to stop them. Indira had become the centre of my world, but I realised I was merely on the periphery of hers. At best, I had amused her for a few weeks. But, like the butterfly she was, she would surely fly away and find new amusement elsewhere.

I tried to halt my thoughts and be grateful at least for the time we had spent together. My mother had chastised me all my childhood for my sudden black moods, saying I had a tendency to be absorbed for some reason by misery. *'You possess a gift for happiness, but you also have the capacity for sudden despair,'* she had once said to me.

'Come on, hurry up. I'm taking you to meet someone else,' said Indira.

I pulled myself valiantly out of my reverie, digging deep to offer her a smile.

'What is it now? Animal, mineral or human?'

It was a game we often played and Indira smiled at the reference.

'Most definitely human. I'm taking you to meet my mother.'

At this, my heart started to pound. There'd been much talk in the Jaipur zenana about the exquisitely beautiful Ayesha, Maharani of Cooch Behar. I'd heard Jameera and her mother cattily suggesting that just because Ayesha had met the Empress of India, Victoria herself, at Buckingham Palace, she seemed to feel she was somehow superior to the other maharanis.

'She speaks English and wears Western clothes in Europe!' Jameera's mother had exclaimed. 'But for all that her clothes are made by French designers and she's covered in the jewels her husband pours on her, these things do not make her a better Indian wife or a queen!'

I knew that none of these things was the real reason why Jameera and her mother sought to belittle Indira's mother. It was because Jameera's father had attended an informal gathering at the Cooch Behar camp four days ago and had arrived home announcing that the Maharani of Cooch Behar was the most beautiful woman he'd ever met.

My child, I have since understood that envy amongst women is rarely inspired by a woman's intelligence, or position in the world, or how many jewels she may have sitting in a vault. No, it is almost always a woman's ability to charm men which arouses feminine jealousy most.

'Ma!' Indira called as we entered the women's quarters of the Cooch Behar camp. 'Where are you?'

'Out here, my darling,' a soft voice replied.

Indira pulled me through a series of tents and then out onto a pretty veranda, shaded from the sun by swaying jacaranda trees. A small fountain played in the centre of the courtyard.

'I've brought my friend Anni to meet you. May we come and say hello?'

'Of course, I was just finishing breakfast.'

Indira's mother was lying on a pile of silken cushions, a breakfast tray spread across her lap. She immediately pushed it to one side, stood up and walked towards us, her arms held open wide to her daughter.

This in itself was an unusual gesture – every time I entered the presence of one of my own maharanis from the zenana, I was always required to walk forward in a low *pranaam*, until given leave to rise from it.

'And where have you been, you naughty girl?' the Maharani said with a smile as she took Indira in her arms.

Whilst she did so, I took a moment to study this woman, the subject of so much gossip in the camp. Indira's mother was completely unadorned by jewels or make-up. Her slim body was clad in a simple silk robe, and her long, dark, curly hair flowed freely around her shoulders. As I stood there, I felt her enormous, intelligent amber eyes – so like her daughter's – flick towards me and appraise me. I agreed with Jameera's father; she was, without doubt, the most beautiful woman I'd ever seen.

'I showed Anni my baby elephant, that's all, Ma.'

The Maharani smiled and kissed her daughter on the top of her head. 'Well, then, you'd better introduce me to your new friend.'

'Yes, of course. Anni, this is my mother, Ayesha. Ma, this is Anahita Chavan.'

'Hello, Anahita.' The Maharani gave me a warm smile of welcome, her perfectly scalloped red lips set around strong white teeth. I stood in front of her, feeling overwhelmed and tongue-tied. Her unprecedented informality, both with myself and her daughter, only added to her charm. Eventually, I put my hands together and bowed my head in the customary *pranaam*. 'I'm honoured to meet you,' I managed to say, and knew I was blushing to the roots of my hair with embarrassment.

'Come, sit down with me, both of you, and take some tea.'

Ayesha led us gracefully towards the cushions and indicated for us to sit on either side of her. I was unsure that I should, as it was unheard of for a maharani to be at the same height as her subjects. In our zenana, we would be on the floor and our maharanis would sit in chairs above us.

As Indira knelt down next to her mother on the cushions, I followed suit, trying to appear as small and low as I could. Ayesha clapped her hands and a serving maid appeared immediately from within the tent.

'*Chai*,' she ordered, and the maid bowed and disappeared back inside. 'Now, Anahita,' Ayesha said, turning her attention to me, 'Indira has spoken of little else but her new friend. She tells me you speak very good English, too. Where did you learn it?'

'From my father, Your Highness, he was a scholar and a teacher,' I managed to reply breathlessly.

'Then you're a lucky girl to have been given the gift of education. Sadly, many fathers still believe that it isn't worthwhile to fill their daughters' heads with knowledge. Perhaps you can instil a little more discipline into my own daughter when it comes to her lessons?' she said, ruffling Indira's hair fondly. 'She's a clever girl, probably far cleverer than her brothers, but at present she has no patience to study.'

'Ma, you know I wish to be a tiger tamer, not a professor!' Indira pouted.

Yet again, I was taken aback by the ease and openness with which mother and daughter spoke to each other.

'Indira tells me too that you live at the Moon Palace in Jaipur?' continued the Maharani.

'I do, yes.'

'Jaipur is indeed a beautiful city.' She smiled.

The tea arrived and when it was poured, I sipped it, hardly believing I was sharing *chai* and a pile of silken cushions with the famous and beautiful Maharani of Cooch Behar.

'Ma, I can't leave my new best friend behind when we go,' Indira declared suddenly. 'So I want her to come and live with us in the palace at Cooch Behar.'

Once again, I blushed deeply and looked down at my feet.

The Maharani raised one perfectly shaped eyebrow. 'I see.'

Her languid gaze fell on me. 'And has Indira discussed this with you, Anahita?'

'I . . . well . . . no, Your Highness,' I stuttered.

'Indira, I hardly think that Anahita would wish to leave her family, her home and her friends behind to come and live with us. You're being selfish again. I do apologise for my daughter, Anahita. She sometimes speaks before she thinks.'

'But, Ma, I'm so lonely at the palace now my brothers and sister are away at school. And you already said that Anni might encourage me to look at my books and help me with my English,' Indira pleaded. 'She's presently companion to Princess Jameera, doing exactly the same for her.'

'Then there's even more reason for Anahita not to wish to move. I'm sure poor Princess Jameera would miss her. You simply cannot steal people, my dear Indira, however much you might wish to.'

I opened my mouth at that moment, wanting to say that there was nothing I would like more than to be 'stolen' by my wonderful new friend. But my tongue simply wouldn't form the words, so I sat there miserably as the Maharani continued to chastise her daughter for her selfishness.

'But, Ma, you don't understand – we are inseparable! If Anni can't come, I might pine away without her,' Indira insisted.

'Then I'm sure we can ask Anni to come and visit us,' the Maharani comforted. 'May I call you Anni too?' she asked me.

'Of course, Your Highness,' I replied hastily. 'And, yes, I would like that very much indeed.'

'Then we shall arrange it, my dear. And now, I must rouse myself and dress. We have a luncheon with the Viceroy.' The Maharani rose, and I hurriedly stood up too. She smiled at me again. 'It was a pleasure to meet you, Anni. I hope you'll visit us in Cooch Behar very soon.'

Indira was also needed for the luncheon, so I trudged back alone to my camp, miserably berating myself for not speaking up when I'd had the chance. I should have told them that I would move to the moon if it meant that I could be alongside my new best friend.

As the Durbar celebrations came to a close, I saw less of Indira. Our own camp was being dismantled and packed up in preparation for the long journey back to Jaipur.

'What's wrong with you today?' asked Jameera. 'You're like a cat that's had its tail trodden on. Have you not had a wonderful time here?'

'Yes, of course.'

'Then you should be grateful I brought you.'

'I am very grateful, Jameera.'

I watched her purse her lips and turn away from me. I knew I had not shown her the degree of gratitude and respect she demanded, but I didn't care. With Indira and her mother, I had felt wanted and valued. It was a wonderful new feeling.

On the last night in Delhi, I crept into bed in the tented room I shared with Jameera and lay there blinking away the tears. I knew we were leaving early in the morning and that there would be no chance to say goodbye to Indira. Tears pricked the back of my eyes and I let them flow freely down my cheeks. We hadn't even thought to exchange addresses, and I wondered whether a letter simply marked 'Princess Indira at Cooch Behar Palace' would reach her.

Besides, I thought miserably, she would go back to her

charmed life as a princess and almost certainly forget all about me. Eventually, I drifted into a restless sleep to the sound of Jameera's snoring.

I thought I must be dreaming when I heard Indira's voice whispering my name.

'Anni! Wake up, wake up!'

I opened my eyes and saw her staring down at me. I jumped up, immediately awake. 'How did you get in here?' I whispered, startled. Jameera stirred in the bed next to me.

Indira put her finger to her lips and held out her hand to pull me from my bed. Like two wraiths in our white nightgowns, we ran from the room and through the sleeping camp until we found a loose tent flap and crawled outside. Indira pulled me in between two tents so we wouldn't be seen. 'I came to say goodbye,' she said.

All the terrible, black thoughts I'd had about her forgetting me vanished. Indira had come through the night to find me before she left, and I felt guilty for doubting her. My eyes filled with tears yet again. Spontaneously, I held out my arms to her and she came into them, wrapping hers around me tightly.

'I will miss you so much,' I cried onto her shoulder.

'Me too,' she said, equally tearful. 'But don't worry, dearest Anni, I'll find a way, and you will come to live with me in Cooch Behar and we'll be together always.'

'Indy, I cannot see a way that—'

'Trust me,' she whispered, 'there's always a way. Now, I must get back before I'm discovered, but –' she removed the small golden Ganesh charm from her neck and placed it round mine – 'this is so you never forget me. Goodbye, my sister, I love you. And I promise it won't be long before we're together again.'

With a last, mischievous twinkle in her eye, Indira sped like a small ghost out into the night.

My hand touched the neck of my bodice a hundred times as we made the long journey home to Jaipur. Inside was hidden Indira's necklace; I did not dare let it show to Jameera – she would immediately have thought I'd stolen it, it was so fine.

Once back at the Moon Palace, everyone around me seemed to settle quickly into their normal routine. But try as I might, I could not. I waited to see what plan Indira would hatch. She had sworn she wouldn't let me down.

But as we entered 1912, several weeks passed with no word from her, even though I stared my clay tiger hard in its eyes and begged Indira to remember me.

In late January, just when I'd begun to lose hope, I was suddenly summoned by Jameera's mother to her quarters.

'Come,' said my mother, washing my face roughly with a cloth and combing my hair. 'The Maharani wishes to see you and you must look your best.'

I was led into her quarters and gave my usual deep *pranaam* of respect.

'Please, sit down, child, and you too, Tira,' the Maharani indicated.

We both sat cross-legged on the floor in front of her.

'I've received a letter this morning from Ayesha, the Maharani of Cooch Behar. She tells me that her daughter Indira became close to you, Anahita, when you were together at the Coronation Durbar. Is this true?'

I considered her question, unsure how to answer it. Perhaps she saw my friendship with another princess as a slight against her own daughter. I looked at her face for clues, but as always, it was impassive and betrayed little emotion.

So I decided I must tell the truth.

'Yes, Highness, we became close.'

'So close, in fact, that the Maharani writes that Princess Indira is apparently refusing to eat until you are allowed to go to her. She has, according to her mother, become quite unwell.'

Whether the Maharani believed this or not, I couldn't be sure.

'Is she very ill?' I asked anxiously.

'She's certainly sick enough for her mother to request of me personally that you travel up to Cooch Behar immediately to see the Princess Indira.'

I turned my glance to my mother, whose face was also impassive.

'How do you feel about this, child?' asked the Maharani.

I did my best to look sombre and concerned, deciding it wouldn't be pertinent to tell her that the fire that had been dimming in my soul had suddenly re-ignited like a thousand fireworks.

'Of course, I'd be honoured to help Princess Indira if it is the case that she needs me,' I said, my head bowed low so neither woman could see the sheer delight I was certain glowed in my eyes.

'And you, Tira?' the Maharani asked. 'Are you prepared to let your daughter go far away for many weeks?'

My mother, being my mother, already knew my heart and where it lay. She nodded. 'Like Anahita, I'm honoured to let her do Her Highness's bidding.'

'I've already spoken to Princess Jameera, and she also agrees that Anahita should go,' added the Maharani.

I stopped myself from raising my eyes to the heavens to give thanks. It was no surprise that Jameera hadn't put up a fight to keep me. She needed a far more malleable companion than me.

'Then if all of us are agreed, Anahita, arrangements will be made by the Maharani of Cooch Behar for you to travel there.'

'Thank you, Your Highness,' I said, bowing my head again. 'When will I leave?' I couldn't stop myself from adding.

'As soon as the arrangements have been made.'

My mother and I backed out of the room. As soon as we were out of sight, she put her arms around me. Tipping my chin up towards her, she stared into my eyes.

'This is what you want?' she asked me.

'More than anything, Maaji.'

9

And this, my darling child, as the astrologer had predicted, really did begin a new chapter in my life. An aide-de-camp had been sent to accompany me from Jaipur to Cooch Behar. As I disembarked from the train, which was set on a single-track railway that had been built to access Cooch Behar, the most north-easterly of Indian provinces, I glanced up and saw the outline of the great Himalayan mountains in the distance scalloped against the sky. With a porter carrying the battered suitcase which once had been my father's, I saw a horse-drawn tonga had been sent to meet me.

Before I had left Jaipur, I had read what I could about Indira's faraway province. It's hard for anyone who has never been to India to imagine how one country can encompass such a vast number of differing climates and landscapes. India is a land of contrasts, each individual state containing a myriad different cultures, languages and people. Even though we are so often lumped together as one country, everything about our great nation is dramatic and varied.

As the driver helped me aboard, my clothes instantly clung to my damp skin. The climate here was hot and humid, so unlike the dry, suffocating heat of Jaipur.

As we drove through the town, I saw the houses were basic, built of bamboo and thatch, their roofs covered with abundant plumes of hibiscus. They were perched on stilts to protect them from the great monsoon floods. No one wasted money here building the solid stone houses of Jaipur, which could last two or three hundred years. In Cooch Behar, their owners were all too aware there might be yet another flood or earthquake that would sweep their homes away without trace.

As the horse clip-clopped along the dusty red roads, I stared eagerly out of the window for my first glimpse of the palace. We were some way out of town by the time I saw it. It looked enormous, with two great wings leading off a huge dome in the centre. We began to drive through the park, its lush manicured lawns stretching away on every side. I heard the trumpeting of elephants from the *pilkhana* and saw a lake which ran the entire length of the palace.

Even then, to my untrained eye, I didn't think the palace looked very traditionally Indian, and I was to find out later that the exterior had been modelled on an English stately home. From the outside, at least, the sturdy brick construction and the lack of delicate Indian latticework at the windows made it look austere in contrast to the prettiness of the Moon Palace in Jaipur.

I've always found the contrast in the atmosphere between the outside and the inside of India's palaces curious; to the onlooker, they seem deserted, because almost all activity takes place within the many shaded courtyards designed especially to shield their occupants from the searing Indian sun. As I write this, it occurs to me that perhaps this is also an apt metaphor for human beings; often, their silent, serene outer skin doesn't betray the liveliness of spirit that exists inside.

And this was certainly the case when I arrived at Cooch Behar Palace. As my tonga came to a standstill and the door was opened for me to dismount, I realized I had not seen a single soul since we had entered the park.

As the driver unloaded my small trunk, I heard a voice behind me.

'Surprise!'

Indira sprang like a monkey onto my back, hooking her slim, brown arms around my neck.

'Ouch!' I said, as she managed to catch my hair in her bracelet. She immediately jumped off and swung me round to face her.

'You're here! I told you I'd make it happen!'

'Yes, I'm here,' I agreed, feeling exhausted from the long journey, and suddenly shy and awkward after so many weeks away from her.

I looked immediately for signs of the sickness that had been described so vividly in her mother's letter. But her eyes sparkled, her thick, black hair shone blue as the sun touched it and her wiry frame seemed no thinner than the last time I had seen it.

'I thought you were very ill,' I chastised her. 'I've hardly slept with worry for you since I heard.'

She put her hands on her tiny hips and rolled her eyes at me. 'Well, I was,' she said. 'In fact, I was so sick that I couldn't eat for weeks. Ma sent for endless doctors to try and find out what was wrong with me. The doctors agreed that I must be pining for something. Or some*one*. And then, once Ma had agreed that you must come, I got out of my bed and suddenly felt hungry and well. Isn't it a miracle?' Indira waved her hands expressively to the heavens. 'Since then, I've been eating like a horse.' Her gaze fell on me and her eyes became serious. 'I've missed you so much, Anni; I think I might well have died if you hadn't come.'

I was overwhelmed by the ruse she had employed to guarantee I would come to her. Naturally mistrustful, especially when it came to royal families and princesses, my feelings must have shown in my eyes.

'Anni, you doubted me, didn't you?'

I bowed my head silently and then looked up at her, reaching my hands towards hers and clasping them. 'Yes, I am sorry to say that I did. But, my dear friend, I will never doubt you again.'

My first few weeks at Cooch Behar Palace with Indira were full of new and wonderful experiences. Palace life and my daily routine could not have been more different from what I'd been used to in Jaipur. I had been warned endlessly by the women of my old zenana that the Maharani of Cooch Behar did not run her female court in a seemly Hindu fashion. Not only did she not adhere to purdah inside the palace walls, but Ayesha had travelled across the water away from India with her family many times. This, in the strictest interpretation of Hindu religion, meant that the entire royal family had broken caste.

The Jaipur ladies had also told me with a grave expression in their eyes that the Maharani seemed more Western than Indian. And that her palace was constantly filled with foreign guests, including European aristocrats and American actors. I had nodded equally gravely in return as I listened to their litany of criticisms. They couldn't know that these descriptions filled me with unimaginable excitement.

As I discovered subsequently, almost all of what they'd said seemed to be true. The Maharani ran her palace and her family in a truly modern way. Every morning, Indira and I would rise at dawn to head for the stables, where two perfectly groomed and saddled horses would be waiting for us. At first, I was playing catch-up with Indira, who proved to be a superb horsewoman. As I galloped at breakneck speed across the park, laughing and whooping as the wind brushed my cheeks, I remember feeling alive and free, and happier than I had ever been.

It took many weeks for me to out-gallop her, but when eventually I did, Indira shouted with pleasure at my triumph.

After breakfast, on weekdays, we would enter a large room where we took lessons with a private tutor. Indira had the attention span of a gnat and it took all my powers of persuasion to make her concentrate on her work. I'd watch her looking longingly outside, waiting for the moment when she would be released to visit her precious elephant, Pretty, to take a short ride on her back, or to play tennis on the beautifully laid-out court.

As for me, I relished the opportunity to continue to expand my education. Our British tutor was a professor of English, who encouraged me in my long-standing love of books. In retrospect, I believe he was as glad to have me in his classroom as I was to be there. My English vocabulary improved enormously and I did my best, as I'd been asked to by the Maharani, to converse with her daughter in the language as much as I possibly could.

The Maharani had also employed an English governess to care for her youngest daughter's needs. Miss Reid was a sweet-natured woman who clearly despaired of ever turning her wild charge into a lady.

On countless occasions, Indira would disobey her pleas not to be late for luncheon, or to sit quietly with a book in the schoolroom afterwards. The moment Miss Reid's back was turned, Indira would wink at me, and we would be off on another adventure outside.

One of my very favourite parts of the palace was the vast library, containing priceless first editions written by famous novelists from around the world. The glass cabinets in which the books stood remained locked at all times; they were simply an impressive ornament, another decoration, and I doubted any one of the titles had ever been taken down and read during all the years they'd been there. I had often glanced at the shelves, my fingers itching to take one out and hold it. I'd had to make do with the tattered copies of *Wuthering Heights*, *Oliver Twist* and Shakespeare's *Hamlet* that my tutor had brought with him from England. During the long, peaceful afternoons I had read and reread them time and again.

Many other afternoons were spent resting in the beautiful, airy bedroom I shared with Indira. I lay on my bed staring at the azure-blue walls, adorned with hand-painted Himalayan daisies, and thanked the gods profusely for bringing me here. Indira, probably because she expended so much nervous energy whilst she was awake, would fall asleep immediately, whereas I would mull over the happenings of the day so far.

As dusk approached, the palace would come back to life. This was the moment of the day I loved more than any other; the sense of anticipation of the evening to come suffused us all. There were always numerous exotic guests from all over the world for dinner. Indira and I used to watch as the servants laid the table in the enormous dining room with solid-gold place settings, heavy knives and forks inlaid with gems, and huge vases full of magnificent flowers. The air was scented by incense which was wafted through the downstairs rooms in a silver *dhuan* by a servant.

On my first night at the palace, after we'd eaten our supper, the next ritual had begun. When Indira had told me where we were going, I had been shocked.

'We are to watch your mother dressing and preparing for the evening? Why?' I had asked.

'I don't know, she just likes us all gathered there.' Indira had shrugged.

On the way across the vast, domed Durbar Hall, which formed the centrepiece of the palace and had an entrance high enough to allow a full-grown elephant to carry a maharaja in a *howdah* through it, I had thought about how much I would dislike having an audience as *I* dressed.

When we had entered the Maharani's private rooms, I had hardly been able to believe the gaggle of people gathered in her boudoir. Maids, relatives, visiting friends and us children filled the room. And there, in the centre of the hubbub, sitting at her delicately carved mother-of-pearl dressing table, was the Maharani herself.

Indira had pulled me straight through the throng and over towards her mother.

'Anni's here, Ma, she's here!' she had exclaimed in delight.

'I can see that.' The Maharani had smiled fondly at us both. 'And I hope now, my Indira, that your health and appetite will return fully to you.' She had glanced at me, and we had shared a look of mutual understanding and amusement. 'Welcome, Anni, I hope you'll be very happy here at the palace with us.'

'Thank you,' I had replied, 'I am sure that I will.'

That first night, I confess I could hardly pay attention to what she said. I was transfixed by her face, her eyes rimmed in kohl, her lips turning red as she carefully painted them with a brush from a small tin of pigment. The scent of the Maharani's favourite French perfume had filled the air as she managed to get ready at the same time as holding court with her entourage, expertly switching between Hindi, English and Bengali depending on whom she was speaking to.

'Come on,' Indira had said, 'I'll show you the rest of Ma's rooms.' She pulled me into the bathroom, which contained a Western-style tub – we girls sat on a rough wooden bench and had water poured unceremoniously from great silver urns all over us – and in her high-ceilinged white and gold bedroom sat an enormous marble bed. Along the entire length of her rooms stretched a shady veranda which opened onto a courtyard full of jacaranda trees, hibiscus and jasmine.

My son, if there was ever a real-life fairytale queen, one who was young, beautiful and kind and who lived in a sumptuous palace, Ayesha, the Maharani of Cooch Behar, was that woman. And I fell completely under her spell, just like everyone else.

Later, when the Maharani – breathtaking in an exquisitely embroidered emerald sari – was finally ready to greet her guests, Indira and I returned to our room, where Miss Reid chivvied us into our nightgowns and into bed.

'Don't you think Ma is the most beautiful woman in the world?' Indira had asked me.

'Yes, the most beautiful,' I'd replied without hesitation.

'And the best part of it all,' she had said as she yawned sleepily, 'is that my parents are so in love with each other. My father adores her. And he is the most handsome man in the world. I can't wait for you to meet him.'

A hand snaked out in the shadows towards me and I offered mine in return. 'Goodnight, dearest Anni,' she had said with a contented sigh. 'I'm so glad you are here.'

10

I realised one morning when I received a letter from my mother that I'd been in Cooch Behar for nearly two months. Of course, initially, it had been agreed that I would stay with Indira only for a few weeks. I'm ashamed to say that I'd allowed myself to get completely swept up in my new life and had lost all sense of time. In her letter, my mother asked me when I was returning. The sudden realisation that my life here was only temporary struck me like a thunderbolt.

Indira and I were virtually joined at the hip by this time, and she noticed my expression immediately.

'What is it?'

I looked up from the letter. 'My mother is asking me when I'll return.'

'To where?' Indira looked confused.

'To Jaipur, of course.'

'But of course you can't leave,' she replied. 'You live here with me now. Perhaps we can arrange for your mother to come for a visit.'

'I doubt she'd be happy to travel the distance.'

'I will speak to Ma and see what she can suggest.'

My heart was in my mouth as Indira dashed off to find her

mother. What if the Maharani had been so busy that she simply hadn't noticed I had not yet gone home? What if – I shuddered with terror – I had to return to the zenana at Jaipur forever?

Indira returned half an hour later and nodded her head in satisfaction. 'Don't worry, Anni. Ma will find a solution. She always does.'

That evening, when we gathered as usual in the Maharani's boudoir, she beckoned me over to her mirror.

'Indira says your mother is missing you and wishes to see you.'

'Yes, that is what she writes in her letter,' I replied nervously.

'I understand completely. No mother wishes to be deprived of the sight and company of her child. So, we must arrange for her to visit you.'

'Thank you, Your Highness.' I bowed to her respectfully. In reality, I wanted to cover her exquisite face with kisses in gratitude.

'I'll send a letter to your mother immediately. I've been meaning to write anyway, as I have another matter I wish to discuss with her.'

My heart leapt with relief. She wasn't necessarily sending me back home.

A few days later, the Maharani appeared in the bedroom Indira and I shared. It was not her daughter she wished to talk to, but me.

'Come and join me, Anni,' she said as she indicated the doors which led to the veranda.

'Can I come too, Ma?' asked Indira plaintively.

'No,' came the firm reply. 'I wish to speak to Anni alone.'

I followed the Maharani to a bench which sat outside in the cool shade of the courtyard. Even in her casual daywear of tunic and trousers, which she wore when there were no guests in attendance, the Maharani looked radiant.

'Anni, there is a reason I wanted to speak to you without my daughter present.'

'Yes, Your Highness?'

'Are you enjoying your life here?'

'Oh yes, Your Highness,' I assured her enthusiastically.

'Do you wish to stay with us for longer?'

'Oh, yes please. I love it here!' The eagerness with which I spoke could give her no cause for doubt.

The Maharani turned her eyes away from me and stared into the distance. Eventually, she sighed. 'I wanted to hear the words from your own lips. I'm fully aware that Indira is head-strong and has been spoilt by the life she was born into. I also know that, being the youngest and petted by her older siblings, she's been allowed more freedom than she should have been. I accept responsibility for that fact. I know she misses her brothers and sister and was lonely here before you came. Still, she cannot simply expect her every demand will be granted, especially if her demand includes a person.'

'I love her,' I said. They were the simplest and truest words I knew.

The Maharani turned back to me and smiled. 'I know you do, Anni. I can see it on your face. And true friendship, which encompasses love, loyalty and trust, is a very rare and precious thing. I hope for both your own and my daughter's sake that your friendship will accompany you into the future. However –' the Maharani reached for my hands and encircled them in hers, her face suddenly serious – 'you too have your own set of thoughts and wishes. And you must promise me that you'll never be afraid to make them felt. Indira is a strong character.' The Maharani paused and smiled again. 'I'm sad to say that I see a lot of me in her. Don't let yourself be ruled by her, will you? That would be bad for you, and bad for my daughter.'

'Yes, Your Highness,' I answered, deeply touched by her considering me worthy of advice. At that moment I realised why Ayesha, the famous Maharani of Cooch Behar, was adored by almost everyone who had the good fortune to meet her.

She understood human nature.

'Now, your mother is coming here in around a week's time. I'll speak to her then.'

'Thank you, Your Highness.'

'I should thank you, Anni.' As she released my hands, she patted them gently with her long, cool fingers before she stood up. 'I think my daughter is most fortunate in having you for her friend.'

A fortnight later, my mother arrived at Cooch Behar Palace.

'Anni, how you have grown!' she exclaimed as I greeted her and then took her on a tour of the palace. I could see she felt overwhelmed by the endless rooms, furnished with priceless treasures collected by the Maharani from all over the world. I had grown accustomed to the sumptuous setting I now lived in.

'Where is the zenana?' she asked me nervously.

'Oh –' I waved airily in its general direction – 'somewhere over there.'

'But surely the Maharani lives with the other women in the zenana?'

'No, Maaji, she has her own separate set of rooms.'

I could sense my mother's feeling of discomfort as I walked with her through the communal areas of the palace. There were a number of aides-de-camp and male servants flitting around who took no notice of us. Even though, compared to many women of her age, my mother's life as a healer and my father's belief that women had a right to education had prepared her better for the relaxed way things worked here, I could still tell that she was ill at ease. She had never before appeared unveiled in front of any male other than my father.

'You and the Princess Indira are approaching the time when you will become women. Will you embrace purdah and live in the zenana then?'

'I don't know, Maaji,' I answered honestly, as we sat taking a cup of tea in the small courtyard outside our bedroom. 'I'd have to ask. Or maybe you could. I know both the Maharaja and the Maharani are great friends with Rabindranath Tagore, whom you know Father admired so much. He doesn't approve of purdah,' I said, trying to make it more palatable for her by reminding her of her beloved husband.

I still remember the anxiety on my mother's face as she struggled between old and new.

'I'd like to take a rest now,' she said eventually. 'It was a long journey.'

I knew that later on that evening my mother was to be taken into the Maharani's boudoir to be presented to her. My heart somersaulted as I thought of what she would see there. It was a high altar to the modern ways, and the high priestess of it all, with her French perfume and Western accoutrements, would only increase my mother's consternation.

What if my mother believed that I was not being brought up in a true Hindu fashion? She would be within her rights to order me straight back with her to Jaipur.

Of course, I needn't have worried. When Indira and I entered the boudoir with my mother, Ayesha herself rose and cut a swathe through a group of women to greet my mother. She was already dressed in a sari of shimmering gold, diamonds adorning her neck and an enormous ruby nose clip catching the light from the Baccarat chandelier above her.

'It's my honour to meet you, Highness,' said my mother, almost doubled over in awe. As I watched the two women, I realised they could not have been more in contrast to each other. One breathtakingly beautiful, rich and independent, the other bowed by the hardship of her life since my father had died.

'No,' answered the Maharani softly, 'it is my honour to meet you. You've given birth to a very special daughter and we are lucky to have her amongst us. Now, come and see my prayer room and we will offer *puja* to Brahma for blessing us with such offspring.'

With that, she led my mother through the surprised onlookers and disappeared into the next room, closing the door behind her.

Fifteen minutes later, when the two women emerged, they were chatting like old friends. My mother's nervousness had completely disappeared and I, too, gave thanks to the gods that the Maharani had known exactly what to do to put my mother at ease.

That evening my mother, just as everyone else, fell under the Maharani's gentle spell. She waxed lyrical about her new friend's taste in furnishings, clothes and her extensive knowledge of philosophy, poetry and the wider world. They shared their thoughts on Ayurvedic medicine and the Maharani was fascinated to hear about my mother's special gift of sight.

'Did you "see" for her, Maaji?' I asked eagerly when she emerged from the Maharani's rooms one afternoon.

'As you know very well, Anni, that's a private matter between the Maharani and myself,' my mother replied.

By the end of the first week, she was relaxed enough to take a walk with me around the gardens in full view of the male residents of the palace. She still wouldn't remove her *ghoonghat* from her face and I respected her for it. But in all other aspects, she'd become as enthralled with Cooch Behar Palace and its denizens as I had.

The day before my mother was to return home, the Maharani called her to her rooms for a private audience. I knew what they would be discussing and Indira and I waited nervously outside.

'What if my mother wishes me to return with her? I think I would die!' I whispered anxiously.

Indira sat calmly next to me, holding my hand. 'She won't ask you to go back, Anni, I promise.'

And, of course, Indira was right. My mother emerged smiling, and took me into my bedroom to talk alone.

'The Maharani has asked me if I would be prepared to lend you to her family on a permanent basis. She's also offered to educate you with Indira, which is exactly what your father would have wished for you.'

'Yes, Maaji,' I muttered.

'She also said she understands it might be hard for me without you, so she's suggested I spend part of my year here with you when the family is in residence at the palace. So, my daughter, do you wish to stay on here when I return to Jaipur?'

'Oh, Maaji, I –' A tear came to my eye. 'I think I do, yes. Even though I'll be away from you for part of the year and will miss you dreadfully. But I do know that Father would be very happy to see me continuing my education. And I can't do that in the zenana in Jaipur.'

'The opportunities you have here are far greater, I agree. And you've always been special, my *pyari*.' She smiled and touched my cheek with her hand. 'You will write every week when we are apart?'

'Of course, Maaji. Every day, if you like.'

'Once a week will be fine, dearest child. And I'll be returning here after the monsoon, in four months' time. I promise it will not seem long.'

'I will miss you.'

'And I you.' She opened her arms to me. 'Just remember, I will always be with you.'

'I know, Maaji,' I said, hugging her tightly.

Even now, I remember that she looked at me in that moment with such sadness in her eyes that I was prompted to say, 'Maybe I should come back to Jaipur with you after all.'

'No, Anni –' she looked up to the heavens – 'I know it is your destiny to stay.'

And so, my mother went back to Jaipur, laden with gifts from the Maharani. And although I'd achieved my heart's desire and could now look upon Cooch Behar Palace as my permanent home, I couldn't help feeling a slight twinge of discomfort that my mother, spiritually gifted and wise as she was, had been so subtly persuaded into giving up her precious daughter.

*

That summer, when the monsoon season came and the hot earth beneath our feet stung even our hardened soles like a thousand bees, the royal party moved with the rest of privileged India up to the hill stations to breathe the fresh, cool air. We travelled to Darjeeling, a magnificent, mountainous region, seven thousand feet high and famous for its tea plantations, whose fields tumbled down the verdant hillsides as far as the eye could see.

That summer was the start of my lifelong love affair with Darjeeling; the distant sight of the breathtaking Himalayas alone sent my spirits soaring. The British had also learned to escape to Darjeeling long ago and had made the town their own. Lines of white bungalows, named after places in England, lined the hillsides and the town was immaculately ordered and laid out, unlike our own chaotic Indian villages. I dreamed of one day visiting the *real* England for myself.

It was in Darjeeling that I met Indira's siblings. All three of them were on holiday from boarding school in England. Aged seventeen, sixteen and fifteen, they petted their younger sister, but, with them being so much more mature than she, I could understand why Indira had felt like an only child. Minty, her fifteen-year-old sister, seemed very grown-up and sophisticated. I listened in fascination as they chatted over dinner about life in England. I learned to play croquet on the immaculate lawns and also became skilled at a myriad card tricks thanks to Indira's gregarious middle brother, Abivanth. I was particularly overawed by Raj, Indira's eldest brother, the Crown Prince, whose good looks and charm rendered me virtually tongue-tied in his presence.

The house we inhabited was tiny compared to Cooch Behar Palace, which meant we lived much more as a family unit. Set way up in the hills, and with only horses or rickshaws able to reach it, it was a place of privacy and tranquillity.

Often, the handsome Maharaja – whom I'd seldom seen in Cooch Behar due to his state duties – would join the rest of his family for a simple picnic lunch in the garden. I saw, in the informal setting of Darjeeling, what I wished for in my own future life: an abiding and true love between husband and wife. I saw it in the way they'd sometimes catch each other's eye over dinner and share a secret smile, in how I'd often see his hand snake surreptitiously to the Maharani's waist. This was the kind of genuine affection that I recalled from my own parents' marriage.

Even though they ruled over a kingdom together, and the demands on their time were enormous, I realised that their true strength flowed from the mutual admiration and trust each felt for the other.

That summer, Indira and I liked to rise very early in the morning and ride up the steep tracks to Tiger Hill in order to watch the sun rising over Mount Everest. We both loved visiting the marketplace in the centre of Darjeeling where Tibetan and Bhutanese vendors in enormous fur hats would sell their wares. I was, without doubt, happier than I had ever been and felt completely welcomed and accepted by Indira's family.

But even though I'd known hardship, I was too young to fully appreciate that the scales of life can tip in an instant. And that great happiness in one moment does not necessarily guarantee the same in the next.

The less fortunate in India, trapped far below our mountain paradise, were not so lucky that season. The dust storms swirled on the plains, covering everything daily in a fine layer; even a chink of a crack in a shuttered window could render the interior filthy by morning. The monsoon rains swelled the rivers and propelled the red earth out of its natural channels, destroying everything in its path.

It was also plague season in India – the time of year every mother dreaded for her children. As I wandered around the graveyard in Darjeeling, I was surprised to see that even a great number of British babies had died here before adulthood. Annually, typhoid, malaria and yellow fever swept through the population, decimating it. That summer was particularly harsh and we had word of plagues breaking out in all parts of the country.

One night in late August, I suffered a series of strange dreams and awoke sweating and with a terrible feeling of dread, which I couldn't dispel. A week later, my heart leapt to my throat when I was called to the Maharani's sitting room. I had never believed it when my mother had told me that I'd inherited her gift. But as I approached the Maharani with a sense of foreboding clutching at my heart, I already knew what it was she had to tell me.

The Maharani was holding a letter in her hands. She beckoned me over and patted the space next to her on the chaise-longue.

'Oh, my *pyari,* I'm sorry to tell you that I have some very bad news for you.'

'How did my mother die?'

It was the only time in my life I ever saw the Maharani lost for words.

'I . . . Has someone told you? I only received the letter this morning.'

'No, I just . . . knew,' I said, fighting back my tears.

'Many say we feel it when a loved one has passed on,' she

said, recovering her composure, 'and you are obviously very sensitive to these things, Anni. I am so sad to tell you that you are right. Your mother had been staying with your aunt and uncle up in the hills to avoid the Jaipur heat. Unfortunately, there was a very bad monsoon, which caused a landslide that swept down the mountains at night. No one in the village survived. I'm so very sorry, my dearest Anni. It seems you've not only lost your mother, but also your aunt and uncle and five cousins.'

I sat there next to her, with her soft palm resting on my small, cold hand. I thought of my mother, her sister and brother-in-law and my cousins, some of them no more than toddlers, and could not reconcile my heart to the idea that they were no longer on the earth.

'If there is anything we can do for you, Anni, you must simply ask.'

I shook my head, too grief-stricken and shocked to speak.

'This happened over a week ago. They are still –' the Maharani's own eyes filled with tears – 'searching for the bodies. If they find them, then you must of course return to Jaipur for the funerals.'

'Yes,' I answered, but we both knew they wouldn't find any bodies. My poor mother would remain in the sun-hardened, red-caked earth for the rest of eternity.

'I'm sure you'll wish to go to temple to offer prayers. I've also found this for you.' She handed me a white tunic, made of the softest silk. 'I've always thought it a comfort that we Indians wear white to mourn the loss of a loved one, not black. There is enough sadness in this time without that. And, dearest Anni, you must not fear for your future. It was I who took you away from your family, and it is I who shall now take responsibility for your care. Do you understand?'

At that moment I understood nothing, but I nodded.

'Remember, even if we can't see them, those we love are always with us,' she added softly.

I stood up, unable at that moment to find comfort in her words.

Once I had dressed in the white tunic, an aide-de-camp was dispatched to take me in the rickshaw to the small Hindu temple in the town. All alone, I sent up the traditional *puja* offerings and prayers to speed the dead on their way. Afterwards, I sat in front of the gods, my head bent forward onto my knees. Even though I wanted to believe, *fool*, that my mother was still with me, as stark reality began to dawn, I also thought of myself. I was now an orphan, with no possessions or money of my own, dependent entirely on the magnanimity of the royal family. It would be doubtful that I'd ever marry – without a family, let alone a dowry, I wasn't a prospect for any man. Even though I would continue to receive an education, it was unlikely that I'd be able to choose my own future path in life.

Along with the tears I cried for my lost family that day, I must confess that I also wept tears for the loss of the future my father had wished for me – a life in which I would use this bright, enquiring mind he had fed and nurtured so assiduously. That life which had been cruelly curtailed.

I felt a hand clasp my shoulder, but I did not stir.

'Anni, Ma told me, and I'm so very, very sorry.' Indira's voice drifted into my thoughts. 'I'm here for you, Anni, I promise, for always. I will look after you. I love you.'

Her hand searched for mine and encircled it tightly. I clung on to it like it was a lifeline.

She hugged me then, her sinewy body shielding mine as I cried. I don't know how long we were there before finally I stood up and said a last goodbye to my family. Then I walked slowly from the temple, arm in arm with the one person in the world who I felt truly cared about me.

Later that evening, unable to sleep, I unwound myself from Indira's warm body, which was tucked up protectively in bed next to me, and ventured out onto the veranda beyond our room. The night air was wonderfully cool and the stars were shining brightly above me.

'Maaji,' I whispered, 'I should be with you up there, not down here alone!' In my grief, it had not escaped me that if I'd still been living in Jaipur with my mother, I, too, would no longer be standing on this earth.

Then I heard a sudden, high-pitched sound in my ears. I turned from left to right to see who it was that was singing so sweetly and clearly. But the veranda and its surrounds were completely deserted. The singing did not abate but continued softly, soothing and comforting me, reminding me of the lullabies my mother would sing to me as a baby.

I suddenly remembered my mother's words from long ago. And I realised that, as she said I would, I'd heard the singing for the first time. As I stood there, I felt my mother close by me, telling me that her gift was being passed over to my keeping. That it hadn't been my turn, and that I had more left to do.

A month later, when the rains had almost stopped and the September air was cooler, we arrived back at the palace. An old lady whom I only knew by sight from the zenana sought me out.

'Anahita, I have something for you.'

I looked at her in surprise, as she led me to a quiet corner and sat me down.

'Do you know who I am?' she asked me.

'No.'

'My name is Zeena and I am a *baidh*. I perform the same role here at the palace as your mother did in Jaipur.'

Her black eyes bored into me and I blinked, comprehending. 'You are a healer?'

'Yes. And when she was here visiting you, your mother may have had a premonition of her own death, for she entrusted something to me. She said I was to give it to you if anything should happen to her.' Zeena held out a small cloth sack tied with a piece of string and handed it to me. 'I haven't looked at what it contains, but I suggest you go somewhere where you won't be disturbed and open it.'

'I will. Thank you for bringing this to me, whatever it may be.' I bowed in gratitude as I stood up.

'She told me that you have the gift of healing too and asked if I would help you.' She looked at me intently. 'And I believe you do have it. I'll teach you all I know, if you wish it.'

'My mother told me when I was small that it would pass to me,' I answered, overwhelmed with emotion. 'I knew my mother was dead before the Maharani confirmed it.'

'Of course you did.' Zeena smiled at me as she brushed my forehead with a kiss. 'You must come and find me when you are ready to begin.'

'Thank you, Zeena.'

I scurried off to my favourite spot in the palace grounds. It was a small pavilion, dedicated to Durga, the goddess of feminine power, hidden in a copse of trees, where I would often sequester myself to read and think. As I sat cross-legged, my hands fumbled impatiently with the tightly knotted string. I was aware that this bag contained the last earthly gifts from my mother, and I had no idea what I would find inside.

I carefully removed the three items from the bag and put them on the hard floor in front of me. There was an envelope addressed to me, a small leather-bound notebook and another, smaller hessian bag, again bound with string. I decided to open the letter first.

My dearest Anni,

Pyari, *I hope I'm wrong, but the night before I was due to leave Cooch Behar Palace, and you, my beloved daughter, the spirits sang to me and told me that I must prepare. As I write, I'm not sure when it will happen. And as we must never live our life in fear of what may be, I'm happy that I do not. Anahita, my own, beautiful daughter, I know that if you are reading these words, I am gone from the earth. But as you will learn in your life, no one who truly loved you is ever far from you.*

You are a special child. I know all parents believe this of their children, but you were put on this earth for a reason. I doubt your journey will be easy, and you must remember that fate can throw many difficult situations at us. But whenever you are uncertain about which is the correct path to take, I beg you to use your gift of intuition. It will never fail you.

Perhaps you heard the spirits singing to you when

*I passed over – that's what happened when my
mother left me. I'm sure that while you read this,
you are feeling alone. Do not, Anni, for you are not
abandoned. Your life is just as it is meant to be, decreed
by the higher powers. Never forget, our destinies
are controlled by them. Maybe,* pyari, *while you read
this, I'm sitting with them now, and beginning to
understand.*

*The gift you have inherited is a blessing and a curse.
It can pull you down into an abyss of darkness when
you foresee the death of someone you love, but equally,
it can lift you to the stars when your unique powers
can help others to heal.*

*As you'll learn on your journey through life, my
daughter, all power can be used for good and evil.
I know you will use your gift wisely.*

*I've left two items with Zeena, whom I trust impli-
citly, and you must too. Have her teach you all that she
knows – she understands who you are. One is my book
of Ayurvedic formulas, the recipes for my healing remedies. It was handed down through generations to me
and is very old and precious. But I hope that what it
contains will aid you on your life's journey. Take care
of it, for it contains the knowledge and wisdom of
your ancestors, women of extraordinary ability.*

*The second item is what your dear father always
called our 'insurance'. At the very least, the contents will
offer you a little security. I should add that your father
never told me about their existence until the night he
died; I don't know their worth or how he came by them.
Perhaps he meant to offer them as a dowry for you one*

*day. If you feel this is an appropriate use of them, then
the power is in your hands.*

*My darling daughter, do not let your grief and
despair at your current fate prevent you from leading
the life that both your father and I desired for you. You
may feel that we have failed you by no longer being with
you, but I can assure you that at the moment you read
this, we are both together, looking down on you and
loving you.*

*As your father said, always try to be true to yourself.
Be a good girl in everything you do.*

I love you,

Your loving mother, xxx

I read the letter many times over, as the first few times, I couldn't see the words for the tears blurring my eyes. Then, with trembling fingers, I opened the small hessian bag.

The string came away easily this time and I tipped its contents out onto the ground.

Inside, were three stones. They looked like any clod of earth I might pull out of the ground anywhere in India. I took the largest in my hands, wondering why my father had called them 'insurance'. Confused, I replaced them in the bag, stood up and walked back disconsolately to the palace.

It was only some weeks later that I discovered their true value; the Maharani had received a delivery from the local gem supplier for her to choose the gift of a new necklace from her husband. The stones – identical pieces of mud to mine – were laid out on a plate, and the jeweller took a special instrument and began to chip away carefully at the dirt. When he finally revealed a twinkle of deep red lying beneath, I grasped what my father had left me: three rubies.

I eventually decided to take the hessian bag back to the pavilion, and there I dug a small hole underneath its foundations with my bare fingers and buried it deep back in the earth. My mother had been right – even though I had little idea how much the stones were actually worth, at least I felt a little more secure that I had something I could call on in a moment of need. And I walked away from the pavilion with my heart slightly lighter.

From that moment on, when Indira was busy being a princess at state functions or dinners, I snatched as many hours as I could in the herb garden with Zeena, determined to learn all I could from her. Even though I had little intention then of becoming a healer, or of putting the concoctions which were listed in my mother's leather-bound notebook into practice, I felt duty-bound to learn what she had wanted me to know. After Zeena had read through my mother's notebook, her gnarled fingers with their long, yellow nails tracing the potions on the page, it seemed to me that she looked at me with new respect.

'You come from a powerful line of *baidh*. There are potions here that are known only to a few.' She turned the pages, until she reached a particular section. 'See, there are even ones listed that can kill a human being outright!' she said, lowering her voice.

I asked her if she had ever used a potion to harm a person.

She stared at me, considering her answer. 'I am a healer, Anahita. The gods alone tell me which potion I should use.'

There was very little I kept back from Indira, but I did not mention my lessons with Zeena. Or the buried rubies. These were secrets my intuition told me to keep to myself.

11

One year later

Indira ran into our bedroom, threw herself upon the mattress and beat the pillow with her fists. 'I won't go! I cannot! I will not!' Then I watched in dismay as my thirteen-year-old friend howled and screamed like a toddler. 'They can't make me! I'll run away! I'll refuse!'

In the past months, I'd often seen these shows of temper when Indira didn't get her way. I sat quietly, watching her until she calmed down. Then I asked gently, 'What is it, Indy? What has happened?'

'My parents wish me to follow my brothers and sister to boarding school in England. I *hate* England! It's dull and miserable and I always get a cold.'

I sat there looking at Indira in abject horror. If they were to send her away to school, I thought selfishly, what would become of me? 'They can't make you go, surely?'

'It's my father who wishes me to go. And as he is "God", his wish is everyone else's command. Including mine. I swear, I will die!' she added dramatically.

Of course for me, the thought of visiting England – the

famous homeland of those who ruled us in India – was an adventure I had always longed for. I imagined seeing Wordsworth's daffodils, visiting the bleak moors of Yorkshire where the Brontës had written their captivating stories, and, of course, London, the Capital of the World. But I knew these were inappropriate thoughts with which to comfort my distraught friend.

'When would you have to leave?'

'I sail in August, and arrive for the start of term in September. I've told Ma that I'll never be any good at lessons, that I wasn't born to sit still – and besides, I know I will wilt like a frozen marigold in that cold, dark place.'

'Oh, Indy, I'll miss you terribly.'

'No, Anni, it's not just me they want to send, it's you too.'

'Me?'

'Of course! Even they wouldn't be so cruel as to send me alone. You'll be coming with me, unless I can think of a way I can persuade them to let us stay here. But Ma loves England and the Season there, so she's not on our side at all. What about Pretty?' cried Indira. 'She'll pine away without me, I know she will!'

I tried to keep my face looking as concerned and as miserable as it had been before Indira had told me that I too was included on this voyage across the sea. 'Is it really that bad?' I asked her. 'Your mother and father seem to love it, and your brothers and sister. They said London is a beautiful city where the streets are lit up with electricity and the women can wander freely, even showing their ankles!'

'We wouldn't be anywhere near London.' Indira hung her head. 'They're sending us off to where my sister went – some horrid school by the cold English sea. Oh, Anni, what on earth are we to do?'

'At least we'll have each other,' I said gently, standing up and going to sit on the bed next to her. I took her hands in mine. 'Please don't cry any more, Indy. As long as we're together, nothing else matters, does it?'

Indira shrugged silently, her eyes downcast. Underneath her bluster, she knew this time she was beaten.

'I'll take care of you, I promise.'

During our last three months in India, Indira sulked continuously and I grew more excited by the day. During the hot season, we moved again up to the royal family's summer residence in Darjeeling.

'This cooler climate is preparing you for when you travel across the sea,' her father, the Maharaja, said to her one balmy evening, when the family were sitting out on the veranda after dinner.

'Pa, *nothing* will prepare me for England,' Indira growled moodily. 'You know I hate it.'

'Just as I hate having to deal with endless affairs of state and never having a day to myself,' her father chastised her. 'Really, Indira, you must learn that life is not simply about pleasure.'

We returned to Cooch Behar Palace from Darjeeling earlier than usual to make ready for the voyage. The entire family was travelling to England together by ship, which required enormous trunks and crates to be packed up – the Maharani insisted on transporting a little bit of home with her wherever she went. Indira entered a slough of despond which even I couldn't rouse her from. She insisted on spending the nights sleeping with Pretty the elephant in the *pilkhana* and no amount of cajoling from me would bring her back inside.

'I can't even say I'll be home for the Christmas holidays,' she said as she stood surveying the half-filled trunks on our bedroom floor, tears flooding down her cheeks. 'There isn't enough time to sail back. I won't see Pretty for almost a year!'

I packed the few possessions I owned: my mother's book of remedies, her *shil noda* and a small selection of dried herbs in case illness beset me in England. After careful thought, I decided to leave my rubies buried beneath the pavilion, believing they were safer there than in my trunk or travelling case.

Four days later, I stood on the deck of the largest and most magnificent ship I'd ever seen as it steamed away from the docks of Calcutta. Little did I know that we would be away for far longer than either of us could ever have imagined.

The royal party was installed in a row of luxurious, above-deck suites on the ship. Indira and I had our own room along the corridor which had been commandeered for the family and the aides-de-camp, butlers, maids and general staff that made up their party. Used to counting in single rupees, I thought that to maintain the lifestyle they did their wealth must have been enough to buy the entire world twice over.

Even Indira managed to raise a smile as we investigated the various modern gadgets in our room. We were also being allowed, now that we were both approaching fourteen, to join the rest of the family for the on-board cocktail parties Indira's parents were holding in their grand suite. Like Indira, I had been fitted out with a suitable Western-style wardrobe – strange-shaped tunics made of muslin and itchy woollen jumpers that I was told I would need once I arrived on England's chilly shores.

As I struggled to fasten the tiny seed-pearl buttons on an uncomfortably tight blouse, I noticed my burgeoning body in the mirror. It had been horribly embarrassing when Miss Reid had suggested to me that it might be time to wear a brassiere. She had also given me some rag-cloths for what she called my 'monthlies'. One had appeared recently, much to my alarm, but thankfully it hadn't happened again since. My new, fuller shape was made even more noticeable by the fact that Indira's body didn't seem to have changed a jot. She had simply grown upwards, not outwards, and was now a good three inches taller than I was. I felt like a fat pomegranate beside a banana.

'Are you ready, girls?' asked Miss Reid as the maid finished combing Indira's lustrous ebony hair.

'Yes, Miss Reid,' I answered for both of us.

'I just know this will be dull,' Indira said, raising her eyebrows as we left our cabin to walk down the corridor towards the salon. We could hear the band playing and a crooner singing Western music as we entered the enormous, ornately decorated room. The glittering jewels adorning the female guests caught the reflection from the chandeliers. All of them were in Western dress, including the Maharani, who was wearing a ravishing sapphire-blue evening gown. I've never been able to decide whether I preferred her in a sari or a cocktail dress – Ayesha, like the chameleon she was, could adjust to either with perfection.

'Stick by me, won't you?' said Indira, pulling me through the crowds towards a waiter.

'Drink, Madam?' A flunkey in a smart white uniform proffered a tray.

Indira winked at me as she chose two glasses of champagne from the assortment on the tray. The waiter glanced at her quizzically, but before he could say anything, Indira had disappeared into the crowd, with me scurrying behind her.

'Go on, try it,' she said, handing me one. 'I quite like it. The bubbles go up your nose.' She lifted the glass to her lips.

'Do you really think we should?' I glanced around nervously. 'It has alcohol in it, Indy. I'm sure we'll get into terrible trouble if anyone sees us.'

'Who's to care, Anni? And besides, we're almost grown-up. Come on,' she urged me.

So I put the champagne glass to my mouth and took a sip. As the bubbles rose into my nose, I choked and spluttered while Indira looked on, laughing.

'Dear me, not on the champagne already are we, girls? And at your age!'

I could have curled up in embarrassment as Raj, Indira's eldest brother, looked down at me in amusement as my eyes streamed. 'Here, Anahita, have my handkerchief.'

'Thank you,' I said as I wiped my eyes and blew my nose, cursing myself for the bad timing. Over the past year, I had developed a crush on Raj; he had arrived in Darjeeling for the summer, having just left Harrow, a school in England which catered to the sons of British and foreign aristocracy. He seemed impossibly grown-up and sophisticated in his Western clothes and was the most handsome young man I'd ever seen.

'May I introduce my friend Prince Varun of Patna. He and I are going up to Oxford together this term. We'll show them a thing or two about cricket, won't we?' Raj made the gesture of bowling a ball.

'Absolutely,' Prince Varun agreed. 'So are you two girls enjoying the voyage so far?'

I turned to Indira, who normally answered for both of us

in these situations. But instead, Indira was staring up into the eyes of Prince Varun, seemingly struck dumb.

'Yes,' I replied hastily, 'it's my first time out of India.'

'Then get ready to be amazed by England, and horrified by the weather,' joked Raj. 'I hope you've packed lots of woollens and Epsom salts. And be prepared for the mustard baths should you catch a cold at school. They're like nothing you could ever imagine.'

Indira was still standing silently, gazing at Varun, so I said, 'Yes, I think we're fully prepared.'

'Good, good. Well, we'll leave you girls to it.' Raj bowed to me, then threw a glance at his sister. 'You're very quiet, Indira. Are you feeling quite well?'

'Yes.' Indira dragged her eyes dreamily away from Prince Varun. 'I'm very well indeed.'

Contrary to Indira's earlier indication that she would wish to leave the 'dull' party as soon as possible, she insisted that we sit in the corner and watch the guests. Eventually, even I was starting to yawn and long for my bed. Finally, I stood up. 'Come on, Indy, I'm tired.'

'Just another five minutes,' Indira said, and I followed her glance to where Raj and Varun were talking animatedly to a couple of young Englishwomen.

At last I managed to drag her out of the salon and along the corridor to our room. We undressed and climbed into bed.

'Indy, you were very quiet tonight. What's the matter?'

Indira's eyes were closed, but she gave a small sigh. 'Yes. I'm absolutely fine. I've just met the man I'm going to marry, that's all.'

'What?!'

'Yes, I saw him, and I just knew.'

'You mean Varun?'

'Of course I do.'

'But, Indy, he's a prince! That will mean it's already been decided by his parents whom he will marry.'

'Just as it's been decided by mine whom I will marry.' Her eyes popped open suddenly, and she cast one of her deep, knowing glances my way. 'I promise you, Anni, one day he will be my husband.'

For the next few weeks, life aboard the ship became a game of cat and mouse as Indira insisted we stalk Raj and Varun, just so that she could catch further glimpses of her 'future husband'. This entailed hanging about surreptitiously outside their cabins when they left to take breakfast or lunch, or indulge in a game of billiards, or play croquet on one of the decks. We would then have to appear as nonchalant as possible, as if it was a coincidence we had found them there, and sit watching whatever game it was they were playing.

Suddenly, the girl who'd never cared a fig for her appearance began to sweat over what she should wear to dinner in the evenings, stealing perfume from her mother's dressing table and lipstick from her sister.

I'm afraid to say that I found the whole thing ridiculous and rather irritating. Indira was simply experiencing her first crush and I knew it would pass soon enough. However, Indy being Indy, she was embracing her new passion as wholeheartedly as she did everything else.

On the last night before we were due to dock in Southampton, the royal party had been invited to have dinner at the Captain's table. Indira's emotions swam ceaselessly between which dress she was going to wear and the fact that this would be the last time she saw Prince Varun. I'd diplomatically refrained from pointing out during Indira's infatuation that she almost certainly could have worn nothing at all, and still Varun would merely have seen her for what she still was: a little girl.

'Look, Minty has lent me one of her old dresses!' Indira burst through the door with a peach chiffon evening dress over her arm. 'And it fits me perfectly.'

'Surely you won't dare to wear it?' I cautioned, thinking of the prim muslin and calico dresses buttoned up to the neck which befitted our still-childish status.

'Yes! Anni, don't you understand? I have to do something dramatic for Varun to notice me!'

'You'll never get away with it. Miss Reid wouldn't let you appear in *that* in public in a million years! And besides, what would your mother say?'

'I'll be fourteen in four months' time. Goodness, many girls in India are married by then,' Indira pouted. 'Anni, you have to help me; I'll get dressed as normal with you, then once Miss Reid has taken us up to the dining room, I'll say I've forgotten something and I'll rush downstairs and change into the dress. How's that for a plan?'

The horror showed on my face. 'Please, Indy, what about your father? Do you want to disgrace him?'

'Honestly, Anni!' Indira put the dress up against her. 'I'm hardly arriving in my vest and knickers. It's simply a more grown-up version of what we normally wear.'

And indeed, I could see that at least the dress was reasonably decorous, with its square-shaped neckline and the bodice cut just below the chest, flowing out beneath the Empire line in soft waves of chiffon to her feet.

'Minty wore it for her sixteenth birthday. So it can't be that bad, can it?'

I sighed, realising that whatever I thought, it was a fait accompli.

Later that evening, as Miss Reid led us up the grand main staircase of the ship and as we neared the dining-room entrance, Indira put her hand to her mouth.

'Oh, Miss Reid! I said I'd lend Lady Alice Carruthers a book, and I promised to bring it up to the table tonight. There's bound to be far too much commotion tomorrow when the ship docks.'

'Would you like me to run down and get it for you, dear?' Miss Reid asked.

'No, don't trouble yourself. I'll go. I know exactly where it is.'

Indira turned and flew down the stairs before she could be stopped, leaving Miss Reid and me standing together in front of the dining-room doors.

I sat myself down in one of the gilt chairs along the corridor. 'Miss Reid, please, I'll wait here for her. I know you haven't eaten yet, and it will be a long day tomorrow. I'll be fine here, really.'

'If you're sure, dear,' she said in agreement. 'Knowing Indira, and the confusion she keeps her possessions in, it could be fifteen minutes before she's back, and I have such a lot of packing to do after supper tonight.'

'Really, don't trouble yourself,' I said, relieved I'd managed to convince her to go to the below-deck canteen where the staff took their meals. 'I promise I won't move until she returns.'

'All right, dear, thank you. I'll be back to collect you at ten o'clock.'

As I watched her walk down the staircase, I knew it had helped that she regarded me as the more trustworthy of the two of us. I'd rarely put a foot wrong in her presence. As I waited for Indira, I amused myself by watching the elegant guests entering the dining room. They spoke in their clipped British accents and I struggled to understand a lot of what they said. It struck me then that learning English in India might be very different to the reality of understanding and making myself understood on their shores.

Finally, as the last guests had passed me and entered the dining room some minutes before, and I was beginning to despair of Indira arriving before Grace – the prayer the English said before every mealtime – a vision in peach chiffon floated up the stairs towards me.

I blinked, hardly believing the change that had been wrought in my tomboyish friend. The dress fitted her tall, slim body perfectly and she'd managed to pile her hair on top of her head, securing it with pins and adding a peach rose to the side of it. She was ravishing, in fact, a younger version of her mother.

'How do I look?' she whispered nervously.

'Beautiful. Come on!' I stood up, heading towards the dining-room doors. We pushed them open, just as the Master of Ceremonies clapped his hands and said, 'My lords, ladies and gentlemen, pray, silence for the Captain.'

Every head turned towards the Captain, who, as bad luck would have it, was seated in the centre of the room only a few yards from the huge doors where Indira and I were making our surreptitious entrance. All eyes moved towards us, and I stood like a rabbit caught in the headlights, my blush as bright as the vermilion adorning Indira's lips.

The Captain adjusted his gaze to that of the other guests. 'Ladies –' he gestured to us – 'kindly take your seats before I say Grace.'

'Thank you.' Totally unabashed, Indira walked towards the Captain's table with her head held high, utterly regal in her bearing and showing no hint of embarrassment at being the centre of attention. For the first time I truly saw her as a princess. We took the two seats which had been left to us at the end of the table, but as I followed in her wake, my eyes fell on Prince Varun. And there was no doubt that he was gazing at her with a different expression in his eyes.

I continued to watch Indira that night, as the peach dress seemed to give her a whole new maturity, elegance and charm. Even her parents, who must have been shocked when their daughter walked in, were now looking on benignly.

Yet again, I thought, as I sat in my muslin dress feeling dowdy and uncomfortable, beauty had worked its magic on all who surveyed it. Far from being angry, everyone had embraced Indira. And once the band struck up, the Maharaja himself took his youngest daughter onto the dance floor. After that, Raj, her brother, followed, and finally, Prince Varun. When Miss Reid arrived at my side at ten o'clock and asked where Indira was, I gestured to the dance floor.

I watched Miss Reid's eyes search her charge out.

'Where?'

'In the peach dress, dancing with Prince Varun.'

I watched her face as recognition dawned. A hand slowly went to her mouth in horror and she looked nervously in the direction of the Maharani. 'I'll almost certainly lose my position over this. Did you know about her plan?'

'Yes,' I said. 'But what could I do?'

'What could either of us do?' Miss Reid sighed heavily. 'She is a princess.'

I lay in bed that night, listening over and over to the details of Indira's triumph, which had culminated in the dance with Prince Varun. He had apparently whispered at the end of it that she was turning into a beautiful young woman, just like her mother. And something inside me – no more than a tiny fissure – began to form at the foundations of my belief that Indira and I would be together always. She was growing up before my eyes, and one day, I thought, as I bit my lip hard to stop the tears, my friendship alone would not be enough for her. She would want the love of a man.

I awoke with a feeling of trepidation the next day, expecting repercussions from Indira's performance the night before. But surprisingly, there were none. Instead, as everyone ran around the ship saying farewell to the friends they'd made on-board, all I heard was how stunning Indira had looked. It seemed that the duckling had turned into a swan and nobody seemed bothered by her disregard for society's rules.

As Indira skipped around from cabin to cabin saying goodbye to her new friends, I took myself out on deck to watch the country I had heard so much about come into view.

Even though it was August, which I'd been told was one of the warmest months in England, I shivered under my thin cotton blouse. It was still early and a low mist hung over the port of Southampton. I inhaled the English air for the very first time and found it noticeable for its blandness. It smelt of nothing except clean, salty wind.

I tried to rouse myself from my dark mood by thinking I was within an hour or so of stepping onto the famous green and pleasant land that had inspired some of the world's greatest writers to produce their finest works.

But I could not.

Perhaps, I comforted myself, I was simply exhausted from the emotional stress of last night, but I knew it ran deeper than that. Still unused to the new and strange feelings inside me that had arrived with the sound of the singing, I stood there as a shudder ran up my spine, my skin tingled and the fine hairs on my arms stood on end. I have learned since, of course, that the sensation was warning me of danger. But that day, as I still struggled to understand what it meant, I simply felt as if every one of my senses was on full alert.

The ship's horn roared a final thunderous note as we docked, and the decks had a carnival-like gaiety about them. On the quay, I could see tiny figures waving Union Jack flags as they waited for the first glimpse of loved ones returned to them.

As everyone else disappeared back into their cabins to collect their belongings and make ready to disembark, the deck emptied and I found myself left in solitude. I shivered again, as much from my sense of aloneness and fear as from the chill. As I reached inside my pocket to find a handkerchief, a pair of warm, brown arms snaked around my waist from behind me.

'What are you doing up here all by yourself? I've been looking for you everywhere.' Indira hugged me tight, her sweet breath melting the ice that had been forming in my veins.

'I was looking at England.'

She turned me around to face her and studied me. 'You've been crying, Anni. Why?'

'I'm not sure,' I replied honestly.

A slim finger reached out to wipe a tear from my cheek. 'Don't cry, Anni, and please don't be frightened. I'm here, re-member?' Indira put her arms around me and hugged me to her. 'And I always will be.'

12

For the following two weeks, we were all installed in a beautiful Victorian house in Pont Street, Knightsbridge. Although it was the size of a rabbit hutch compared to the palace we were used to, it somehow didn't matter, as there was so much to see and do outside. Contrary to Indira's remonstrations about how much she hated England, she immediately commandeered the family chauffeur and was determined to show me the delights of London. We drove down The Mall to see Buckingham Palace and the Changing of the Guard. We visited the Tower of London, where Indira enjoyed regaling me with lurid details of how Henry VIII, King of England, had once chopped off the heads of two of his wives because he kept wanting to marry another one.

'How silly that they're only allowed to marry one woman at a time and have to kill them if they want someone else!' She giggled. 'You know Pa could have up to eight wives if he chose to.'

We went to Trafalgar Square and fed the pigeons bustling around Nelson's column and took a riverboat along the River Thames. But in truth, Indira's favourite place in London was only a few yards from our Pont Street home.

As she led me through its front doors, she informed me that we had just entered the most famous shop in the world.

'I love Harrods; it sells everything, from new keys for a broken lock, to cheese, to clothes – even Indian elephants! And,' she added as we journeyed up in the lift, 'Ma has an account here, so anything you want, just say.'

Indeed, the Harrods shop, or department store as she called it, was an Aladdin's cave. Sometimes Indira would play a game with one of the stern-faced assistants by asking if they stocked parakeets or jacaranda trees.

'Well, Madam, you'll find the parakeets in the pet department and the trees in the gardening department. If they don't stock what you desire, I'm sure Harrods can order one for you,' the assistant would reply.

'Oh, Indy, please don't tease them!' I begged her as she walked away giggling and I grappled with embarrassment.

She took me upstairs to the spectacular toy department, where the sales assistants greeted her like a long-lost friend.

'When I was very small, I used to sneak out of our house and come here to place my orders for anything I wanted. I put them on Ma's account, and she didn't notice for ages.' Indira laughed as she led me out back down the astonishing moving staircase she called an escalator.

'You're not buying anything there today?'

'No, I think I've rather grown out of toys, don't you? Let's go to the womenswear department – I've never tried on a ready-made dress before. It'll be fun!'

Having rallied a gaggle of assistants to bring her a collection of beautiful dresses, I followed Indira into the changing room so that she could try them on. After we'd been there for two hours, my patience began to wear thin.

'Are you sure your mother won't mind?' I said as Indira twirled in yet another stunning creation and told the assistant to add it to her already enormous pile.

'Not until she gets the account in a few weeks' time.' She grinned.

On our way down to the front entrance, we passed the books department and I paused longingly for a second. Indira noticed and, perhaps because she was feeling guilty for keeping me so long as she tried on her dresses, she suggested we go to take a look.

And it was here I found myself in a wonderland of my own.

In front of me, in the Harrods shop, were endless rows of the same books I'd coveted behind the glass doors of Cooch Behar Palace's library. And they were freely available for me to pick off the shelves. I stood with copy after copy in my hands, caressing the gilt-embossed titles.

'Choose anything you want, Anni,' said Indira, as restless beside me here as I had been in the womenswear department.

For once, I didn't protest, and chose three: *Bleak House* by Charles Dickens, *Jane Eyre* by Charlotte Brontë and *Pride and Prejudice* by Jane Austen. I hugged them to myself as we left Harrods, hardly believing that I owned them and would never have to give them back.

In the bedroom that Indira and I shared on the top floor of the house on Pont Street, I cleared a space on a shelf and proudly displayed my three books. I swore then and there that, one day, I would earn enough money to own as many books as I wished.

Even though I was filled with wonder at the new sights and sounds of England, my time in London heightened my sense of dependence on the Cooch Behar royal family. At the palace, my needs were small and I was just one of hundreds who were fed and cared for. But here in London, I became acutely aware of it. Even though Indira always had plenty of money and was generous to a fault, I didn't like to ask her for anything. In the small prayer room which had been set up in one of the quieter rooms at the back of the house, I sat on my knees and offered *puja* to Lakshmi, the goddess of wealth, in the hope that one day I would find a way to be financially independent.

A few days later, our return visit to the Harrods shop took me and Indira, under the watchful eye of Miss Reid, to a very different department – that of school uniforms.

'We have to wear a tie – like men!' cried Indira as Miss Reid showed her how to fasten it around her neck. 'Aargh!' Indira put her hands to her throat, her eyes full of mock terror. 'I feel as though I'm being strangled.'

There then followed a selection of blouses, smocks and jumpers that were so itchy it was as if a thousand fleas were jumping on my skin.

'And these,' said the sales assistant, 'are for the girls to wear for games, such as netball and hockey.' She held up a shapeless maroon tunic and large matching pants.

'Netball? Hockey? I don't wish to know how to play these games,' said Indira haughtily.

'I'm sure you'll love them once you have tried them, dear,' said Miss Reid, a fount of endless patience. 'And you're so good at outdoor pursuits. You'll take to English ball games like a duck to water.'

'I'm very sure I won't,' said Indira sulkily.

Miss Reid and I shared a look as she stomped into the changing rooms to try on the hideous tunic.

*

A week later, we were motored down to Eastbourne in Sussex. Indira sat next to me in the back of the plush Rolls-Royce, staring out miserably at the leafy English countryside, which I thought very beautiful. Autumn had begun to make its appearance; the leaves were turning gold and the softness of the early-morning mists had a soporific effect on me. Miss Reid was accompanying us on the journey and sat in the front seat, chatting with the chauffeur. Eventually we arrived in front of an austere grey building, which reminded me, perhaps unfairly, of Dotheboys Hall, the school where the young Nicholas Nickleby secures an assistant master's post in Charles Dickens's story.

The chauffeur unloaded our trunks from the boot at the front of the car, while Indira refused to move from the inside of it. Miss Reid and I climbed out and surveyed the school.

'Don't be nervous, dear, I'm sure your time here will benefit you greatly. And,' she added as an afterthought, lowering her voice, 'Indira is without her maid for the first time. She will have to *do* for herself whilst she's here. Remember, you may not be a princess, but you are a well-bred young lady in your own right, a cousin to a maharani no less. Don't let her treat *you* like a servant, will you?'

'I'm sure she won't,' I said loyally.

Miss Reid had no time to say more, for a petulant Indira had followed us out of the car at last and was now sitting cross-legged on the gravel drive.

'Get up, dear!' chided Miss Reid. 'And start acting like the young woman you've been so desperate to become in the past few weeks.'

Indira didn't move. She simply crossed her arms tighter as

if to make her point more thoroughly and stared silently into the distance.

I walked around the side of the car and crouched down next to her. 'Come on, Indy, the other girls might see you and think you're a baby. Besides,' I added, 'it might be fun.'

'I hate it,' Indira growled, and I saw that her eyes were full of tears. 'No one in my family cares that I've gone. Pa was too busy even to say goodbye. They just wanted to get rid of me.'

'You know that isn't true. They all adore you; and your father especially would want you to make him proud. Listen,' I whispered, thinking on my feet, 'you have plenty of money, haven't you?'

She nodded.

'Right.' I used the last weapon in my armoury. 'Then if we don't like it, we'll simply run away and get on the first ship back to India. How about that?'

At this, she turned to me and her eyes lit up at the thought of such an adventure.

'Yes,' she said as she stood up finally and dusted the chalky whiteness of the gravel from her skirt. 'Now that would make them sorry, wouldn't it?'

'Yes. Ready?' I asked her.

'Ready.'

And, fingers grasped tightly in each other's hands, we walked up the steps and into the school.

Miss Reid had already warned us that we would be objects of fascination to the other pupils. Indian girls were still very much a rare sight at an English boarding school. For the first week, we steeled ourselves against the stares and whispers our presence engendered, and the giggling we heard when we were served chicken instead of their beef in the dining room. As the girls cold-shouldered us, we clung together for support. Especially at night in the draughty dormitory of ten, when Indira would climb into my bed so we could give each other a hug of warmth and comfort.

'I want to go home,' she would cry as her tears fell onto my nightgown. 'Please, Anni, let's do as you said and run away.'

'We will soon, I promise, but we have to stay long enough for your parents to realise that you really have given it a try.'

Indira wasn't the only one who was miserable. I, too, found my new life terrifying. I loathed the chill of the English dawn, when my bones froze and my body covered itself in involuntary goosebumps which didn't disappear until Indira's warm body curled around me at night. The bland English food, which seemed to be cooked in leftover dishwater, with no spices added, made me feel sick. And even though I had thought that my command of the English language and my comprehension of it was good, I struggled to understand the staff and the girls, who spoke so quickly and pronounced even familiar words so differently. When they asked me a question, I would stand, speechless, only realising later what they had meant. The outdoor games with wooden sticks, conducted on wet, muddy fields, with a set of rules that were as confusing as they seemed ridiculous, were beyond me. I was never a ball player, so these were the hours in the day I dreaded most.

Due to the incessant English rain, everything smelt of damp. At night, no incense hung in the air as it had in the palace at Cooch Behar; all that shone above us was the harsh light of a naked electric bulb.

By the time the first two weeks were over, it was *me* who wanted to run away.

And then the history teacher, who had apparently been on leave of absence due to a stint abroad, arrived one morning in our freezing classroom to teach us. He was younger than the other teachers we'd had so far, and his skin was tanned a deep nut-brown.

'Good morning, girls,' he said as he entered the classroom. Dutifully we all stood up and chanted, 'Good morning, sir.'

'Well now, I hope you all had a good summer break. I certainly did. I went out to visit my parents in India.'

The rest of the girls looked bored, but both Indira and I were immediately alert.

'And, it seems, we have two new pupils from that country. I believe that one of you is a princess. Now –' his gaze fell on Indira and me – 'which one of you two would that be?'

There was sudden animated whispering in the classroom, as all the girls turned to stare at us, trying to second-guess which one of us it was. Indira raised her hand slowly. 'I am, sir.'

'Her Highness, Princess Indira of Cooch Behar.' The teacher smiled knowingly. 'I visited Cooch Behar whilst I was in India two years ago and saw the wonderful palace your family lives in.'

This prompted another round of excited muttering and much staring from the girls.

'Yes, sir.' Indira lowered her eyes.

'Perhaps, Indira, you would at some point like to tell us the history of your family and how you live. I think all the girls here would learn a lot from your account.'

'Yes, sir.'

'And you?' he asked, his gaze falling upon me. 'Where do you live?'

'I live at the palace too, sir.'

'I see. And yet you are not a princess?'

'No, sir, I'm not.'

'Anni's my best friend,' said Indira gallantly. 'And my companion.'

'Jolly good, jolly good. Well now, girls, I hope you're helping Princess Indira and Miss Chavan feel at home. I'm going to tell you what I saw during my travels through British India.'

Once the lesson was finished, we were sent out to collect our yellowing bottle of milk for 'elevenses', as the girls called it, and for a blast of invigorating sea air, which the British seemed to think was so essential. Normally, Indira and I would stand in a corner of the courtyard, surreptitiously pouring our milk away into the bushes. Today it was different. The girls followed us.

'Are you really a princess?'

'Do you live in a palace?'

'Do you have lots of servants?'

'Have you ever ridden on an elephant?'

'Do you wear a crown when you're at home?'

The excited girls clustered around Indira as I stood on the sidelines and watched her as she smiled graciously and answered as many questions as she could. Later, when the lunchtime bell rang and we filed into the dining room, a girl named Celestria, who was the person everyone else in our class wanted to know, came over to Indira and me.

'Will you come and sit with us for luncheon, Princess Indira?'

'Of course.'

I watched as Indira moved away from me, talking to Celestria. Then she turned around and beckoned to me. 'Anni must come too.'

Celestria nodded, but when we reached the long trestle table, the girls bunched up on the benches to make room in the centre for Indira and Celestria. I was left at the end hanging off the edge.

In that hour, I watched Indira blossom with the attention and admiration she received. I couldn't blame her for it. She'd spent her entire life surrounded by other people showing their subservience and acquiescing to her every whim. She had been born 'special'. And I, Anahita, had not.

I will remember that first, harsh English winter as one of the most desolate periods of my life. As Indira grew in confidence, her exuberant personality began to assert itself and all the girls vied for her attention. She rose swiftly through the ranks to take her rightful place as queen bee as naturally as the sun rises in the sky every morning. Even though she did her best to include me, the other girls made it obvious that they weren't interested in a mere companion, who didn't exude the kind of sparkling charm that came naturally in spades to Indira. I became increasingly isolated, and spent many lunchtimes in the library reading by myself, not wishing to embarrass Indira with my uncomfortable, hovering presence.

To make matters worse, as Indira's body grew more swan-like, with all the bits that attached themselves at puberty fitting her height in just the right proportions and only adding to her elegance, hormones and the stodgy English diet merely made me sprout even further sideways. I had also noticed that when I was reading in dim light, I could hardly make out the words. I was sent to the school doctor, who prescribed a pair of ugly, thick-lensed glasses for reading.

Occasionally, Indira would still crawl into my bed at night and hug me.

'Are you all right, Anni?' she'd whisper softly in my ear.

'Yes, of course,' I'd lie.

She rarely noticed me in the daylight hours, when she spent time with her new aristocratic English friends. I felt keenly that I had somehow become a burden and an embarrassment to her. So I shut myself off into my world of books, and longed for the moment in June when we'd return to the palace and all would be as it had been with Indira and me.

My heart lightened as spring came to England and we returned to the house in London for the Easter break. But even there I saw less of Indira than I did at school, for she was invited endlessly to stay at her new friends' houses and for tea at smart hotels.

One afternoon, she returned from such an event and found me reading on the bed in our room.

'Anni, I wonder if I could ask you an awfully big favour,' she began in her newly acquired English accent.

I removed my glasses and looked at her. 'Yes, Indy, what is it?'

'Well, the thing is, Celestria's parents are off to France and she was saying how terribly boring it would be staying at their house in the country with simply her governess for company. She's asked me if she could come and stay here at Pont Street with us. And Ma has said yes.'

'How nice,' I managed to say.

'Well,' she sighed, exaggeratedly, 'the problem is, the only spare room we have is the old box room along the corridor. I can hardly put Celestria in there – she is the daughter of a lord, after all. So I was wondering, if you don't mind *awfully*, whether just for the week she's here, you'd consider moving in there?'

'Of course,' I answered.

In essence, I didn't mind – I wasn't concerned by moving to a servant's room. But that moment compounded the growing sense of fear and dread I'd had in my heart all winter. I couldn't blame Indira; it was natural she would grow away from me. She was destined to join the ranks of the highest in society and one day become the wife of a maharaja, whereas I . . .

I didn't know.

To make matters worse, as Celestria took her place in my old bed next to Indira, the rumblings of impending war grew louder. Everyone in London was assuring everyone else that of course the Kaiser would not be stupid enough to launch an unprovoked attack on a neighbouring country. All I could think was that if war did break out, we would surely be unable to travel back to India when the summer holidays began in two months' time.

Indira's parents sailed home a few days after Easter. Her father had state business to attend to in Cooch Behar. On the journey back to school at the end of the holidays when I finally had Indira to myself, I broached the subject with her.

'Everyone says there won't be a war,' she said, brushing my comment aside airily, 'and besides, I'm sure we could stay at the house in Pont Street if needs be. The Season is meant to be fun in London, so I hear.'

I was shocked at her nonchalance. Could this really be the same girl who, only a few months ago, had cried over the fact that she'd miss her pet elephant? The air of faux sophistication, which Indira, being the great mimic she was, insisted on copying from her English friends, made me want to shake her hard in frustration.

Later, when we arrived back at school, and Indira asked if it was all right if she moved into a dorm with Celestria and her other friends, I agreed without protest. I had to accept that Indira had changed irrevocably.

The summer term passed much faster than the previous two, partly due to the fact that I had realised that Indira, at least for now, was lost to me. Charlotte, the girl who now occupied Indira's former bed next to me, was sweet and friendly. Her father was an army vicar in the Christian church, serving abroad. Although I could never have another friendship like the one I'd shared with Indira, I felt that at least Charlotte and I had things in common. As her fees were paid for by the army, she took her education seriously, unlike many of our English classmates, who saw school as a place to pass the time until they were launched into society and a grand marriage. Charlotte had decided to become a governess when she left school.

'Father earns a pittance from the church, which he saves to use as a pension for when he and Mother retire. But there's nothing over to keep me, so I must stay at home with them, or work for a living,' she'd confided to me one night.

This led me to think that perhaps I too could have a future as a governess. By the end of my time at school, I would certainly be educated well enough to teach small children. But then, I thought, sighing, who on earth would want me? In India, it was seen as a sign of status to employ an English gentlewoman, but no family on *either* continent would want an Indian to teach their children, no matter how qualified she was.

As each day passed, I realised that I was stranded in

no-man's-land. I'd been brought up in a palace, yet I was poor; I was being educated in England, but I was the wrong colour to use my skills. I was not of the working class, but I wasn't aristocratic enough to warrant a good marriage. I thought of the little hessian sack hidden beneath the pavilion in the grounds of Cooch Behar Palace and prayed to all the gods and goddesses I knew of that it was still buried there, its contents safe and undisturbed.

13

Further rumours of war abounded at the beginning of June. There was no question of us returning home to India. Nor was there the possibility of Indira and I spending the summer in the house in Pont Street – it had been shut up and many of the staff had already joined the services. Besides, Indira's mother was frightened of the very real possibility of bombs dropping on London, so it was arranged that Indira and I would spend the summer as far away as the Maharani could get us. We were to journey down to a county called Devon in southern England. The widow of the ex-Resident of Cooch Behar – the most senior British official present in every princely state – had offered to accommodate the two of us over the holidays.

'I can't believe Ma is making us go there! War hasn't even been declared yet,' grumbled Indira as she threw clothes haphazardly into her trunk. 'I begged her to let me go and stay with Celestria, but she said no. What on earth am I going to do with myself for a whole summer, stuck out in the middle of nowhere with no friends?'

I *wanted* to say – wanted to, but of course didn't – that I'd be there to keep her company. But as we set off on our journey down to Devon, she sat as far from me on the black leather seat as she could, her face turned away from me. As usual with Indira, her body language said everything that her words did not. I only wished that I'd been able to stay at school, as some of the other girls whose parents were abroad had done. Including my friend Charlotte. But how could I have explained to the Maharani that her daughter no longer wanted me as her companion?

These were thoughts I could not voice to a woman who had taken me in and then paid willingly for my expensive education, because she believed her daughter loved and needed me.

I looked at Indira sulking and knew she needed me no longer.

When we drove into the park that surrounded Astbury Hall it took a good few minutes before the house came into view. I gazed at it with fascination, for it strongly resembled Cooch Behar Palace in its shape and form. It was as though they were twin souls: one fashioned from heat, the other from ice. I was later to discover that the architect had modelled the palace partially on Astbury Hall, so it wasn't surprising that the cold monolith of a building in front of me, with its domed cupola forming the centrepiece, felt familiar.

When we came to a halt in front of the enormous stone steps that led up to the front door, I saw it swing open and members of the household staff started to stream out. They lined up along the steps as we both climbed out of the car. Princess Indira was certainly getting a royal welcome. She walked up the steps past the servants towards a woman, stern and wide-hipped, who was wearing an old-fashioned Edwardian dress.

'I'm Maud Astbury. Welcome to Astbury Hall, Princess Indira.'

'Thank you, Lady Astbury,' Indira replied politely.

I followed in their wake as she led Indira inside.

'I hope your room will be suitable for you, my dear. We're so short-staffed here, what with all the young men going off to join up.'

Indira, gracious to a fault when she was treated royally, nodded in agreement. 'Of course, I understand. It's awfully kind of you to have me.'

'My son, Donald, is coming home in a few days for the holidays too. At least he may be able to keep you amused.'

As usual, I was standing behind Indira, feeling uncomfortable. Eventually, Lady Astbury's eyes fell upon me. 'I see you've brought your own maid with you?'

'No,' said Indira quickly. 'Anahita is my friend and companion.'

'I see.' There was some consternation on Lady Astbury's face as she led Indira away from me to the bottom of the grand staircase. She bent her head towards Indira and the two of them whispered together.

'Of course, I'll see that it's arranged. Now, Princess Indira, the maid will show you and your . . . companion upstairs to your rooms. Please do tell me if there is anything that you will need during your stay. I will see you at dinner tonight.'

'I'm sorry, Anni,' Indira said yet again as she looked around the dim little attic space where I'd been billeted. 'Obviously Ma was in such a state she forgot to mention that you'd be coming here too. Lady Astbury promised that she would prepare a room on the main floor for you tomorrow. Do you mind awfully staying in here for tonight?'

'Of course not,' I said, gratified by what I felt was Indira's genuine concern. 'The view is lovely from here.'

Indira peered out of the small pane of glass, set between the eaves of the great house. 'Yes, you're right, it is. Anyway, if you can't bear it in here, my bed is big enough for at least another four people.' She grinned at me.

'I'll be fine up here.'

'Well, then, I'll be downstairs if you need me. Anni,' she said, taking my hands in hers, 'I'm sorry if I've abandoned you at school. I haven't meant to, really.'

And then, Indira threw her arms around me, like she used to in the old days when it was just the two of us against the world.

'Come down when you're unpacked,' she said, giving me a tiny wave as she left.

A week after we'd arrived at the house, Lady Astbury seemed to have conveniently forgotten about my impending move to the lower floor and I was still lodged in my tiny attic bedroom. I found it impossible to sleep beyond six o'clock, as the sun rose through my uncurtained window and bathed the room in blinding light. I peered outside and saw it was another beautiful day. Restless, I washed my face in the basin provided for me and took the back stairs down through the kitchen to enjoy the sunrise outside.

As I walked along the enormous terrace, which didn't need a veranda to shade it from the weak English sun, I could smell the sweet scent of newly mown grass. I trod lightly down the steps into the gardens beyond and wandered around, admiring bed after bed of magnificent roses. As I luxuriated in the stillness and calm of the early morning, my mind flashed to a typical summer dawn in India. Here in temperate and steady England, the weather did not dominate and destroy. The thermometer dropped in the winter, making life less pleasant, but as far as I was aware, there had never been a monsoon, earthquake or, in fact, any particularly dramatic natural disaster on the British Isles.

India, I thought, was the polar opposite. Everything about it was vibrant, colourful, with drama aplenty. The temperatures soared, the wind blew, the rivers broke their banks; all was violent and unpredictable.

I was beginning to understand, too, that, unlike my countrymen's fiery natures, as a rule the British were an unemotional people. Sitting down on a bench, I thought back to when my friend Charlotte had learned of her mother's death just before the end of term. She took the news stoically, with acceptance and few tears. Then I thought of myself two years before, weeping and wailing for the loss of my mother that terrible day in the temple.

I also knew that, even though the British were always at war in some far-flung foreign part of the world, the solid English ground on which I stood had not been invaded for more than two hundred years.

But all that might change in the next weeks or months. Would the Kaiser stamp his heavy leather boots across Europe and shake his fist at this tiny nation, which had somehow managed to conquer so much of the world and build an empire on which, as the English loved to remind each other, the sun never set?

'Hello there, are you our Indian princess?'

I'd been so engrossed in my thoughts that I hadn't heard anyone approach me. I looked up into a pair of the bluest English eyes I'd ever seen. They were contained within a face that still had the undistinguished features of adolescence before the final contours of adulthood appeared. The boy's hair, to my Indian eyes, was the colour of straw and just as coarse. He had the usual pale pink-and-white complexion of the English that so many Indians longed for.

To me, that sunrise, he looked like the Adonis in the Greek myths I had read during history lessons.

'I—'

As I began to answer him, the faint sound of singing started in my ears and I found it difficult to concentrate. A now-familiar shiver ran up my backbone. Someone, or something, was telling me that this stranger would play a part in my future.

'Do you understand English?' he prompted me.

'Yes.' I tried to shut out the sound in my ears by telling them that I understood what they were trying to say to me. That the message had come through loud and clear. 'I speak good English,' I replied.

'And your name is Indira?'

'No, I'm her companion. My name is Anahita Chavan – Anni for short.'

'Hello, Miss Chavan, or Anni for short,' he said, holding out his hand, 'I'm Donald Astbury. How do you do?'

As with all the English, his manners were impeccable.

'Very well, thank you,' I replied demurely.

He sat down companionably next to me on the bench. 'So may I ask what you're doing out in the garden at such an early hour?'

'The sunrise through my window wakes me. And you?'

'Oh, I arrived home from school late last evening. The bell there rings at six-thirty, so I woke up here on the dot. It's such a glorious morning that I decided to get up and go and check on my mare in the stables.'

'I love horses,' I said wistfully.

'You ride?'

'Yes, I learned before I was able to walk on my own two feet.'

'I didn't realise they taught riding from the cradle in India the way they do here.'

'Of course! How else would we have got about for thousands of years?'

'Good point, good point,' Donald said with a smile. 'Then how about I show you our stables?'

'I'd love to see them,' I agreed eagerly.

'Come on, then.' He helped me up from the bench and we started to walk across the gardens. 'So, how are you finding England?'

'There are some things I like, and others that I do not.'

He looked at me suddenly. 'You're awfully sensible and your English is excellent. May I ask how old you are?'

'I'll be fifteen in a few months' time,' I answered, exaggerating a little.

'Goodness. Most of the English girls I meet of your age are still silly little children.'

'Thank you.'

'Not at all,' he replied as we approached the stables. 'Now, look here, this is my mare, Glory. My mother had her named Gloria after some maiden aunt, but I really didn't think the name suited her, so I changed it. What do you think of her?'

I looked at the horse and saw that Glory was indeed glorious, and a thoroughbred. By my reckoning, she stood sixteen hands high. I offered her my palm, and put it under her chin as I stroked her long, sleek face.

'Gosh, I'm impressed,' Donald commented. 'Normally she's whiney and complains when a stranger strokes her. You obviously have the touch, Anni.'

'I seem to understand them, somehow.'

'Well, how about a ride? I'd love to see if Glory would stand you on her back. Normally, she bolts and throws unknown riders off. Let's see if she'll allow you to mount her.'

'I'd love to try,' I said eagerly.

'Lead her out and I'll saddle her up,' my new friend instructed. 'I'm sure she'll let us know if she's in a mood to oblige us.'

I did as he requested, then, once Glory was still, I jumped onto her back, hitching up my long skirt as far as modesty would allow me to sit astride her.

Donald smiled. 'It seems she's perfectly happy to have you up there. I'll get the stallion.'

Five minutes later, we were trotting companionably together across the park. He brought his horse up short and looked at me. 'Are you up for some rougher terrain? Dartmoor is literally a few minutes that way,' he said, gesturing to his left. 'It's the most wonderful hack and I think you're good enough to cope.'

'Of course.' I agreed, not knowing what this 'Dartmoor' place might be, but feeling happier and freer than I had for months. 'I'll follow you.'

'Righty-oh,' Donald agreed, and immediately cantered off, with Glory and me doing our best to keep up with him.

As we left the park and flew out onto the moor, a warm breeze pulled through my hair and I felt the heaviness that had recently assailed me begin to lighten. At first, I concentrated on steering our way through the rocky, uneven terrain. But Glory seemed to know exactly where she was going and, realising that she was in charge, I relaxed, sat back and enjoyed the ride.

Forty minutes later, we arrived back at the stables, both horses and riders panting with exertion.

'My goodness,' said Donald, as he climbed off his horse and handed him to the yawning stable lad for attention, 'you're by far the best girl in the saddle I've ever seen.'

I realised he was looking at me with genuine admiration.

'Thank you. I'm sure you'll find that Princess Indira is equally competent,' I added loyally.

'Then I'll look forward to putting her to the test too, but I doubt she could possibly be better than you.' He offered me his hand to help me dismount. 'Well, Anni, I hope you'll join me on further rides,' he said, as we walked back together towards the Hall. 'Tomorrow morning, perhaps? Six-thirty sharp?'

'I'd love to, yes.'

I floated upstairs to wash before breakfast, feeling happier than I had for months.

Despite my misgivings about being unable to return to India, that first summer at Astbury was one I will never forget. Even though Britain had officially declared war on Germany on 4 August, we remained relatively untouched by it. As food shortages began, we hardly noticed, as the estate, with its thousands of acres of fertile farmland, was self-sufficient.

Although Donald himself was too young to join up, one

particular event that brought home to me the suffering and change others were facing was when Selina, Lady Astbury's daughter, came back home to live with us. Her husband, a captain in the British Army, had been posted to France. They had only been married for just over a year and Selina was eight months pregnant with their first child.

Sometimes in the afternoons I would find her sitting in the Orangery, which housed the many exotic plants that generations of Astburys had brought home from their travels to foreign climes. I recognised some of them from my mother's leather-bound notebook of remedies, and began to take cuttings from them, then grind them with my *shil noda*, laying them out on the tiny eave-top edge outside my attic window to dry in the sun. On my forays around the garden and sometimes out onto Dartmoor, I'd found further unusual herbs and plants, and having asked for spare jam jars from the kitchen, my collection was growing.

'What do you do with all these cuttings you take, Anni?' asked Selina one humid afternoon in the Orangery as she fanned herself in her chair and watched me with apparent interest.

I was unsure how to answer, but I decided to tell her the truth. 'I make healing medicines from them,' I said.

'Really? Did you learn how to do this in India?'

'Yes. My mother taught me.' I didn't want to enlarge on the subject, worrying she might think me some kind of witch doctor.

'My goodness, how clever you are,' she replied with genuine admiration. 'I know my father was a great believer in the local remedies when he was posted in India. Well, if you have any special potion to hurry this baby into the world, I, for one, would be grateful.'

I studied the shape of her belly, saw that the child she was carrying had dropped lower in the past few days, which meant the head was already down.

'I don't think it will be long now.'

'Really? You can tell?'

'Yes.' I smiled. 'I believe so.'

Sadly, despite her heartfelt protestations the day we had first arrived, I saw Indira less frequently than ever. Lady Astbury had consented to her plea that friends should be invited down from London to keep her company. I had a feeling Lady Astbury had an ulterior motive in this; after all, it would soon be time for Donald to choose a bride from the ranks of well-bred young British women. The introductions Indira provided on his very doorstep were likely to be valuable.

'Never have so many delightful young girls' – Lady Astbury pronounced it 'gels' – 'flooded through our doors before,' she announced to me one day as I encountered her on the grand staircase. 'Anahita, dear, would you run upstairs and just check that the maids have remembered to put flowers in Lady Celestria's bedroom?'

'Of course,' I said, and scurried off to see if they had.

I didn't like Lady Astbury, and I knew she didn't like me. She had lived in India when her husband was the Resident of Cooch Behar, and I gathered from the things she said that she had loathed every second of it; she treated me as little more than a serving maid. Her superior attitude to my countrymen and women – 'dirty little heathens', I'd heard her call us once

– exacerbated her disdain for me. I knew she was a strict Catholic and went to Mass in the Hall's chapel every day.

For me, her rigid formality and intrinsic arrogance summed up the very worst of the British. Indira, of course, was royalty, and had been brought up in a Western style. Lady Astbury was able to treat her as an equal . . . *just*.

Despite the fact that I too was related to Indian royalty, more and more I found I was running errands for Lady Astbury. She would often ask me absent-mindedly to 'run along' and find her embroidery for her, or collect a book from the library.

This situation was intensified because of the staff crisis in the house. With so many of the men from the servants' hall leaving to fight in France, the maids had double their usual workload. Not wanting to appear rude and ungrateful, I always acquiesced to Lady Astbury's requests. It wasn't a hardship helping the maids, who were a sweet, friendly bunch and glad to have another pair of hands to change a bed or dust a room.

In the first few days at Astbury, I'd gone down to dinner in the formal dining room with Indira but found myself ignored, which made me uncomfortable. Then, on the fourth night, a tray had been brought up to my room in the attic, and I'd taken the hint. I was not unhappy about it, as my wardrobe did not contain the plethora of formal English clothes needed for such nightly occasions, and I didn't like to mention my lack of them to Indira.

Tilly, one of the maids, on her nightly journey up the endless staircases to bring me my tray in the attic, commented that I must be lonely eating my supper all alone. She suggested I might prefer to eat with the rest of the staff in the kitchen. As

I knew this would also save her legs from the climb upstairs, I agreed. From then on, I ate downstairs with the servants every night, answering their constant questions as all of them were fascinated by my life at the palace in India.

On one occasion, the cook, Mrs Thomas, complained of the arthritis in her hands. I asked her whether she would like something to help with the pain and inflammation.

'I doubt it'll help,' she commented, 'but it'll do no harm either, I'm sure.'

Using my *shil noda*, I ground down a calamus root I'd found growing in the Orangery and then added water to create a paste. That night, I showed Mrs Thomas how to apply the paste to her hands.

'You must do this twice every day for a week, and I think it will help.'

Sure enough, a week later, Mrs Thomas was telling everyone what a 'miracle worker' I was. This quickly engendered a stream of kitchen 'customers', who would ask me to mix them a remedy to help with all manner of aches and pains. I was happy to help, and it gave me a chance to put what I'd learned from Zeena and my mother into practice. I also enjoyed the other servants' genuine warmth and acceptance – it had been a long time since I'd felt that.

But the main reason I was so happy that summer, so happy that even Indira's cold shoulder and Lady Astbury's treatment of me could not lower my mood, was my morning hacks with Donald Astbury.

The day after our first ride, I'd sprung out of bed the next morning, wondering if he would be at the stables as agreed.

'Anni!' he'd said, smiling. 'Up for another ride?'

'Yes.' I'd nodded eagerly, and we had saddled up, then

flown off across Dartmoor in the soft sun of the early morning. From then on, we met almost every morning. During those rides, we began to form a friendship.

In complete contrast to his mother, Donald was warm and open, and I felt I could talk freely with him about my life. He was genuinely fascinated to hear about India, its customs and culture.

'My father always loved India and its people,' he explained. 'Unfortunately, my mother didn't, and that's the reason they returned to England when Selina and I were very young. Sadly, my father died five years later. Mother always blamed India for killing him, and admittedly, he did suffer from recurrences of the malaria he caught there, but in the end, he died of pneumonia. He said it was the English weather that didn't suit him. He was a very good chap. Always trying to help somebody or other.'

'Are you like him?' I asked, as we lay on the rough Dartmoor grass, allowing our panting horses to take a drink from the brook.

'My mother always says so. I don't think she approved of what she termed his bleeding heart – Father was always on a mission to help the less fortunate, often to the detriment of our own bank account. He also held no account of creed or colour, whereas my mother is a little more . . . traditional in her thinking.'

During those rides on the moors, he talked to me of his fears for his own future because of the war, and how he worried about his ability to take over the management of the Astbury Estate in a few years' time. It would pass to him when he came of age, at twenty-one.

'There's hardly enough money to pay the costs on the estate

as it is,' he sighed, 'let alone restore the Hall – some of which hasn't been touched for a hundred years. Mother inherited it, you see. Father wasn't really a businessman, nor was it ever imagined that he should die whilst I was so young. So I rather think that Mother's buried her head in the sand. Or, should I say more accurately, the chapel. I don't want to be the one to tell her how difficult things are, but it's doubtful that even her God can help us.'

I looked at him and felt humbled that, though he was only sixteen, the weight of the world seemed to be on his shoulders.

'So many lives depend on me to earn their family crust.' Then he rolled over and grinned at me. 'Well, looks like there'll be nothing for it but to marry a rich heiress! Come on, it's time to ride back.'

After Donald had disappeared into the house to change for breakfast, I'd rarely see him until the following morning. His daytime activities were taken up with amusing Indira and her friends with luncheons, tennis parties and riding far more sedately than we did together through the park. I doubted he ever spoke of our morning rides – I certainly didn't. It was another secret I kept to myself during those long, balmy English summer nights.

14

At the end of August, a couple of days before Indira and I were to return to school, Selina went into labour. The maids were up and down the stairs with towels and hot water. The atmosphere in the kitchen was tense with the normal mixture of anticipation at the arrival of a new baby and trepidation that all might not go well for her.

'Doctor Trefusis is returning from the hospital in Exeter. Only Lady Selina would have picked a Sunday evening to go into labour. Let's hope he arrives here soon,' Mrs Thomas said, rolling her eyes.

An hour later, Tilly, Selina's maid, came downstairs looking pale. 'She's in a terrible state up there, rolling around the bed in agony and screaming her head off. I don't know what to do to calm her down. What can I give her, Mrs Thomas? I'm worried the baby's stuck or something.'

'Have you called for Her Ladyship?' Mrs Thomas asked.

'Yes, but you know you won't get Lady Astbury anywhere near the birthing room. I reckon she paid someone else to give birth to hers for her!'

'Lady Selina must be tired,' I commented from my usual chair in the corner of the kitchen.

'She's exhausted, Miss Anni, she's been going at it for the past six hours,' Tilly explained.

'Then you should take her some sugar water to help keep her glucose levels up,' I advised quietly. 'And have her move around as much as possible.'

All eyes in the kitchen turned to me. 'Have you ever seen a baby being born, Miss Anni?' asked Mrs Thomas.

'Oh, yes. I watched my mother many times when she went out to help the local women during their labours.'

'Well, any port in a storm,' said Mrs Thomas. 'Miss Anni, would you go upstairs with Tilly, who'll ask Lady Selina if she'll see you?'

'If you're sure,' I replied, rising nervously from my chair.

'She can only say no, can't she? Sounds to me like she needs all the help she can get. Off you go, dear.'

I followed Tilly up the stairs, and as I waited outside Selina's door, I could hear the moans from within.

Tilly poked her head around the door and beckoned to me. 'She didn't seem to understand what I was saying, so come in anyway.'

I walked into the bedroom and saw Selina lying flat on her back, her face white, sweat matting her hair.

'Lady Selina, it's Anahita. I've helped bring babies into the world before. Would you mind if I tried to help you?'

Selina raised an exhausted hand, which I took as a sign of her consent.

'First, we must prop her up on her pillows so she can drink the sugar water, and then run downstairs for some damp flannels to place on her forehead. Tie her hair up as well,' I told Tilly, 'she'll be cooler.'

Once we had both gently persuaded Selina upright and

Tilly had forced some of the sugar water down her, I felt for her pulse, which was racing.

'Lady Selina, may I examine you? I need to know how far on you are.'

She gave a reluctant nod, her eyes still closed.

I lifted her nightgown, and examined her and felt immediately that she was only four fingertips dilated. She needed to be ten before she could even think of pushing.

'Lady Selina, the baby is ready to come, but your body is not ready for it. I want you to stand up with me and walk. I promise you gravity will help. Can you do that?'

'No, no . . . the pain, the pain . . .' she moaned.

'Well, let us at least try.'

Putting my arm underneath her back, I heaved her upright, turned her legs to the side of the bed and, with all my strength, lifted her to a standing position. 'There, now we will walk,' I instructed. 'It will also help the pain.' Slowly, I made her put one foot in front of the other and we began to pace to the other side of the bedroom.

'There, you're doing very well,' I encouraged.

For two long hours, I led Selina up and down her bedroom floor, breathing with her, whispering words of encouragement. The perpetual motion calmed her and her pulse began to steady.

'I need to push!' she announced suddenly.

This was the moment I knew all should be ready and I motioned for Tilly to lay towels on the bed. I helped Selina lie down on top of the towels. 'Don't push for now, Lady Selina, pant instead, like a thirsty dog . . . like this . . .' I made a series of quick, shallow breaths and smiled encouragingly at her as she began to imitate me. I quickly checked she was dilated sufficiently to let the baby come through. Satisfied that was indeed the case, I instructed her that the next time she felt she must push, then she should, as hard as she possibly could. A scream shattered the still night air as I saw the baby's head appear at the opening.

It took a number of pushes – with Selina squeezing my hand so tightly that I felt the bones might be crushed to powder – before the baby's head shot out. Then I helped the rest of its tiny, perfect form to slither out of its mother.

'Is the baby all right, Anahita?' Selina asked, trying to raise her head to look down, but failing.

'Oh, oh!' Tilly clapped her hands to her face as the baby lay squawking between Selina's legs. 'It's a little girl! Congratulations, Lady Selina!'

I picked up the baby and put it immediately in Selina's arms. At that moment, the door opened and the doctor arrived.

'Well, well,' he said as he walked to the bottom of the bed and gazed at mother and child, calm now with exhaustion and triumph. The doctor opened his medical box and took out an instrument with which to cut the cord. He glanced at me and gave me a gruff smile. 'Shall I take over from here?'

'Of course.' Knowing I was no longer needed or wanted, I moved to leave the room. But Selina immediately threw out a hand towards me. 'Thank you, Anni, you were wonderful.'

Next morning, as I went down for breakfast in the kitchen – so exhausted that I'd failed to get up for my morning ride with Donald – I was treated to a heroine's welcome.

'You saved her life! Well, that's what Lady Selina says, anyway,' said Tilly. 'Miss Anni was amazing,' she announced to the kitchen. 'She knew exactly what to do and calmed her down no end. I hope that old battle-axe upstairs is grateful to you, Miss Anni. Can you believe, she went nowhere near her poor daughter while she was in all that agony? And then I heard her telling the doctor on the landing afterwards that Lady Selina was fortunate it had been a straightforward birth. All I can say is, she should thank her lucky stars you were here and knew what to do.'

Later on that day, I was invited upstairs by Selina to view the baby. Selina was lying contentedly with her daughter nestled in her arms. She gave me a glowing smile as I walked in.

'Hello, Anni. Come and see my adorable, perfect baby.' She patted the space on the bed next to her and I sat down on it tentatively.

'Oh, she is beautiful!' I said, as I reached out a finger to stroke the baby's velvety skin. 'What have you named her?'

'I'm afraid I didn't have much of a choice in that one. She's called Eleanor, after her father's mother. She's an absolute peach, don't you think? Would you like to hold her, Anni?'

'I would love to,' I said, and she passed the baby into my arms.

'I just want to say, dear Anni, that you were a wonder last night. I told all my family this morning that I don't know what I'd have done if you hadn't been here. Thank you, from both of us.'

'Not at all.' I smiled at her. 'It was my honour to be part of the miracle of new life.'

'Yes, I only wish this little one's father was here to see his daughter. We've sent a telegram to France, of course, but Lord knows when he'll get the message.'

Suddenly, the faint sounds began in my ears and my heart felt laden with blackness. I knew then that this baby would never see her father. Shakily, I forced a smile back onto my face. 'He'll be here soon enough,' I lied.

'I can only pray that he will be. Now, Princess Indira tells me you're leaving tomorrow to return to school?'

'Yes.'

'It's such a shame, Anni. I wish you could take care of us both, rather than that ancient nursemaid whom Mother has employed. I find your way so much more comforting. Promise you'll return soon?'

'Yes,' I said, handing the baby back to her.

'Goodbye, then, Anni, and thank you again.'

'Goodbye. And good luck with your beautiful little one.'

As I stood up and walked towards the door, Selina said, 'Are you really only fourteen, Anni? I can hardly believe it. Last night, it felt as though I was with a woman at least three times your age and experience.'

'Yes, I am.' I gave her a small smile of farewell and left the room.

We were to leave for school at eleven the following morning, which gave me time to go out for my last ride with Donald. He, of course, had heard the story of my helping his niece into the world.

As we sat in our usual spot by the brook, he asked me how I'd known what to do.

'It's really very simple,' I explained. 'You must always follow nature. Your sister's body knew everything, I just tried to help her trust it.'

I could see there was new respect for me in Donald's eyes today. 'My goodness, if only more of the world would think like that. My father had huge respect for nature. You're awfully wise, Anahita, for one so young.'

'Sometimes,' I said as I dug the heel of my boot into the solid, parched ground, 'I think it's as much a curse as a blessing.'

'What do you mean?'

'Well, to have a mind that wishes to make sense of the world.' I looked at him. 'For most women, to be pretty and to have many new dresses is enough to satisfy them.'

'Well, I can't help you with the dresses,' he chuckled, 'but I can tell you that you are pretty. Very pretty indeed. Now, we'd better head for home.'

As we walked back to the house from the stables, Donald said suddenly, 'I shall miss our morning rides together.'

'Me too,' I said, meaning it with all my heart.

He leaned towards me and kissed me gently on the cheek. 'Goodbye, Anni, come back soon to visit us. You're a very special young lady, and it's been a pleasure knowing you.'

My heart sang with joy all the way back to school in Eastbourne. Even Indira's chatter about how much she was looking forward to seeing Celestria and the rest of the girls, and the thought of being incarcerated and lonely once more, could not pull my spirits down.

For I had met someone who liked me simply for myself. We were friends, that was all. Or at least, I tried my best to make myself believe that, but the memory of his lips on my cheek told a different story to my heart.

15

Over the following two years, the war in Europe raged on and Indira and I were unable to return to India. I remained at school for the holidays, whilst Indira went to stay with her various friends. I didn't mind, as many of the girls were in the same boat, including my friend Charlotte. I used the time to study for my upcoming matriculation.

Indira and I celebrated turning sixteen with a low-key event at school, based around cakes which tasted like rock due to the powdered egg. Indira fell in and out with her friends, and turned to me for sympathy if one of them had said something particularly nasty. I'd finally accepted her see-saw approach to our friendship, knowing that when her confidence waned, she would be back to me, needing comfort.

However much it hurt, I told myself that my position in her life was providing me with the education my father had always wished me to have. I was one of the brightest in my class, or, at least, the most dedicated and hard-working pupil, and the teachers began to talk to me about university. Of course, this was an impossibility, but it was heart-warming to know they thought so highly of me.

Christmas of 1916 was spent at Astbury – I remember it as

a sombre affair. As I had known she would be, Selina had been notified that her husband had been killed in France back in October. A household in mourning was not a place to expect celebration.

Selina looked thin and pale in her black widow's weeds. She managed a smile when she saw me.

'Hello, my dearest Anni, how cheery to see your bright face back here at Astbury.'

The following afternoon, she sought me out and asked me to accompany her on a walk.

'I was so sad to hear of your husband's death, Lady Selina,' I said as we walked through the frost-laden garden. A heavy mist had descended and the frail winter's sun seemed to be retreating in front of night's rapid advance.

'Thank you,' Selina said. 'At present, I'm struggling to make sense of it all. Hugo was so young, Anni, with his whole life ahead of him. And now –' she paused – 'he's gone. Mother insists that I should find comfort in God and prayer, as she does. But if I'm truthful, I'm just repeating hollow words that have no meaning. I can't bring myself to go to the chapel. Is it dreadful to admit that now, when I need it most, my faith seems to have left me?'

'No, of course not. Sometimes it's impossible to understand why loved ones are taken from us,' I agreed. 'But whilst the gods took, they also gave. You have your beautiful daughter, and she carries part of Hugo in her.'

'Yes, and I thank God – or the gods, if you prefer – for her,' Selina said quietly. 'But would it also be dreadful to admit that Hugo's death has left me a widow at twenty-two, living back at home, with only my mother as a companion and little chance of escape in the future?'

'Lady Selina, there will be another chance of happiness in front of you, I promise,' I said, my instincts suddenly alert. It wasn't the appropriate time to tell her about a new love waiting for her just around the corner, but I knew with every bone in my body that it was true.

'Do you really think so, Anni?'

'Yes, I do. And remember, it isn't necessary to pray in a church every day. We are all part of God. There is a little of him inside each of us. *He* will hear you, wherever you are.'

'Thank you, dear Anni.' Selina laid a gloved hand on mine as we walked back towards the Hall, ready to escape the cold.

There were no morning rides that Christmas. Donald, having been called up for military service some weeks before, was training somewhere with his battalion.

One frosty December morning, as I took my breakfast in the kitchen, I was handed a letter addressed to me.

> *Chelsea Barracks*
> *London*
>
> *19 December 1916*
>
> Dearest Anahita,
>
> *I do hope you don't mind me writing to you. I could think of no one else whom I could trust with my innermost thoughts. My training (or the few weeks of marching round and round and learning how to shoot a rifle) is completed and I'm about to be shipped off tomorrow to some unknown destination, which all us fellows suspect is France. I have, of course, written a*

formal letter to my mother and my sister, letting them know of my imminent departure and have sounded as I must – brave and strong.

Even though all the chaps I'm with are gung-ho about the jolly time we will all have in the trenches, I know we're all ignoring the fact that many of us won't return. So, as I write this to you tonight, only hours before I leave, I want you to know, Anni, that I don't want to die just yet. Or live, as so many poor souls are having to, maimed for life.

Forgive me, I've never written a letter like this one before. But I know from what the servants say about you, and from our own private moments together, that perhaps you have certain powers. If you do, please, Anni, send whatever you can to protect me. If you tell me I will be all right, I know I will be. You are my talisman.

Could you write back to me at the address above? I would very much like to hear from you. I hope you don't think that I'm less of a man, or a coward, for writing this. But I keep thinking back to those glorious sunny mornings when we lay by the brook together and all was peaceful. Perhaps I am being selfish, but I want to have more days like that.

I trust you to keep the contents of this letter private. I hope you are well, and please pray for me.

Yours affectionately,

Donald Astbury

I read and reread Donald's letter many times. Then I walked out into the gardens, away from the house. If Donald was to

leave this earth soon, I knew I would feel it and hear it. And
. . . I felt nothing. A clear, pure nothing.

My heart lifted with joy, for now I knew he would survive
his ordeal and return home, unharmed.

Therefore, I was able with complete faith to write the letter I would have penned whether I'd sensed bad news or not.

Astbury Hall
Devon

30 December 1916

Dear Donald,

Thank you for your letter.

*Please do not be afraid. I'm absolutely sure you won't be
taken from this earth just yet. I hope I will see you soon,
when you return from France.*

Best regards,

Anahita Chavan

Even Indira's friends did not arrive to visit her at Astbury over
the Christmas break. Petrol rationing prohibited long journeys
from the southern counties where most of them lived. Given
the dark mood in the upstairs drawing room, on New Year's
Eve, Indira resorted to joining me below stairs with the servants. There was a piano, on which Mrs Thomas bashed out
some old English tunes. Without a doubt, as 1916 turned to
1917, it was the cheeriest place in the Hall to be.

One night, just after New Year, there was a knock on my
attic door.

'Come in.'

Indira appeared, her eyes red from weeping, and held out her arms to me. Reluctant to get out of bed – there were no fires lit on my attic floor – I wound the covers around me, stood up and went to her.

'What is it?' I asked.

'Oh, Anni, I'm so homesick for Ma and Pa . . . and India. I hate it here. It's no fun and so cold. Really, I feel just as much of an orphan as you do!'

'I'm sure the war will be over soon and you will be able to see your family,' I comforted her calmly.

'And – oh Anni, I've realised I've been so mean to you, ignoring you, and,' Indira gesticulated, 'making you sleep in this freezing cold attic without saying anything to Lady Astbury. Listen –' she shivered suddenly – 'come downstairs with me and sleep in my bed. There's a fire at least, and we can talk.'

I acquiesced to her wishes, as I always did, and once we were wrapped in blankets in front of the fire in her bedroom, she stared into it and sighed. 'You know, I'm dreaming of the palace every night. I never used to appreciate it. Or you,' she added. 'I know I've been a cruel friend, and I'm probably a bad person. Can you forgive me, Anni?'

'Of course I can forgive you.' I smiled at her.

'We will get back to India, one day, won't we?'

'Of course we will. We're winning the war and it won't be long now, everybody says.'

'You know,' Indira sighed, 'I don't belong in England really, I belong in India. I miss it so terribly. Pretty must think I've deserted her completely.'

The thought of her pet elephant prompted another round of tears.

'Perhaps this war is teaching all of us to think about what we have, instead of what we lack,' I soothed.

She looked up at me, her amber eyes wide. 'You are so wise, Anni. Ma told me I should always listen to you, and perhaps she was right.'

'I'm not wise, Indy, I am just accepting. We cannot change what *is*, no matter how hard we try.'

'And,' Indira bit her lip, 'I was thinking that my prince may have forgotten me.'

'As I told you, if the two of you are meant to be together, you will be.'

'Yes, you're right,' Indira agreed. 'Anni, will you sleep with me in here tonight? I don't want to be alone.'

'Yes, if you'd like me to.'

So the two of us huddled together in Indira's big bed, just as we used to when we were children.

'Are you sure you forgive me, Anni?' she asked, as I turned out the light.

'I love you, Indy, I will always forgive you.'

True to her word, when we arrived back at school, Indira spent much more time with me than in previous terms. This was partly because her best friend, Celestria, had been taken out of the school. There was now the real possibility of England being bombed, and her mother wanted her daughter safely home with her. Other girls had been removed too, and although London had been the primary target for air attacks so far, the entire country remained in a state of heightened tension and trepidation.

At Easter, we packed for the holidays, expecting to catch the train down to Dartmoor. We were surprised when a chauffeur arrived in a Rolls-Royce to collect us on the last day of term.

'Where are we going?' asked Indira, not knowing the roads well enough to tell. The driver remained silent, and it was only when we reached the familiar streets of London that Indira's face broke into a smile. As the car drew up outside the Pont Street house, Indira threw herself out of it and ran up the steps to the front door.

The door opened and there was the Maharani herself.

'Ma!' I watched Indira throw herself into her mother's arms.

'Surprise!' the Maharani said as she hugged her daughter to her. 'I didn't want to tell you I'd be here for definite until the ship had docked safely in England. Which was only yesterday.'

'But how? I thought it was impossible to travel, with all the ships being requisitioned for troops?' asked Indira, as we walked inside.

'I'll tell you all about it. It was quite an adventure!' She laughed, as her gaze finally fell upon me. 'Anni, how you have grown! Why, Indira, our Anni is turning into a beauty!'

I ignored her remark as a kind pleasantry and followed them both into the elegant drawing room, where a welcoming fire was lit in the grate.

'So, Ma, tell me how you made it all the way to England?' Indira said as we sat down and the Maharani called her maid to bring tea.

'I said that it was a matter of urgency that I travel here. I told the Resident that my youngest child was seriously ill in London, and I had to come, whatever the consequences. So, the captain of one of the British India troop ships agreed to take me on-board. He warned me very sternly that he couldn't guarantee my safety –' the Maharani smiled, obviously very pleased with the adventure – 'and that I might have to sleep in a hammock alongside the soldiers! Of course, they found me far more comfortable quarters than that and I ate very well every night with the delightful Captain and his officers.'

'Oh, Ma,' cried Indira, her eyes wide, 'you might have died on the way! You know how many ships have been lost already.'

'I know, my *pyari*, but I couldn't bear to go another day without seeing my daughter. And besides, the ship was full-steam ahead – top speed all the way to get us here without incident. We arrived in half the time it usually takes. So how are you both?' Her gaze passed to me and then settled back on her beloved daughter.

'Anni and I have been as unhappy as the birds in monsoon season,' Indira moaned. 'The food has been terrible, the cold unbearable and everyone here is miserable. Ma, I don't think you know what England is really like. It's a dreadful, dark country and I can't wait to come home.'

'Things are difficult in India too. We have many of our own young men fighting for England in the war.' The Maharani sighed. 'These are worrying and difficult times for us all. But,' she said, rallying, 'we must make the best of it. So, while I'm here in London, we will do just that.'

She was as good as her word, and the house was filled with guests drawn from a London starved of pleasure, guests who were eager to enjoy her opulent style of entertaining. She threw dinners and cocktail parties – although quite where she procured delicacies such as quails' eggs, smoked salmon and caviar in wartime London, I have no idea.

The Maharani was horrified at the state of my wardrobe, which had not been replenished for almost two years. I had grown out of almost everything I owned, so she packed me off with Indira to Harrods to buy what we wanted. This time, I found myself far more interested in the womenswear department. I wouldn't have gone so far as to agree with the Maharani when she had kindly told me I'd become 'a beauty'. But even I could see, when I tried on the beautiful dresses and looked at myself in the mirror, that my puppy fat had left me, revealing a shapely and quite acceptable figure.

'Anni, you should have written to me!' she said, berating me again. 'Please, don't feel shame in asking for what you need in the future.'

The Maharani also sent me to an optician for a new pair of glasses to replace the one pair I owned, which I had clumsily repaired with fuse wire when they'd broken. Indira and I had long-overdue haircuts and emerged from the salon proudly with our hair styled in the new modern bob. We were also treated to our first manicure by the woman who came to the house for the Maharani. That night, as I walked down to dinner in my beautiful new silk dress from Harrods, I even think I may have garnered some admiring glances from the other guests.

In the middle of the holidays, Indira was ecstatic with happiness when Prince Varun appeared at one of the Maharani's soirées. He was in London on two weeks' leave from his regiment.

Since they had last met, Indira had grown into a startlingly beautiful young woman. I watched them closely that evening, having no idea if anyone else around the table noticed the chemistry between the two of them.

That night, after dinner, Indira arrived in our bedroom just as I had climbed under the blankets. Her eyes were alight and she was tingling with excitement from top to toe.

'Oh, Anni, isn't he beautiful?' she said, as she sprang full-length onto her bed and lay, eyes closed, with a dreamy expression on her face.

'He is very handsome, yes.'

'And guess what? He wants to meet me again whilst he's in London. Can you believe it?' She clasped her hands together in delight. 'Of course, Ma will never let me go unchaperoned. So would you, darling Anni, accompany me for tea at the Ritz, then leave me by the hotel entrance and go for a walk for an hour? Please,' she begged me, 'I have no idea when we will see each other again. I *must* go.'

'Indy, I can't. You know you should *never* be seen out in public alone with a man. You are a princess, there are rules.'

'I don't care!' Indira sank her face into the pillow, then turned to look at me, a glint in her eye. 'After all, I hardly think we can get up to much over a cup of tea and some cucumber sandwiches, can we? Unless he takes me upstairs, of course . . .'

'Please, don't even say it!' I rolled my eyes in horror. 'If your mother finds out, which she almost certainly will, as she has spies everywhere, we'll both be in terrible trouble.'

'Well, that's nothing new for me, is it? What's she going to do, put me back into purdah? *Please* say you'll cover for me, Anni, just this once.'

'All right,' I sighed heavily, 'just this once, and only for an hour.'

'Thank you!' Indira, having got her way, threw her arms around me. 'You truly are the best friend a girl could have.'

*

The following afternoon, we both dressed up in suitable attire for taking tea at the Ritz and called for the chauffeur to drive us there. Indira, sitting in the back next to me, could hardly control her excitement. 'You understand the plan, Anni, don't you? We'll tell the chauffeur to collect us at four. And you'll pretend to come inside, but leave me at the entrance.'

'Yes.' I frowned, this being the hundredth time she had told me. 'Good luck,' I said as we alighted in front of the grand entrance to the Ritz and I saw the chauffeur pull away. She blew me a kiss as she stepped inside. I turned round and walked towards Green Park, not looking forward to an empty hour sitting alone in the chill of a spring day in London. I happened to glance across the street and saw an elegant, stone building that proclaimed itself to be the Royal Academy of Arts. Crossing the road, I studied the board outside. Apparently there was an exhibition of new artists, so I walked through the grand portico and up the steps. Inside, I approached the desk which sat in the middle of the impressive hall.

'I'd like to see the exhibition. How much is it?' I asked the woman sitting behind it.

'Are you a member of the Royal Academy?'

'No. Do I need to be?'

She paused for a moment, then answered, 'Yes. You do.'

'Then I'm sorry to trouble you,' I said and began to walk as elegantly as I could back towards the exit. As I did so, the two Englishwomen who'd been waiting behind me stepped forward to the desk. The receptionist asked if they were members and they replied, as I had, that they were not.

'Then that will be five shillings each,' the receptionist replied. The women paid and walked on inside.

That moment, without the cloak of Indian royalty around my shoulders, was my first taste of racial prejudice in Great Britain, the country that had ruled us for over a hundred and fifty years. And sadly, it wouldn't be my last.

Subsequently, I spent the following three afternoons shivering in Green Park waiting for Indira to complete further trysts with her prince. Even though Fortnum and Mason and the delights of Piccadilly were only a stone's throw away, I was too frightened by the reaction of the woman at the Royal Academy to venture anywhere else alone. I realised how odd I must have looked out of context, without the rest of the royal party: with my brown body and face encased in Western dress, I certainly garnered many stares as people passed me on my park bench. I lowered my eyes to my new friend, Thomas Hardy, and concentrated on *Far from the Madding Crowd*.

When Indira and I met at the appointed time at the side entrance to the Ritz, and climbed into the car to return home, we were in polar-opposite emotional states: she, in the first flush of love; I, realising even more clearly that I belonged nowhere.

'Oh, Anni,' she gushed, as I listened yet again to the flood of superlatives about her prince. 'I'm so in love, and today he told me he is in love with me!'

'I'm very happy for you, Indy, but' – I had done my research on Indira's prince – 'he's already married. You know he is.'

'Of course I know! He is a prince, after all. It was arranged for him before he even took his first steps. But it's official, that's all. It is not a love marriage.'

'Just as your own marriage has been arranged to the Maharaja of Dharampur,' I reminded her brusquely. 'And surely, Indira, you couldn't bear being only the second wife? Besides, we both know that your father takes a particularly modern approach to your mother. Prince Varun would almost certainly expect you to stay at his palace in purdah as he travels.'

'Yes, maybe at first, for the sake of form,' Indira countered, 'but then he'd wish me to become his companion and travel the world with him, just as Ma does with Pa.'

'Are you –' I cleared my throat – 'telling me that you and Prince Varun have discussed this?'

'Of course! He wants to marry me. Today he said he'd known from when he first saw me that one day we would be married.'

I stared at her in shock. What Indira was telling me was ridiculous. She was already betrothed to another, and a marriage arranged years ago between two princely states and their ruling families could *not* simply be cancelled.

I also knew all too well that Indira was used to getting her own way, but surely this would prove a step too far, even for her. To add insult to injury, I was equally furious with myself for abetting their romance.

'Indy, please,' I begged her, 'you must know that you and Prince Varun can never be together?'

'Don't say that!' she snapped at me irritably. 'Of course it's possible, anything is possible with love . . .'

As usual, when I wasn't in full agreement with Indira's thoughts and feelings, she distanced herself from me. I had refused to be a party to her deception any longer, but I knew full well that in the afternoons, whilst she told her mother that she was off to visit a friend, she was seeing her prince. I would be glad to return to school and to remove both myself and Indira from London.

A week later, Varun left to return to his regiment and Indira sank into a deep depression, refusing to leave her room, citing illness as the reason.

Two nights before we were to return to school in East-bourne, the Maharani called me into the drawing room to see her.

'Dear Anni, I think it's time that we discussed your future.'

'Yes, Your Highness.'

'Please –' she indicated a chair by the fire which she always had burning in the drawing room – 'sit down. Tea?'

I accepted a cup and waited to hear what she had to say.

'Indira doesn't know it yet, but I'm taking her back to India with me when I leave in a few days' time. Her illness in recent days has made my mind up. I wish for my family to be together during these difficult times and India, for the moment at least, is a safe place to be. Now, unlike my daughter,' she smiled, 'I know you're doing exceptionally well at school – I do read all your reports, you know. You're a clever girl, just as I knew you were when you were younger, and a very good influence on Indira.'

I tried to hold back my blushes, berating myself for the deceit of the past two weeks. 'Thank you, Your Highness.'

'So, it's time to ask *you* what you want, Anni. You have your matriculation and the completion of your formal educa-tion coming up in the next few weeks. For Indira –' the Maharani sighed – 'it hardly matters. She will be married to the Maharaja of Dharampur within the next eighteen months. Of course, there'll always be a place for you in my home and I don't doubt that Indira will wish for you to accompany her to her new palace when she marries. But I feel I should ask you, Anni, if it is your wish to return to India with us? Or whether you want to stay in England and complete your education?'

'I don't know, Your Highness.'

'I've also had a letter from Lady Selina at Astbury Hall. As I'm sure you know, she's an old friend of Minty, my daughter. She says you assisted her when she gave birth to her child.'

'Yes, Your Highness, I did.'

'So,' the Maharani continued, steepling her beautifully manicured fingers, 'if you do decide to stay in England, Selina has offered you a position at Astbury Hall taking care of her baby daughter. It seems she is struggling to find a good nursemaid during this crisis.'

I admit that my heart leapt at the thought of living in the house Donald would one day be returning to, when the war was finally over. 'It's very kind of her, and I will certainly think about it.'

'It must, of course, be your choice,' she continued, 'but I do feel that perhaps your horizons should be set beyond being a mere nursemaid.'

I knew I had only a few moments to assimilate what she was saying. This woman, who didn't need to ask me what I wanted for my future, but had the grace and integrity to do so, was offering me my freedom. 'I miss India terribly,' I answered honestly, 'and if I did stay here, I'd miss Indira too. She's like my sister.'

'We all miss India and our friends when we are away,' the Maharani agreed, 'but the life you would have there as a grown woman is perhaps not what you would wish. Even though it will pain my daughter to lose you, I wouldn't want to see you shut up in a zenana for the rest of your life, unable to use that clever brain of yours. And –' the Maharani sighed – 'forgive me if I speak the truth, but even though I will, of course, endeavour to help you, your marriage prospects will be . . . limited.'

'Yes, I know.'

'So, Anni, it is for you to decide. I'm happy if you wish to stay here in England and complete your education – I feel it would be unfair for you to have worked so hard without doing so – or if you want to return to India with Indira and me. Your passage home is already booked, but I can easily cancel it.'

'Your Highness, I need a little time to think,' I answered.

'Of course,' she said. 'We will talk tomorrow morning. Let us hope Indira has recovered from her illness and can travel.'

'Yes.'

As I rose and walked to the door, the Maharani followed me and put her hand on my shoulder. 'Remember, Anni, I know my daughter very well. She is far too much like me. Her heart rules her head.'

I knew the Maharani was telling me that she was aware of Indira's crush on Prince Varun and would deal with it. I was sure that was part of the reason she was taking Indira home with her and I felt relieved that the burden had been lifted from me.

That night, I silently paced the bedroom floor while Indira slept. I was flushed with the new and rare feeling of making my own decisions – I held my destiny in my own hands. To stay on alone in England and complete my education would be a brave step, whereas if I returned to India with the Maharani and Indira I'd have the protective shield of the royal family around me. I thought of the moment at the Royal Academy of Arts and shuddered. But if Indira's arranged marriage went ahead, my future would, as the Maharani had subtly pointed out, be limited to the confines of Indira's new zenana. And I would almost certainly remain a spinster for the rest of my days.

And then again, in England lay freedom and also – I forced myself to be honest about why the position Selina had offered me was so tempting – Donald.

I knew we were merely friends and I understood that, given our positions in life, we could never be more. But if I returned to India, I would surely never see him again.

Eventually, I did what any young adult does when they have a difficult decision to make: I consulted my parents. I sat cross-legged on the floor, looked up to the heavens and asked them what their daughter should do. Then I waited for a response . . .

'I have decided I wish to stay in England and complete my education.'

The Maharani smiled at me. 'I thought that might be your answer, Anni.'

'I think . . .' This was the first time I'd voiced the thoughts that had been coming into my head for a while now and had crystallised last night after I'd consulted my parents, 'I think I might like to train as a nurse.'

'Yes, I can see that it might suit you, given your gifts.' She gave me a sweet, reassuring smile.

'But what about Princess Indira? We haven't been apart for almost six years. I don't want her to feel that I'm deserting her.'

'As we both know, Anni, my daughter's heart is elsewhere for the present. She sees and feels nothing else.'

'Yes,' I said, and we shared a moment of understanding.

'Leave her to me, Anni, trust me to take care of the situation. I think it's right that you forge your own life. I will send you a monthly allowance, which should be adequate for your needs and, if you wish me to, I'll write to Selina telling her you would like to accept her offer.'

'Yes, but, Your Highness, just for the summer,' I said. 'After that, I feel I would like to join the Voluntary Aid Detachment as a nurse and help in the war effort.'

'That's very admirable of you, Anni, and it will prepare you well for your future. So, we are decided?'

'Yes. I cannot begin to thank you enough for all you have done for me. You have been so generous, so kind.' Tears welled in my eyes and I bit my lip to stem them.

'Dearest Anni, please remember that I promised your mother I would take care of you when she handed you over to me. I wish you to remember that I'm here in her place. If there is anything that you need, you must promise to write to me, for I don't know how long it will be before we see each other again. Come.'

The Maharani opened her arms to me and I went into them. 'I love you like you are my own, dear Anni. Never be afraid of asking for my help if you need it in the future.'

'Thank you, Your Highness,' I whispered, my eyes full of tears. I gave thanks to the heavens that they'd brought this wonderful woman – such a rare combination of power and goodness – into my life. At that moment, I felt truly blessed.

As the Maharani had predicted so accurately, Indira was not particularly perturbed when I told her that I was staying in England and returning to school to take my matriculation.

'You will write?' she asked me. 'Every day?'

'Maybe not every day, for I'll be studying hard,' I said, smiling, 'but certainly very often.'

As my trunk was shut and taken downstairs, she looked at me suddenly. 'I thought you hated it here in England. Why on earth would you want to stay?'

'Because I know it's the right thing to do,' I replied.

It was only after I'd kissed the Maharani goodbye and hugged Indira to me for one last time, before climbing into the back of the car that would take me away from them – perhaps forever – that I realised the enormity of the decision I had made.

Astbury Hall,

2011

16

Ari sat in his car on the side of the narrow road that cut through Dartmoor and thumped the satnav with his fist in frustration. Not that it would help, he knew; the signal had gone haywire ten minutes ago – which was approximately the last time he'd seen any form of signpost. He was completely lost.

For want of something better to do, Ari climbed out of the car and took a deep breath of fresh, moorland air. It was a hot day for England and as he gazed across the undulating land-scape, he appreciated the beauty his great-grandmother had described so vividly in her story. The stillness was what struck him most; barely a hint of a breeze, the silence only broken by the call of a buzzard flying over the rugged, empty moor – he doubted it had changed since Anahita was last here.

Due to his hectic work schedule in London, coupled with jet lag, Ari had yet to finish her story. But what he had read so far on the plane had intrigued him enough to hire a car, drive down to Devon and take a look at Astbury Hall for himself. Even before reaching his destination, he'd already begun to second-guess what had taken place here.

As he stood surveying the moors, Ari realised that these

next few days would be the nearest thing to a holiday he had taken in the past fifteen years. Even if he discovered his great-grandmother's story wasn't worth pursuing, it would at least give *him* time to clear his own thoughts before he returned to face the mess he had made of his life in India.

'*Because . . . it is also your future.*'

Anahita's last words had drifted back to him as he had driven towards Devon that morning.

Ari climbed back into his car and restarted the engine. He would simply have to drive until he came across a village where he could ask for directions. For once he had no deadline to meet, so he sat back, relaxed and began to enjoy the scenery.

An hour later, he stopped in front of a pair of wrought-iron gates and glanced along the drive that led beyond them. He couldn't see a building from the road, but he noticed the gates were firmly closed with a security guard standing beside them. As he wondered what to do, a white van arrived on the other side of the gates. The guard nodded and opened them to let the van through.

'All right, mate?' the man in the van said as he drove past Ari.

'Yes, this is Astbury Hall, isn't it?'

'Yes, a nightmare to find as well. I've just delivered some extra cable and it took me the best part of an hour to locate it. You here for the shoot?'

'Yes,' Ari lied.

'If you're looking for Steve Campion, the production manager, head straight up the drive and turn right when you reach the house. You should find him in the courtyard.' The driver set off. As the gates began to close, Ari took the decision and drove swiftly through them.

'I was told to find Steve Campion in the courtyard,' he said to the security guard.

The guard nodded uninterestedly and waved him on. As he passed through the parkland surrounding the house, Ari guessed the estate must now be used for business purposes, probably a hotel or conference centre. This was certainly what had happened to many of the grand old palaces in India.

When Astbury Hall finally came into view, it wasn't just the grandeur of it that made Ari catch his breath. Gathered on the front steps were a number of men attired in top hats and tails, and women in an array of period evening dresses. There was a vintage Rolls-Royce parked outside the house and a man stood next to it, wearing an old-fashioned chauffeur's uniform.

Ari slowed the car and blinked hard, for the scene in front of him was plucked from another era. It was only when he noticed the camera equipment surrounding the people that he chuckled, realising that the white van man had meant shooting a *film*, not a brace of pheasants.

He saw someone waving at him urgently, indicating that he should drive round to the right of the house. They were obviously in the middle of shooting a scene. Doing so, Ari arrived in a courtyard humming with activity. Finding a space to park his car, he stepped out alongside a throng of crew and actors dressed in costume, queuing at a catering van. No one took any notice of him as he moved amongst them. He spied an open door at the side of the house and tentatively moved through a lobby and found himself in a large, deserted kitchen.

Ari stared at the long, scrubbed pine table, the old-fashioned range and an upright piano against the wall. A threadbare chair sat near the fireplace. He wondered if this was the same kitchen that Anahita had sat in almost one hundred years before.

'Can I help you?'

A female voice stirred him out of his reverie.

The sturdily built, middle-aged woman looked at him questioningly. 'There's no food supplied in here, my love, all the film people eat outside from the catering van. And there are Portaloos round the back,' she added.

'Forgive me,' Ari said, 'I'm not part of the film.'

'So why are you standing in my kitchen?'

'I've come to see Astbury Hall.'

'It's not open to the public, so you can't.' As she stared at him, her eyes narrowed suspiciously. 'You're not one of those journalists, are you? How did you get in here? There's meant to be security on the gate.'

'No, no,' said Ari hastily, wondering how on earth he *was* supposed to explain his presence. 'It's a . . . family connection I've come about.'

'Really?'

'Yes. One of my relatives used to work at Astbury Hall many years ago.'

'Who?'

'Her name was Anahita Chavan.'

'Never heard of her,' the woman replied.

'It was over ninety years ago that she was here. I've been in England on business for the past few days and I thought it would be interesting to see the place I've heard so much about.'

'So you just walked straight in here without so much as a "by your leave", did you?'

'Please accept my apologies – I wasn't sure whom I should speak to. Is there a current Lord Astbury?'

'There is, but he'll be far too busy to see you without an appointment.'

'Of course,' Ari agreed. 'Then perhaps –' he reached into his jacket pocket and dug out a card – 'you could give him this? It has both my cellphone number and my email on it.'

As she studied it, Ari became aware of another presence in the kitchen. He turned to the interior door and saw a young woman, tall, slender and beautiful, standing by it. She was dressed in a vintage gown of the softest silk, which draped elegantly to her slim ankles.

'Am I interrupting, Mrs Trevathan?'

Ari noticed the young woman spoke with a soft American accent.

'No, dear, not at all. This gentleman was just leaving.' The older woman turned her attention back to Ari. 'Lord Astbury doesn't have email and rarely uses the telephone. I suggest you put your enquiry in writing and post it here for his attention. Now, Miss Rebecca, what can I do for you?'

'I was just wondering whether you have any antihistamine? My nose is itchy and my eyes are watering. Is it ragweed season here?'

'I don't know what ragweed is, but June is certainly hay-fever time. His Lordship suffers from it sometimes too.' Mrs Trevathan walked to a dresser and pulled out a plastic box from a drawer. Finding some tablets, she handed the packet to the young woman.

'Thanks, Mrs Trevathan. I'll take one at lunch. I'm due on set right now.'

'I'm sorry to trouble you,' Ari said. 'I'll do as you suggest and write to Lord Astbury. Goodbye.' He followed the young woman towards the door. 'May I?'

'Thank you,' she said, surveying him with her enormous brown eyes as he opened it for her.

'Forgive me for being presumptuous,' said Ari as they stepped into the bright sunshine of the courtyard, 'but you seem very familiar. Is it possible we've met before?'

'I doubt it,' she replied. 'A lot of people seem to think they know me. Are you part of the production team?'

'No, I'm here on family business. I had a relative who worked at the house a long time ago. I'd obviously like to gain an audience with Lord Astbury, but I get the feeling that it might be a struggle.'

'Mrs Trevathan's very protective of him, so your instinct is probably right,' the young woman replied as they paused beside Ari's car.

'It's a shame, actually,' said Ari, 'as he might well be interested in a slice of his family history he knows nothing about. Anyway, I'll do as that woman in the kitchen suggested and put the details in writing.'

'I see Lord Astbury quite often, so perhaps I could mention that you were here?' she said.

'That would be very helpful, as it's doubtful I'll be in England for much longer.' He pulled out a pen and another card from his wallet, and wrote on it. 'Could you give him this? That's me, Ari Malik, and the name of my great-grandmother who worked here. You never know, he might have heard of her.'

As Ari unlocked his car, the young woman studied the card. 'Anahita Chavan. Sure, Mr Malik, I'll see he gets it.'

'Thanks.' Then, on a sudden instinct, Ari reached through into the back seat of his car and grabbed the plastic file containing his great-grandmother's story. He separated the pages he had read from those he hadn't and handed them to her. 'Perhaps you could give him this too? It's a photocopy of part of my great-grandmother's life story. If nothing else, it's a fascinating glimpse of Astbury Hall and its residents in the 1920s.'

'That's the era of the story we're filming here,' she mused, taking the pages from him. 'Will it reveal some skeletons in the Astbury closet? I'm sure this place has secrets to hide.'

'I haven't reached the end of the story yet, but I have a feeling that it might, yes.' Ari smiled at her.

He climbed into the driver's seat. 'By the way, I didn't get your name.'

'Rebecca, Rebecca Bradley. See you around, Mr Malik.' And with a smile and a wave, she floated away from him.

Ari watched her in his rear-view mirror, still pondering why she seemed so familiar. She was certainly a beauty, although blondes were hardly his preference, he thought, as he turned the car out of the courtyard and made his way back down the drive to search for a nearby hotel.

Once she had finished filming for the day, Rebecca walked across the entrance hall and into the dark study that contained the one telephone in the house. Closing the door behind her, she sat down in the torn leather chair and dialled Jack's number. It was ten o'clock in the morning in LA and even Jack should be in the land of the living.

'Hello?' His familiar voice sounded drowsy still.

'Hi, it's me, Rebecca.'

'Jeez, Becks! I was beginning to wonder whether you were still alive.'

'I've left you voicemail messages, Jack. Didn't you get them?'

'Yeah, sure I did . . . how are you? Is it raining there?'

'No, why?'

'It always rains across the pond, doesn't it?'

'Not all the time, no,' she responded, irrationally irritated by his comment. 'So, how are things with you?'

'Oh, you know, looking through scripts, searching for a good project – I got a couple of things that look okay, but my agent's not happy with my billing.'

'I'm sorry.'

'And you, Becks? You missing me?'

'Of course I am. I'm staying in an awesome house where the media can't get to me. It's really peaceful. The filming's going well and I think Robert Hope is happy with my performance so far.'

'Good, good. So, how long are you there for?'

'Another month, I think.'

'That's a helluva long time, honey. How will I survive without you?'

'I'm sure you'll cope, Jack,' she replied brusquely.

'Well, maybe I'll just fly over and see you. After all, we got plans to discuss, dates to set.'

'Jack, I . . .' Rebecca's voice trailed off and she sighed inwardly. He seemed to have conveniently forgotten it was the media who had declared them engaged, while she was still yet to give him her final answer. 'Let's see how it goes, okay? My filming schedule is so tight for the next few weeks. You know how it is.'

'Yeah, sure, but I really miss you, baby.'

'Me too. I've got to go – I'll try to give you a call over the weekend.'

'Yeah, do that, please. It seems crazy I can't get hold of you when I want to speak to you. You sure you're telling me the truth about the lack of signal there?'

'Of course I am, Jack. Why would I not? Listen, I really have to go.'

'Okay, love you.'

'You too, bye.'

Rebecca put the receiver down and walked slowly up the stairs to her bedroom. She slumped down into the chair by the fireplace with a sigh. What was wrong with her? A few months ago she'd been hopelessly in love with Jack. Yet, just now, she could hardly bring herself to speak to him, let alone whisper loving endearments or tell him she missed him.

Perhaps, she told herself, it was because she'd been backed into an irreversible corner. Like a deer in the headlights, she felt trapped. And here in England, she was spending time in the company of men who seemed to take themselves far less seriously than Jack did.

Rebecca had never got used to the fact that he used more moisturiser and skin-care products than she did. She giggled at the thought of Lord Anthony doing the same. Probably his only nod to personal grooming was a cut-throat razor he'd owned since his first shave.

That reminded her, she must find Anthony and hand him Mr Malik's card and the pages he had given her. She glanced out of the window and saw that Anthony was in the garden, pruning the roses. Leaving her bedroom, she made her way downstairs to the terrace. As she stepped outside, he spotted her, and she saw him head across the garden and up the steps towards her.

'How are you, Rebecca?'

'It was a good day,' she said. 'You?'

'Oh, the same as ever really,' he said amiably.

'Did Mrs Trevathan mention you had a visitor earlier today?'

'No, who?'

'A young Indian guy called Ari Malik, who told us a relative of his had worked here many years ago. He asked me to give you these pages. They're written by his great-grandmother about her time at Astbury Hall in the early 1900s. This was her name.' Rebecca proffered the card and Anthony studied it.

'Anahita Chavan . . . I'm afraid it doesn't ring a bell. But if she was a servant, her name would be listed in the old staff-wages ledgers that are kept in the library.'

'Well, maybe these pages will tell you more. Mr Malik said you might like to read them.'

Anthony glanced down at them and Rebecca noticed that he looked uncertain. 'Not really my thing, delving into the family history. What's the point of reliving the past when it contains so much pain?'

'I'm sorry, Anthony, I didn't mean to upset you.'

'Forgive me.' Anthony rallied and gave her a weak smile. 'It's as much as I can do to survive in the present.'

'I understand. Then, would you mind if I read them? It might give me more of an insight into the era Elizabeth lived in.'

'Elizabeth?'

'My character in the film,' Rebecca clarified.

'Oh, of course. By all means, go ahead,' Anthony agreed. 'Perhaps you'd do me the honour of joining me for a drink when your filming schedule permits?'

'Of course, I'd love to.'

'I'll look forward to it. Goodbye for now,' he said as he

stuffed the card she'd given him in his pocket and ambled off back down the steps to his precious garden.

Rebecca spent the next half an hour watching the filming of the village fête scene, which had been set up on the parkland at the front of the house. Young children – locals from the surrounding villages – dashed around excitedly to the various stalls, and Rebecca spotted the nurse she had seen that first day in the kitchen pushing an old lady in a wheelchair. She watched in awe as Marion Devereaux – legendary star of the British stage and screen – completed a long and complicated section of dialogue in one single, perfect take.

Yawning suddenly, Rebecca returned to her room. She curled up on the bed and ran through her lines for half an hour, then found her attention wandering to the plastic file Ari Malik had handed her.

When she next looked up, she saw it was past midnight. She climbed under the covers and fell asleep immediately, dreaming that night of maharajas, rubies and an exotic Indian prince with blue eyes . . .

17

For the next three nights the weather was warm and dry, with a full white moon shining bright in the star-filled sky. Consequently, Robert had decided to shoot the night scenes, so it had been past two in the morning by the time Rebecca had sunk wearily into bed. Tonight, sighing as she waited next to James for them to elope together in the vintage Rolls-Royce, it looked as if it would be even later.

'And they say being an actor is a glamorous profession,' James said, yawning in the darkness. 'I'm more than happy to run away with you anytime, Becks. Although repeating it seven times at one in the morning and only getting as far as thirty yards each take is trying my patience. What a ridiculous way to earn a living.'

'At least we're outside in an amazing location, not stuck in an over-air-conditioned soundstage on a Hollywood backlot,' Rebecca reminded him.

'True, true. So, is it possible that our American sweetheart is falling in love with England? I saw you chatting with our host the other day in the garden. What's he like? He seems rather aloof.'

'Anthony's a nice guy, actually. Just a little shy, I guess.'

'"Anthony", is it? Not Lord Astbury? Very chummy, aren't we?' quipped James. 'How do you fancy a title, Becks? You'd be following in the footsteps of your wealthy American fore-bears. Many heiresses swapped their family fortune for a place in the British aristocracy. Come to think of it, "Lady Rebecca Astbury" has a certain ring to it,' he teased her.

'Ha ha,' Rebecca muttered under her breath, as the sound technician indicated they were finally ready to go.

'Twenty seconds!'

'Seems to me this old place could do with a shiny new American fortune. I'd watch out if I were you, darling. Lord Anthony may be after your money.'

'Ten seconds!'

'He's sweet, but hardly my type,' Rebecca whispered.

'Five seconds!'

'What *is* your type?'

Rebecca had no time to answer further as the clapperboard slammed in front of the windscreen and once again James steered the car down the drive.

After a few minutes the assistant director announced it was finally a take and they were wrapping for the night. Steve opened the door for her and she climbed out of the car.

'Okay?' he asked her.

'Yes, thanks.'

'I'm afraid you've got an early call again tomorrow morning, but after that, we all have a couple of days off at the weekend,' he said as the three of them mounted the giant steps up to the front door of the house. 'Are you happy to stay here at the Hall, or would you like me to ask Graham to drive you to London?'

'Yes, come with me to London,' suggested James. 'I'll take you sightseeing.'

'It's kind of you, but I have a heavy schedule next week,' Rebecca explained. 'So I think I'll just stay here and learn my lines in peace, and maybe do some exploring locally.'

'No problem. Graham will be on call to take you anywhere you want to go,' Steve assured her. 'Right, then, I'll see you at six a.m. tomorrow.'

'Are you absolutely sure you don't want to come with me, Becks?' asked James. 'I don't like to think of you here all alone, at the mercy of the mysterious Lord Astbury and the Hall's very own version of Mrs Danvers,' he teased. 'Anyway, if you do change your mind, I'm leaving straight after the shoot ends tomorrow afternoon.'

'Thanks. Goodnight, James,' she replied, heading inside towards Wardrobe to change out of her costume. Perhaps it was simply that she was exhausted tonight, but currently she had no inclination to leave Astbury Hall. Besides which, knowing her present luck, she and James would be spotted together and immediately there would be a shot of the two of them beamed around the globe.

The cast and crew left the house at teatime the following afternoon, and Rebecca took the opportunity to have a leisurely soak in the bath. She decided that tomorrow she'd ask Graham to drive her into the nearest town so that she could purchase a few more clothes and some stronger allergy drugs for her hay fever.

Climbing out of the bath, Rebecca walked back along the corridor to find Mrs Trevathan waiting for her outside her bedroom.

'I brought you some of my home-made chamomile tea, my love.'

'Thank you,' said Rebecca.

'Well, it will help relax you after your long week. His Lordship has also invited you for a drink with him on the terrace tonight. He said you discussed it earlier in the week.'

'Yes, we did. What time would suit him?'

'Seven-thirty? And he said you're welcome to join him afterwards for dinner, too, if you'd like,' Mrs Trevathan added.

'Not tonight, thank you. My hay fever is very bad right now.'

'You poor thing. Well, nothing a good night's rest can't cure, I'm sure. I'll tell His Lordship you'll be down at seven-thirty, dear.'

Making quick work of the delicious chamomile tea, Rebecca spent an hour immersed in the scenes she would be playing the following week. She then got dressed, grabbed a cardigan and made her way downstairs and outside to the flagstone terrace that stretched almost the entire length of the main block of the house.

Anthony was sitting at a wrought-iron table off to one side that offered a splendid view of the flower gardens and the sweep of green lawn and parkland beyond. 'Good evening,' he said, and smiled as he stood up and pulled out a chair for her.

'Thank you,' said Rebecca, sitting down. 'What a gorgeous sunset. Nature's really putting on a show for us. You know, I'd never really appreciated the skies until I came here to Astbury. The stars seem so bright here too.'

'Well, perhaps one doesn't notice in a city,' said Anthony, holding a jug aloft and pouring an amber-coloured liquid filled with fruit and ice into her glass.

'What are we drinking?' Rebecca eyed it with suspicion.

'Pimm's – it's what we British drink on rare summer evenings like this one. I promise there's plenty of lemonade in it, so it won't get you tipsy.'

Rebecca put the glass tentatively to her lips and took a sip. 'It's very good, thank you,' she said.

'I'm glad you like it. Mrs Trevathan tells me you're suffering from hay fever.'

'Yes, I've had it since I was a child and it really gets me down sometimes. By the way, last night I read the first pages of the story that Mr Malik left with me, the ones written by his relative who used to work here. No skeletons so far.' Rebecca smiled. 'But Donald, who I think you said was your grandfather, does make a memorable appearance.'

'Does he, indeed?' Anthony sipped his Pimm's thoughtfully. 'I did check the staff ledgers in the library and I can't find any trace of someone named Anahita Chavan during the time frame you suggested.'

'Well, according to her story, she most definitely worked here, if only briefly,' Rebecca elaborated. 'She was nursemaid to Eleanor, the daughter of your grandfather's sister.'

'Selina Fontaine. From what I was told by my mother, she was the black sheep of the family. She married some French count and moved to France. After that, she never spent much time here again.'

'I'm surprised,' said Rebecca. 'She sounded like a nice person in the story. Excuse me for saying so, Anthony, but I'm amazed you don't want to find out more about your family's past. I'd love it if I could discover even a little bit more of my own.'

'Forgive me if I don't agree,' he answered, seeming agitated.

'In the case of my family history, as Mrs Trevathan is always telling me, it's better to let sleeping dogs lie.'

'That might be true, but what I've read happened almost a hundred years ago. Surely it can't do any harm to learn more about those who lived here before you?'

Anthony gazed into the distance, then turned towards her. 'So you think it would help me if I did, Rebecca?'

'I . . .' She looked at him, the expression in his eyes reminding her of a child turning to a mother for advice. She shrugged. 'Maybe it's the American way, but I always want to know the facts,' she replied.

'Well, maybe you're right and I should read this document you seem so enthralled by,' he finally agreed.

'My apologies, Anthony, this is none of my business. I really don't mean to interfere.'

'Did this Mr Malik seem like a good chap?'

'Well, he didn't seem to be looking for anything from you other than to have a conversation about his great-grandmother,' Rebecca confirmed.

'I'll think about it, certainly. Now, what plans do you have for the weekend?' Anthony said, abruptly changing the subject. 'I must admit I'm enjoying this short hiatus of having my home back to myself.'

'I'm sure you are. I promise I'll be out of your hair as well tomorrow,' she said hastily. 'I'm going to ask Graham, my driver, to take me to the nearest town. I need to buy some more things to wear. I brought so few clothes over with me and it's warmer here than I expected. And then I thought that maybe I'd do a little local sightseeing. Any place in particular that you think I should visit?'

'Of course, but when I said I wanted the house back to

myself, please don't feel I was including you. In fact, I'd be happy to show you around personally. It's doubtful that anyone knows this part of the world better than I.'

'Really, Anthony, that won't be necessary,' Rebecca assured him. 'I'm sure the last thing you want to do this weekend is play tour guide.'

'No, I insist. Seriously. I don't find your presence here obtrusive at all and it would be my pleasure. Mrs Trevathan says you're too weary to join me for dinner tonight, so, shall we reconvene here on the terrace tomorrow morning at, say, ten o'clock?'

'Okay, if you're sure,' agreed Rebecca, 'but I really don't want to put you to any trouble.'

'It won't be any trouble at all. So, tell me how the film is going?'

Rebecca chatted to him about the film, glad to see the earlier tension leave Anthony's face as he listened.

'Of course the real star of the show is Astbury Hall itself. Everyone feels privileged to be here and it's going to look just wonderful on the big screen.'

'At least it's earning its keep for a change,' sighed Anthony. 'Rather ironic that the fact that there've been no funds to modernise it has made it so appealing as a backdrop for your film.'

'I love it here, Anthony, no matter how old-fashioned the bathroom facilities are,' she added with a smile.

'Do you? Do you really?

'Yes, really,' she confirmed.

'That pleases me.' A look of almost child-like pleasure crossed Anthony's face.

When Mrs Trevathan appeared on the terrace to announce that Anthony's supper was ready, Rebecca felt guilty at how grateful she was that she could slip away upstairs for a light meal quietly by herself.

Rebecca woke the following morning feeling groggy and with the kind of headache that made her question whether she had drunk too much alcohol the night before. She wondered just how strong the Pimm's drink Anthony had given her had been. Mrs Trevathan arrived in her bedroom promptly at nine and placed a tray laden with tea, toast and a boiled egg on her lap. Rebecca sat up in bed feeling queasy and tried but failed to eat much of the breakfast. She swallowed down some ibuprofen for her head, pulled on a T-shirt and jeans and went downstairs.

'Good morning.' Anthony was already on the terrace waiting for her. 'Shall we?'

The two of them walked round to the front drive, where an ancient Range Rover was parked. 'Climb aboard. I'm sorry it's hardly what you're used to,' he said apologetically.

Rebecca sat inside as Anthony started the engine, wondering at her host's never-changing uniform of checked shirt and ancient tweed jacket. Perhaps they were the only clothes he owned. She hoped Mrs Trevathan washed them occasionally.

'I thought I'd take you into Ashburton. There're a couple of boutiques, although I've no idea whether what they sell will be to your taste,' commented Anthony as they drove off. 'Then we'll drive to Widecombe-in-the-Moor and have lunch at the pub there. After that, maybe you'd like to see Dartmoor? The most pleasant way is on horseback, but perhaps you don't ride.'

'I love riding, actually,' said Rebecca, brightening at the thought. 'I had to learn for a part I played in a film a few years ago. It was set in Montana and I was taught by a couple of real-life cowboys. So I'm sure my riding style isn't as polished as you're used to.'

'Well, well, there we are,' said Anthony, obviously surprised. 'Sadly, our stables aren't quite what they were in the old days. I rent them out to the girl who runs the local riding school, in return for her keeping a couple of my horses there. Never was much of a rider when I was younger, and my back plays up these days, so they don't get much exercise. So, please, feel free to take one out as often as you wish whilst you're here. It really would be a help if you did.'

'You know what? I just might,' Rebecca agreed.

'By the way, I thought about what you said last night. I contacted Mr Malik this morning and asked him to come to the Hall for lunch tomorrow. On one condition,' Anthony added.

'What's that?'

'You join us. After all, it's you who's persuaded me I should meet him.'

'Of course, I'd be glad to,' Rebecca agreed. 'And, Anthony, if Mr Malik is coming for lunch tomorrow, I do think you should perhaps read the start of his great-grandmother's story before he arrives. It really is fascinating.'

Anthony glanced at her nervously. 'Can you promise there really are no skeletons in the family wardrobe that might shock me?'

'None at all, from what I've read so far, anyway. Most of it is about Anahita's childhood in India. I truly felt I was entering a different world and it's made me want to go visit. She lived in an amazing palace as companion to a princess, before they both came over to England to boarding school.'

'Presumably, that's the family connection,' mused Anthony as he drove. 'I know my great-grandfather was Resident out in Cooch Behar State before he died.'

'Yes. And I get the feeling that he loved it, but your great-grandmother, Maud, didn't feel the same way.'

'I'm sure. Sadly, there wasn't much she approved of. Certainly not us men,' he added with feeling.

'Well, I guess you'll just have to read it for yourself.'

'Then I will. And I'll let Mrs Trevathan know about lunch tomorrow. Right,' Anthony said as he parked the car in a space along a pretty, bustling high street, 'let's go shopping.'

The morning turned out to be more pleasant than Rebecca had expected it to be. Walking along in the sunshine flanked by her male protector, with her newly dyed hair, Rebecca enjoyed the freedom of being in public without being recognised. After she had nipped into a few shops and picked out a couple of new shirts, and grabbed more antihistamines from the chemist, they drove on to Widecombe-in-the-Moor.

They sat outside in the sun at the Rugglestone Inn, enjoying a fresh crab salad.

'It's like a picture postcard of how I imagined England to be,' said Rebecca, taking in the quaintness of the chocolate-box cottages that dotted the narrow street. 'In fact, speaking of postcards, I might send some.'

'It's certainly a beautiful part of the world. And it's good for me to see it through fresh eyes. I've never travelled much, and I suppose one becomes a little jaded with the familiar.'

'Were you sent off to boarding school when you were small, like your grandfather Donald?' Rebecca enquired.

'No. I was home-educated. My mother didn't approve of boarding school,' he explained.

LUCINDA RILEY

'Really? I'm surprised. From the film script and my research on the era, I thought it was a rite of passage for all boys
from British families like yours.'

'Mother would have missed me too much. You can imagine how lonely she'd have been rattling around the Hall by
herself.'

'Of course.' Rebecca had noticed there was a whisper of
girlishness about him every time he spoke of his mother. She
wondered suddenly if the reason Anthony had never married
was because he was gay. 'From what I hear about boarding
school, you had a lucky escape. I can't understand why anyone
would have a child and want to send them away.'

'Mother always thought it rather a joke that we young
Brits were sent away to school to fit us out to run the empire.
By the end of the 1950s when I was a boy, there was no empire left to run.' He sighed. 'Still, everybody tells me boarding
school is far kinder now. Apparently they even provide hot
water these days.'

'I'd never even consider it for one of my kids.' Rebecca
shuddered.

'As you rightly said, it's tradition, my dear. Well now, perhaps you'd like to take a ride on Dartmoor this afternoon?'

Having eaten lunch, Rebecca was now feeling queasy and
could feel her headache returning. 'Maybe tomorrow. I'm still
feeling a little tired today.'

'Then how about we head home and I'll show you the family chapel?' he suggested. 'It was designed by Vanbrugh, a very
famous English architect. It's tucked away inside the house off
the long gallery.'

'Yes, if that's okay with you, Anthony,' Rebecca replied.

Twenty minutes later, back at the Hall, Rebecca followed

Anthony through the elegant long gallery. He stood in front of an oak door and used an oversized key to unlock it.

Rebecca stepped inside and looked up with wonder at a soaring forest of gilded columns ascending towards a small dome, whose sides were adorned with clouds and cherubs.

'It's so beautiful,' she breathed, turning to Anthony.

'Yes, but sadly wasted these days. I rarely come in here. Please,' he said, sitting down in a pew, 'feel free to wander around.'

Rebecca did so, enjoying the calm atmosphere and feeling the weight of history the chapel contained. She looked down at the well-worn marble floor, tangible evidence of the many souls who had come here over the years to find solace.

She turned and looked back at her companion. Anthony was staring straight ahead, obviously deep in thought. Seeing him sitting there alone, she felt his vulnerability. She walked over and sat down next to him in the pew. 'Do you believe in God, Anthony?'

'My great-grandmother Maud was very religious. She brought my mother up as a strict Roman Catholic. Since Maud was still alive when I was born, I was as well. Personally, I don't believe in any of it. Never did, to be honest, although I paid lip-service in front of her. Do you believe?'

'I've never really given religion any headspace. It wasn't part of my childhood, that's for sure.'

'It was rather a large part of mine, although I gave it no more thought than you have. It was simply a routine with no meaning. Deadly dull, like a science or maths lesson. To be frank, I can only see the mayhem it's caused throughout the centuries. And certainly Maud's obsession with it didn't help my family either. She wasn't a . . . warm person. Anyway, there we are.' He turned to Rebecca with a sad smile. 'Are you ready to go?'

'Yes. Thank you for bringing me here, I feel privileged to have seen it.'

'It's been my pleasure,' he assured her earnestly.

'Where are your ancestors buried?' Rebecca asked, suddenly hoping the answer wouldn't be in a vault beneath their feet.

'In what I consider to be a ghastly building in a copse in the park. I could take you to the mausoleum now, if you wanted,' Anthony offered as they walked back down the long gallery.

'Actually, I really do have a bad headache. Maybe another day.'

'Well, I do hope you'll feel well enough to join myself and our young Indian friend tomorrow. Mrs Trevathan always puts on a decent roast lunch.'

'Yes, of course. I'm sure I'll feel better after a rest.'

'Rebecca, I . . .' Anthony stared at her for a moment and then shook his head. 'Nothing. I hope you feel better tomorrow. Is there anything you need?'

'Just some sleep, I'm sure.'

'Well, I'm back to my garden. Thank you for a pleasant day.'

Anthony walked off in the direction of the terrace as Rebecca made her way up the stairs. Closing the door behind her, she took some more ibuprofen and lay down on the bed, wishing for once that she was in a hotel and she could put a 'do not disturb' sign on the door. Closing her eyes, she did her best to relax.

18

'Rebecca . . . Rebecca . . . ?'

She heard a voice calling her awake. Opening her eyes, she saw Mrs Trevathan staring down at her.

'You've been asleep for over three hours. I thought I should wake you as it's almost seven in the evening, and you'll never get your rest later if you sleep any more now. I've brought you up some tea and scones.'

'Oh – thank you.' Rebecca felt disorientated and shaky.

'His Lordship said you were suffering from a bad headache. Is there anything else I can get you? You look very pale, dear.'

'No, I'm okay, thanks,' Rebecca replied, swinging her legs off the bed and walking over to the table. 'I feel better now after my nap.'

'Shall I pour the tea for you?'

'Yes please.'

'I hear we have an extra guest for luncheon tomorrow. Apparently, you told His Lordship about the Indian gentleman who came calling.'

'I did, yes.' Rebecca glanced up at Mrs Trevathan's expression and saw the disapproval there. 'Is that a problem?'

'No, no. It's just all so hectic at the moment. I suppose we're just not used to having our usual routine disturbed.'

'I can imagine,' Rebecca said sympathetically. She paused. 'Anthony's been so kind to me. But he also strikes me as a very lonely person. I'm sure it's none of my business, but I wonder, has Anthony ever had a girlfriend?'

'Not really, no. I suppose you could say His Lordship is what's called a confirmed bachelor. He's a one-off, he is, and that's for sure.' Mrs Trevathan allowed herself a fond smile.

'I don't know whether I'd want to go through my life forever alone,' sighed Rebecca, taking a sip of her tea.

'Well, each to his own, I always say. We can't all be lucky in love, can we? Besides, he's always got me for company, dear. Right then, I'll leave you to it.'

'Oh, by the way, I promised to give Anthony the manuscript Mr Malik handed to me so he can read it before tomorrow.' Rebecca took the pile of pages from the night table by the bed and handed them to Mrs Trevathan.

She looked at the file suspiciously. 'What's all this about, then?'

'It's mainly about life in India. And, of course, about Astbury Hall too.'

'I see. There's nothing in it that'll disturb His Lordship, is there? He's very –' she searched for the word – 'sensitive, and I don't want him upset.'

'Not at all.'

'But what does this Indian fellow want, do you think?' Mrs Trevathan persisted.

'Simply to find out more about his great-grandmother's past. What else could it be?'

'Nothing . . . nothing,' murmured Mrs Trevathan, clearly

unconvinced. 'Right, I'll leave you to enjoy your tea in peace.'

As Rebecca ate the delicious scones, she thought about the territorial way Mrs Trevathan spoke of Anthony. In fact, they could almost have been husband and wife. After all, she performed all the domestic duties a wife traditionally would, and they'd obviously been together a very long time. Rebecca then wondered how Mrs Trevathan would feel if another woman *did* enter the equation. She couldn't help finding the relationship between them strange. It was so – *intimate*, in some ways, each of them relying heavily on the other, yet so distant in other respects. Perhaps, she thought with a grimace, it was how many marriages were.

Rebecca placed her empty plate on the tray and left it outside her door as a signal that she didn't wish to be disturbed. She sat in the chair and rationally tried to consider what her life would be like if she were married to Jack. There would be no 'master and servant' relationship, because they'd both be equals. But was that possible? Jack's ego was the size of the *Titanic*, and because her own was less pronounced and it was in her nature to avoid conflict at all costs, she supposed it would be she who would surrender first.

Rebecca stood up and went and had a bath, then climbed into bed with her script. She found it difficult to concentrate, her thoughts returning constantly to Jack and his proposal. Eventually, as her eyes grew heavy and she prepared for sleep, she realised the one thing she knew for certain was that she was not ready for a lifetime commitment yet.

'Ah, Rebecca, I was just about to send up Mrs Trevathan to call you downstairs.' Anthony stood up from the dining-room table to greet her. 'You look much better today. Headache gone?'

'Yes, it has, thanks,' Rebecca confirmed as she walked into the room.

'I believe you two have met before. Rebecca, this is Mr Ari Malik,' said Anthony.

'Hello again,' said Rebecca, smiling and reaching out her hand to Ari.

'Rebecca,' Ari said, embarrassed, 'I must apologise for insisting that I knew you when we last met. I've subsequently realised who you are.'

'Really, it's not a problem. Actually, it's a refreshing change,' she said with a laugh.

'I saw a photograph of you and your fiancé in a newspaper only yesterday,' Ari continued. 'May I offer my congratulations?'

'Thanks.' Rebecca blushed uncomfortably.

'You're engaged to be married?' Anthony stared at Rebecca in surprise. 'I didn't realise that.'

'I . . . yes.'

'I see. Shall we sit down?' Anthony said abruptly. 'Mr Malik, I'm not sure if the fare will be quite to your taste. My housekeeper tends to cook along traditional English lines.'

'Please, call me Ari. Don't worry, I got used to English cookery when I was at Harrow.'

'You were at Harrow?' Anthony seemed somewhat taken aback.

'Yes, my parents believed a British education was the best in the world. And so . . .'

As Ari continued speaking, his words drifted past Rebecca as she found herself taking proper note of his physical beauty.

He had thick, wavy black hair that shone with strands that almost looked blue in the sunlight streaming through the window. It was long enough for a few tendrils to touch the collar of his shirt, but not to stop him from appearing masculine. His skin was a light honey-brown, and he wore an immaculately pressed and starched white shirt. But it was his eyes that held Rebecca's attention – she couldn't think how to describe the colour because they were blue, but also contained flecks of green and amber, reminding her of looking into the kaleidoscope she'd had as a child.

'What do you think, Rebecca?' Anthony was asking her.

'Excuse me.' She dragged her attention back to the conversation. 'I'm afraid I missed that.'

'I was saying to Ari that since the decline of the British Empire, perhaps many of our traditions are not held in quite the same high regard as they used to be by the world.'

'Oh, I'm not sure about that.' Rebecca smiled. 'We Yanks still love you Brits. I mean, here I am, making a film about your aristocracy for the American market.'

'I agree with Rebecca,' said Ari. 'Many of my country's most ingrained customs come from all those decades of British rule. These days, though, I think we may be better at some of them than you are over here. Look at our cricket, for example,' he teased.

'Do you live in India?' asked Rebecca as Mrs Trevathan placed soup in front of all of them.

'Yes. I'm based in Mumbai, but I spend a fair amount of my time travelling abroad.'

'What is it you do, exactly?' asked Anthony.

'My company provides technology solutions for businesses. Simply put, we design bespoke software.'

'Really? I'm afraid I'm a dinosaur,' said Anthony. 'Don't own a computer and never will. To be blunt, they terrify me.'

'Yet my six-year-old nephew can change programs on a computer as swiftly as he can turn the pages of a book,' said Ari. 'Like it or not, the digital world has altered all of our lives irrevocably.'

'Except for mine,' Anthony replied without rancour. 'As you may have noticed, my home and myself are both outdated and happily so. Now, please, dig in.'

Throughout lunch, Rebecca was content to sit back and listen with interest as the two men discussed British and Indian history and the strange but enduring intertwining of the two such different cultures it had produced.

When the meal was over, Anthony said, 'Shall we move into the drawing room for coffee?'

Once they were all settled in the drawing room and Mrs Trevathan had poured coffee for the men and a chamomile tea for Rebecca, Anthony retrieved the pages from a bureau and handed them back to Ari.

'Thank you for letting me read this. I found it fascinating, especially the insight into the India of 1911. It's the world my great-grandfather was part of.'

'Yes, I learned many things about my own culture from these pages too,' Ari agreed.

'But,' Anthony continued, 'having read what I have so far, I can't quite see what relevance it would have to my family or Astbury Hall.'

'No, I can understand that,' said Ari. 'However, now that I've read my great-grandmother's story in its entirety, I can assure you that there is great relevance in it.'

'Your great-grandmother describes how she worked here,

yes, but as I said to Rebecca, I couldn't find any record of her in any of the staff-wages ledgers from that period.'

'It wouldn't surprise me if you found no trace of her at all documented at Astbury Hall. Sadly, her time here did not have a happy ending for anyone involved.'

'Then I'm not sure I want to know,' Anthony stated flatly.

'Actually, the reason I came to Astbury was to see if you could help me with a missing piece of the jigsaw from my own family's history,' said Ari.

'And what might that be?'

'To cut a long story short, just after Violet Astbury's death, Anahita was told her son had died. But for the rest of her life she refused to accept it.' He indicated the folder containing the rest of the story. 'It's complicated, but I really think she explains it all far better than I possibly could. Would you like to read the rest?'

'Perhaps.' Anthony stood up suddenly, obviously agitated. 'Rebecca, you mentioned yesterday that you'd like to take a ride across the moors.'

'Yes, I did.'

'Do you ride, Ari?' Anthony enquired.

'Yes.'

'Then why don't the two of you go and blow away some cobwebs? I have some work to do in the garden.'

'It's such a beautiful day, I'd love to take a ride,' Rebecca said. 'Do you want to join me, Ari?' she encouraged. It was obvious Anthony wanted them to leave.

'Yes, of course, if you're both sure. The lunch was delicious, Anthony, thank you for your very kind hospitality,' said Ari, taking the hint and following Rebecca across the room to the

French doors that opened onto the terrace. 'But I don't have any boots or other riding clothes with me.'

'Turn left and the stables are about half a mile past the courtyard,' Anthony said. 'Tell Debbie I sent you. She has riding togs down there. Enjoy.'

'Thank you,' said Rebecca, 'see you later.'

'I've obviously upset him,' Ari said to her when they were out of earshot.

'Maybe he knows more than he's telling?' She shrugged.

'Possibly. Are you staying here with him?'

'Yes. I know Anthony comes across as a little peculiar, but he's been very kind and hospitable to me. Thanks for agreeing to come riding, anyway,' she said as they entered the yard. 'I think he needed some time alone.'

'It's my pleasure.' Ari smiled at her.

'Wait here and I'll go and find this Debbie,' she said, and walked along the row of horses, patting their velvet noses.

Debbie, the stable girl, suggested a sleek grey mare for Rebecca and a chestnut stallion for Ari. Saddling up the horses, she pointed them in the direction of the moors. 'Follow the bridle path when you get there,' she advised. 'Until you know the area better, I wouldn't go off piste. You may have a devil of a time finding your way back otherwise. I'll be here until six,' she said as the two of them clopped out of the stables.

'What a gorgeous afternoon,' commented Ari. 'The English climate is so temperate – it rarely goes to extremes. Much like the people who live in it,' he added with a hint of irony in his voice.

'I seem to recall your great-grandmother writing much the same thing. Certainly the English are far less demonstrative than us Americans.'

'And we Indians, too. But I was educated here, and taught to hold my emotions in check.' He smiled. 'Now,' he said as they reached the edge of the moor, 'how are you feeling? Are you up for a canter?'

'I'll give it a try, but if I lag behind, you carry on ahead if you want to.'

Ari tapped the horse's flank and his chestnut stallion galloped off. Rebecca gave a slight pressure with her heels and followed behind him at a more sedate pace. As she gathered confidence, she began to speed up and was soon flying along by his side. Neither of them spoke as the horses let rip. Eventually, when all four of them were panting, Ari spotted a brook running in a crevice of moorland.

'Shall we let the horses have a drink and take in some of this wonderful scenery?' he suggested.

'Sure,' Rebecca answered, dismounting and leading her grey to the brook's edge. She flopped down onto the coarse grass and stared up at the cloudless sky. Ari did the same and they lay next to each other in comfortable silence.

'Can you hear that?' said Ari.

'What?'

'Exactly.' He smiled at her. 'Nothing.'

'And I love it.' Rebecca sighed in pleasure. 'How long will you be staying in England?'

'I'll give it a few days and see if Anthony is inspired to read more of Anahita's story. There's some local investigation I can do myself to try to trace her so-called lost son. As a matter of fact, it was good timing. I needed to get away from India for a while.'

'Why's that?'

'I suppose –' Ari sighed – 'I've arrived at a turning point, in every area of my life. Perhaps I'm having an early mid-life crisis, but everything that used to matter, that seemed important, suddenly doesn't any more.'

'Do you know what triggered it?' Rebecca asked him gently.

'Sadly, yes. I let a wonderful girl go because I was obsessed with my career and success. It's only in retrospect I can see what I had and lost.'

'Then why can't you tell her that?'

'She was married two weeks ago to someone else. I can't blame her for giving up on me. She was beside me all the time I was building my business and I just didn't notice her. Anyway,' he sighed sadly, 'what's done is done and it's no good wishing for what might have been.'

'Well, I didn't come here to find answers,' said Rebecca, propping herself up on an elbow and resting her cheek on her hand, 'but I guess this place is providing me with some, anyway.'

'Such as?' Ari prompted her.

Rebecca took a deep breath. 'Between you and me, I've decided I don't want to be married just yet.'

'I see. Isn't that going to cause a problem or two? From what I read the other day in the newspapers, the world is already planning your wedding.'

'Yes, but I'd prefer to have that problem now than that of a messy divorce in five years' time. Perhaps Jack and I can just stay engaged for a while, but' – Rebecca rolled over onto her front and picked at the rough grass – 'I'm not sure that's the answer either.'

'Do you love him?' Ari asked bluntly.

'I . . . don't know any more.'

'Well, find out for sure before you decide.' Ari turned onto his back, closed his eyes and rested his arms behind his head. Looking at him, Rebecca thought again how attractive he was. She was at the same time relieved and a little disappointed that he had made it clear that he was mourning the loss of someone he had loved. He wasn't interested in her, that was obvious. She too turned over to lie on her back and closed her eyes, mulling over this unusual state of affairs. After years of men hitting on her at the first opportunity, it was refreshing that Ari seemed content just to talk.

'You're smiling,' he said suddenly. 'Why?'

She opened her eyes and saw Ari staring down at her. 'I'm feeling calm and happy.'

'Enjoying the moment, as all the gurus will tell you, is the key to a happy life. So, are you up for more riding? I'd like to explore a little further.'

'Sure,' she agreed and they remounted the horses.

'Now –' Ari's eyes swept the horizon – 'if this is the brook my great-grandmother describes in her story, I'm sure there's a cottage somewhere close by. Let's look around and see if we can spot it.'

Rebecca followed Ari off the bridle path and onto the moor itself. Something seemed to be guiding him, for after a few minutes of searching, they saw the chimney tops of a building, half hidden in a dip by the rugged surroundings.

'That's it,' said Ari, 'I know it is.'

'What?'

'The cottage where Anahita lived. Come on!'

'But I thought she lived up at the Hall. You can't say something like that and then not tell me what you mean!' she called as Ari set off.

'All in good time,' he shouted back over his shoulder. Rebecca trotted after him, making her way down the slope and round to the front of the cottage.

'This has to be the one,' Ari said as he jumped off his horse. 'Let's take a look around.' Helping Rebecca dismount, he walked with her up to the gate. The garden beyond it had long ago been overtaken by the moorland grass and wild plants.

'It's almost as if the moors have reclaimed it,' he commented as he forced the gate open with all his strength. 'Looks like this place hasn't been lived in for years. Maybe not since Anahita was here ninety years ago,' he mused as he trampled down the grass to make a path for them to the front door.

Every inch of the cottage was covered in thick ivy, so he used his hands to try to tear it away from the windows, but it was impenetrable. Then he attempted the door, using all his weight to punch it open through the ivy, but that also failed.

As Rebecca waited, waist-deep in brambles and grass, a sudden deep colour caught her eye amidst the tangle. Parting the weeds, Rebecca gasped as she saw a small, perfect rose, identical in colour to the one Anthony had given her when she'd first arrived at Astbury. As she bent to take a closer look, she realised there were other tiny buds on the plant, desperate to blossom, and felt a sudden sense of sadness that something so beautiful could still be blooming in the choking chaos surrounding it.

'Maybe we should smash a window pane?' he suggested. 'Or perhaps there's another door at the back?'

'I don't think we should be breaking and entering,' said Rebecca nervously. 'Someone must own this.'

'Yes, Anthony,' Ari confirmed.

'Then let's ask him for a key,' Rebecca suggested, eager to leave. There was something about this place that made her feel uncomfortable.

'I'm going round to the back to see if there's another way in.' Ari turned tail and walked past her towards the gate.

'We ought to ride home now,' she said, 'it's past six already and we promised Debbie we'd be back by then.'

Ari checked his watch. 'Yes, you're right. At least now I know where the cottage is. Perhaps I can ask Anthony's permission to come back and investigate.'

'What is it you want to see?' she asked him as they climbed back onto their horses, feeling a palpable sense of relief as they trotted away.

'If there's anything left inside to indicate the presence of my great-grandmother.'

'Surely if it was ninety years ago, there won't be?'

'You're probably right, but I'd like to satisfy my curiosity anyway.'

Arriving at the stables, they turned the horses over to Debbie with profuse apologies for having kept her waiting and walked back towards the Hall. As they took the steps to the terrace, Rebecca saw that Anthony was working in the walled garden. He waved them over.

'Good hack?' he asked.

'Yes. Thank you for the loan of the horses,' said Ari.

'No problem. The poor nags see so little action these days. Feel free to take one out whenever you wish. How long are you staying for?'

'I'm not sure,' said Ari.

'Well, I've been thinking as I've been out here digging, that I really shouldn't shy away from my family's past. So I'll continue reading your great-grandmother's story. And when I have we'll speak again.'

'Thank you, I'm so glad. Then I'll wait to hear from you.'

'And by all means, feel free to wander Astbury's grounds in the meantime. They really are at their best this time of year. Goodbye for now.' Anthony retreated back down the steps to the garden.

Rebecca grinned at Ari. 'Be careful. If you come by here tomorrow, you might end up in the film.'

'Hardly, unless there's a walk-on part for an Indian manservant. Right, I'll be off. And thanks, Rebecca. It's entirely down to you that Anthony saw me at all.'

'No problem. See you, Ari.'

'Yes, I hope so.' He smiled as he walked away.

19

'Are you okay, Rebecca?' asked James as they stood on set early Monday morning. 'You don't seem your usual cheery self.'

'I'm not sure.' Rebecca glanced down at her shaking hands and knew the tremor was not from nerves about the scene they were about to shoot. 'I do feel kind of weird, even though I've had a couple of days off.'

'Probably caught a bug, or maybe our heavy British food isn't suiting your delicate constitution. We can ask Steve to call a doctor if you need one.'

'It's this headache I can't seem to shake. I thought it had gone yesterday, but today it's back. Maybe it's a migraine, but I've never had one before. Thanks, I guess I'll just see how I go,' she said, smiling weakly at him.

'Thirty seconds, everyone!'

Rebecca was glad she was sitting down for the scene. As well as the headache, she felt nauseous and dizzy. She'd have to take some more ibuprofen when they broke for lunch.

An hour later, as Rebecca was hurrying towards her bedroom to find the pills, Steve waylaid her.

'The production office had another call earlier this morning from your fiancé. He sounded pretty concerned, as apparently you said you'd contact him over the weekend and you didn't.'

'It's impossible to get a cellphone signal here and I don't like to use the house phone,' Rebecca explained.

'Look, I understand completely, but obviously your fiancé doesn't. I've told you, the company is paying all the bills, so go ahead and use the landline in Lord Astbury's study.'

'Okay, I'll call him later. I'm sorry if he's being a bother.' She turned away from Steve and made her way wearily up the stairs.

Luckily, Rebecca wasn't needed on set that evening. Having felt no better during the day, she returned to her room and sank down gratefully on the bed.

Mrs Trevathan appeared a few minutes later, her face full of concern.

'Are you not well, my love?' she said as she bustled over and put her hand on Rebecca's forehead.

'I'll be fine. I've just got a bad headache, that's all.'

'You don't feel as if you've got a temperature. Why don't I bring you up some nice soup in a bit and then you can have an early night?'

'Thanks, but I really couldn't eat anything,' she said, wishing Mrs Trevathan would leave the room so that she could close her eyes.

'All right, dear, but I'll come up and check on you later.'

'That really won't be necessary.'

'You want some peace and quiet,' Mrs Trevathan said, lowering her voice to almost a whisper. 'I understand. Goodnight then, dear.'

As she left the room, Rebecca wondered if those who'd

lived at Astbury in the past had ever felt smothered by the cloying attentions of their servants. There was simply no privacy. She sighed as she removed her clothes and slipped between the sheets. She hadn't called Jack yet, but she felt too sick to do so. After a good night's sleep, she was sure she'd feel more up to it.

Rebecca dreamed strange dreams that night. She was in the cottage on the moors and there was danger, but the door was stuck fast and when she tried to open the windows, the ivy covering them curled round her hands and held her fast. Once again she smelt the heady scent of perfume as a hand closed over her nose and mouth and she could no longer breathe . . .

Rebecca jumped awake with a start, her heart banging against her chest. She reached for the light, knocking over the glass of water on the night table beside her. Climbing out of bed and reassuring herself that it had simply been a nightmare, probably born of a fever – she certainly felt warm when she touched her brow – Rebecca opened the door and stumbled along the corridor to the bathroom to refill her glass. Washing her face in cold water, she emerged and walked back in the dim light towards her room.

She stifled a scream as a shadowy figure accosted her by her door.

'Are you all right?'

'I –' She managed to focus her eyes on the shape and saw it was Anthony, clad in a paisley dressing gown. 'I wasn't expecting to meet anyone,' she said as she tried to catch her breath.

'I'm sorry to have startled you. I heard someone cry out from along the corridor and came to investigate.'

'I guess I just had a nightmare. I'm sorry to have disturbed you.'

'Don't worry about that, I rarely sleep soundly,' Anthony comforted her. 'Well, if you're sure everything is all right, I'll say goodnight.'

'Goodnight.' Rebecca opened the door to her bedroom and closed it firmly behind her.

'Jack's called again,' said Steve, finding Rebecca the next morning. 'Go to the study and call him now whilst you have a break, before I end up in the tabloids accused of thwarting your fairy-tale romance.' He grinned at her and walked away.

Rebecca left the set on the terrace where she'd just finished filming and walked towards Anthony's study. Her headache had cleared this morning and she finally felt able to cope with speaking to Jack.

As was typical, both his home number and his cellphone went straight to voicemail. Sighing in frustration, Rebecca wandered back to the far end of the south terrace, where location catering had set up tables in the sunshine and joined the rest of the cast for lunch.

'Come here, darling, and sit next to me,' Marion Devereaux said, patting the empty seat beside her.

'Thanks,' Rebecca said, smiling, and feeling a flutter of nerves in her stomach. So far, she'd been too shy to approach the legendary actress, whose career had brought her every award and accolade under the sun.

'I was watching you on set this morning, darling, and I want to tell you that you're good. In fact, you're very good.'

'Thank you.' Rebecca blushed with pleasure.

'Yes, you have a lovely, natural quality in front of the camera. Have you done much stage acting?'

'I did when I was at Juilliard in New York, but since I graduated I've only appeared in films.'

'I hope you'll find a chance to be on the stage again. Nothing like a live audience to make the adrenaline run and pull the best out of an actor.' Marion smiled as she lit a slim cigarette. 'Mind you, one is paid a pittance.'

'I don't care about the money, I never really have.'

'No, darling, I don't suppose you would, what with all those big Hollywood films under your belt,' Marion commented drily.

Rebecca reddened at the obvious inference. 'Would you have any advice for me? Any ways I can improve as an actress?'

The old lady's famous violet eyes turned to her. 'Yes, darling, simply *live*. Gather experiences and know yourself. Understanding of the human psyche brings gravitas and emotional substance to a performance that technique can't replicate. Act from your soul as much as your brain,' she said, clasping her hands to her considerable chest.

Part of Rebecca wanted to giggle, but she agreed solemnly. 'Thank you, Marion. I'll try to do exactly that.'

'How I wish I was you, just starting out, with a whole host of wonderful parts in front of me.' She sighed. 'However, I'm a far better actress these days than I ever was at your age. We must have dinner together one evening before the shoot ends. Now, I'll take my leave,' she said, rising. 'The sun is playing havoc with my make-up.'

Rebecca sat where she was, relishing the praise, the warmth of the day and her current headache-free state. James appeared and sat next to her in the chair Marion had vacated a few seconds earlier.

'Feeling better?' he asked. 'You certainly look it.'

'Yes, I am, thank you.'

'Well enough to join me for dinner tonight? We could drive out to that great pub you told me about.'

'Why not?' Rebecca replied, feeling that perhaps she did need a break from the confines of Astbury Hall.

'Great, we'll have to be there by eight, mind you. Everything closes so early out here in the hinterlands.'

'Spoken like a real city boy,' teased Rebecca.

'Yup, not really cut out for the country – more of a smoky nightclub at two a.m. sort of chap myself. But when in Rome . . .' With that, James strolled off.

'Where are you off to this evening?' asked Mrs Trevathan as Rebecca let her into her room. 'You're all dressed up.'

'Not really, this is just a new shirt I bought on Saturday. I'm going out to the pub with one of the actors.'

'So, you're not in for supper tonight?'

'No, not tonight.' Rebecca was tempted to add, 'As long as I have your permission, that is,' but she held her tongue.

'Lord Astbury was hoping you'd join him. He wanted to speak to you about that story the Indian gentleman gave him and he's invited him here again for dinner tomorrow night. You will be available then, won't you?'

'Yes, of course. Please send my apologies and tell him I look forward to seeing him tomorrow.'

'Right then, I'll see you later, dear. I'll be waiting up until you're safely home. His Lordship always likes me to lock and bolt the house before I go to bed.'

'There's no need, I don't want to keep you up. Perhaps I could borrow a key just for tonight?'

'That really won't be necessary,' Mrs Trevathan said firmly.

'Okay,' Rebecca conceded. 'I won't be very late, I'm sure. By the way, I have something to ask you,' she added tentatively. 'What part of the house is His Lordship's bedroom in?'

'In the west wing corridor, on the other side of the main staircase. Why do you ask?' Mrs Trevathan looked both surprised and defensive at Rebecca's question.

'Oh, it's nothing, I just thought I heard someone talking outside my door last night, but I was probably dreaming.'

'Yes, I'm sure that was the case. Have a nice evening, dear.'

As Rebecca walked across the drive towards James, who was waiting for her in Graham's car, her mind was awhirl. If Anthony slept at the other end of the house, he couldn't possibly have heard her cry out last night. So what had he been doing standing outside her bedroom door?

James jumped out to open the passenger side door for her. 'Darling, you look so – modern!' he exclaimed jokily.

They gossiped about the shoot on the drive to the Rugglestone Inn. On arrival, they were seated in a discreet corner.

James went to the bar and returned with a bottle of wine. He sat down and poured some into the glass in front of Rebecca.

'That's enough!' she countered when it was half full. 'After my terrible migraine, I don't want to risk doing anything to bring it back.'

'Not much of a drinker, are you?'

'You say that as if it's a bad thing,' she chided him.

'Of course not. When I went to Hollywood I noticed all the American actors seemed to be teetotallers. Whereas the British are a bunch of raging alcoholics. Cheers.' James clinked his glass against hers. 'Here's to celebrating one's vices. So,' he continued with a smile, 'how's life at Astbury Hall?'

'Well, between you and me, the longer I stay there, the weirder it seems to me,' Rebecca confessed. 'For example, the housekeeper, Mrs Trevathan, is so protective of Lord Astbury it borders on obsessive.'

'Maybe she's in love with him; female servants often fall head over heels for their employers. It's a cliché, but it happens.'

'Possibly, but also, she's constantly in my room, fussing over me, bringing me things to eat and drink.'

'Sounds like heaven to me. I rather enjoy an attentive woman fussing over me,' James said, grinning.

'I know she's only trying to be kind, but I feel like she never leaves me alone.'

'I would have thought it was rather wonderful living like a princess in a palace and being waited on hand and foot. We don't even have room service past ten o'clock at our hotel.' James raised his eyebrows. 'Anyway, surely it's done you good to have some peace for a while, given the circumstances?'

'Yes, that part has been wonderful. Sorry if I'm sounding like a brat. I guess I just haven't been feeling very well.'

'And what about the enigmatic Lord Astbury? He hasn't tried to jump you yet, has he?'

'God no!' Rebecca rolled her eyes. 'I get the feeling he isn't very interested in girls – or boys, or any relationship really.'

'Well, I can't make him out at all,' agreed James. 'Living in that great house alone for all these years, no Internet or modern conveniences – he's a strange one, that's for sure.'

'I like him actually, and I agree, he's unusual, but there's something so sad about him. I sometimes just want to throw my arms around him and give him a hug,' Rebecca admitted.

'So you *are* falling for him?'

'Absolutely not! I just feel kind of protective of him, that's all. It's like he doesn't really understand the modern world. Oh God, I'm sounding just like Mrs Trevathan!' She groaned.

'Well, given what you say, it's a good thing that he has the unnaturally devoted Mrs Trevathan to care for him,' said James equably.

'I'm beginning to wonder if that isn't half the problem.' She sighed. 'Even if he did meet somebody, I doubt they'd stand a chance with her watching their every move.'

'From everything you say, she *is* obviously in love with him. Perhaps they've been secretly shagging for years.' James grinned. 'I'm picturing clandestine rendezvous in the linen cupboard or behind the potting shed.'

'Stop it!' she begged, squirming at the thought. 'Anyway, it's none of my business, is it?'

'No, but it's always interesting to imagine other people's lives. And we *are* actors after all, darling, so analysing human behaviour is a big part of our job.'

'Another thing that bothers me is the way Anthony keeps telling me how much I look like his grandmother, Violet. It's very unsettling.'

'Do you?' asked James.

'I've seen her portrait, and yes I do, especially with my hair dyed this colour.'

'Curiouser and curiouser, as Alice once said. You're not related to this Violet, are you, by any chance?'

'No. My relatives were certainly not connected to the

English aristocracy at all, I'm sure.' Rebecca took a sip of her wine. 'Quite the opposite, actually.'

'Well, from the sounds of things, the goings-on at Astbury Hall are the basis for a much more interesting plot than the one we're currently filming,' James surmised.

'You know, sometimes, when I'm in costume, I have this weird sensation that I really *am* Violet, the woman I look like, living her life at Astbury back in the twenties. It's all rather surreal.'

'Well, try not to lose your marbles just yet, darling, it isn't a good idea to start getting fantasy and reality confused. Any time you require bringing back to the real world, I'm your man. Now, shall we order?'

A middle-aged woman appeared shyly by their table. 'Excuse me for interrupting, but aren't you James Waugh and . . . oh my God! You're Rebecca Bradley! I didn't recognise you with the different hair colour.'

'Well spotted,' said James, smiling at the woman. 'What can we do for you?'

'Well, I'd love both your autographs, and a photo, if possible.'

'Of course.' James took the proffered napkin and pen and wrote his signature on it. He was just passing the napkin to Rebecca when a flash went off in their faces.

'Thank you so much. Sorry to bother you both, and I hope you enjoy your time in England, Miss Bradley.'

As the woman left their table, Rebecca looked at James in horror. 'You let her take a photo? I never allow a fan to do that without signing a release stating it won't be for public use and will only be for their private album!'

'Calm down, Rebecca, I doubt very much whether she's

going to send it off immediately to the nearest tabloid newspaper.'

'Well, that's what usually happens to me when someone takes a photo without signing anything,' Rebecca retorted, feeling sick.

'I suppose you're far more newsworthy than I am.' James shrugged. 'Let's keep our fingers crossed that she doesn't.'

After that, the two of them were interrupted constantly by a stream of excited locals seeking their autographs.

'I think it's time to remove ourselves, don't you? I'm so sorry, Rebecca,' he said as he guided her out of the pub and into the waiting car. 'I obviously underestimated the extent of your fame, even in a sleepy little village like this one.'

'Never mind,' said Rebecca shakily. 'Forget every bad thing I said about life at Astbury earlier, I'm so glad to be going back there now, returning to the security of it. I'd almost forgotten what it's like going out to eat in public.'

'God, your life must be hell.' James rolled his eyes. 'How on earth do you cope?'

'I don't and the truth is, I haven't even agreed to marry Jack yet! It's the media who've gone into a frenzy.' She bit her lip. 'I'm not at all sure what I'm going to do.'

'I see,' said James quietly as they drove through the majestic moors under a star-filled sky.

'Anyway,' Rebecca sighed. 'I'm sure I'll sort it out when I get back to the States. I'm not saying things are over between us, I just don't want to be rushed into a wedding.'

'Well, if you ever did decide to bin him, I'd be very willing to put myself forward as an alternative suitor.'

'Well, thank you, kind sir,' Rebecca replied lightly, 'but I don't think that'll be necessary.'

'No, more's the pity.' As they pulled up in front of Astbury Hall, he said, 'I gather it's probably not very appropriate to invite me in for a coffee or a nightcap at your place, so I'll say goodnight here.'

'Goodnight, James, and thank you for supper.'

Rebecca opened the car door, but before she could get out, he grabbed her hand and pulled her back towards him to give her a warm hug.

'Remember, darling, I'm always here if you need to talk.'

'Thanks.' Releasing herself from his grasp, Rebecca climbed out, blew a kiss at him and waved as Graham and he drove away. Turning to walk up the steps and into the house, she did a double take as she recognised who was standing at the front door.

'Jack,' she said, faltering as she walked slowly up the steps towards him. 'What in the world are you doing here?' She could see his face was like thunder.

'I did try to contact you to tell you I was coming on over to see you, but you never got back to me. And I think I've just understood why. Who's lover boy in the car?' he asked her in a furious tone.

'No, Jack –' Rebecca shook her head – 'he's not – I mean, really, I –'

'Well, at least it makes me understand why I've hardly heard a peep from you in the past two weeks. So, I guess the best thing is for me to leave right now.'

'Jack, please! It's not what you think at all!'

'Then what the hell is it? If it's not him, then tell me the reason why I haven't spoken to you more than once since you left and we agreed to get married!'

'We didn't! Look, please,' Rebecca was aware that they

were standing with the front door wide open so anyone inside the house could hear the conversation. 'Please, can we at least go into the house and I can explain?'

'Jesus Christ!' Jack gave her a sudden cold smile. 'You sound just like me when I've been caught in a sticky situation.'

Mrs Trevathan appeared at the doorway, looking fraught. 'Perhaps it's best if you come in. His Lordship is asleep and I don't want him disturbed.'

'I'm sorry, Mrs Trevathan,' said Rebecca, 'I didn't know my . . . friend was arriving.'

'No, that's because you were probably in the arms of your new lover and couldn't be bothered to return my calls!'

'Please, sir, I'd be grateful if you could keep your voice down,' hissed Mrs Trevathan.

'Would you prefer that we go to a hotel?' Rebecca asked her as they followed the housekeeper in. 'My driver can take us there.'

'I doubt you'd find anywhere open at ten-thirty at night,' she said tartly, leading them along a corridor and opening the door to a small sitting room right at the end of it. 'I hope you can resolve your differences in here.' She pulled the door shut as she left.

'Is she out of Central Casting, or what? So –' Jack crossed his arms – 'would you like to tell me what the hell is going on? Is it over between us, and you just haven't had the balls to tell me?'

'I told you, Jack, I have no cellphone or Internet signal, and there's only one telephone here, which I don't like to use.'

'Well, from the looks of things, you weren't lying about that,' he conceded. 'This place is like something out of a history book. However, even if it has been difficult to get through to me, when

I've left message after message with the production office to tell you to call me, you either haven't, or you've called at a moment you know I won't pick up. I want to know why, Becks.'

Rebecca sank down onto the sofa, feeling shocked, exhausted and unprepared for this showdown. 'I guess I just wanted some time to think.'

'Think about what? Us? The night before you left I gave you an engagement ring and asked you to be my wife!' he shouted. 'Then you run off the next day and don't tell me where you are or what's going on in that head of yours, Becks. And the one time we *do* speak, you sound so distant, like you couldn't wait to end the call. I've been out of my mind ever since.' Jack swept a hand through his hair and paced back and forth. 'Can't you see what you've done is cruel, just leaving me hanging, not knowing what you were thinking? I love you, Becks. That night I was asking to spend the rest of my life with you! So why *did* you run off?'

'I didn't,' she replied, trying to remain calm. 'If you remember, I was always catching a flight to England the next day. I just decided to get on an earlier plane, that's all.'

'Come on! This is me you're talking to! Don't fob me off.'

'No, I'm sorry. I guess –' she searched for the right words – 'I got frightened. Marriage is kind of a huge deal and we've had some problems lately.'

'What problems? I didn't think we had problems, otherwise I wouldn't have asked you to marry me that night.'

'Well –' she took a deep breath – 'it's the drugs issue, Jack. It's been bad the past few months.'

'*What*? Goddammit, Becks! I can't believe you think I have a problem. Most of Hollywood is using on some level. It's normal. You're making me out to be some kind of addict!'

'I'm sorry, I just hate it, that's all.'

'Surely everyone's entitled to a little fun occasionally? Especially while I'm going through a rough patch with my career. But, of course, you wouldn't know about that, would you?' he remarked bitchily.

'Jack, please try to understand that I just needed some time to think. When I got off the plane here, I was greeted by a whole heap of journalists congratulating me on my engagement. I felt blindsided.' Rebecca wrung her hands in despair. 'Did you announce to the media we were engaged?'

'No, I didn't say anything!'

'Really? So where did they get your quotes from?'

'Where they usually get them, honey, as you well know. From my publicist, who went off the reservation with this thing.' Jack rolled his eyes. 'Come on, Becks, don't act all naive. You know how it works and I'm hurt you could have blamed me.'

'I'm sorry,' she said again, lost for anything else to say.

'But you know what really bugs me?' He stood, glaring, in front of her. 'Even if I *had* confirmed that I'd asked you to marry me, would that really have been so bad? I mean, I guess I got it wrong. I was kind of hoping you'd be happy.'

'It's a big decision and—'

'Well, you've sure had plenty of space and time here. So, can I ask if you've reached a decision?'

Rebecca remained silent, struggling with how to reply.

'Okay,' Jack sighed. 'I guess that response says it all. And that guy I saw all over you in the car – he's been comforting you while you decide, I take it?'

'No! James is an actor in the film. He's nice. I like him, but

I've hardly even seen him off set. He asked me out for something to eat tonight and that's as far as it's gone.'

Jack stared at her. 'And you really expect me to believe that? Screwing your co-star on location is the oldest story in the book. Don't patronise me by denying it. I turn up here after two weeks of silence from my girl and find her in the arms of another man. What am I *supposed* to think? You can't seriously expect me to believe that the two things aren't related?'

'Well, I can assure you they're not,' Rebecca reiterated, exhausted now. 'Ask Mrs Trevathan, if you want, she knows I've been here every night. I know how it must look to you, Jack, but it's simply not the truth.'

'Christ, you're even sounding different. That English accent of yours is another thing you seem to have acquired since you've been over here.'

They both sat in silence for a while, stung by each other's words. 'So you're saying that we're still together?' Jack said finally.

'Yes, everyone here knows we are.'

'The question is, Becks, do *you* know? Have you made up your mind yet about my proposal? Because you sure as hell have had enough time to think about it now. And if it's a "yes", it might go some way to convincing me you haven't been screwing that actor guy either.'

Rebecca's mind was a jumble of confused thoughts. 'I . . .' She put her fingers to her temple. 'Jack, I'm still in shock from your being here. Can we just both calm down and talk about this tomorrow, when we've had some sleep? I've been sick with a terrible migraine and—'

'Please don't play the sympathy card on me, Becks. You were well enough to take a trip out to dinner with lover boy earlier. Okay –' Jack sighed – 'I think I've seen all I need to. I guess the best thing for me to do would be to head back home.'

'Jack, please! Don't go,' she begged. 'We need to sort this out. Just because I ran scared about your marriage proposal doesn't mean I've decided we're over. One of our problems is that we never have enough time or privacy to really talk to each other. You're always in one place and I'm in another. Right now, we actually have those things. For both our sakes, don't you think we should take advantage of that?'

Jack slumped onto the sofa next to her and shook his head. 'I don't know what I want at this moment, Becks. Marrying you was the one thing keeping me going. My career is a mess, the good parts aren't coming in like they used to, I'm starting to think maybe I'm all washed up. I –'

Jack began to weep. Rebecca reached over and took him in her arms.

'I'm sorry, Jack, I really am. Of course you're not washed up. You've just been going through a rough patch, which I'm sure will happen to me in the future.'

'Yeah, but you've got a good few years ahead playing the lead, whereas I'm obviously past that point. And yes,' he admitted, 'I probably have been using too much recently, but I swear, Becks, I'm not an addict. I've just been feeling kind of down lately and wanted a quick fix. You believe me, don't you?'

'Yes, I believe you,' Rebecca answered. What else could she say? She'd been on the back foot since the moment Jack had appeared at Astbury.

'And it hurts me, Becks, hurts me bad that you obviously didn't think I was serious when I asked you to be my wife. That you felt I was playing a game, and you don't realise how much I love you.'

Rebecca stroked his hair gently. 'I'm sorry for hurting you, Jack. I really am.'

'Thanks. I could really use a drink. Any alcohol in this god-forsaken place?'

'If there is, I wouldn't know where to find it. Why don't we go upstairs and try to get some sleep? We can talk some more tomorrow, although I'm due on set early.'

'If you're sure you want me back in your bed,' he shrugged. 'And you can swear to me that you haven't been screwing that actor as much as you like, because as sure as hell the rest of the cast and crew will know and I won't hang around to be a laughing stock.'

'No, Jack,' Rebecca replied wearily, 'I swear that I haven't.'

Eventually, Jack gave a flicker of a smile. 'I guess I'm going to have to believe you. So, take me up to your tower, fair maiden, where I intend to make up for lost time.' He drew Rebecca to him and kissed her.

'Come on, let's go,' she said, taking his hands and pulling him up from the sofa. 'The chances are that Mrs Trevathan is still around somewhere. She refuses to go to bed until every-one else has.' Rebecca led him along the maze of shadowy cor-ridors until they arrived in the entrance hall. Mrs Trevathan appeared like a ghost beside them. 'Is your . . . *friend* wishing to stay the night?' she enquired.

'Yes, if that's okay with you and Anthony,' said Rebecca.

'Well, I can hardly ask His Lordship for permission at this time of night, can I? He'll be tucked up in bed and fast asleep. I will, of course, tell him in the morning of your young man's presence in the house. Goodnight.'

'Goodnight, ma'am, and thank you. I'm sorry to have made such a racket earlier.' Jack gave her one of his legendary killer smiles, but Mrs Trevathan's expression remained unmoved.

'Jesus, she's a weird one, isn't she?' Jack said when they'd gone upstairs and were behind Rebecca's closed bedroom door. 'Hey, is there really no lock on that door?' he asked from where he was sitting on the bed.

'Sadly not,' Rebecca replied, feeling suddenly awkward as Jack reached out his arms to her.

'Come here.'

She walked towards him and he took her into them.

'I'd forgotten how gorgeous you are. You make a beautiful blonde, that's for sure. I've missed you, Becks.'

As they made love, she tried to relax and enjoy it. Afterwards, Jack fell asleep and Rebecca padded out of bed to use the bathroom. Returning quietly, she climbed in next to him and switched off the light.

In the early hours of the morning, he woke and reached for her again in the darkness. As her body arched towards him, she had the uncanny feeling there was another presence in the room, someone watching . . .

While she rested against Jack's broad shoulder, she let the idea drift out of her head and sank into a dreamless sleep.

20

Jack's unexpected night-time arrival was the buzz on set the following day. The make-up girls went into a swoon when he arrived in their room looking for Rebecca. She watched as he charmed them and they all fell under his spell.

'You lucky, lucky girl,' said Chrissie, the chief make-up artist. 'He's even more gorgeous in real life than he is on-screen,' she commented after Jack had kissed Rebecca on the top of her head and headed off to find some breakfast from the catering van.

'When did *he* appear, then?' asked James as they took their marks on set an hour later. 'You didn't mention last night that he was coming.'

'I didn't know he was. He was waiting for me when I got out of the car. Unfortunately, he saw you give me a hug and imagined the worst.' Rebecca sighed.

'I see. Well, before it's pistols at dawn over your honour, m'lady, I'll be happy to put him straight on that score,' James joked. 'I'll tell him honestly that I'd have been delighted to avail myself of your charms any time, but sadly you would have none of it.' He gave her the benefit of one of his mischievous grins. 'He's certainly a handsome chap. If I was the competitive type, I'd feel threatened. But thankfully, I'm not.'

By lunchtime, Jack had regained his usual ebullience and was revelling in the attention he was receiving.

'I'm happy I came over here, Becks,' he said, knocking back the beer Steve had managed to procure for him. 'This is a nice crowd you're working with.'

'Yes, everyone's been very welcoming.'

'And I can't wait to put my hands up your skirt later and feel those silk stockings and that garter,' he whispered to her. 'Dig the hair colour too. It's like I got myself a whole new girl.'

After lunch, Jack pulled Rebecca inside the house. 'Come on, time for a little nap,' he said as they began to mount the stairs to her bedroom.

'Rebecca, will you be so kind as to introduce me to your visitor?' said a stern voice from behind them.

'Hello, Anthony,' said Rebecca turning round, trying not to look guilty. 'I'm sorry I haven't had the chance to introduce my boyfriend to you. He arrived unexpectedly very late last night and Mrs Trevathan said you were already asleep. This is Jack Heyward. Jack, meet Lord Anthony Astbury.'

'Hi, sir . . . I mean Lord Anthony,' said Jack, his normal confidence deserting him. He walked back down the stairs and held out his hand to Anthony. 'Thank you for letting me crash here without prior notice.'

Anthony surveyed him, stony-faced. 'It doesn't seem as though I have any say in the matter, but you are welcome nonetheless.'

'Thank you. And I'm happy for me and Becks to move out to a hotel if that would be more appropriate.'

'Mrs Trevathan has found you a bedroom here already, I presume?'

'Oh no, sir – Your Lordship. I slept with Becks – that is, in the same room.'

Rebecca wanted to giggle at Jack's obvious embarrassment.

'I see.' Anthony raised an eyebrow. 'Well, if there's anything else you require, please speak to Mrs Trevathan. I presume, Rebecca, that you won't be dining with me tonight? You do know Mr Malik is joining me?'

'No, I'm sorry, Anthony. Jack and I have a few things we need to discuss.'

'Very well.' He nodded at them and walked away across the hall.

'Jeez, if I thought the housekeeper was weird, that guy takes the cake!' Jack commented as they remounted the stairs.

'Honestly, he's nice when you get to know him. I guess he's just no good with people.'

'You mean he's a sociopath?' Jack laughed as he opened the bedroom door.

'I mean that he spends his life living alone here and doesn't interact with other people too much,' she replied defensively.

'As I said, a total weirdo. He obviously doesn't approve of me sharing a room with you. Don't tell me he only believes in sex after marriage?' said Jack, his hand snaking up her thigh to the top of her stockings.

'I don't think he believes in sex at all,' chuckled Rebecca as Jack threw her onto the bed and silenced her laughter with a kiss.

*

Later that afternoon, Rebecca was due to shoot a complicated scene which would take a couple of hours. Jack said he'd take a trip to James's hotel to use his Wi-Fi.

'You weren't joking when you said there was no signal here, were you?' he said as he kissed her on the nose. 'James suggested I have a drink with him to make up for giving me the wrong impression last night. It's okay, Becks, I believe you and I'm sorry I jumped to the wrong conclusion.'

'It's understandable you did. I'm sorry too.'

'James says I have to try a pint of bitter. Personally, I'd prefer a vodka shot or two.'

'Have a good time,' she said as he left, smiling to herself over the irony that Jack seemed to have bonded with James. In a way, they were very similar and she dreaded to think of the reaction of the local female populace when they hit the hotel bar together.

'You look perkier tonight, darling.' Robert winked at her as she arrived on set half an hour later. 'I've just watched the rushes and you're positively glowing on-screen. Perhaps we should have your fiancé's presence written into any future contracts. Only teasing, darling. Right, let's get started.'

For a change, they managed to fly through the scene, and by seven-thirty, Rebecca was back in her jeans and downstairs looking for Anthony. She wanted to find him and apologise for Jack's unexpected arrival before he had dinner with Ari. Thinking she might spy him in the gardens, she walked down the terrace steps. Instead, there, sitting on the bench in the rose garden, was Ari. He glanced up at her.

'Hello, Rebecca.'

'Hi, what are you doing sitting outside?'

'Mrs Trevathan told me Anthony wasn't down yet and to take a stroll in the gardens whilst I waited. To be honest, I don't think she likes me.' He sighed.

'I don't think she likes anyone who disturbs her routine,' said Rebecca.

'Shall we take a walk?' Ari stood up.

'Why not?'

'It's so beautiful here, isn't it? The English countryside has such a –' Ari searched for the word as they strolled across the lawn – 'serenity to it, a quality one finds so rarely in Mumbai.'

'Or in New York,' said Rebecca.

'Is that where you live?'

'Yes.'

'Well, it's the sense of space here that's so different from India. The cities of my homeland are so overcrowded – everyone fighting for their own few inches of room. And the noise on the streets never ceases day and night. Even in our temples, people sing and chatter, just as they do in the streets outside. To find any peace is almost impossible.'

'I've never been to India,' said Rebecca. 'In fact, I've hardly travelled outside the States at all. It's interesting you talk of it being so hectic. All the books I've read tell of people going there to find some sort of inner peace.'

'Oh, there's an awful lot of that,' Ari agreed. 'But then, if you're living in one room with your elderly relatives, your husband and your children and only have a few rupees to buy rice, you need a strong sense of faith. Here in the West, perhaps faith in something larger than oneself isn't so necessary any longer. Physical comfort – materialism, if you like – is the enemy of any serious spirituality, I think. When we're warm and well-fed, our souls can be empty and we still make it through the day. And that, as I've discovered recently, is the greatest poverty of all,' he added with a sigh.

'I've never thought of it like that, but you're right.'

'Well, perhaps I've come away to England to seek my soul,' Ari said with a glimmer of a smile, as he stared at the deepening amber glow of the sunset.

'It's sad, but I know of very few people who are truly *happy*,' said Rebecca. 'Everyone is so greedy. They're never satisfied with what they have.'

'In my country, we're taught that nirvana is achieved by letting go of worldly possessions. Conveniently, if you're a poor Indian, you rarely have any to begin with. I think that so much depends on our expectations of what our life should be. The less you expect, the more content you are. See?' Ari opened his arms wide to the universe. 'We're creating our very own ashram on the grounds of a stately home in England.'

Rebecca smiled at the thought.

'It's turned chilly,' he said, 'shall we walk back?'

'Yes.'

'Are you joining us for dinner tonight?'

'No, I have a guest staying. My boyfriend arrived last night out of the blue,' she explained.

'I see. And, given our conversation on the moors the other day, how do you feel about that?' Ari asked her.

'It feels . . . okay. Better than I thought it would.'

'Good. Well, wish me luck over dinner. I hope Anthony's not too unsettled by my great-grandmother's story.'

'Well, as I don't know what happened next, I can't comment,' said Rebecca as they entered the main hall.

'I'll tell you about it sometime, but if I don't hurry up, I'll be late for my host, which won't help my quest for information.'

'Good luck,' she said as she walked towards the stairs.

'Thanks.'

Ari turned and walked into the dining room.

Anthony looked up as he entered. 'Hello, Mr Malik. Please close the door before you sit down – I would prefer that we are not overheard. How are you?'

'I'm well, thank you,' replied Ari, following Anthony's instruction and coming over to join him at the table. 'And you?'

'To be blunt, shocked by what I've read so far.'

'Yes,' Ari said, sensing Anthony's tension.

Anthony poured some wine into Ari's glass. 'So,' he sighed, 'we must talk about the past . . .'

England,

1917

21

Anahita

Back at school, I concentrated hard on my exams, knowing that if I were to dare to try to enter the British medical profession, then my results would need to be above exceptional. My matriculation exams took place in a blur of late nights, headaches and worry. I thought I had acquitted myself well, but I wouldn't know my results until late summer.

Immediately after the end of term, before I took up my post as nursemaid to Selina's baby, I left Eastbourne with my friend Charlotte, the vicar's daughter, to journey up to her home in Yorkshire. I had professed to her many times my wish to see the parsonage where my beloved Brontë sisters had lived.

Charlotte's father was away in Africa preaching, and you may remember that I've already told you that her mother had died the previous year. Charlotte's twin brother, Ned, was sweetness itself, and they both accompanied me from the rectory on the bus up to Haworth Moors.

That evening, the three of us sat outside in the pretty rectory garden and ate supper together.

'What will you do now your education is finished?' I asked Ned as we drank coffee.

'Sadly, unless this war ends pretty damned quickly, and now we all doubt it will, I'll be in the army within six weeks. Not really my bag, fighting,' Ned added complacently, 'I'd rather follow the Brontës down their writing line.'

'You're not interested in becoming a vicar like your father, then?'

'No fear! If I had any faith before this war began, sadly, I've lost it now.'

'Oh, Ned,' countered Charlotte, 'don't say that, please, I'm sure it'll be over soon.'

'And we must never lose faith, Ned,' I added. 'What else would we have if we did?'

The next day, as Charlotte went off to visit a relative, Ned and I walked together on Keighley Moors. We talked of literature, a little of philosophy, and he asked me about my former life in India. I liked his thoughtful, gentle nature, and I admit to thinking of him quite often in the following months. The next morning, I said a tearful goodbye to Charlotte at Keighley railway station and began the long journey down to Devon.

'Anni! Dear Anni, welcome!' Selina threw her arms around me and gave me a smile of genuine pleasure, as I climbed down from the trap. 'Do come in, and many apologies for not being able to send a car to the station for you. Petrol rationing really has bitten here, and as we live so far from anything useful, we've had to safeguard it with all our might. I've put you in the room next to the nursery on the main floor,' she said as she led me up the stairs. 'Little Eleanor mostly sleeps through the night, but I thought it would be nice if you were close to her in case she does wake.'

'Thank you,' I said, overwhelmed by her warm reception. 'You do know I have little experience looking after young children?'

'Anni, you helped bring Eleanor into the world! I trust you completely. There now,' she said as she threw open my bedroom door, 'will this suffice?'

I looked around the room with its superb view over the gardens and the moor beyond. 'Yes, it's lovely, thank you.'

'May I ring for some tea to be brought up to you here?'

'Actually, I'd prefer to go down and see all my friends in the kitchen. I'll take tea there.'

'I'm so glad you are here, Anni. You can't know what a nightmare it's been to find someone suitable to help me with Eleanor. The ancient nursemaid Mother found me was ghastly, so I sent her packing, which didn't please Mother at all.' Selina rolled her eyes. 'For the past few months, I've been taking care of Eleanor myself. Now, when you're settled and have said hello to everyone in the kitchen, come and see us both in the nursery.'

As I unpacked my trunk, I couldn't help but smile at the notion that a mother would consider it outrageous that she should have to take care of her own child herself. When I had tidied myself up, I went downstairs to see the kitchen. The staff clustered around me, Mrs Thomas pressing cakes and tea on me, Tilly hugging me tightly, and I felt a warm glow of belonging.

After that, I went back upstairs to see Eleanor in her nursery. Now almost three years old, she was a delightful, pretty little girl and she took to me immediately. With her mother watching, I bathed her, put her in her nightgown and sang her to sleep in her bed.

'You are a wonder,' said Selina as we tiptoed out of the room, 'Eleanor seems to adore you already. I was just thinking, Anni, that perhaps when she's settled with you, I might go to London. I haven't been out of this house for a year and there are so many friends I'd like to see.'

'Of course, Lady Selina. That's what I'm here for. As long as you trust me, you can go anywhere you wish.'

'Then I just might! It's been so miserable here. Later on, I'd like you to join Mother and me for dinner. I'm longing to hear how Minty, Indira and the Cooch Behar family are getting along.'

I put on my best dress from Harrods and went down to have dinner in the formal dining room. Lady Astbury treated me with her usual disdain and hardly uttered a word directly to me. I knew she was uncomfortable having me, a mere nurse-maid, at the table. Selina, however, enjoyed my stories of the time Indira and I had spent in London when the Maharani had managed to come to England on the troop ship.

'Mother, as Anni is now here to care for Eleanor, I thought I might go to London next week, if I may?' Selina suggested over pudding.

I felt terribly sad for her, having to ask permission from her mother when she herself had been a married woman and had run a household of her own. Fate had decreed that Selina's in-dependent life had ended before it had properly begun.

'If you must, Selina, dear.' Lady Astbury looked disap-proving. 'Are you sure you're comfortable with the child, Miss Chavan?' she asked me. 'I certainly shan't have time to see to it.'

'Of course, Lady Astbury. Eleanor and I will be fine,' I replied.

A few days later, Selina was ready to set off to London. Her face was a mixture of excitement and trepidation as she donned her travelling gloves and climbed up into the trap to ride to the station.

'You enjoy yourself, Lady Selina. You're young and beautiful and deserve to have some fun after such a difficult time,' I told her.

'Thank you, Anni, you always know the right thing to say. Please do send a telegram to our London address if there are any problems with Eleanor.'

'I will, I promise,' I said as I waved goodbye.

As it turned out, Selina, content that all was as it should be with her daughter, extended her stay in London for almost a month. *And who could blame her?* I thought to myself one evening. Astbury had a pall of despair hanging over it. Even I, who was not given to notice inconveniences such as the lack of hot water or the crumbling masonry on the exterior of the house, was aware of the fact that it was falling into a state of disrepair.

Added to which, the son and heir of the house, my beloved Donald, was still away fighting abroad. No one had heard from him in weeks, and as I wandered down to the stables with Eleanor to pet the horses, I rested my head against Glory's sleek mane.

'Your master will be home soon, I promise,' I whispered to her.

As August came, I watched the glowing fields of corn turn brown as they were left uncut, because there was not enough manpower to harvest and thresh the crop. The sheep out on the moors had remained unsheared, sweating through the summer in their heavy woollen coats when their warmth could have clothed many a soldier in freezing foreign parts.

At the head of this chaos sat the stoic figure of Maud Astbury. I watched her sometimes, as she took tea on the lawn at three-thirty p.m. sharp every day, then walked to the private chapel in the house at six, her routine undisturbed as the estate drew to a standstill about her.

I tried to be understanding, reminding myself that when she had married Donald's father twenty-five years before, it had been a different era. She hadn't been raised to single-handedly take charge of such a huge responsibility as Astbury. I explained this to the servants, who had started to grumble at their mistress's seeming inability to improve the sorry state of affairs.

'Then Her Ladyship should blinking well *learn* how to run things,' commented Mrs Thomas. 'If she doesn't do something soon, there'll be nothing left here for the young lord to return to!'

'Let's hope it's not all down to you, Eleanor,' I whispered to her one afternoon as I took her for her afternoon walk across the park. 'I only pray my spirits were right, and your uncle will return safe and sound.'

I received the results of my matriculation in the middle of August. I had passed with flying colours and the slow, dreary summer had convinced me that, unlike the other residents of Astbury Hall, I was not prepared to sit around and wait for the war to end in order to begin my life.

A couple of days after Selina returned from London, I went to see her.

'Lady Selina,' I began, 'I've decided that I do indeed wish to help in the war effort. I've applied to join the Voluntary Aid Detachment.'

'Oh dear.' Selina looked despondent. 'The Maharani did mention you might wish to do so at the end of the summer, but I was rather hoping you'd forgotten about the idea.'

'I'm afraid I haven't. I begin my nursing training in London in September. I understand you'll have to find someone else to take care of little Eleanor, but I've noticed that Jane, the new young maid from the village, has a particular liking for her, and Eleanor seems fond of her, too. I think you might find she can care for her very well indeed.'

Selina gave a long sigh. 'Well, Anni, I hope you know what you're letting yourself in for. One of my friends joined the VADs and lasted a week. She had to empty bed pans!' She wrinkled her nose. 'I suppose it would be against King and country to ask you to reconsider, so of course you must go. So I shall just sit here in this godforsaken pile of ours and make up a four for the weekly game of bridge with Mother, the priest and his seventy-year-old sister!'

On instinct, I took one of her small, pale hands in mine. 'Lady Selina, I can promise you that there's much happiness coming in your future. In fact, I think you may have already sensed it whilst you were in London.'

She stared at me in amazement. 'Oh, Anni, how can you know these things? Yes, there was one man, but, of course, I'm only widowed nearly a year, and Mother certainly wouldn't approve of him. He's a foreigner, a French count who's working in London as liaison on behalf of the French government.'

She blushed prettily and looked up at me shyly. 'To be perfectly blunt, Anni, I like him far more than I should.'

'I promise you, Lady Selina, if you follow your heart and don't let others persuade you otherwise, then all will be well.'

'Thank you, Anni, thank you. You seem to give hope to everyone around you.'

'I only say what my instincts tell me.'

'Well, may *I* say that you deserve someone special too.'

'Thank you, Lady Selina.' As I walked away, I doubted that even *she* would approve if she knew who I wished that person could be.

22

November 1918, Northern France

My child, I don't wish to go into detail about what I saw during my time nursing our poor boys in France. You will have read in the history books, I'm sure, just how dreadful it was. I can only say that anything they might report can never describe the true horror I witnessed.

I was sent out to France a few weeks after my initial training. I'd proved adept and they were desperate for nurses to care for those wounded on the front line. Like everyone else who was present at that time, it left memories which remain indelibly imprinted on my soul. The utter despair that comes from watching the human race destroy itself tested my faith. I was merely grateful that my mother had taken me when I was young out to the villages in Jaipur and that I'd seen true suffering before. At least I was more prepared for it than most.

I will tell you, though, that I bumped into Ned, my friend Charlotte's twin brother. He was in my field hospital for a few days with a deep gash to his forehead. I bound it for him, and it was a pleasure to see a familiar face from a more tranquil time in my life.

Ned must have felt the same, and as he was stationed near our hospital behind the lines, during our rare time off he used to take me to the local town of Albert, where we'd have at least a few hours' respite. We talked about books, art, theatre – anything that wasn't to do with the dreadful reality we both faced daily.

I was with him on the day the Armistice was finally declared. By then, the trenches were half empty, partly due to the horrific second battle of the Somme and the fact that there seemed little point in shipping in replacement cannon fodder, as it became more apparent that the Germans would have no choice but to surrender.

We were among a crowd of nurses and soldiers who drove in a jeep to Albert, none of us daring to believe it could actually be true. Soldiers of all nationalities were pouring into the town square from along the front line – English, French, American and even Indian – and a makeshift band played together that night in a euphoric cacophony of joyous sound.

I vividly remember someone letting off fireworks, and the entire square quietening suddenly. Our senses were alert, afraid that we had been wrongly informed and it was the sound of German rockets. But as the fireworks blazed into the sky, the sparkling colours and patterns of light assured us that it was not.

And it was just after the fireworks that I received a tap on my shoulder.

I was in Ned's arms at the time, dancing to the tunes of the Dixieland Jazz Band. We paused and I glanced round, and there, looking like an aged shadow of his former boyish self, was Donald Astbury.

'Anahita? Is it you?'

'Donald?' I was holding my breath, hardly daring to believe it.

'Yes.' He smiled. 'Selina wrote and told me that you'd joined the VADs, but what a coincidence to find you here tonight!'

Ned was standing to attention – Donald was a senior officer – so I dutifully made the introductions and the two men shook hands.

Donald looked down at me with affection in his eyes. 'Do you know, Sergeant Brookner, the last time I saw this young lady, she was nearly fifteen years old. And now look at you, Anni!' His eyes swept up and down my body admiringly. 'All grown up. I hardly recognised you. And,' Donald continued explaining to Ned, 'it was also Anni who told me I would see the war out safely. Many were the times I'd be in the trenches and look at your letter, Anni, and believe that I would get through. So,' Donald smiled suddenly, his weary, grey face lighting up, 'here I am!'

The musicians began to play a chorus of 'Let Me Call You Sweetheart'.

'Would you mind, old chap, if I had this dance with Anni?' Donald asked Ned.

'Of course not, sir,' said Ned with a trace of sadness in his voice.

'Thank you. Come on, Anni, let's go and celebrate this happy occasion.' Donald took my hand and swept me off into the crowd.

I'm ashamed to say that I didn't return to Ned's arms that night. Donald and I danced the night away together in that village square of northern France as though our lives were just beginning. And perhaps, in many ways, they were.

'I can't believe how you've grown up!' he said to me a hundred times. 'Anni, you're so beautiful!'

'Please –' I blushed each time he said it, 'my dress is three years old and my hair hasn't been cut in over eighteen months.'

'Your hair is glorious,' said Donald, running his fingers through it. '*You* are glorious! We were meant to meet here tonight.'

I understood that everyone was carried away that night on a kind of euphoria which is impossible to describe. As Donald showered me with compliments and told me that he'd thought about me every day for the past three years, I sealed them in a box away from my heart, because I understood why he was saying them.

As the square slowly emptied on that frosty November night, Donald and I sat on the edge of the fountain in the centre of it and gazed up at the stars in the clear bright sky.

'Cigarette?' he offered.

I took one and we sat close together, smoking companionably.

'I really can hardly believe it's over,' he said in wonder.

'No, although I must be returning to the hospital soon. I still have many sick and wounded patients who need me, Armistice or not.'

'I'm sure they've all flourished under your care, Anni. Truly, you were born to be a nurse.'

'In the future, I'd prefer to see more of my patients survive.' I shuddered. 'I did all I could, but on so many occasions I simply couldn't help. I think I might like to continue it once the war is over.'

'It *is* over, my dearest Anni,' Donald teased me, and we

both chuckled at the phrase the world had used every day for the past four years.

'I really must be getting back now. Matron will flay me alive as it is.'

'I doubt it, not tonight. But if you must go, then I'll accompany you.'

'Surely it's out of your way?' I said as I stood up.

'No matter. Tonight, I feel I could walk a million miles.'

We strolled out of the village arm in arm and along the deserted road, the air still acrid from months of shellfire.

'You know, I really do believe that you were my talisman,' said Donald as we neared the entrance to the camp which contained my hospital. 'I went over the top countless times and yet never received so much as a scratch.'

'I knew you were born lucky.' I grinned at him.

'Maybe, but you helped me believe it. And that was the important bit. Goodnight, Anni.'

Donald bent down then, and he kissed me. And I'm embarrassed to say that the kiss didn't stop for a very long time.

The following two weeks were busy for me as we patched up the men still in our hospital in preparation for their journey back to England. Donald arrived every night in his jeep to take me out. The other nurses raised their eyebrows and tittered amongst themselves.

'Our Anni's got herself a young man, and an officer at that! And he's got two legs and two arms left as well. Lucky you!' said one of the nurses, not unkindly.

I tried desperately to seal my heart from Donald and the damage I was aware he could do to it. Neither of us, in that precious moment in time we shared together – a world without rules or convention, or society telling us how we must behave or whom we should love – talked of the future. We simply lived in the moment, relishing every second of it.

As it drew to a close, and I was due to travel back across the Channel to England on a hospital ship with some of my patients, the intensity between us grew to a fever pitch.

'I'll see you in London, won't I?' Donald asked me desperately on our last night together. 'And you will come down and stay at Astbury? You know how everyone adores you there.'

'Apart from your mother.' I rolled my eyes as I sat comfortably in his embrace in his jeep.

'Don't mind her, she doesn't like anyone. God, I couldn't wait for the war to be over when it was raging, but now I have to contemplate facing dear Mama and the estate, I'm feeling far less euphoric.' He grimaced. 'Astbury legally passed over to me on my twenty-first birthday a couple of weeks ago. So now it's entirely my responsibility.'

'I think you'll have some work to do there, yes,' I replied, the queen of understatement.

'Where will you be staying when you get back?'

'There's a nurses' hostel near the hospital where I'm being sent with my patients,' I answered. 'It's in Whitechapel, and I'll be working there for the foreseeable future.'

'Anni,' Donald said, a sudden urgency in his voice, 'don't go back tonight. Come with me to the village. I have a room there. At the very least, we can be together for a few hours more.'

'I . . .'

'Really, Anni, I'm a gentleman, and I wouldn't do anything to compromise your virtue.'

'Hush,' I interrupted him, unable to stop myself. 'I'll come with you.'

Of course, it was as impossible that night, as it has ever been the world over, for two people in love not to wish to be joined in our special, human way. In that small darkened room, the soft light from the square seeping in between the shutters, as Donald gently removed my clothes, I didn't feel one iota of guilt. As he kissed me all over my body, and we became one, I felt my faith in the gods and in humanity restored.

'I love you, my darling Anni, I must be with you,' he moaned, 'I need you, I need you . . .'

'I love you too,' I whispered into his ear as our urgency increased, 'and I always will.'

23

I didn't see Donald for the first month after we returned to England. It was Christmas – the first he'd had with his family at Astbury Hall for three years. But he wrote to me every day; long, heartfelt letters, telling me how much he missed me, loved me and couldn't wait until he was with me again.

I wrote back in return, letters full of my daily life at the hospital. Even though my heart was fit to burst with love for him, I restrained myself from letting it flow as completely onto paper as he did. Now I was back in England, the pragmatic side of me knew that I couldn't allow myself to become completely swept up by him, for I simply couldn't see a way in which we could be together in the future. I was kept very busy, thank the gods, at the London Hospital in Whitechapel, and one afternoon just after the New Year, I was called into Matron's office and asked to sit down.

'Nurse Chavan, I've been discussing you today in my weekly meeting with the doctors. We all agree you have a special aptitude for nursing. Your record in France goes before you and your work here so far has been of the highest standard.'

'Thank you,' I said, feeling gratified by her praise. It didn't come often.

'Before you left for France, you were only given basic training as an auxiliary nurse, is that correct?'

'Yes, Matron, but when I was in France, it was all hands to the pump and I learned many things from the doctors as I worked. I can suture professionally, dress wounds, give injections, and I also assisted the doctors with the many emergency operations they had to perform.'

'Yes, I'm aware of all that. You also have the air of calm authority which gives confidence to your patients. I already see that the more highly trained nurses look up to you and respect you. So what we at the hospital would like to suggest is that you train further and achieve the qualifications you need to become a nurse, and then perhaps a ward sister.'

I was overwhelmed, I had no idea my prowess had been so remarked upon. 'Thank you, Matron, I'm honoured.'

'You would still be based here at the hospital, but three days a week you would go to our on-site college to learn the appropriate technical side of the nursing you missed out on. You would officially qualify as a nurse in a year's time. How do you feel about that?'

'I'd very much like to take the course,' I replied.

'Good. I shall enrol you immediately and you can start next week.'

'Thank you, Matron,' I said as I stood up and left the room. Outside, I gave an involuntary whoop of pleasure and excitement, thinking how proud my father and mother would have been of me. Two days later, to complete my happiness, Donald arrived in London. He was staying at the Astburys' London house in Belgrave Square, where Selina was currently installed with little Eleanor and her nursemaid Jane, the girl I'd suggested take over from me.

Knowing he was coming, I'd already booked the day off from the hospital, and I took a bus to Selfridges and spent some of my hard-earned wages on a new and very modish coat for the occasion. As I approached Piccadilly Circus – we had agreed to meet under the statue of Eros – my heart began to beat very hard against my chest. Perhaps Donald had changed his mind and wouldn't come, I thought as I searched the crowds for his familiar face. But, eventually, there he was, looking around for me as anxiously as I had been for him. He walked towards me and swept me into his arms.

'Darling, oh God, I've missed you so much!' He tipped up my chin and studied my face. 'Have you missed me?'

'Of course I have, and I have so much to tell you. Shall we have tea somewhere?' I suggested.

'Yes,' he nuzzled his face into my neck, 'although at this moment, a cup of tea is the last thing on my mind. But, hey ho, it'll have to do.'

We sat together in Lyons' Corner House on Shaftesbury Avenue, talking avidly until it had grown dark outside. Sweetly, Donald seemed to be just as thrilled as I was about my career promotion.

'You're a wonderful nurse,' he said admiringly. 'All of the chaps I know that passed through your tender hands in France remember you. And of course, my sister adores you. Talking of which, I told her I was meeting you today and she said that she and Eleanor would love to see you, too. Can you possibly come to the house tomorrow night? You could see Eleanor and then stay on for dinner with Selina, myself and her new *amour* – Henri Fontaine.'

'Lady Selina has fallen in love? I knew it!' I clapped my hands in delight at the news.

'Yes, very much so,' confirmed Donald. 'Although, for reasons you can well understand, presently Mother knows nothing about it. She wouldn't approve at all.'

'I shall have to check my roster, but yes, I'm sure I can manage it. It'll be much easier once I'm at college next week. I finish my classes at four o'clock. Does Lady Selina know about . . . us?' I asked him tentatively.

'Well, I haven't gone into detail, especially over Christmas with Mother around, but Selina certainly knows I saw a lot of you in France. And of course,' he smiled, 'she'll guess the minute she sees us together.'

'And you don't mind her knowing?'

'Anni, why on earth would I mind? Selina adores you, and besides, she's yet to tell Mother what brings *her* so often to London,' Donald added.

'Your mother doesn't like foreigners in general,' I agreed quietly.

'My mother lives in the past, in a different era. You know that, Anni.'

'Yes, I do. But—'

'Hush!' Donald put a finger to my lips. 'She isn't here now and I don't wish the spectre of her to spoil this rare time we have together.'

I checked my watch and realised curfew in the nurses' hostel was in less than an hour. 'I must go,' I said.

'Must you?'

'Yes.'

Donald signalled for the bill and we stepped outside into the crisp night air. As we walked back up to Piccadilly Circus

LUCINDA RILEY

so that I could catch my bus, he pulled me into a doorway and kissed me passionately.

'So,' he said, finally releasing me, 'I'll see you at our house tomorrow night? Belgrave Square, number twenty-nine. I have an appointment at my club with the family bank manager tomorrow at six, so depending on how ghastly the finances look, I might be a little delayed.'

'Are they very bad?'

'Put simply, Anni, if the bank refuses to extend the loan any further, I'll have no choice but to sell the entire estate – the Hall and all the land. So yes,' Donald said with a sigh, 'I hardly doubt they could be worse.'

'Don't give up hope yet. I'll see you tomorrow.' I kissed him and rushed off to climb aboard the bus.

The following evening, I travelled to Belgrave Square. Selina and Eleanor were just as pleased to see me as Donald had said they would be.

'Anni, what a pleasure it is to have you here,' Selina said as she led me over to Eleanor, who was looking at a picture book on the rug in front of the fire. 'Eleanor, look, it's Anni.'

Eleanor was soon on my knee as Selina called for the maid to bring tea. 'Now, whilst Donald is gone, I want you to tell me all about your adventures in France. And of course,' she smiled at me conspiratorially, 'how you came to meet him there.'

I gave her a carefully edited version of my time working behind the front line, and an equally brief outline of my renewed acquaintance with Donald. Selina called for Jane to take Eleanor upstairs to bed and once we were alone, she continued her interrogation.

'Oh, Anni, so you and Donald re-met on Armistice Day, then danced the night away together in France. How wonder-

324

fully romantic. But' – she leaned towards me and lowered her voice – 'I don't think you're telling me everything. I know my little brother very well, and the minute I saw him I knew he was in love. Oh please, Anni, you can trust me. If it's with you, I think it's adorable!' She gave her bell-like laugh.

'I think you would have to ask Donald that question.'

'Don't you worry, I will. Remember, it was you that said there was someone waiting for *me*. And you were right, Anni, there was. I'm so very happy.'

'I'm truly glad for you, Lady Selina.'

'Please, just call me Selina; one way or another, it feels as if we're almost family.' She smiled. 'Anyway,' she continued, 'I will trust you to tell you that I'm madly in love with Henri, and that we plan to be married as soon as possible, whatever Mother has to say about it. I do hope you'll like him, he'll be here at any minute. You know, Anni, sometimes I feel dreadfully guilty. I don't think I ever felt for Eleanor's poor, dead father the way I do about Henri.'

'Yes, but we can never choose who we truly love, can we?' I replied.

'No, it seems we can't. Hugo was a good man, and perfect for me in terms of position, as Mother always said, but he didn't ever grab at my heart.'

'So will you stay here in London or move to France?'

'A bit of both, I think. Henri has a château down in the south of the country, which is apparently beautiful, but he also loves London.'

At that moment, Donald entered the room. He looked weary, but his eyes lit up as he saw me. He made to come to me, but then noticed his sister sitting opposite and checked himself.

'Selina, you look as beautiful as ever tonight,' he said. 'And Anni, how are you?' He took my hand in his and kissed it, his eyes saying all he felt that his body could not.

'I'm well, thank you, Donald,' I answered formally, a twinkle in my eye.

I could see that Selina was watching the two of us in fascination, but there was no time for her to question either of us further. The drawing-room door opened again and the maid ushered in a diminutive man with a moustache and hair of a length that was considered downright bohemian in England.

'Henri, welcome.' Selina went to him and they, too, went through the machinations of formality. 'May I present to you Lord Donald Astbury, my brother, and our friend Miss Anahita Chavan.'

'*Enchanté, mademoiselle*,' the count said as he kissed my hand.

'Now then, who would like what to drink?' said Selina.

Once we had all settled and the wine had flowed over dinner, our reserve slipped. The four of us began to discuss Selina and Henri's plans for the future.

At one point, Henri leaned across to me and whispered, 'Is their mother really as frightening as Selina describes to me?'

'Sadly, yes. And she doesn't like foreigners.'

Sharing a mutuality of situation, we threw back our heads and laughed at the irony of the dinner tonight. As Donald's hand snaked under the table towards me and rested on my knee, Henri continued to confide in me.

'I'm to go with Selina to Devon in the next two weeks to tell "*Madame le Dragon*" that I wish to marry her daughter. Will I be eaten alive?'

'There's every chance you may come back short of a finger

or two. But I doubt she'll touch the rest of you. You are French, after all, and wouldn't be to her taste.'

After dinner, as was the custom of the time, Donald and Henri stayed at the table for brandy and cigars and Selina and I departed to the drawing room.

'Isn't Henri wonderful?' she said, as she sat down contentedly in the chair by the fire.

'I like him very much indeed. I think he'll make you a good husband,' I assured her.

'And as for you, I can see that Donald adores you just as Henri adores me. Perhaps we could have a joint wedding?' she said, bubbling over with laughter.

'Selina,' I said, suddenly sombre, 'I think your circumstances are very different from those of Donald. He's the heir to Astbury. As he once told me, he must marry someone who can help him save it. You know all too well how much in need of repair it is.'

'I'm sure you're right, but I'm not involved in the business side, you see.'

'Well, Donald has told me the family finances are desperate.'

'But surely what he needs is someone strong like you next to him, who can give him support as he tries to put the estate right?' countered Selina.

'Unfortunately, we both know your mother won't see it like that.'

'Do you love him, Anni?'

'More than the earth and sky,' I replied honestly. 'But I don't wish to ruin his future, Selina. I have no dowry, and mixed-race marriages are still very much frowned on in England. Not that Donald has asked me, of course,' I added hastily.

'Nonsense! Only a week ago, I received a letter from my friend Minty, Indira's big sister, saying one of her friends had recently married an Englishman.'

'Yes, and perhaps her friend was a princess, not a mere nursemaid.' I sighed. 'We both know your mother would be horrified.'

'Damn my mother! Donald is of age, he's Lord Astbury and in charge of the estate *and* his own destiny. You make him happy, Anni. What else matters?'

We discussed the situation no further as the men arrived in the drawing room to join us. I checked my watch and saw that it was past eleven o'clock. I had a late pass, but I had to be back at the nurses' hostel by midnight.

'I must go,' I said to Donald quietly, not wishing to break up the party.

'Of course. I'll call a taxi to take you home.'

I said my goodbyes to Selina and Henri, and Donald escorted me down the steps of the house. As we stood in Belgrave Square waiting for a taxi to pass by, I turned to him.

'How was your meeting with your bank manager?'

'As dreadful as I expected,' he said. 'The estate is on the verge of bankruptcy and I was told categorically tonight that the bank can't extend the loan. Mother has let it go to rack and ruin, with no thought for prudence.'

'I'm so sorry, Donald,' I said softly.

'Well, as the bank manager said to me, I'm not the only one who's arrived home after four years of war to find a situation like this. The trouble is, the rot had set in long before. My father died ten years ago. The upshot is that the estate will have to be sold. It's as simple as that.'

'It may be simple to you, but do you think your mother will accept it?' I asked him.

'She'll have to, like all of us. There is no choice. Sadly,' Donald sighed, as he hailed a cab for me, 'nothing is as it once was.'

I gave the address to the driver and Donald pressed a bank note into my hand as he held me close.

'Shall I see you tomorrow?' he asked.

'I don't finish my ward shift until eight.'

'Then I'll come and see you and we'll have dinner somewhere in Whitechapel.'

'I don't think you'll like it there,' I said, as the taxi prepared to move off.

'I didn't like France much either until I met you again.' He smiled. 'I'll see you outside the hospital at eight, Anni. Goodnight.'

I sank back onto the soft leather seat, my mind turning over the events of the evening and what Selina had said. If the Astbury Estate was to be sold because it had to be, then maybe, just maybe, there was a possibility of a future for Donald and me.

Dangerously, for the first time, I began to imagine it.

One way or another during the next two weeks, Donald and I contrived to see each other every day. Selina had returned to Astbury Hall to prepare the way with her mother for Henri's imminent arrival and announcement of their engagement, so Donald and I had the London house to ourselves.

'You know, Matron may decide to strike me off for appearing undedicated,' I said as Donald and I lay contentedly together in the big bed one night. 'I've had seven all-night passes in the past two weeks.'

'But she knows too that your "aunt", a cousin to the Maharani of Cooch Behar herself, is over in England and wishes to see her niece,' Donald teased, stroking my hair softly as he did so. 'Listen, Anni.' He looked at me, suddenly serious. 'I have to return to Devon very soon to speak to my mother about selling the estate. I wanted to leave it until after Selina has announced she's marrying Henri. Too many shocks at once, well, it might be all too much for her.'

'Of course.'

'And then, there's you and me –'

'What do you mean?'

'Anni, please, you *know* what I mean. You and me,' he repeated. 'I love you, Anni. You're my best friend, my lover and the wisest and most beautiful woman I've ever met. And I want you to be my wife.'

I stared at him in amazement. 'Your wife?'

'Yes, Anni, my wife. How can you look so surprised? I just couldn't bear the thought of living without you. What better reason is there to marry than that?'

'There isn't one. But—'

'No buts.' Donald put a finger to my lips. He wrapped his arms round me and we wriggled into a new and more comfortable position. 'I know you're aware of the problems I'm currently facing and I must deal with them one at a time. However, I want you to know that I'm determined to marry you. I hope you realise that, with things as they are, you won't be the chatelaine of a great house. There really won't be a lot left even after the Hall is sold, especially as I'll have to buy Mother somewhere suitable out of the proceeds. I was thinking that perhaps we should live here in London and think about buying a smaller house in the country when the little ones come along.'

'Oh, Donald.' At this point, I began to cry.

'Darling, what is it?'

'It's just –' I blew my nose and tried again. 'It's just that I'm shocked you've seriously considered a future with me.'

'Why? Haven't you?' Donald looked astonished and a little upset.

'Donald, don't you understand that I haven't dared to contemplate it? We're from such different worlds: I'm a penniless Indian nurse and you're a lord of the realm.'

'You're of high birth in your own country, Anni,' he reminded me.

'Yes, but like yours, our family fell on hard times. My mother married for love, you see.'

'There we are, then.' He smiled.

'But, Donald,' I steeled myself to say the words, 'you must realise it won't be just your mother who will object to our marriage. I've suffered from prejudice because of my race and the colour of my skin many times in England. Are you sure you can live with the stigma of having an Indian wife?'

'I adore the gorgeous colour of your skin, my darling,' he said as he kissed my neck. 'To be frank, whoever doesn't, I wouldn't care to know anyway.'

I stared up at him, never loving him more than I did at that moment. 'You're a very unusual man, Donald Astbury.'

'And you're an extraordinary woman. I adore you.'

When he left for Devon the following day, I actually began to imagine our future. And little by little, the box in which I'd buried my true feelings for him began to splinter and crack.

24

While Donald was in Devon, I was determined to immerse myself in my nursing course. I knew I hadn't concentrated fully on it. No matter what the future held for the two of us, this was an achievement I wanted for myself.

Perhaps it's true to say that when one is loved by another person it creates a glow of happiness and confidence that others find irresistible. Never before had I been asked out to so many dances and outings by the doctors at my hospital.

'Quite the girl of the moment,' said one of the nurses, as yet again I refused an invitation from an eligible young surgeon.

For the first time in my life, it seemed as if she might be right.

I've since learned that one must never be complacent about a special time in one's existence. It's always so fleeting, that moment when one feels invincible, and I'm sad to say that my moment came to an abrupt halt very soon afterwards. A week after Donald had left for Devon, I received a letter at the nurses' hostel, forwarded to me by Selina.

Cooch Behar Palace
Cooch Behar
Bengal

December 1918

My dearest Anni,

I have no idea where you are living since you returned from France a few weeks ago, but I thought the Astburys might. Maybe you have since written with your new address, but we both know how slow the Indian post can be. I can only say how proud we all are here of your nursing work on the front line. And I hope you are well and finally able to find your path, after the turbulence of the past four years.

Therefore this letter is hard for me to write, as I hate to call your attention away from your own life. But I need your help.

As we both know, Indira fell in love a long time ago with Prince Varun. Since the war has now ended, preparations for her marriage are going ahead. But she is point blank refusing to marry the Maharaja of Dharampur. We have all tried pleading with her, telling her that she has no choice – you can imagine the scandal if she declined at this moment – and the Maharaja is a good man, if a little older than she. Indira must do her duty for her family, whatever her heart is telling her.

She is currently refusing to eat, or, in fact, to rise from her bed at all. She tells me she wishes to lie there and die rather than marry a man she doesn't love. No one at the palace can bring her to her senses, and I beg you, Anni, as someone she loves, trusts and respects, to

333

come back home, even if just for a short time, and help
us try to make her see where her duty lies. We all feel
that you're perhaps the only person on this earth to
whom she will listen.

I enclose in this letter a first-class passage back
home. It is an open ticket, as I have no idea how long
this letter will take to reach you, but all you need to do
is contact the P&O office and arrange the exact date
you wish to leave.

I know this is a lot to ask of you, but besides, it's a
long time since you visited the country of your birth,
and we love you dearly.

My dear Anni, we need you.

With love, and very best regards . . .

The letter was signed '*Ayesha*' and bore her royal stamp beneath it.

I sat on my narrow bed in the hostel, my mind reeling as thoughts from the past assailed me. My immersion in my new English life had been so complete, it was difficult to even visualise the palace, or the faces of the people who had once meant everything to me.

Numerous thoughts ran through my head, the foremost one being: what would Donald say?

Surely it was too much to ask of me to throw up everything and return, even for a short time, to a life I'd long ago said goodbye to? I paced up and down my dormitory, realising that even if I only went to stay for two weeks, the voyage there and back would take just under two months. The timing was dreadful, could not have been more so.

But I also knew that everything I was and everything I had in my life now, I owed to the Maharani and her family, who had supported and cared for me when no one else had. The last time I had seen the Maharani, she had presented me with a choice, but this time, I knew I had none at all.

'It's a great pity,' sighed Matron the next morning, when I told her I had to return urgently to India on family business. 'Have you any idea when you'll be back?'

'I would hope within three months,' I reassured her.

'Well, what I suggest we do is put you on compassionate leave. This means we are still able to hold a place open for you both at the hospital and on your nursing course. We wouldn't want to lose you here.'

'Matron, I'm so very sorry to let you down, but I must go. It's a family matter.'

'Well, just make sure you *do* return, won't you, Nurse Chavan?'

'Of course I'll return.' I smiled at her confidently as I stood up to leave the room. 'My whole life is here in England now.'

As the Maharani had asked me to, I visited the P&O office and booked myself onto the next available passage. I sent a telegram to her letting her know when I'd be arriving and then steeled myself to tell Donald, who was due to return to London from Devon within the next few days. As I knew he would be, he was aghast when I told him.

'Oh, Anni,' he said when I broke the news on his first evening back, 'must you go?'

'Yes, I must. They're the nearest thing to family I have. The Maharani was so kind to me when I was a child and lost my mother. She was the one who sent me to England in the first place and paid for my education here.'

'But, Anni,' he persisted, 'what can you do? If Indira has made up her mind not to marry this maharaja, I hardly think that anyone, not even her oldest friend, will be able to change it. No one could tell me to stop loving you,' Donald added with a sad smile.

'You're right, I doubt I can do anything, but the Maharani has called for me and I cannot let her down.'

'How long will you be gone?'

'About three months, I think.'

Donald grabbed my hands and held them tightly. 'Promise me, not a day longer?'

'All I can promise is that I will return to England the first moment I can,' I said, frowning.

'You haven't been home to India for a long time. Maybe its charms will persuade you to stay.'

'That won't happen,' I said firmly. 'Now, tell me about Devon and how your mother took the news of Selina's engagement?'

'I've had the most ghastly ten days,' Donald admitted. 'When I arrived, Selina told me Mother virtually fainted from shock when she said she was going to marry Henri and in all likelihood live in France. Mother, of course, forbade it; said she'd never welcome her at Astbury again and would cut her off without a penny if she dared to marry Henri. Not that she has a penny to give to Selina,' Donald added morosely. 'By the time I arrived a few days later, she'd taken to her bed and re-fused to leave it. She said she was sick and didn't want to see anyone. Granted, she had a cold, but when I managed to gain entry, she was hardly at death's door. However,' he sighed, 'given the fact that she took Selina's news so badly and was obviously unwell, I hardly thought it appropriate to tell her the estate would have to be sold. Or that I was in love with you, my darling,' he added.

'No, that would definitely have been a shock too far,' I agreed.

'So, we're at an *impasse* at present. And now, hearing your news, I think that when you leave for India, I'll go down to Devon and begin to look for a buyer for the estate. And try to choose the right moment to tell Mother.'

'I don't envy you, Donald. Where is Selina now?' I asked.

'She's sailed off to France with Eleanor and Henri. He's taking her to see his château in Provence. Lucky her,' Donald mused. 'I only wish I could sail for India with you.'

'So do I,' I answered with feeling.

We sat in silence for a while, both contemplating the hand that fate had dealt us.

'You will write, won't you?' Donald urged.

'Of course I will. And it won't be for long. I'm sure the sale of Astbury will keep you busy.'

'Don't remind me. The thought of only Mother for company every day for the next few months sends shivers down my spine. And I do mean to tell her, Anni, not just about the estate, but about us and our plans for the future,' he explained. 'I had actually planned to ask you formally to marry me once I'd told her. Do the whole thing properly, go down on bended knee, produce a ring. But at the very least, I want you to understand before you leave just how serious I am about you and our future. We will be married, Anni, I swear it. It is what you want, isn't it?'

'Yes, so very much that it scares me,' I said honestly.

'So you do love me, darling?'

'*Of course* I love you, Donald.'

'I sometimes think you're far more English than I am, in the way you are able to hold your emotions in check,' he teased me. 'As you know, I've never been any good at that. I wear my heart on my sleeve and I always have. So can we say for now that we're unofficially engaged?' He kissed the tips of my fingers gently with his lips.

I looked at him with all the love I felt burning in my eyes. 'Yes, I would like that. I would like it very much indeed.'

For the following few days, with all my barriers broken down by the threat of separation and Donald's unwavering determination for us to be together, I showed my love for him openly and honestly. Already on leave from the hospital, I had to move out of the nurses' hostel, so I brought my suitcase with me and moved into Belgrave Square with Donald. He in turn gave the maid a week off so that we could have complete privacy.

We behaved just like any two young people in love, spending our days strolling through the beautiful London parks and the nights entwined in his bed. I threw caution to the wind in that regard, not taking the care I should have to protect myself, but nothing at that moment mattered more than our unfettered love.

Donald drove me down to Southampton on the day I was to leave for India. He came on-board ship with me and admired the smart cabin I'd been allocated.

'The princess returns to her palace.' He grinned as he pulled me onto the enormous bed and held me in his arms. 'Do you think anyone would notice if I hid beneath your mattress and stowed away?'

'I'm sure they wouldn't.'

'Oh, how I wish I could,' he sighed, as the ship's bell rang out to indicate that it was time for all non-passengers to leave as the ship was preparing to depart. 'But I suppose I'd better go home and try to find a way to support you in the manner to which you're obviously accustomed,' he said, making an attempt to lighten the atmosphere.

'You know I don't care about luxuries, Donald.'

'Well, that's a jolly good thing, because when you become my wife, you won't have any,' he teased.

Our mood changed as I walked with him along the corridor and out onto the deck where we would say a last goodbye.

He put his arms around me and held me tightly. 'I love you, my Anahita. Come back to me as soon as you can.'

'I will, I promise,' I said, and saw there were tears in his eyes as there were in my own.

'Right, then,' he said, after a last, lingering kiss. 'Goodbye, my darling. Take care of yourself until I can do it for you.'

'And you.' I was so choked with emotion, I could hardly speak.

He gave me a small wave as he turned from me and began to walk down the gang-plank with the last remaining guests. Just before he reached the bottom, I called out to him.

'Wait for me, Donald! However long it takes, please wait for me.'

But it was a windy day, and my words were lost on the breeze.

25

The voyage back to India was uneventful and would have been pleasant if I hadn't been missing Donald quite so much. There were any number of amusements to keep me occupied and also young men, both English and Indian, who requested my company next to them for dinner and asked me to dance with them afterwards.

I began to realise on the voyage that the gawky thirteen-year-old who had travelled across the water to England six years before had shed her skin and become an elegant and not unattractive young woman. This pleased me as it would please any woman, and for that simple reason it made me feel a little more worthy of Donald. He sent sweet telegrams to the ship full of love and humour, telling me how he had managed to sell a painting and acquire some new sheep, that a second threshing machine had been going cheap at auction. And that his mother still lay in bed, pretending to be sick. His latest telegram had made me smile:

Mother refusing to attend Selina's wedding Stop Next week in London Stop I'm to give her away Stop Us next, my darling Stop Donald xx

As the ship steamed through calm seas on its way to my homeland, I began to focus my thoughts on Indira. Knowing how stubborn she was, I doubted I could do anything to change her mind. I was hoping my attempts to make her see sense would show themselves to be fruitless and that the Maharani would thank me for at least trying. And, having done my duty, I'd be able to return to England and Donald as quickly as I could.

I did not wish to hear the voices who sang to me as I lay in bed in my cabin, rocked by a gentle sea, who told me this wouldn't be the case. I was in charge of my own destiny now, I whispered to them. I would *make* it happen, whatever the cost.

On the morning the ship docked in Calcutta, I packed my heavy woollen jumpers away at the bottom of my suitcase and put on an old summer dress that had seen better days. Then, I went up on deck and smelt the hot sultry air. Below, a colourful, noisy mass of people were waiting on the quay for their loved ones.

I was home.

The Maharani had sent Suresh, one of her aides-de-camp, to meet me and escort me by train from Calcutta to Cooch Behar. As he spoke to me in rapid Hindi, I struggled to follow him. It had been many years since I'd last conversed in my native tongue. On the long train journey up to Cooch Behar, I realised it would take time to re-acclimatise to a culture I'd almost forgotten. I suffered from the overwhelming heat, and my ears rang from the incessant noise that India and its inhabitants made. There was an urgency, an intense atmosphere which I found difficult to adjust to, so used was I now to the more measured pace of England and its residents.

I realised I had also forgotten the staggering beauty of the Cooch Behar Palace. As the chauffeur drove me through the spectacular grounds, I devoured every detail, as my eyes had been long-starved of such dramatic surroundings.

'The Maharani requests an audience with you at sunset,' Suresh informed me. 'She will come to your room. Until then, please take time to rest.'

I was given a beautiful suite in the opulent guest quarters, and as the maid bowed out of the room, I realised that perhaps Indira had no idea of my presence here. I lay down on my bed and I wondered how I, a woman currently embroiled in a clandestine affair herself, could try to persuade another that she should act against the dictates of her heart?

At six o'clock, as I smelt the *dhuan* being wafted about the palace and watched the many oil lamps being lit, the Maharani appeared in my doorway.

'Anahita,' she moved forward with her usual grace, looking as beautiful as I remembered, and took me in her arms, 'welcome home,' she said, then stood back to survey me. 'Why, you're a beautiful young woman and, I think I'm right in saying, a woman who has had many new life experiences since I last saw her. I heard about your bravery in France through Selina's letters to Minty.'

'Thank you, Your Highness, but I was only one of thousands who did what they could. I must apologise to you for not having appropriate clothes to wear here at the palace. These days, I only have Western dress,' I said, embarrassed, as I studied her exquisite sari, fashioned out of a deep purple cloth embroidered with delicate gold hibiscus flowers.

'No matter, I will have my dressmaker come to you tomorrow. Now, let us go outside and talk.'

We walked together to a courtyard full of sweet-smelling frangipani flowers and jacaranda trees. And as the sun set over the great central dome of the palace, the Maharani told me about Indira.

'She refuses to leave her room unless her father and I agree to cancel the marriage contract with the Maharaja of Dharampur and allow her to become the wife of Prince Varun. We both know that Indira is capable of being very headstrong, and I understand she believes she loves this man. But it is simply impossible, do you see?' the Maharani said, gesticulating wildly, her ringed, elegant hands betraying her tension. 'It would cause a scandal amongst the princely states in India and I do not wish for my daughter *or* my family to be at the centre of such a thing.'

'Does Indira know I'm here?'

'No, I didn't tell her. I thought it might be better if you arrived unrequested, simply wishing to see your old friend.'

'Please, Your Highness, forgive me,' I replied. 'Indira is many things, but she isn't stupid. She'll know you have sent for me.'

'Yes, you are right, of course,' the Maharani shook her head in despair, 'but you were the only person I could think of whom she might listen to. What Indira does not understand is that love can grow. My marriage to Indira's father was also arranged. He was not my choice, but I learned to love him as he did me, and we are very happy.'

'I know you are, Your Highness. Everybody sees and feels it.'

'I have also come to see that Indira was given the kind of childhood I didn't have. She's spent time in and embraced the freedoms of Western culture. She's a young woman who's grown up between two worlds. And while her father and I believed we were widening her horizons, the truth is, we confused her. We allowed her to believe she had choices that weren't ever going to be hers to make.' The Maharani stared into the approaching dusk with sadness in her eyes. 'But you, Anni,' she turned her attention back to me, 'you must know all about that.'

'Oh, I do. You find you belong in neither world.'

'At least you have no arranged marriage and can follow your heart. Sadly, Indira cannot. So, please go and see her tonight. Try to persuade her that she must see sense, that she cannot bring the shame and scandal upon her family that this would cause.'

'I don't hold out much hope.' I sighed. 'But I will do my best.'

She patted my hand. 'I know you will.'

An hour later, I was taken to Indira's room. As I entered, I saw the empty bed that I'd once slept in as a child. Indira was lying in hers next to it, her eyes closed.

'Indy?' I whispered. 'It's me, Anni, I've come to see you.'

'Anni?' Indira opened one eye and looked at me. 'Goodness, it really is you! Oh, Anni, I can't believe you've come.'

'Of course I came.'

'I'm so happy to see you.' She held out her stick-like arms to me and I put my own around her tiny frame. This time, no one had been exaggerating about the state of Indira's health. From the look and feel of her, she really was starving herself to death.

'Your mother wrote and told me you were sick, Indy,' I said as I sat down on her bed and she nuzzled into my shoulder.

'Yes, I'm sick. I don't wish to live any more,' she sighed.

There was a part of me that wanted to giggle, for Indira hadn't changed a jot. When she was a child, the world would come to an end over a simple thing she needed or wanted. I realised then that even though our problems might become more serious in adulthood, our behaviour and attitude towards them can remain much the same as from the day that we were born.

'Why is it you don't wish to live?' I asked her quietly as I stroked her hair.

'Please don't patronise me, Anni,' she sighed, removing her head from my shoulder and staring at me, her eyes luminous in her thin face. 'I know my mother sent for you and has probably already talked with you since your arrival, so you know why I'm like this. And if you've come to try and convince me otherwise, then please, just go away now. Because I won't listen. I won't listen. Oh, Anni, I –'

Indira cried then, great racking sobs that shook her frail body. I sat with her calmly, just as I did with my patients, saying little and waiting until the wave of emotion subsided.

'Here, have a handkerchief,' I said eventually, as the sobs diminished.

'Thank you,' she snuffled.

'Yes, I do know why you're sick. And yes, your mother did send for me,' I admitted. 'But it was my choice to come. I've left many things behind in England to be here, Indy, and I did so because you're my friend. I love you and I want to try and help you if I can.'

'How can you help?' asked Indira, as she blew her nose hard. 'Even you, with your wisdom and your special foresight, can't change the fact that in exactly four months I'm meant to marry an old man I've only met twice in my life, then spend the rest of it in his zenana, and his ghastly, godforsaken palace that no one ever visits. So, I might as well die here, where at least I'll be in my own home, rather than locked up there, all alone.'

'Well, I don't think that's the whole truth, is it? You're miserable because you're in love with someone else,' I said gently.

'Yes, the fact that I could have such a happy life with Varun, who's not that much older than me, whom I love and want in all the ways any woman should, just makes the thought even worse.'

'I can understand that,' I said softly. 'I know what it's like to be in love.'

'Do you? Well, I only wish my parents could understand too.'

'Indy, I'm going to ring for some food – I'm hungry, even if you're not – and while we eat it, I want to hear all about your prince.'

I rang the bell and spoke quickly to a servant, who nodded and disappeared from the room.

'Now,' I said, 'let's have you out of that bed, and we'll go and sit outside, where we can be sure no one will be listening, and you can tell me all about him.'

Shakily, Indira climbed out of bed and I helped her outside onto comfortable cushions placed on the veranda.

She told me how she and Varun had contrived to see each other as often as possible in the past three years. During the war, it had been difficult, but in the last five months, Raj, her older brother, had invited Varun to visit the palace and their passion for each other had grown.

'Anni, neither of us is willing to live without the other,' Indira declared.

As she spoke, I fed her mouthfuls of the soup the maid had

brought up – I'd often found a diversionary tactic worked for a patient whose appetite was poor. With a heavy heart, I also realised that Indira's mind was made up and it was fruitless to even begin to try to change it. All I could do was listen, and, as the professional nurse I was training to be, help her to grow stronger physically. The sorry state she was in at present was not conducive to helping her make any kind of logical decision.

In reality, my heart went out to my beloved friend. The idea of being forced to marry a man she didn't love, and then being shut away in purdah and a zenana for the rest of her days, sent shudders through me.

'So, that is where we are,' Indira said as she finished her story – and the last mouthful of soup in the bowl.

'I still remember that day on the ship when you first set eyes on Varun and told me he was the man you were going to marry,' I recalled.

'Yes, and I will! I must!' Indira turned to me. 'Oh, it's so good to talk openly and freely with someone who understands how I feel.'

'Sadly, I do.'

At that, Indira threw her arms around me, and held me to her. 'Anni, it's so wonderful to see you. I'd forgotten how special you are. And I think,' she drew back and looked at me suddenly, 'that you've not only grown into a beauty, but you are also even wiser than you used to be. So,' she said, picking up a chapatti from the plate and tearing a piece off it, 'you won't try to persuade me to marry the Old Man?'

'How could I possibly do that?' I asked her with a smile. 'Remember, I know you very well and I realise it's a futile endeavour to try to change your mind. The task at hand, Indy, is to discover how you *can* marry the man you love without causing civil war between two princely states.'

My eyes twinkled and, thankfully, so did hers. We both giggled like the children we'd once been.

'Do you think the Old Man will come after my father and demand a duel at dawn, like they do in England, because his honour has been betrayed?'

'Perhaps,' I agreed, 'and I feel it would be better if no one died because of your love for Varun.'

'Yes.' And at last I saw that a little of the old sparkle was returning to Indira's eyes. 'But how?' she asked me.

I, too, chewed on a chapatti as I pondered the situation. 'Would you let me think about it?'

'Just promise me, please, dear Anni, that you're really on my side?' Indira implored. 'You won't go reporting back what I've said to Ma?'

'Of course I'm on your side, and I won't say a word. But you must do me one favour in return, Indy. If we're to make a plan, you need to be well enough to carry it out. Lying here being a martyr and refusing food is not getting you anywhere. If I am to help you, I want you to promise me that you'll start eating. That means three full meals a day and no lying around in bed feeling sorry for yourself any longer.'

'My,' she rolled her eyes, and smiled at me, 'you've grown bossy since I last saw you!'

'Well, looking at you now, even if we do manage to find a way for you to marry Varun, I doubt he'd want you. There's nothing left of you! You'll lose your looks completely if you carry on like this.'

'You're right,' she agreed. 'I look and feel awful. But until you arrived, there wasn't any point in being anything else.'

'Well, there is now,' I confirmed. 'So do we have a deal?'

'Can I really trust you, Anni?'

'Indy,' I said, suddenly irritated, 'have I ever let you down before? I've travelled halfway across the world to try to help you. And may the gods forgive me, but, for my own reasons, I want your problem sorted as soon as it can be. For I, too, have someone I'm desperate to return to back in England.'

'Really? How exciting! Tomorrow you must tell me all about it.'

'I will. So?' I looked at her questioningly.

'Yes.' She held out her hand. 'Deal.'

26

My nursing experience told me Indira's return to strength would take time – she was seriously underweight and her constitution was weak. So, in the next few days, with encouragement from me, Indira would rise from her bed and eat breakfast. We would take a short walk around the gardens and she would rest before lunch. I had asked the kitchens to prepare simple, nourishing dishes. Anything rich would not stay inside a stomach that had been starved for so long. In the evenings we dined together on the veranda outside her bedroom. By way of an incentive, I told her that I wasn't prepared to reveal my plan for her future until she was stronger and able to enact it.

What that plan was, exactly, I had little idea yet, although thoughts were beginning to formulate in my mind. The Maharani came to see me every day when Indira took her afternoon nap, her eyes full of wonder at the difference in her daughter.

'You truly are a miracle worker, Anni, and I'm so thankful you've come. Maybe soon, she'll start to see sense.'

'She's found the will to live again, let that be enough for now,' I cautioned.

At night in my bedroom, I wrote to Donald, telling him of Indira and life at the palace. I warned him that it was going to take longer than I'd initially expected before I could contemplate returning to England. I missed him unbearably, and it took all the patience I possessed to oversee Indira's slow progress back to health.

A month on, and at last Indira was beginning to look much more like her usual self. She was showing some of her old zest for daily life and had grown strong enough for us to take short horseback rides out in the park in the mornings. It was during those rides that, finally, I told her of my own love for Donald, and the life we were planning together when I returned to England.

I confided in her my worries about Donald's mother and her prejudices.

'But from the sound of him, Donald doesn't care *what* his mother thinks,' said Indira. 'The estate is his and he can marry who he wishes.'

'Well, he hasn't dared to tell her about me yet.'

'Well, I'm sure he will, and the two of you will live happily ever after. Besides, you've only got a grim mother-in-law to deal with, whereas I have a possible war between two princely states. You're so lucky, Anni, you're free to do anything you want.' She sighed.

I managed to take a little comfort from Indira's words, although I understood that she couldn't fully see or understand the complexity of my situation. And currently there was one thing in particular which was concerning me. I'd chosen to ignore it, hoping, like any girl in my situation, that I might be mistaken.

Once I'd settled Indira to sleep that night, I paced up and

down, trying to think just how I could help her. I knew that if she were forced to marry a man she didn't love and be closeted in his zenana for the rest of her days, she would simply waste away again. And I wouldn't be there to help her.

I asked the stars for guidance that night – my mother had instilled in me that I must always be careful when interfering in other people's destinies.

'Take care, little one,' she'd warned me once, 'because, in giving help, *you* will become part of their destiny.'

And even though I knew any plan I conjured up would almost certainly be seen as a betrayal by the Maharani – the woman who was the nearest thing to a mother I had on this earth – there was nothing else to be done.

The following day, before I went to join Indira for breakfast, I rode out across the park to the pavilion where, six years ago, I'd buried my inheritance. I retrieved the hessian bag from the hole I'd dug underneath it and was relieved to see that the three stones were still inside it. I tucked the two smaller rubies into a pocket of my sari, placing the last and largest ruby back in its hiding place.

Later, on our afternoon walk, I took Indira to a spot in the gardens where I knew no one would hear our conversation. She looked at me, eagerness in her eyes, as I settled her on the grass under a jasmine tree.

'Well? Have you come up with a plan?'

'I don't know whether it's a plan exactly,' I answered, 'but I do believe that often in life, if you present people with a *fait accompli*, they'll eventually come to accept it. Indira, do you know where Varun is at the moment?'

'I think he's somewhere in Europe,' Indira rubbed her nose

thoughtfully, 'but his servants will forward the letter to him wherever he is.'

'Then you must write and tell him you will come to join him in Europe in a few weeks' time. Perhaps Paris,' I suggested. 'You must name a day and a place where you'll be and ask him to meet you there.'

She looked at me in amazement. 'You're telling me I should run away?'

'I can't see you have any other choice. I'll tell your mother that I believe you need to recuperate from your illness in Switzerland. That the fresh mountain air and change of scenery will not only build up your strength, but take your mind off Varun. That you've agreed that, after a time of recuperation, you're prepared to return to India and marry the Maharaja of Dharampur.'

'Oh, Anni,' Indira clasped her hands to mine, 'but will Ma believe you?'

'I'm sad to say that your mother trusts me completely, Indy. I'll play my part to the hilt and tell her that I've convinced you that you must do your duty. But you, too, will have to convince her you're prepared to accept your marriage.'

'But surely,' Indira chewed her lip anxiously, 'they'll never give me their blessing to marry Varun?'

'No, they won't. And if you go ahead with this, then that's something you must simply accept,' I said firmly.

I watched her mentally walk through what I was suggesting. And I wondered if losing her parents' love and enduring their inevitable fury and disappointment would be a step too far for her. It was a terrible choice for her to have to make. But she had to realise fully the consequences of her actions before she agreed to the plan.

'So, I'd have to marry Varun in secret?'

'Yes. And if Varun is as passionate about you as you are about him, then he too must accept this is the only way. It might not be the grand ceremony which befits the joining of two princely states, but it will have to suffice for now. Indy,' I sighed, 'if you want to be with your prince, I can't see that you have any other choice.'

'But I have no money of my own at all. Not even enough to buy a wedding dress!' Indira laughed nervously as the further ramifications of her plight struck her. 'Once they hear, I know Ma and Pa will cut me off without a rupee.'

'I have some money put by,' I said, thinking how ironic it was to be sitting in a palace owned by two of the wealthiest people in the world and offering to help their daughter financially.

'Will they ever forgive me?'

'I can't answer that. It's a chance you simply have to take if you're set on being with Varun. One of the things I learned when I was working out in France as a nurse, Indy, is that life is too short. And we all have to make sacrifices to do what we believe is right for us.'

'Well, I know it is right for me and Varun to be together. So I'll write to him, and tell him we must meet in Paris.'

'Yes, and if he responds positively, then I'll speak to your mother.'

Indira stood up, then paced up and down for a while in an agony of indecision. Finally, she stopped and turned to me. 'I'll do it. I'll write to him now, and perhaps you could post the letter for me this afternoon?'

'Of course.'

Later that day, after I'd posted Indira's letter to Prince

Varun, and one to Donald too, I emerged and walked down the noisy, crowded street in a daze, coming to terms with the fact that my part in Indira's deception would almost certainly mean that I'd never be welcome at the palace again.

But I had a new life, a life that would be spent elsewhere. And as I walked into a jewellery shop, the love I felt for Donald gave me the strength to hand over the two rubies to the man behind the counter.

I returned to the rickshaw half an hour later, having gleaned from the man's eyes how special and precious my stones were. He had almost certainly paid me only a quarter of their true value, but tucked inside my pocket was enough money for Indira at least to buy a wedding dress and also for me to know I had enough to see me through a year or so if I needed it. Which I was beginning to realise I might.

For over two weeks, Indira and I lived in anguish waiting for Varun to reply. When finally he did, I took the letter to Indira immediately, and her eyes burned with trepidation and excitement as she opened it. Reading it quickly, she looked up at me, her eyes now shining. 'He too agrees that it's the only way. He says he can't live without me! So, what now?'

'I'll speak to your mother as soon as I can.'

'Oh, Anni!' Indira threw her arms around me. 'How can I ever repay you for helping me?'

'One day, I'm sure the moment will come.'

That evening, I took a deep breath and requested to see the Maharani. I told her the plan I had devised and, as her beautiful dark eyes gazed upon me, filled with trust and appreciation, I was horrified at how easily I was able to lie to her. When I finished speaking, she took my hands in hers and smiled at me. 'Thank you for helping, Anni. I suspected that you might be the only one she'd listen to. We're all very grate-ful to you.'

I left the Maharani's rooms feeling like the liar and the cheat that I was. I dispatched Indira to see her mother and she, too, played her part to perfection. The following day, our pas-sage to Europe was booked for us to travel in ten days' time.

Meanwhile, I had another urgent situation that I knew I must steel myself to resolve. The following day saw me in the zenana with my old friend and teacher, Zeena. We walked out-side into the gardens together and she took my hand and felt my pulse. Then she looked at me and nodded.

'I know why you're here to see me.'

'Yes. Can you help me?' I asked, hearing the desperation in my own voice.

'You don't want the child?'

'I do, but not at this moment. There will be others . . .'

She inclined her head. 'Come to me this afternoon and we'll see what we can do.'

I returned later as she'd requested, my nerves jangling as she examined me.

Then she sat me upright, looked at me sternly and shook her head.

'You're over twelve weeks along. If I try, it would put your life in danger, and I'm not prepared to take the risk. You know as well as I do that it's too late to be safe.'

I *had* known of course. I was a nurse, after all. But I'd been burying my head, as cowardly and frightened as the next young woman in my predicament.

Zeena gazed at me. 'The father loves you?'

'Yes.'

'Then why are you here?' She smiled at me.

'It is . . . complicated.'

'Love is always complicated.' She chuckled and then shook her head. 'Tell him you have a precious gift for him. If he loves you as he says he does, he will be happy.'

As the full ramifications of my situation took hold, I was gripped with sudden terror. 'Zeena, you don't understand. I don't know what to do.'

'You'll find a way, Anahita, I'm sure.'

I walked away from her, my eyes blurred with tears. I headed straight for the stables, had the groom tack me up a horse, and rode off at full pelt, screaming to the hot, dusty air at my own stupidity. I'd known for weeks. Why, oh why, had I refused to acknowledge the facts earlier? I was a nurse, a 'wise woman', perfectly able to help others with their lives, yet I'd managed to destroy my own.

As I urged my horse faster, I wondered if I should perhaps throw myself from its back rather than face the terrible consequences of my ruined future. However much Donald loved me, if I returned from India pregnant when the union we both wanted so much was already fraught with difficulty, surely even he would feel it was a step too far? I thought of his mother, a devout Catholic, who would undoubtedly prefer to see any baby born out of wedlock drowned at birth – let alone one produced from a union between her son and a 'heathen' Indian girl.

I brought the horse to an abrupt standstill, slid off and fell to my knees and wept. For I knew there was no one to blame but myself.

Finally, standing up, I comforted myself with the thoughts that at least I'd have a few weeks on-board the ship to think about what I should do next and the money from the rubies to enable me to enact whatever decision I took. The one definite was that the baby inside me would be arriving in my arms in six months' time.

I'd often said to my patients that they should accept the will of the gods and pray for strength and acceptance. This was the mantra that I must follow now if I was to survive.

The following week, we sailed for Europe. Indira's hand searched for mine as we stood on the deck watching India disappear from view as the ship pulled out of port. We were both sombre, lost in our own thoughts.

Indira soon came to life and danced the night away with the many young beaux who were eager to escort her. Finally I had the solitude I needed to think about my future and I began to formulate a plan.

When the ship docked at Marseilles, we took a train to Paris and checked into the Ritz. Immediately, I sent a telegram to the Maharani, telling her of our safe arrival and that we would be travelling by train to the clinic in the Swiss Alps in the next few days. Prince Varun was expected the following morning, and Indira was in a state of high excitement as she tried on dresses and discarded them haphazardly onto the bed.

'I haven't got a thing to wear! It's so long since I shopped in Europe. Everything I own is old-fashioned.'

'Your prince will love you whatever you're dressed in.'

That night, we both lay sleepless in our beds.

'Have you any idea where you and Varun will go from here?' I asked.

'He said in his letter we must be married as soon as possible and then stay in Europe until the dust settles at home. Oh, Anni, do you think what I'm doing is wrong? It will break Ma and Pa's hearts.'

'They'll get over it eventually. As I've said to you often, Indy, we must try to do what we can to be happy.'

'Even if it involves hurting the people we love?'

'Sometimes, yes. But hopefully, it won't be for long. Your parents love you too much to let you go, although I doubt your mother will ever forgive me,' I said into the darkness.

'Of course she will, because she'll say that I forced you into it. It's me they'll blame, Anni, I promise. I'll make sure they do.'

'And you'll have a handsome prince who loves you for a husband, just as we both dreamed of that first night we met.'

'And you'll return to yours, and we'll both live happily ever after.'

As I tossed and turned through the long hours until dawn broke, I knew that my *own* fairytale was fast becoming a nightmare.

The following day I sat with Indira as we waited for her prince to arrive. Eventually the door to the drawing room opened and in he came. Indira gave a cry of joy and ran into his arms. I withdrew as subtly as I could.

I returned a few hours later to find Indira sitting at the writing bureau, a pen in her hand, deep in thought.

'Thank goodness you're here, Anni. I need your help. Varun says I must write to my parents as soon as possible to tell them we're to be married. By the time the letter reaches them in India, it will be too late to stop us. And,' Indira's brow furrowed with anxiety, 'I don't know what to say.'

'Of course I'll help you write it. But tell me first, did your prince live up to your expectations?'

'Oh yes, yes,' said Indira, her eyes dreamy. 'He's already

obtained a special marriage licence for us. He says there's no time to waste, as my family has many spies in Paris and may hear of what we're doing. So, the ceremony is set for the day after tomorrow. We're going to the town hall, and I'll need a witness. Will you do that for me, Anni?'

'In for a penny, in for a pound,' I replied, using a very British expression. 'Of course I will. Now, let's get on with this letter.'

Varun came to visit Indira the following day and the three of us took tea together in Indira's suite, discussing their plans. I was at least gratified to see that Indira's love was so obviously reciprocated by her prince. They were both aglow with happiness at their reunion.

'Where will you be taking Indira when you're married?' I asked him.

'I have a good friend who has said we can use his house down in Saint-Raphaël for as long as we like,' Varun explained. 'Both our families will need some time to get used to what we've done. I don't wish to upset them further by flaunting our marriage in European society, so we'll lie low for the time being.'

'I'm sure most of Europe will think it's terribly romantic,' I said, smiling. 'A prince and a princess running away together has all the elements of a fairytale, doesn't it?'

'Varun says I must write a nice letter to my jilted Maharaja.' Indira pouted from the writing bureau. 'What on earth do I say? "*Dear Old Man Prince, you are fat and ugly and I've never loved you. I'm afraid to tell you that I've married someone else. Yours, Princess Indira*"?'

We all chuckled at this, then Varun put an arm round Indira protectively. 'I know you don't want to write to him, my darling, but we're hurting a lot of people. We must try, within that, to behave with as much integrity as we can.'

'Yes.' Indira sighed. 'I know.'

Varun stood up and turned to me. 'Thank you, Anahita, for everything you've done for my princess. We're both deeply in your debt. I shall leave you now to write my own letter home. And I shall see you, Indira, tomorrow morning at the town hall.'

'*Bon nuit, mon amour*,' she said, blowing him a kiss. Then she turned to me. 'I can hardly believe that tomorrow will be my wedding day. I'd always imagined the great state occasion of my marriage in Cooch Behar, with my prince arriving in the Durbar Hall on an elephant, dressed in his ceremonial robes. Instead, we'll take a taxi to the town hall!'

'Does it matter to you?' I asked.

'Not one tiny bit, nor does it to him.'

'I think Varun is a good man, Indy. You're lucky to have found him. And most importantly, I can see he loves you.'

'I know,' she said gravely. 'I must do my best to stop acting like a spoilt child – which we both know I can be sometimes – when I'm his wife.'

'Agreed,' I said, smiling at her self-awareness. 'Now, what does the bride-to-be feel like for her pre-marriage supper?'

The following day, despite the fact that Indira didn't go through hours of being bathed, oiled and dressed in the complex layers of a traditional marriage sari and only had me to attend to her, I thought she looked as pretty as a picture in her white lace dress, with tiny cream rosebuds placed in her inky hair. As I sat in the dreary room at the town hall with Varun's manservant and watched my dearest friend marry her prince,

I felt the circle of our young lives had been completed. Our futures would not be the fairytale we had dreamed of as little girls, when we had lain on the grass and gazed up at the stars together; love had touched both of us and changed us in ways we could never have imagined.

After the ceremony, the newly-weds had champagne sent to the honeymoon suite Varun had taken for them.

'Darling Anni, you must give me your address before we go our separate ways,' said Indira.

'Yes, of course. I'll write to you with it at your Saint-Raphaël address when I get back to London.'

Twenty minutes later, I took my leave, as I could see that the two of them were desperate to be alone. I gave Indira an encouraging smile, knowing she was both apprehensive and excited by the intimacies she would experience for the first time with her prince that night. As I left, I felt both fearful and relieved that, tomorrow, I could finally concentrate on my own future.

The next morning, when the couple emerged from their suite at midday, I was already packed and ready to leave. Indira's face fell at the sight of my closed suitcase. 'Are you sure you don't wish to accompany us down to Saint-Raphaël for a while?'

'No, I think the two of you will have plenty to keep you occupied. You won't want me hanging around. Besides,' I said with far more gaiety than I felt, 'I must go back and see my own love.'

'Of course. I can never tell you how grateful I am to you for helping me find mine.'

'So now we must say goodbye.'

Both of us shed tears as we embraced.

'Be happy, my dearest friend,' I said, as the porter arrived to take my suitcase downstairs.

'I will be. And you too, Anni. I'll never forget what you've done for me. I'm not sure I can ever repay it, but if there's ever a time that you need me, all you must do is ask.'

'Thank you.' I nodded, too choked to say much more. 'Goodbye.'

Taking a deep breath, I turned away from her and walked through the door. I didn't look back, knowing that if I did, I would break down completely.

Outside on the Place Vendôme, I stood for a few moments trying to compose myself. I walked towards the nearest post box and slipped the letter I'd written to Donald – explaining that I'd be away for some time – into it. Then I picked up my suitcase and took my first step towards the unknown.

Astbury Hall,

July 2011

27

'Would you like a brandy? I certainly would,' Anthony asked Ari, as Mrs Trevathan broke the silence between the two men, arriving to clear away the dessert plates in the dining room.

'Thank you,' replied Ari, watching Anthony as he took a decanter from a tray on a sideboard, poured the brandy into two glasses and handed one to him.

'Your health,' Anthony toasted.

'And yours. I sincerely apologise if the story has upset you.'

'I admit I had to stop reading after the revelation of Anahita's pregnancy. I just don't know whether I can believe that everything your great-grandmother has written is the absolute truth,' Anthony replied.

'I am sure it is the truth as she knew it. Love is a strange thing, I suppose,' Ari mused.

'The one thing that does ring true, however, is Anahita's description of Maud, my great-grandmother. She was terrifying. Mother and I both lived in fear of her until the day she died.'

'I can tell you that Maud certainly played her part in the tragedy that subsequently followed,' sighed Ari.

'Well, the fact remains that there isn't a single shred of

evidence to confirm either your great-grandmother's relationship with my grandfather, or her presence here at Astbury.'

'If Donald did father a child with Anahita, surely, given the scandal it would have caused, any trace of her and her son would have been well hidden?'

Ari saw Anthony physically shudder. 'But the child died anyway – you've told me your great-grandmother received his death certificate from Indira, her friend?'

'Yes, and so far I have no proof to suggest that he did survive,' admitted Ari. 'In that sense, I'm almost certainly here on a wild goose chase. Still, I'm glad I came, it's been wonderful to get to know a place that was so important to her.'

'I wish I could help you further with your investigations, but I can't,' Anthony stated flatly. 'Surely, you must have considered the fact that much of your great-grandmother's story might well be fantasy? It was written thirty years after the event and we all know how memories become confused with the passage of time.'

'I agree there may well be some exaggeration in the pages. However, there was just one more thing I wanted to investigate further. Later in her story, she mentions a cottage which was a very happy place for her for a year or two.'

'Which particular cottage? There are any number of them on the estate,' said Anthony.

'The one on the moors in the dip by the brook. Rebecca and I passed it when we were out riding. I'm sure that's the one Anahita was talking about.'

'Good grief! That old place is completely derelict, nothing left inside it at all. I'm about to order its demolition.'

'You've seen inside it?' asked Ari.

'Yes,' Anthony replied firmly.

'Well, in any case, if I may, I'd like to take up your offer of borrowing a horse again for a last hack across the moors, if that still stands?' he added.

'Of course,' agreed Anthony, as he drained his glass. 'So, when are you thinking of returning to India?'

'It depends. I'm turfed out of my bed-and-breakfast the day after tomorrow. It's high season and the landlady has a two-week family booking, so I must find somewhere else to stay.'

'Well then,' Anthony stood up abruptly, 'do come up to the Hall and say goodbye before you go.'

'I will, thank you.' Recognising that the evening was over and he was being dismissed, Ari stood too.

Anthony walked towards the door, then turned round as if in afterthought. 'If you do take a horse out tomorrow, I need you to promise that you won't enter the cottage near the brook. It's been condemned and I won't be held responsible for any accident that might befall you if you did. Do you see?'

'I do.' Ari followed Anthony out of the drawing room and into the main hall. 'Thank you for dinner.'

'The front door is unlocked; do see yourself out.' Anthony nodded as he headed for the stairs. 'I'm sorry your journey here to Astbury Hall has been fruitless. Goodnight.'

'Goodnight.' Ari walked across the hall and went out of the front door into the still, starlit night. As he walked to his car in the courtyard, he mused on his conversation with Anthony. He didn't know the man well enough to decide whether he was simply ignorant of the past and therefore so protective of his ancestors that he couldn't bear to contemplate the truth. Or if, in fact, he knew far more than he was letting on.

*

Arriving back in her room after having a bath, Rebecca saw that it was past ten o'clock and Jack was still not back from his evening out with James. Realising that she could easily have joined Anthony and Ari downstairs for dinner if Jack had told her he'd be out so late, she stifled her irritation and tried to concentrate on her script.

At eleven-thirty, there was a tentative knock on her door.

'Come in,' she called.

Mrs Trevathan's head appeared round it. 'Sorry to disturb you, Miss Rebecca, but is your young man due back tonight or not?'

'I'm so sorry, Mrs Trevathan, Jack's out with James Waugh in Ashburton. Why don't you go to bed and I'll wait up for him?'

'That won't be necessary, dear, but if he's to stay here for a while, perhaps in future he could inform me of what time he'll be arriving back?'

'Of course. I was expecting him much earlier.'

'Never mind. Sleep well, dear, and I'll see you tomorrow morning.'

Mrs Trevathan closed the door and Rebecca decided that if Jack was staying on longer, the best thing they could do would be to move to a hotel. Yes, there'd be a media frenzy at their presence together in England, and very likely the paparazzi would be camped outside the hotel, but she didn't want to abuse Anthony's and Mrs Trevathan's hospitality.

Today, she'd been feeling more sanguine about their relationship. It had been good to see him and their love-making had reminded her of the intensity of their bond. Maybe she *had* underestimated his true feelings for her. The very fact that he'd arrived here in England to find her was surely obvious testament to how much he cared about her.

At midnight, Rebecca gave up and turned out the light. She had another early call the following morning.

She was disturbed from sleep in the early hours by a clattering in the room. She switched on the light and saw Jack sprawled on the floor, having tripped over the coffee table.

'Sorry,' he giggled. 'I was trying to be quiet and not wake you.'

Rebecca peered at him from her vantage point on the bed, her heart sinking. It was evident that he was very drunk.

'You had a good night, then?'

'James is a guy who sure knows how to party. I left him with some woman who was going up to keep him company in his room. Right . . .' He tried to stand up and, failing the first time, managed it the second. He made it to the bed and lay on it fully clothed. His eyes opened as he gazed up at her from his prone position. 'Do you know how gorgeous you are?' he slurred.

Rebecca saw his tell-tale enlarged pupils. 'Jack, you've done some lines tonight, haven't you?'

'Only a couple. Now come here.' He reached for her, but she pulled away abruptly.

'I need to sleep, please, Jack, I have a call in –' Rebecca glanced at the clock – 'four hours' time.'

'Come on, baby, I'll be quick, promise,' he said as he groped inside her T-shirt for her breasts.

'Please, no!' Rebecca wriggled out of his grasp and reached to turn off the light.

'Spoilsport, I just wanted to make love to my girl. Just wanted to make love to my girl. I . . .'

Rebecca waited, knowing from experience that he'd be asleep within two minutes. And sure enough, she soon heard the familiar sound of snoring.

Tears pricking the back of her eyes, Rebecca did her best to doze off too.

Early the following morning, Ari drove to the Astbury stables. Debbie saddled up the chestnut stallion for him and he set off across the moors. It was a glorious morning and he rode hard. Arriving at the cottage by the brook twenty minutes later, he slid off his horse and walked towards a high wooden fence with a gate set to one side of the building. It seemed in relatively better repair than the rest of the exterior and behind it, he thought, perhaps there might be a door to the rear of the cottage. He tugged at the black ring in the centre, but it didn't budge and he saw the lock beneath it. He made a couple of fruitless attempts to jump up and clamber over, but it was too high.

Leading his horse to stand against the fence, Ari mounted him and grabbed the top of the fence with his hands. He heaved himself up, swung his legs over and jumped down. Landing smoothly on the ground below him, he looked around and saw that he was standing in a courtyard containing a number of small outbuildings. He took a quick look in them and found them empty, apart from an old horse-drawn trap resting in the corner of one.

Turning his attention to the back of the cottage itself, he walked over to the one door and tried the handle. He was amazed when it turned easily and the door sprang open. Tentatively, he stepped inside and found himself in a kitchen.

From the impenetrable ivy-covered exterior of the cottage,

and from what Anthony had said last night, Ari had presumed that he would enter a filthy, cobwebbed interior. But no. He ran his finger across the surface of the wooden table which stood in the centre of the kitchen; there was a layer of dust upon it, but certainly not the filth of ninety years of neglect. As he wandered around it, he saw that cups were hung neatly on hooks, the old black range had no rust, and the plates in the dresser were cracked but clean. Looking down, he saw his feet were not making footprints in the dirt that surely would have settled over time on the tiled floor.

Then he saw a modern electric kettle sitting atop a counter to one side of the range. Ari pulled out a chair from the table and sat down abruptly. Clearly this was not an abandoned cottage which was so unsafe it was about to be demolished, as Anthony had described.

Standing up, suddenly aware that there could actually be an occupant elsewhere in the cottage, Ari walked quietly towards the kitchen door and opened it. In the hallway, he listened for sounds, but heard nothing. Opening a door on the left, he saw the small sitting room. It was dark, due to the ivy that covered the window panes, and Ari struggled to adjust his eyes to the gloom. The fire grate showed only minimal black dust, which had recently dislodged itself from the chimney. The chair in front of it was threadbare, but clean.

Walking over to the bookshelves, he saw they were full of old copies of some of the British literary classics. The books Anahita had said she loved.

Ari made his way up the narrow stairs and stood on the tiny landing before tentatively pushing open one of the two doors. He entered a neat bedroom, with faded flower-sprigged curtains at the windows and a worn patchwork quilt covering the brass bedstead. The pillows sat snugly in pillowcases and the sheets and blanket seemed prepared for its occupant to slide beneath them. On the dressing table stood various feminine lotions and potions, and a large bottle of perfume.

Ari scratched his head, feeling unsettled. Everything he saw made it obvious that the cottage had a current resident.

But who?

The cottage was the perfect hiding place, Ari thought to himself as he left the bedroom to investigate the room on the other side of the landing. No one would possibly suspect from the exterior that anyone could be living in it.

A new rush of emotion assailed him as he glanced at what this bedroom contained. A rusting iron cot took up most of the space in the tiny room, a moth-eaten baby blanket still covering the mattress. A pair of mournful eyes gazed up at him from within it and Ari reached for the ancient teddy bear and hugged it to him like a child.

'My God,' he whispered. He now believed that his great-grandmother's story was true.

28

Jack hadn't stirred when Rebecca had climbed out of bed the following morning. Blocking his behaviour from her mind, she pulled on a pair of tracksuit pants and went downstairs and into Make-up.

It was a long, hard day's shoot and she felt drained by the time she arrived back upstairs past six that evening.

'Are you leaving?' she asked in surprise as she entered her bedroom to find Jack re-packing his shirts into his overnight bag.

'Yes, but only to go to London. My new best pal, James, let me know of a film that Sam Jeffrey is making. I used the telephone in the study and got my manager to call him this morning to say I was over here, and he wants to see me to-morrow morning. Isn't that great, honey? The guy is a serious young director and already has a couple of BAFTAs under his belt. So I got a taxi booked to take me to London. I'll be back sometime tomorrow evening.'

'Right,' Rebecca replied, startled.

'Chasing across to England to find you is turning out to be a good move.' He came over to her, put his arms around her and kissed her. 'So wish me luck and promise me you won't fall into the arms of my new best buddy while I'm gone,' he said as he picked up his holdall and walked towards the door. 'I know where he's been. Love you, baby, bye.' Jack winked at her and closed the door behind him.

'I thought you'd come here to see me,' she whispered to herself as she sat down in a daze on the bed. After a few minutes of getting used to the idea of Jack's abrupt departure, Rebecca stood up and went to take a bath. It was a beautiful evening, and having been cooped up inside under the hot lights all day, she decided to take a walk and get a breath of fresh air. She met Mrs Trevathan on the main staircase.

'Don't pass me, Rebecca. It's very bad luck to cross on the stairs,' she said.

'Really? I guess that must be an English custom.' She shrugged.

'I expect you're right,' Mrs Trevathan said. Rebecca thought she looked extremely flustered. 'Has your young man gone now?'

'Yes, but he'll be back tomorrow.'

'I see. So, will you be wanting supper tonight?'

'No, thanks, I ate a big lunch earlier on set.'

'Then I'll leave you some sandwiches and the chamomile tea you like in your room for later.'

'Thank you, Mrs Trevathan.'

The crew had moved off to the village for the evening's filming, so the house and gardens were quiet. Rebecca went to sit on the bench in the walled garden. The roses were coming into full bloom now and the smell was heavenly.

'Hello.' Anthony's voice snapped her out of her reverie. 'Your young man gone off to London, I hear?'

'Yes. But he'll be back tomorrow. Really, if it's a problem, please say so and we'll move to the hotel.'

'No, it isn't a problem, really. Although . . .'

'What?'

'I suppose he wasn't what I expected,' Anthony admitted. 'Forgive me, I'm hardly one to talk about relationships between men and women.'

'It's okay, Anthony, really.'

'As long as he looks after you and you're happy, that's all that matters.'

'Yes.' Rebecca refrained from comment; at present she didn't trust herself not to say something negative.

'So what do you think of our young Indian friend?'

'I like him,' said Rebecca honestly.

'Yes, he seems like a nice chap, but personally, I'm struggling to believe his story. If I did, it would alter my perception of Donald and Violet, my grandparents, and I'd find that most upsetting,' he confessed.

'I'm afraid I don't know the full story, but I can't see why either he or his great-grandmother would make it up,' said Rebecca.

'No, not unless he wants something,' muttered Anthony darkly.

'What could he want?'

'Money? A claim to the estate?'

'Anthony, I haven't read any more than the first hundred pages, so I can't comment. But Ari seems to me like an honourable kind of guy. I don't think he's come here to cause trouble, just to find out about his own family's past.'

'Even if he was after money, he's now fully aware there isn't any to be had,' Anthony replied morosely.

'From what he's told me, Ari is a very successful business-man. I really don't think that's why he's here, Anthony.'

'You don't think so?'

Again, Rebecca felt Anthony's almost childish need for re-assurance from her. 'No, I really don't.'

'Then, in that case,' Anthony said, visibly relaxing, 'I feel I haven't been terribly hospitable. He told me last night he has nowhere to stay around here as from tomorrow. So shall I offer him a room here until he leaves for India in a few days' time?'

'I think it would be a very sweet gesture,' she agreed.

'Goodness, this house won't have seen so many guests within its walls for years,' said Anthony.

'Are you enjoying the company?' she asked him.

'Yes, I think I am. Although Mrs Trevathan doesn't approve, of course. Well, now, thank you for your advice, Rebecca. I'll go inside and telephone Mr Malik.' He smiled briefly at her and walked off in the direction of the house.

Rebecca turned towards the park at the front of the Hall. She wanted some time to clear her head and consider what to do about Jack. It had taken her less than twenty-four hours in his presence to remember why she had struggled to say yes to his proposal. As she wandered across the sun-dappled grass through the great chestnut trees that dotted the park, she realised that the two weeks she had spent here at Astbury had changed her. She was able to see things much more clearly, as if the physical space around her mirrored the space in her mind. And the honest truth was that last night, when Jack had turned up in the bedroom drunk and stoned, he had disgusted her.

Against the backdrop of Astbury, everything about him looked and sounded like a stereotypical Hollywood cliché. In

Tinseltown, Jack's behaviour, his ego and self-indulgence might be seen as normal. But in the real world – in the world where ordinary people simply got on with their lives and struggled through day by day – it most certainly wasn't. No matter how many times she tried to excuse it, Jack's dependence on drugs and alcohol was not something she could live with. She knew from bitter experience it was a road to nowhere.

There was simply no way she could accept his proposal. So what if the world didn't understand? It wasn't the world who had to live with him. Rebecca knew she must tell him it was no-go unless he cleaned up his act. At least, she thought, if she told him now while she was staying at Astbury, she would be protected within its secure surrounds from the media fall-out. Her agent would go wild, but Rebecca was also beginning to acknowledge that too many other people – most of them men – had been in control of her destiny for the past few years. She had to be responsible for herself again, whatever it took.

Perhaps her refusal to marry him would be the shot across the bows Jack needed to help him face his demons. But somehow she doubted it.

She looked up then and realised she had wandered into a part of the park she had never visited before. In front of her, surrounded by a copse of trees, was a building reminiscent of a Greek temple, out of place in its pastoral English setting. Walking towards it, she climbed up the steps between the white marble columns. She expected the vast door to be locked, and was surprised that it opened when she turned the handle.

Stepping into the cool, shadowy interior, Rebecca shivered as she remembered Anthony mentioning that his ancestors were buried in a mausoleum in the grounds. Her instinct was to leave immediately, but as she looked around the walls at the great stone plaques naming those whose bones lay behind them, she was intrigued. She read of Astbury ancestors dating back to the sixteenth century; husbands and wives interred together for all eternity. Rebecca moved to the more recent tombs and stood in front of Lord Donald and Lady Violet Astbury's resting place.

DONALD CHARLES ASTBURY
b. 1 December 1897 – d. 28 August 1922
aged 25

VIOLET ROSE ASTBURY
b. 14 November 1898 – d. 25 July 1922
aged 23

A frisson ran up Rebecca's spine as she double-checked the date of Donald Astbury's death. He'd died so young . . . and only a month after Violet. Was it a coincidence? Rebecca wanted desperately to know. Next to Donald and Violet's memorial stone – having survived for thirty-three years longer than her son, dying at the age of eighty-three in 1955 – was Lady Maud Astbury. She was interred with her husband, George, who had predeceased her by forty-four years, dying in 1911. The most recent stone was that of Anthony's mother:

DAISY VIOLET ASTBURY
b. 25 July 1922 – d. 2 September 1986
aged 64

ANTHONY DONALD ASTBURY
b. 20 January 1952 – d.

The final date below Anthony's name had not yet been carved.

Below the stone stood a large vase full of fresh roses. Rebecca knelt down and smelt their scent, pondering the fact that Anthony's father was obviously not buried with Daisy, his mother. Instead, it would be Anthony's bones that would eventually lie with her. Shivering suddenly from the chill, Rebecca left the mausoleum wondering why Anthony had chosen twenty-five years ago to be buried with his mother, rather than alongside a possible wife he might take in the future.

As she walked back across the park towards the Hall, Rebecca thought again that Anthony must surely be gay. Or perhaps he was simply not interested in either sex and had always known it.

Whatever his predilections, the visit to the mausoleum had confirmed one thing in Rebecca's mind, and that was that life was too short to worry about the consequences of doing the right thing. When Jack returned from London, she would tell him what she had decided.

29

The following morning, Rebecca felt the now-familiar nausea and the beginnings of another headache. Taking two ibuprofen with the cup of tea Mrs Trevathan had brought her, she went downstairs into Make-up.

'You're looking peaky again, Becks,' James commented as they walked towards the drawing room together to shoot their next scene.

'I just can't get rid of this headache,' she said, 'but I'm okay.'

'You know, I really think you should get Steve to call the doc to come and check you over. You're not yourself at all, are you, sweetheart?'

'Please don't say anything,' Rebecca pleaded. 'I don't want them thinking I'm a typical hypochondriac American.'

'I doubt anyone would think that, given your current state,' said James, reassuringly. 'You have goosebumps all over you, even though it's boiling in here.'

'I promise I'll see a doctor if I don't feel better soon.'

'When's my new mate Jack back from London, by the way?'

'I'm not sure. I heard you had a fun night out together,' she replied sarcastically.

'We did indeed. A man after my own heart, your fiancé. Mind you, on the alcohol front, I take back all I said about the Hollywood crowd not drinking. Jack makes me look like an amateur.' He grinned.

After lunch, Rebecca was at a loose end until the evening, when the cast would be having a special dinner together on the terrace for Robert Hope's birthday. She wandered downstairs and, on a whim, headed for the library. Entering it, she walked to the fireplace and stared at the portrait of Violet Astbury above it.

'Yes, the likeness is extraordinary,' said a voice from behind her.

Rebecca turned round and saw Ari Malik smiling at her from behind a high-backed leather chair.

'You startled me, I didn't see you there.'

'Sorry.' Ari stood up and came towards her. Standing next to her, he gazed up at the portrait. 'The obvious question is: are you related to Violet Astbury?'

'As I told Anthony when he first showed me the painting, my folks hail from Chicago and they weren't wealthy. So, as far as I know, I'm not.'

'One way or another, poor Anthony must really feel that his family's past is coming back to haunt him just now.' Ari sighed.

'Yes, I spoke to him last night and he's definitely unsettled by it all. He seems to worship the memories of Violet and his mother, Daisy,' Rebecca said. 'Are you meeting him here today?'

'At some point, yes, I should think, although I haven't actually seen him since I arrived. I received a call out of the blue from him yesterday evening to invite me to stay here until

I left for India. Mrs Trevathan didn't look too happy when she showed me to my bedroom earlier, mind you.'

'Did you find what you were searching for here?'

'I've seen enough to be pretty certain my great-grandmother *was* here and that most of her story is true. I didn't come here to upset any apple carts, and understandably, Anthony is very sensitive about revealing too many facts about his family's past. I think he believes I have some kind of ulterior motive in all this.'

'And do you?'

'No,' Ari said, shaking his head, 'other than to confirm my great-grandmother was here at Astbury and her son really did die in childhood as his death certificate states.'

'Do you think Anthony knows more than he's telling?'

'Sometimes I think he does, but on the other hand, when I saw him for dinner after he'd started to read the story, he told me he couldn't bear to read on and I believed him. The whole affair was a tragedy for everyone involved,' Ari sighed. 'I actually think that Anthony might be right when he talks about the death of his grandparents, Violet and Donald, being the catalyst for the fall of the Astbury fortunes.'

'Ari, I don't know the full story, but from what I've read so far, I'd guess that maybe Anahita and Donald's relationship was at the root of everything that happened afterwards. Would I be right?'

'You would,' Ari said in agreement.

'I don't want to pry, but does it mean that you and Anthony are somehow related from way back when?'

'It's complex, Rebecca. It opens the door to so many questions.'

'The first one that springs to my mind is whether the fact that you may be related means that you could have a legal claim on this estate,' she ventured.

'That's not something I've even contemplated,' Ari said, a genuine expression of surprise on his face.

'Well, maybe Anthony *has*. It might be an idea to reassure him. As you can see, Astbury is his life.'

'You're right. To be honest, I can't work Anthony out at all.'

'Maybe the subject matter is just too painful for him. Sometimes the past is,' Rebecca replied.

'I promise I'm not going to push him any further. At least there are some lines of investigation I can follow myself. Anyway, enough of me and the mysteries of the past. How are you? Is the film going well?' Ari asked her.

'I'm okay, and yes, filming has been going well. Although I've been suffering from some bad migraines since I've been here.'

'That's strange. Are they something you've experienced before?' he asked, gazing at her thoughtfully.

'No, it's the first time I've ever had them. But I'm determined not to let them ruin my stay in England.'

'And how is your fiancé?'

'He's in London just now, seeing a director about a film. If I'm completely honest, Ari, we're not in a good place.' She sighed.

'I thought you said that things seemed better between the two of you when he got here?'

Rebecca shook her head slowly. 'I think that's just what I wanted to believe. And I guess that I have to start trusting myself and making my own decisions.'

'You've more or less just quoted a line from a poem I read recently. "If" by Rudyard Kipling. It's my father's favourite. Do you know it?'

'No,' said Rebecca, 'I'm afraid I don't.'

'Well, you should have a read sometime. The poem's all about being true to yourself.'

'I'll look it up,' she said. 'Anyway, I'd better get going. There's a big dinner on the terrace tonight for our director and I need to get ready.'

'I'm off to investigate the local graveyard to see if I can find any sign of Anahita's son there and then on to Exeter to see if his death was officially registered.' He walked towards the door and Rebecca followed him.

'Will you let me know if you find anything? It may sound stupid, but I somehow feel involved. I suppose it's partly because of my resemblance to Violet. Did your great-grandmother know her?'

'Yes, apparently she did,' Ari said as they left the library and walked towards the hall. 'Have a nice evening, Rebecca, and if those headaches don't get better, see a doctor soon, won't you?'

'I will, yes. Thanks.'

Ari watched her as she floated gracefully up the main staircase. He could understand why Anthony had been so affected by her presence here. Even he, an outside observer, couldn't help but be unsettled by her likeness to Violet. There was also, for all her success and fame, an innate vulnerability about Rebecca. He felt that fate had placed her here at Astbury, like an innocent pawn in a complex game of chess.

It was impossible for him – let alone Anthony – to ignore the fact that it felt as if history was repeating itself: Donald and Anthony, the bachelor heirs to the Astbury Estate, Violet and Rebecca, the beautiful, rich Americans and he and Anahita, from an exotic, far-away land . . .

Ari looked above him at the great central dome and thought that if Anahita really *was* up there amongst the spirits she'd insisted had guided her during her life, she must be looking down now with great interest as a new generation of human players went about the intricate game of life.

Even though Rebecca had taken as many painkillers as she'd dared to defeat her headache, she still found it a struggle to get through Robert's birthday dinner on the terrace that evening.

'You're very quiet, darling,' said James as he placed an arm around her shoulder. 'Still not feeling any better?'

'I'm okay, James, really. Thanks for asking.'

'Bad-boy Jack is due back later tonight, then?'

'I think so, but he can't contact me here at Astbury to tell me when he'll arrive.'

'I'd take it as a real compliment that you've tamed him, Becks. That night in the bar he had women coming on to him left, right and centre and he didn't look twice at them. He really loves you, darling.'

'Does he?'

'God, yes!' James took a slug of champagne. 'I mean, it's going to take some kind of serious woman to have me plighting my troth to her forevermore, I can tell you.'

'I think I can take that as a compliment,' said Rebecca. 'I'm going to slip away now and get some sleep. I'll see you in the morning.'

Walking upstairs to her room, with the sound of laughter echoing from the terrace, Rebecca thought about James's comments. Jack might have loved her, he might have been pre-pared to ignore the overtures of other women – for now – but the fact remained, he had problems that were insurmountable unless he faced them.

Or was she being too hard on him?

Feeling too ill to make sense of anything further tonight, but not wanting her earlier determination to confront him to ebb away, Rebecca undressed and flopped into bed. Taking a sip of the still-warm chamomile tea which Mrs Trevathan had left her, she looked at her watch and wondered where on earth Jack was. As she turned off the light, half of her hoped he wouldn't make an appearance tonight so she could get an uninterrupted night's sleep.

It was past midnight when he appeared in the bedroom.

'Hi, baby.' He walked buoyantly across the room, kissed her, then put his arms round her shoulders. He stank of stale alcohol and Rebecca, already nauseous, turned her face away.

'Are you okay, Becks? You're a strange colour.'

'It's this headache again, it's making me feel sick. I'm going to see a doctor if it hasn't gone away tomorrow.'

'Yeah, you do that.' Jack sat on the edge of the bed and took her hand in his. 'Poor baby,' he crooned. 'Hey, you don't think by any chance I got you pregnant, do you?'

'No, Jack, that's impossible. I'm on the pill, remember?'

'I know, but wouldn't it be great if you were? It'd be the best-looking child in the world, I reckon. And I promise that, if you are, I wouldn't have a problem. No sir. It's about time I was a daddy.'

'Jack, I'm almost one hundred per cent sure I'm not,' Rebecca replied wearily. 'So how did the meeting go?'

'Great. Me and the director guy got on a like a house on

fire. Then afterwards, we went for lunch and had what you might call a male bonding session,' he said, smiling in reminiscence.

'So when will you hear about the part?'

'In the next few days. Right, I'm going to take a bath in that old tub down the hall, since there's no shower here. Christ, what a crazy place to be staying.' He kissed her on the nose. 'You just relax while I'm gone.'

Rebecca nodded and closed her eyes as Jack picked up his toiletry bag and left the room.

He was back fifteen minutes later and climbed into bed next to her.

'Could you find the energy to try and make a baby tonight?' he whispered, his hands reaching for her.

'Please, Jack, I really don't feel so good. Can you leave me to go to sleep, please?'

'Spoilsport.' As he leaned over to kiss her, to her horror, she saw a smudge of white powder sitting just inside his nostril.

'I'm sorry, Becks, but you gotta realise that I'm climbing into bed with the woman that every man in the Western world wants to screw, she's so goddamned beautiful. It's no surprise I get turned on.'

'Please! I said I'm not feeling well and I've got to sleep.'

'Sorry,' he said, offended, as she rolled away from him and switched off the light.

In the morning, Rebecca asked Steve to call a doctor. Unable to stay in bed, as she hardly wanted to greet him with a fiancé who was still passed out cold from drugs and alcohol next to her, she staggered downstairs and waited for him in the drawing room.

Twenty minutes later, a tall, middle-aged man holding his Gladstone bag entered the room with Steve.

'I'll leave you to it,' Steve said to her from the door as the doctor walked over and sat down next to her.

'Hello, Miss Bradley. My name is Dr Trefusis. What seems to be the problem?'

Rebecca explained her symptoms and then the doctor subjected her to a thorough examination.

'Right,' he said, having completed his investigations. 'Your pulse is faster than I'd expect and your blood pressure is also up. However, that can often be due to stress, especially when one has to see a strange doctor to find out what's wrong,' he said, his kind eyes smiling down at her.

'I don't understand it, I'm almost never sick,' she said, sighing.

'Well, sadly, we're human and it happens to all of us. Now, I want you to give me a urine sample and I'd like to do some blood tests to eliminate a few possibilities. Please try not to worry, Miss Bradley. You've almost certainly got a virus of some kind. You don't have a temperature, but that could be because, as you told me, you took some ibuprofen earlier.'

Rebecca took a specimen jar to the bathroom and did as requested, then looked the other way as the doctor stuck the needle into her vein. The sight of it brought back memories of her mother.

'Right, all done. Now, here's my cellphone number, just in case you feel worse. I'll be in touch as soon as I have the results of your tests. Be warned, though, it could be a few days before we get them back. Until then, I want you on bed rest. Drink plenty of fluids, keep taking the ibuprofen, and we'll see if you improve.'

'Bed rest? But I can't do that! My filming schedule is full for the next two days, Doctor, and I won't hold up the shoot,' said Rebecca, horrified.

'You can't help being sick, Miss Bradley. You're certainly in no fit state to be filming anything at present. Why don't I have a word with the chap who showed me in? I'll explain the situation.' Dr Trefusis closed up his bag and walked towards the door, pausing suddenly in afterthought. 'You don't think you could possibly be pregnant, do you?'

'I'm on the pill,' said Rebecca.

'Nonetheless, we'll do a pregnancy test from your urine sample this afternoon, just to rule it out for sure. Goodbye, Miss Bradley.'

Rebecca lay back on the sofa, feeling ill *and* guilty for being ill in equal measure. She wished she could go upstairs to her bedroom, shut the curtains and go to sleep. But the thought of having to face Jack whilst she felt so fragile was not palatable.

Ten minutes later, Steve came into the room. 'Right, all sorted, darling. I've had a word with Robert and we're currently rescheduling so you can take a couple of days off and recover.'

'I'm sorry, Steve, I feel so bad for causing all this trouble.'

'Rebecca, stop being paranoid. Everyone on set loves you and they've already seen how dedicated and hard-working you've been. We're just sorry that you're not well. Anyway, let's hope that with a couple of days' rest you'll be on the mend.'

'Yes,' she said gratefully. 'Thank you.'

'Now, why don't you go up to your room and try to sleep?' Steve suggested.

'Jack's still resting. He was exhausted after London. I'll just stay down here until he's woken up.'

'Okay –' Steve shot her a strange look – 'but our priority is you and you need to be tucked up in bed. I'll have a word with Mrs Trevathan and see if she has another room you can use in the meantime.'

As he left, Rebecca squirmed in embarrassment. Here she was, too sick to work and with a liability of a boyfriend sleeping in her bedroom upstairs.

'Hello, my love.' Mrs Trevathan arrived in the drawing room a few minutes later with a sympathetic look in her eyes. 'How are you feeling?'

'Awful,' said Rebecca, her reserve crumbling at the sight of the motherly figure. Her eyes filled with tears and she wiped them away.

'There, there, dear.' Mrs Trevathan put a kindly hand on Rebecca's. 'Steve explained the situation, so I've organised another bedroom for you in the meantime.'

Half an hour later, Rebecca was lying in an enormous, canopied bed while Mrs Trevathan bustled in and out with water, tea and toast and some magazines she thought Rebecca might like to read.

'I think you're in a couple of them,' she said teasingly as she handed them to her.

'This is such a lovely bedroom. I guess I've been upgraded,' Rebecca said with a forlorn smile.

'It is, isn't it? This was Lady Violet Astbury's suite of rooms and certainly, in the forty years I've been working here, I've never known it used. It was His Lordship himself that suggested you should move in here when I asked him where I should put you this morning. It has the best view over the gardens and moor and is the only bedroom with an en-suite bathroom. There's also a private sitting room and a dressing room through that door,' she said, indicating it.

'Well, please thank Anthony for me. I promise it's only temporary until Jack wakes up.'

'If I were you, I'd stay here until you're feeling better. You get some shut-eye, dear.'

'Thank you so much for all your kindness.'

'Don't be silly, that's what I'm here for.' Mrs Trevathan smiled at her and left the room.

Rebecca woke later feeling a little better and sat up in bed sipping the tea Mrs Trevathan had brought her. For the first time, she took in the details of the room she was occupying. It was hard to believe it had remained empty of human presence for so many years. Everything in it was immaculate – even the paintwork on the skirting boards looked fresh and new. Her glance fell on the highly polished Art Deco dressing table and she saw perfume bottles, a hairbrush and a string of beads hooked over one side of the three-faced mirror. Climbing out of bed, she walked over to it, picked up a perfume bottle and sniffed it. With a start, she realised it was familiar . . . it was the light, flowery scent she was sure had hung in the air some nights in her room.

Padding barefoot next door, she entered a bathroom. Again, the pristine fittings took her by surprise. The bathtub was old, but without a sign of the wear that was so prevalent in other parts of the house. A long line of mirrored wardrobes took up the entirety of one of the walls. Rebecca opened one and gasped as she saw the array of beautiful clothes, immaculately preserved in clear plastic hanging bags.

'Violet's clothes,' she murmured. Closing the door hastily, she wandered back into her bedroom and across to the other door. Beyond it was a small but beautifully furnished sitting room. Photographs in silver frames stood on a bureau and she saw Violet's face – her *own* face – staring back at her. Next to her stood a handsome young man in evening dress; it had to be Donald, Anthony's grandfather.

Another door led to a starkly furnished smaller room – a male room, containing none of the accoutrements of femininity. Realising this must have been Donald's dressing room, she saw there was a narrow wooden bed, a mahogany wardrobe, a chest of drawers and a packed bookshelf. Rebecca studied the titles on the shelf, everything, ranging from children's books to Thomas Hardy. One in particular caught her eye: the name 'Rudyard Kipling – *If*' was embossed in gold on the spine of a thick brown leather volume. Remembering the poem 'If' that Ari had mentioned to her only yesterday, which was written by the famous writer, she drew it out carefully. There was an intricate gold insignia stencilled on the front of it. She sat down on the bed and opened it carefully. On the inside cover was an inscription in faded ink:

Christmas 1910

My dear Donald, this very special gift was given to me by His Highness, the Maharaja of Cooch Behar, when I left to return to England after spending five years as Resident there. He had it commissioned especially for me, as he knew Rudyard Kipling was my favourite author and poet. It contains a beautifully handwritten poem at the front of the book, but it is in fact, a diary. Use it as you wish.

Your devoted father,

George

Rebecca remembered from the stone plaque in the mausoleum that George Astbury had died only a few weeks later, in January 1911.

She turned the first yellowing page and saw the poem, as Donald's father had indicated, handwritten, with exquisite gold decoration on the page. She read through the verses, and knew that there could never be a more poignant last gift from a father to a son.

The words, one hundred years on, made *her* feel empowered too. She stood up, about to return the book to the bookshelf, when an ink stain on the bottom of one of the later pages made her turn the following leaf over.

She sat back down as she read the first immaculately written entry.

January 1911

*Father died four days ago. I was told at school and am
now at home for the funeral. Mother is at chapel most
of the time and insists we go with her. Frankly, just now,
I don't have much faith in HIM, but I will do my best
to support her in her grief. Selina, too, is distraught. I
understand that I'm the man of the house now and must
be brave and strong. Father, in truth, I miss you awfully
and do not know how to comfort the women.*

The rest of the page was blank with no further entries, but turning over, Rebecca saw the diary restarted in 1912, with occasional entries during the following three years, and then again in earnest in February 1919, which Rebecca realised was just after the First World War had ended.

Rebecca heard her name being called. She reluctantly returned the diary to the bookshelf and walked swiftly back to the bedroom.

'How are you feeling, dear?' said Mrs Trevathan, who had just walked in.

'I'm a little better.'

'At least you have a bit more colour in your cheeks now. Rebecca, Jack is awake and wishes to see you. I've said you're asleep for now. I wanted to ask whether you're up to a visitor?' The look Mrs Trevathan gave her let Rebecca know she understood.

'Not really, no,' she said truthfully.

'Well, would you like me to make sure he's occupied until tomorrow? I could suggest he goes out to the hotel in Ashburton with his actor friend later. Mr James enquired after you earlier by the way, and sends his love,' she added.

'That would be very kind of you. But if Jack does go out with James, he may be in late. And—'

'Yes, dear, I understand,' said Mrs Trevathan. 'Don't worry, I'll deal with him.'

'Please, if he causes a problem, send him to me.'

'I can assure you that I've dealt with far worse than your young man in my time,' she interjected crisply. 'Now, I've left you some supper, plenty of water and a glass of warm milk that His Lordship insisted I bring you. He, too, sends you his regards, by the way, and wishes you a speedy recovery. Oh, and that Indian gentleman we now have staying was also very concerned and wanted to see you,' she added. 'Well, now, I'll go and make sure that you're not disturbed tonight by any of your male admirers.' Mrs Trevathan's eyes twinkled. 'If there's anything you need, ring the bell by the side of your bed.'

Rebecca looked at it. 'It still works?'

'Oh yes, dear, it still works,' Mrs Trevathan replied. 'Why don't you take a nice long soak in that tub and then have an early night? I can bring you some of your things from your old room.'

'Thank you, I will. And you're right, I do need some peace.'

'I know, my love, I can see it. As I said, leave it to me.'

On instinct, Rebecca went to Mrs Trevathan and gave her a hug. 'Thank you.'

Clearly surprised and embarrassed by such a display, Mrs Trevathan quickly extricated herself from Rebecca's arms and walked briskly to the door. 'Goodnight, dear, sleep well.'

'I will.'

Feeling calmer now that she knew that Jack was not going to appear at any moment, Rebecca took a bath, then retrieved the leather-bound diary from Donald's dressing room. Climbing into the bed, she turned to the pages after the First World War. The first entry talked about 'A' boarding a ship for India.

Surely, Rebecca thought suddenly, *Donald must be talking about Anahita?*

If he was, then this innocent-looking book, which had sat unnoticed on the shelves amongst the rest for decades, could contain the proof Ari needed to confirm Anahita's story.

Rebecca only had to read another two entries before she knew for certain that 'A' *was* Anahita. She glanced upwards and gave an ironic smile to the heavens.

'You led us both here, Anni, and I found it,' she whispered as she made herself comfortable and let Donald's words pull her back into the past . . .

Donald

February 1919

30

1 February

A left today on the ship that will take her to India.
I'm so completely miserable I can't explain. She's so
wonderful in every way – so warm, and wise, unlike
any other girl I've ever met. How I'll cope without
her in the next few weeks I don't know. And tomorrow
I must return to Astbury to try and tell Mother
that we have to sell the estate. Dreading her
reaction, quite frankly.

19 February

At Astbury. Mother still refusing to leave her room,
saying she's dying of some terrible sickness, but the
doctor can't diagnose anything physically wrong. The
entire household knows that she's still sulking about
Selina's marriage to Henri. Received a beautiful telegram
from A, who turned nineteen on-board ship three days
ago. Her words of love keep me going. She arrives in
Calcutta in two weeks' time. I can only hope she's back
home soon. Have sent telegram back telling her how

much I love her. Anyway, whether she likes it or not,
I'm going to speak to Mother today. We can't go on like
this any longer.

Bracing himself, Donald knocked on the door of his mother's
bedroom. He heard the clatter of china, and finally, a weak
'Enter'.

'Hello, Mother, could I open one of the curtains? It's so
dark in here I can't even see you.'

'If you must, but the light hurts my eyes,' Maud answered
in a quavering voice.

Donald pulled back one of the curtains and walked over to
his mother. 'May I sit down?'

'Pull up a chair beside me.' She indicated with a laboured
movement of her fingers on top of the sheets.

Donald did so. 'How are you?'

'No better.'

'At least you have some colour.'

'That's probably the rouge I asked Bessie to put on my
cheeks this morning,' replied Maud abruptly. 'I feel worse every
day.'

Donald took a deep breath. 'Mother, I understand
you're not well, but there really are some things we must discuss.'

'Like your sister marrying that ghastly little Frenchman?
Your father would turn in his grave.'

Donald thought back to his warm, loving father and knew
how happy he would have been that Selina had found someone to share her life with after suffering such tragedy.

'What's done is done, Mother, and there's nothing either of

us can do to change it. Selina is an adult and must make her own decisions.'

'If you don't approve, then why will you attend their sordid little wedding?' Maud retorted. 'No one in London society is going, and that's a fact.'

'She's my sister, Mother. And as a matter of fact, I happen to like Henri. I think he loves Selina and will take good care of her and Eleanor.'

'In that case, what is it you wish to discuss with me?' Maud changed the subject.

He steeled himself to tell her what he must. 'Mother, the estate is in the most dreadful financial mess, and if I don't do something about it soon, the house will literally fall down about our ears. The bank may even decide to repossess it, we're in such debt.'

His mother did not respond, so Donald ploughed on.

'Tragic as it is, the only thing I can do is sell up. I must pray I can find a buyer who has enough money to see its potential and take it on.'

At this, Maud's eyes darted to her son. Even in the dim light, Donald could see they were full of abject horror.

'*Sell* the Astbury Estate?'

He watched as his mother threw back her head and laughed.

'Donald, although I recognise the house is in need of some renovation, I think you're being a little overdramatic. Of course we can't sell it! It's been in the family since the sixteen hundreds!'

'Well, Mother, I've spent the past month talking to our bankers, the accountant and the estate manager, who all sing to the same tune. The estate is bankrupt and there is an end to it. I'm sorry, but that's how it is.'

'Donald –' Maud's voice rose suddenly from the depths of her debilitating illness – 'I can countenance many things, but I will never, ever agree to sell the Astbury Estate.'

'Mother,' Donald answered as calmly as he could, 'you may remember that three months ago, when I came of age, it was legally handed over to me. Therefore, it's my decision as to what is best to do. However sad or distasteful this situation is to all of us, sell we must. Or face the bailiffs coming in to forcefully remove us.'

At this, Maud fell back onto her pillow and clutched at her heart.

'How can you be so cruel? I'm a sick woman, and you bring me this news! I have a terrible pain in my chest; please, call Bessie, call the doctor . . .'

Donald looked down at her and saw that her face had indeed turned a ghastly pale colour.

'Mother, please, I don't mean to upset you, but really, we simply have no choice.'

She was panting now, trying to catch her breath. Donald stood up. 'I'll call for Dr Trefusis. I'm sorry to have distressed you like this.' He sighed and left the room.

Dr Trefusis came immediately. He examined Maud and found Donald waiting nervously outside.

'She's suffering from some form of nervous attack. I've given her a sleeping draught, and I'll be back in the morning to see how she is. However, for all our sakes,' he said firmly, 'I suggest you leave whatever it was you said to her earlier well alone for now.'

10 March

*Received a telegram from A to tell me that the boat
docked safely in India and that she is en route to
Cooch Behar Palace. Mother is still refusing to leave her
bedroom or allow me entry to it and I rattle round the
Hall in a constant state of anxiety and despair. Spent
this afternoon writing a long letter to A at the palace to
comfort myself. The pall of gloom that's presently cast
over Astbury is palpable. Servants are always the first to
smell trouble, and I think they all know something's up.
This morning, I had a property agent call round. The
estate has been valued and amounts to precious little,
considering what it contains. But at least it will be
enough to service the debt and buy myself and A a
much smaller country house. And enough, too, so
my mother can afford similar.*

April arrived and Donald was glad of the bright spring days
which brought the garden to life and caused the gorse on the
moors to begin to turn a vivid yellow. But as he trotted Glory
out of the stable one morning, a nagging fear assailed him. He
hadn't heard from Anni for almost a month, not since she'd
arrived at the palace in Cooch Behar. As he urged Glory to pick
up speed and cantered out across the moors, small demons
began to tap holes in his confidence.

Had she returned to India and met someone else? After all,
she was a beautiful, accomplished woman – not a princess, no,
but aristocratic with the sort of upbringing, grace and intelligence that any man would find attractive. He was a lord of the
British realm, yes, but a penniless one who, as soon as Astbury
was sold, would be without a kingdom to rule.

In the past month, Donald had begun to realise his education had only fitted him to become a member of the gentry and to run his estate and his staff. Unless he returned to the army – a thought which horrified him – what would he do with his future if the estate were sold? Dismounting by the brook where Anni and he had talked together that first summer, he lay down in the grass to think.

After his experiences in the war, a life lived in leisure with no purpose seemed pointless. And he felt guilty – guilty because it was *he* who would be the one to erase so many hundreds of years of the history of the Astburys at Astbury Hall. He found himself trying to think, yet again, if there was a way that the estate could be saved, but no plausible ideas revealed themselves. He knew that if there *were* a way, he would want to take it, not only because of the family history, but also because at least then he'd be doing something worthwhile by giving the two hundred or so local staff and tenant farmers a livelihood – not to mention his mother, who, despite her current histrionics, was genuinely devastated about having to leave.

Donald stood up and remounted Glory. He told himself he would simply have to accept it and concentrate his energies on his new future with Anni, and through that discover a new purpose to his life.

15 May

Yesterday (at long last), Mother emerged from her bedroom. But no word from A for almost ten weeks. I've written numerous letters to the address she gave me at the palace, but have heard nothing in reply. Where can she be? Never felt so damned low. Perhaps she's

*forgotten me. Perhaps she, too, like her friend Indira, has
met an Indian prince and has run away with him . . .*

Donald threw down his pen, stood up and gazed sullenly
through his bedroom window. The sun was high in the sky and
the day was beautiful, but he couldn't appreciate it. Dreadful
thoughts about Anni and reasons for her not replying to him
filled his mind constantly. Or perhaps, he reasoned, it was as
simple as her letters not getting through. The post between
England and India was notoriously difficult. But he knew he
wouldn't settle until he'd heard from her.

Downstairs at breakfast, he found his mother eating her
way through a plateful of bacon and eggs.

'I'm pleased to see you looking so much better, Mother.'
With an effort, he conjured up a tight smile.

'Well, you know how the winter affects me. But summer is
almost here and there's much to do.'

'Really?' said Donald, wondering what on earth she meant.

'Yes.' Maud passed him a letter across the breakfast table.
'Some old friends of your father's have suggested they might
like to come and visit us. Of course I have said yes.'

Donald perused the letter, which had a New York address.
'It says they'll be arriving in about seven weeks' time. Who are
the Drumners anyway?'

'Ralph Drumner is head of one of the oldest and, might I
add, wealthiest families in New York. I believe he owns a bank,
and his wife, Sissy, from what I remember of her, is delightful.
They also have a daughter, Violet, who's about the same age as
you. She's apparently on her European tour, but will join her
parents here at some point during the summer.'

Donald was surprised at her apparent enthusiasm. Maud regarded most Americans as 'common'.

'Well, as long as you'll be well enough to entertain them, Mother, I'm happy the thought of old friends visiting has perked you up.'

'Yes, I do believe it has.' Maud smiled happily at her son.

As she was in such a good mood, Donald decided to tackle the Selina question. 'Perhaps, whilst your visitors are here, you might consider having Selina down to visit. I know little Eleanor is missing her grandmother, and Astbury.'

'As you well know, Donald, so long as she is married to that man, Selina will never be welcome here in this house. Have I made myself clear?'

Donald sighed, knowing that as Lord Astbury and the legal owner of the estate, he was perfectly entitled to overrule her and invite his sister to visit whenever he chose. However, the inevitable aftermath of upsetting his mother again when she seemed so much brighter was not a situation he felt he could currently stomach.

9 June

Been to London to see the bank manager again. More bad news – time is running out now and I must make plans to put the estate up for sale soon. I also went to visit Anni's matron at The London Hospital in Whitechapel, who told me she hasn't heard a word from her either. Saw Selina briefly and she said she met Indira and her new husband in the South of France. Anni had told Indira she was returning directly to England when she left Paris in May. I really am beside myself with anxiety. Without her, what is there left?

14 July

*Ralph Drumner and his wife, Sissy, arrived to stay at
Astbury a week ago. They seem sweet enough and,
despite the dilapidated state of the house, are charmed
at staying in a real stately home with an English lord
present. Sissy actually curtsied to me when they arrived!
I think that Ralph Drumner is far shrewder than he
pretends. He's obviously as rich as Croesus; Sissy is in
all the latest Paris fashions and is dripping in diamonds.
They're here for two months, 'doing England', as they
put it, and tomorrow their daughter Violet arrives. Still
no word from A. My heart slowly turns to ice, as really
I can think of no good reason why she hasn't contacted
me, except for one.*

'The Drumners will be back here at three-thirty, in time for
afternoon tea,' announced Maud. 'I suggest we take it on
the terrace. You know they went to London to collect their
daughter? She arrived last night from Paris.'

'Yes, Mother,' Donald answered distractedly over breakfast.

'As you're of a similar age to her, it might help if you joined
us and entertained her.'

Donald folded *The Times* and stood up from the table.
'Don't worry, I'll be on parade.'

That afternoon, Donald took a ride around the estate. The
tenant farmers he visited at least seemed cheerful, having had
the perfect weather conditions for a bumper wheat crop, which
would be harvested within the next few weeks. This was news
they thought would please him; little did they know of the fate
about to befall them.

A prospective buyer for the estate had been found. Mr Kinghorn, a Cornish man by birth, was a businessman who'd done extremely well in tin during the war. He seemed a decent enough fellow and was eager to buy his way up the social ladder by acquiring the Astbury Estate. He was purchasing it for a song simply because there was no competition for it in the financially grim post-war years. Donald was yet to give his final handshake on the sale. But at least, he thought, comforting himself as he handed his mare over to the groom and walked back towards the Hall, he knew that the estate would probably be run in a far more efficient and businesslike way under the new owner's watchful eye.

Walking into the garden, Donald spied the Drumners and his mother sitting on the terrace taking tea and realised he was late. They would have to suffer him in his riding breeches rather than him face his mother's further displeasure. He strode up the steps and as he did so, the young woman at the table caught his eye. The masculine in him recognised immediately that Violet Drumner was a beauty. Her slender body was enclosed in a pretty tea dress, her blonde hair cut into a modish bob. As he drew closer, he could see that she had vivid brown eyes and perfectly shaped bow lips set in flawlessly pale skin.

'Good day to you,' he said as he arrived on the terrace at the table. 'Mother, Ralph, Sissy, my apologies for being late and, Miss Drumner,' Donald said, turning to the young woman, 'welcome to Astbury. May I call you Violet?'

'Yes, please do.' She smiled, revealing a glimpse of her perfect teeth.

'I'm delighted to make your acquaintance,' he said as he sat down and the maid hurried to pour him a cup of tea. 'How was your journey down here?'

'Extremely pleasant,' Violet answered. 'I haven't really seen outside London before. All the dances I attended here in England at the beginning of the summer were in town.'

'And, of course, Violet made her debut in New York last year,' said Sissy.

'Indeed,' said Maud, with a barely perceptible raise of her eyebrow.

'Did you enjoy the Season here too?'

'My, yes! I met so many interesting people. I simply adore England,' Violet added in her chirpy New York tone.

'Violet was quite the belle of the London Season by all accounts,' said Ralph. 'Had a heap of titled young men chasing after her. And don't say you didn't, Violet.'

'Oh really, Pa.' Violet blushed prettily. 'All the girls were popular.'

'Was there one young man in particular who caught your eye?' asked Maud.

'I think I'm too young to settle down just yet,' she answered diplomatically.

'Do you ride, Violet?' Donald asked, changing the subject.

'Oh yes, in Central Park, quite often, and when we go to our summer cottage in Newport, I have my own horse there.'

'Then whilst you're here, you must allow me to take you out for a ride across the moors.'

'I'd like that very much, Donald.'

24 *July*

Took V riding again this morning. She's technically proficient but rides like a girl, whereas A rode like a man. Still, she is sweet, bright and well educated and her pleasure at being here in England makes me smile. She's

also very pretty and I look at her sometimes, thinking
how her pale skin and blonde hair could not be more
in contrast to A's exotic, sultry looks. At least her being
here has helped me take my mind off A, as her natural
energy is infectious.

Donald realised that at least he'd been walking with a little more of a spring in his step in the past two weeks. With their typically American enthusiasm, the Drumners had lifted the atmosphere of gloom that had hung over Astbury of late. His mother had roused herself and invited some local gentry round for a rare dinner party a few days ago. Even the servants seemed genuinely appreciative of the additional work they had to do because of the visitors. Maids hurried up and down the stairs preparing baths for the two American women and caring for their enormous wardrobes. The guest bedroom corridor smelt permanently of Violet's perfume, light and summery, like herself.

Their bright faces greeted him at the breakfast table that morning, as Ralph extolled their plan to 'take in Cornwall' in the next few days.

'Mother,' Violet said, 'would you mind if I don't accompany you? Amy Venables is having a dance in London and has written to ask if I can attend. It would be lovely to see some of my English friends from the Season one more time before we leave for New York.'

'I'm sure it would, my dear, but you can't possibly go to London alone. It's simply out of the question,' replied Sissy.

'We have plenty of room at our London house,' Maud said. 'You can stay there, Violet dear.'

'That would be most kind of you, Lady Astbury.'

'And didn't you say you had to go up to town in the next few days, Donald?' added Maud.

'I . . . yes, I will be in London,' he replied uncomfortably, not wishing to appear rude.

'Why, it's perfect – you can accompany me to the dance! I'm sure Amy Venables wouldn't mind,' said Violet, clapping her hands together.

'What a splendid idea!' said Maud. 'Right, that's settled then.' She smiled at the assembled company.

After breakfast, Donald retreated into the library with *The Times* but was unable to concentrate. Despite the fact that it was now five months since he had last heard from Anni, he felt uncomfortable at the thought of accompanying Violet to a dance. However, it seemed he'd been out-manoeuvred by his mother, and it would look churlish to try to back out now.

Musing on his mother's sudden new lease of life and unusually accommodating manner, for the first time Donald wondered if the Drumners' sudden arrival at Astbury had been as random as it had seemed. After all, there was no doubt about the Drumners' wealth, and Ralph had talked only the other day about the large trust fund he looked after for Violet until she came of age in three months' time – the amount, of course, that would come with her when she married.

'Damn you, Mother!' Donald slammed *The Times* down on the table, stood up and walked to the window. He berated himself for being so naive; how could he not have seen the web his mother was spinning around him?

'I will not be bought or manipulated,' he said through gritted teeth as he looked out at the warm August sunshine bathing the park in soft light. Besides, one thing Maud could not control was Violet's feelings for him. With her fortune, attractive personality and undeniable beauty, Donald supposed she could have any eligible man she chose. It was doubtful she'd be interested in him. Yet he thought of the way she smiled at him from under her long lashes, how she seemed eager to join him in any activity he suggested . . .

During the long train journey up to London, Donald listened as Violet chatted about her life in New York, the beautiful house on Park Avenue where she lived with her parents and the wonderful things she had seen on her European tour.

'I fear it will be awfully hard to return. Americans can be so insular, you know,' she added, as though the experiences of her three months in Europe had made her a citizen of the world.

'So you prefer England?' Donald enquired politely.

'Oh yes, I've always had a great passion for your literature. I just adore the countryside here. Everything is so quaint.'

Arriving at the house in Belgrave Square, Violet was taken upstairs to her room by a maid and Donald walked into the drawing room to find Selina sitting at the bureau writing a letter.

'Donald.' Her face lit up as she saw him and she stood to embrace him.

'How are you, Selina?'

'I've just arrived back from Henri's château in France. He's still over there, attending to some business. Eleanor and I are staying here for now until our new house in Kensington is ready for occupation. Tea?'

'Lovely,' said Donald sitting down in a chair while Selina rang for the maid.

'So how is everything at Astbury?' she asked him.

'Well, Mother has certainly improved; she is positively

lively compared to how she was when you last saw her.' Donald raised a knowing eyebrow at his sister.

'Any sign of my being forgiven?'

'To be honest, I haven't broached the subject recently. She's been so much jollier lately I haven't wanted to raise anything that may disrupt her mood.'

'Besides, you've probably been busy escorting your young American heiress around the delights of Devon.'

'I've done my duty, certainly,' he said in agreement. 'Tonight I have to go to some ghastly dance with all her ingénue debutante friends.'

'Do you like Violet, Donald? I'm looking forward to meeting her.'

'Yes, she's a very nice girl. But –' Donald's face darkened – 'you understand that's as far as it goes.'

'Yes, of course. Have you heard anything from Anni?'

'Not a peep.' He sighed. 'I even wrote to Scotland Yard to see if they could make inquiries as to her whereabouts, but they've come back with nothing. She's literally vanished into thin air.'

'Well, surely that's something?' comforted Selina. 'At least we can presume she isn't dead?'

'Selina, she could be anywhere. She may not even have returned to England as she said she would. In fact, I'm starting to think she may have stayed in India and simply couldn't bring herself to tell me.'

The two of them were silent in contemplation as the maid brought in the tea tray. Selina poured a cup for each of them, eyeing Donald thoughtfully.

'Donald, darling, I hate to say it, but—'

'I know, and please don't,' he halted her. 'I'm beginning to realise that I may have no choice but to try to move on.'

'Yes, I'm afraid so,' Selina agreed. 'I know how you loved her but—'

'*Love* her,' interrupted Donald.

'Yes, love her,' Selina corrected herself, 'but any marriage between the two of you was never going to be easy. You know what English society is like, and the two of you would have struggled to be accepted.'

'I care nothing about that,' said Donald angrily. 'I stood toe-to-toe in the trenches with men of all manner of creed and colour, saw their bravery. *And* watched them die just as painfully as anyone with white skin did, might I add.'

'Well,' Selina replied quietly, 'it's all credit to you that you carry no prejudice, but you know very well that many others do, and always will.'

'Are you saying that Anni has left me to protect me from that?'

'No, I was just suggesting it as a possible reason. I'm as baffled as you that she hasn't contacted you.'

'I hope that Anni never felt any discomfort about her skin colour from me.'

'Donald, darling,' Selina tried to calm him, 'I'm not saying she did from you, but perhaps from others. Look at our own mother, for example. And what about if you'd had children? They would have been half-caste and—'

'Enough!' Donald clattered his cup into the saucer.

'Forgive me.' Selina was on the brink of tears. 'I was only trying to point out the pitfalls if all had worked out as you'd planned it.'

'None of them would have mattered if we were together.'

Donald stood up. 'I'd better go and change for this damned party.'

Donald walked upstairs to his bedroom and sank onto the bed, his head in his hands. Could Selina's theory be right? Had Anni, to save him from himself, decided it was best if she stayed away?

He simply refused to believe that this could be the case. Anni had known that he despised prejudice in any form.

Time and again, Donald came back to the same conclusion. He was now convinced she had simply realised she didn't love him as she had thought. Or perhaps she loved someone else more, he thought with a shudder.

Tears came to his eyes as, for the first time, he seriously contemplated a future without her. And realised that he was beginning to give up hope.

31

25 August

Enjoyed the dance last night more than I thought I would. A couple of my old friends from Harrow were there escorting two of the girls. It was remarkably good to see them and we chatted about old times. They're both due to be married in the next few weeks and have invited me to attend. They both, of course, ribbed me about V, saying what luck I had to be dancing with the most beautiful girl in the room . . .

Violet had decided to stay on in town for a little longer than planned. And Donald was loath to return to Devon to give Mr Kinghorn his final decision on the sale of the estate, so he decided to put it off for a short while. In between escorting Violet to various dinners and to see some of the sights in London, Donald went to his club in Pall Mall. He enjoyed renewing old acquaintances and chatting late into the night about the war.

More and more he realised that, when he'd been in London after the Armistice, his entire world had revolved around Anni and his love for her. Nothing else had mattered except being with her, and he'd had little time or inclination for anything else. It was as if he'd lived in a bubble, and though his heart still ached for her, at least the current social diversion was welcome.

Admittedly, he enjoyed the fact that his friends envied his relationship with Violet, who really did seem to be the belle of the social whirl in London. She was beautiful, quick-witted and, as Donald began to discover while she was away from the smothering cocoon of her parents, was possessed of both a vivacious character and a wicked sense of humour.

Even he found himself being charmed by her sense of fun and her genuine pleasure simply at being alive. Where Anni had been deep, passionate and dark, Violet was merry, frivolous and light. He also noticed she was endlessly generous, often arranging thoughtful surprises to please her many friends.

The invitations came in thick and fast and she was welcomed at any London dinner table, the men vying to sit next to her and enjoy her company. Donald found himself chaperoning her most evenings to social gatherings, and, he had to admit, he began to enjoy it.

Towards the end of Violet's time in London, they were invited to a dinner at Lord and Lady Charlesworth's house near Hyde Park. Their son, Harry, was heir to one of the largest and most prominent estates in the country. He was also extremely handsome, with a charming and exuberant personality. As usual, being the girl of the moment, Violet was seated next to her young host at dinner, and Donald watched as Harry and she whispered to each other in an intimate fashion. It was obvious that he was very taken with her, and she with him.

Over pudding, a territorial pang hit his heart and Donald realised with a jolt that he was jealous.

Taken aback by the sudden realisation, he was in a contemplative mood on the drive home. Violet was in her usual high spirits, full of chatter about Harry and how he had invited her to visit his country estate in Derbyshire when the shooting season began in a few days' time.

The following morning, a letter arrived on the tray in the hall for Violet. Donald, passing through for breakfast, turned it over and saw the Charlesworth seal on the back. That evening, Violet did not ask Donald to accompany her as usual; instead one of her girlfriends arrived to escort her and she left in a stunning new Paquin dress and a haze of perfume. He didn't manage to sleep until he heard her light footsteps tap-tapping up the stairs in the small hours.

She didn't appear for breakfast the next morning, but at luncheon she was present at the table, yawning.

'Did you have a good evening?' Donald asked her politely.

'Wonderful,' she said dreamily. 'Harry knows all the best places to go in London. He took me to an underground club where they play the best Jazz music! We danced all night, so much that my feet hurt this morning. And his crowd were wonderful.'

'Are you seeing Harry again?'

'I do hope so. He's such fun.'

'Well, I must think of returning home to Devon. Shall I leave you here in London?' Donald suggested. 'You seem more than capable of taking care of yourself.'

She looked at him from underneath her long lashes, suddenly vulnerable. 'I'm not sure I'd enjoy travelling all that way back alone.'

'Far be it for me to spoil your fun,' he replied, feeling double his years. 'Why don't we compromise and leave for Devon at the end of the week?'

'Yes, that would be just perfect! I've had such a wonderful time in London. Thank you, Donald.'

'Not at all. I'm glad you've enjoyed yourself. Now, you must excuse me, I have an appointment at my club.' Donald stood up and moved towards the door, then paused and looked back at her. 'Perhaps before we leave, you could take me to one of these new places that Harry knows?'

'Oh, Donald, I'd be delighted!'

And suddenly, the tables were turned. In his desire to please Violet, for the next three nights Donald found himself learning to dance to the new Jazz music which was so popular in America and causing a stir in England. They would arrive home in Belgrave Square sometime before dawn, sweating and giggling. Donald would kiss her goodnight sedately at the bottom of the stairs and she would smile at him, then tap-tap in her intrinsically feminine way up the stairs to bed.

On their last night in London, Violet had disappeared upstairs as usual and Donald walked into the drawing room to pour himself a brandy. As he took a sip, he knew that tonight he had wanted to kiss her properly. With a sigh, he realised he was actually looking forward to travelling back to Devon the following day and having her to himself.

'Anni,' he whispered to the air, sinking guiltily into the chair. 'Forgive me.'

On the train journey home, Violet, obviously exhausted from her London exertions, fell asleep for most of the way and Donald used the time to take stock of his feelings.

He wasn't sure whether his growing keenness on Violet was simply a reaction to the misery of losing Anni, but neither could he ignore the fact that in her beautiful eyes lay an alternative key to his future. If he was to sell Astbury, it would leave him without a purpose in life. When he had first contemplated this scenario, Anni had been included in his equation and the thought of beginning anew with her by his side had made the thought bearable. But now, Donald thought with a sigh, if he were to sell up and be alone, what point would his life have?

On the other hand, if he married Violet, of whom he was fond and who would undoubtedly make Astbury Hall come alive again with her money, personality and social contacts, would it really be such a terrible alternative?

And perhaps, he thought, to some extent Selina had been right; in the few months after the war, he'd been mentally and emotionally ravaged, scarred by the terrible things he'd seen. Sharing that experience with someone who understood had been vital. But in the long term . . . Donald stared out of the train window and asked himself bluntly whether it could really have worked. Had he been living in a fool's paradise?

He also admitted to himself that he had enjoyed his old world during the past month in London. However shallow it might have been at times, at least he *belonged* in it. He was sure he could never love anyone the way he loved Anni, but who of his class *could* enjoy the luxury of marrying for love? He was certain his parents hadn't – they'd simply formed a successful partnership.

And he could hardly ask for a prettier bride, Donald reflected as he gazed at Violet across the table in the first-class carriage. It wouldn't be a hardship to make love to her, surely? There was no doubt he already desired her physically.

Of course, he knew there was every chance Violet would turn his proposal down. He was only one of a number of her suitors, and a virtually penniless one at that.

But by the time the train pulled into Exeter, Donald had made up his mind to ask her.

Over dinner that night, the Drumners talked of their passage home in a week's time.

'We'll all be sorry to leave England's shores. Isn't that right, Violet?' Sissy asked her daughter.

'Extremely sorry,' said Violet with a sigh. 'I seem to have taken to England so well.'

'And England's certainly taken to you,' Donald heard himself saying with a smile.

Later, over brandy and cigars in the library with Ralph Drumner, Donald girded his loins to say the words he needed to say.

'Mr Drumner—'

'Please, Lord Astbury, call me Ralph.'

'Then you must call me Donald,' he responded. 'Ralph, it can't have escaped your notice how very fond I've become of Violet.'

Ralph raised an eyebrow. 'Really? Then, obviously, your relationship has progressed in the past month.'

'Yes, it has,' Donald agreed. 'Violet is extremely special and –' Donald thought carefully of the right words to choose – 'has endeared herself to me in many ways.'

'She is indeed special.' Ralph scrutinised him. 'And with a very large fortune to boot. You can understand I wouldn't want to see my daughter taken advantage of by any man because of it.'

'Of course not,' Donald said hastily, 'and I can assure you, it is not in my nature to do so.'

'Even if the Astburys are currently in need of a serious injection of cash?' Ralph eyed him. 'Believe me, Donald, I'm not blind, or stupid. I've taken the time to look around and I've seen with my own eyes the amount of money this place needs to set it back on its feet.'

'Ralph, forgive me for saying so, but I'm talking about my feelings for your daughter here, not my financial position,' Donald replied steadily. 'In truth, I currently have a buyer for the estate and have seriously been thinking of accepting his offer.'

At this, Ralph looked genuinely surprised. 'Really? You'd be prepared to sell your birthright, your own family's history? This place which, excuse me if I'm wrong, has belonged to your family since the sixteen hundreds?'

'If I have to, yes. At present, it's a rope around my neck, and if I'm unable to find the financial means to pay off its debts and restore it, I'd prefer to be realistic, have done with it and sell it.'

At this, Ralph was silent and Donald could see he was thinking things through. 'Where would you live if you did sell up?'

'I've no idea, but to be honest, that's secondary to making sure myself and my mother, plus any wife I choose to take and the subsequent children we might have, are financially secure.'

'I guess I've underestimated you, young man. I spend my days making difficult financial decisions which cannot and must not be affected by emotions. In my experience, I've encountered few people who can face these kinds of concerns pragmatically. Especially when they relate to the family home.'

'I can only assure you, Ralph, that I'm visiting Mr Kinghorn, my prospective buyer, at the end of this week. I intend to give him my final decision then.'

'Which is to sell?'

'Yes,' Donald answered. 'Put bluntly, I have no choice.'

'But it will break your mother's heart if you do, surely?'

'As you yourself said, I can't allow my emotions to come into it. I must be pragmatic, above all.'

'Have you mentioned this situation to Violet?' Ralph asked.

'No, but I'm presuming that if she wishes to marry me, she'll love me enough for where we live to be an irrelevance.'

Donald couldn't help but smile to himself as his comment hit home.

'Of course,' Ralph agreed after a pause. 'Once you've paid your creditors, will there be anything left over from the sale of Astbury?'

'Enough to buy a decent enough sort of house in the country and to keep our London place.'

'I see.'

'I'm hoping this should be enough to satisfy your daughter's future requirements,' Donald added.

'Do I take it you're asking for my daughter's hand in marriage?'

'Yes,' Donald agreed. 'Though I can understand after what we've just discussed that you may feel it unwise to consent to it. After all, I can't give her what other suitors might be able to.'

'Well, listen here, young man, despite what I've just said, even I must realise that money is not the most important consideration here. It's my daughter's heart and her future that matter to me. Have you spoken to her of your feelings?'

'No, I felt it was inappropriate until I'd talked to you.'

'Well now, Donald, you've sure given me something to think about. But I guess, at the end of the day, it's Violet's decision, one way or the other.'

'So, do you give me permission to ask her?'

'Yes. However, I'd prefer you not to mention to her the fact that you're considering selling Astbury. We both know that won't be the case if she consents to your proposal. I'm a father, and I want my little girl to have the best.' Ralph drained the rest of the brandy in his glass and looked hard at Donald. 'Young man, I have to admit I wasn't sure about you, but your honesty during this conversation has won me over. I think you'd make a fine husband for my daughter.'

'Thank you, Ralph. I'm glad that you feel that way.'

'I'm happy if my girl's happy. Now, shall we go and join the ladies in the drawing room?'

Perhaps it was emotional osmosis, but all three women looked up expectantly at Ralph and Donald as they came into the room.

'I'm ready for my bed. Sissy, will you join me?' Ralph said pointedly to his wife.

'Of course,' said Sissy, who kissed Violet goodnight before she left the room.

Maud also followed suit, wishing both Violet and Donald pleasant dreams.

'So, here we are, then,' said Donald awkwardly when finally they were alone.

'Yes, here we are,' said Violet.

Donald sat down in a chair opposite her. 'You know, I was just saying to your father how much I'll miss your company when you return to New York next week.'

'Will you?' asked Violet, wide-eyed. 'Oh, my!'

'Yes, I will. In the past month, you must have noticed that I've grown exceedingly fond of you.'

'Well, that's very sweet of you to say, Donald, thank you.'

'And I was just discussing with your father a way in which I could perhaps persuade you to stay longer.'

'Such as?'

'Well –' Donald took a deep breath. 'Violet, I'll understand if you feel this is an inappropriate suggestion, for I've no idea about your feelings for me. But I found that I've rather fallen for you. So, I was wondering if I could – er – ask if you wished to be my wife?'

She glanced at him, a glimmer of a smile on her lips. 'Donald Astbury, are you trying to propose to me?'

'Yes, and I apologise if I seem a little awkward. Don't do this sort of thing every day, you know.' Donald took another deep breath and went down on one knee in front of Violet. He took her hands in his. 'Violet Drumner, I am asking you if you would make me the happiest of men and do me the honour of marrying me.'

She looked down at him but did not reply.

Feeling embarrassed and uncomfortable in the ensuing silence, Donald continued. 'I completely understand if there's another who has stolen your heart, and I promise I'll take your refusal like a man.'

At this, Violet threw back her head and laughed. 'You mean Harry Charlesworth?'

'Yes, as a matter of fact, I do,' he replied, not seeing the joke.

'Oh, Donald, excuse me.' Violet tried to compose herself. 'Harry has no romantic interest in me whatsoever. In fact, he has no interest in any girl at all, if you understand my meaning.'

'You mean he's a homosexual?'

'Why yes! Of course. Isn't it obvious?'

'Not to me, no.'

'Well now,' Violet said, regaining her composure, 'I'm sure that Harry will continue to be one of my best friends in the future. As a matter of fact, I spoke to him a lot about you.' Suddenly, Violet's eyes were serious. 'He told me that you were a dark horse.'

'Did he now?'

'Oh yes, apparently there was some talk last year in London about you.'

'Really?'

'Yes, something about you having a mystery woman and hiding her away.'

'My goodness.' Donald showed his genuine surprise. 'I didn't realise my movements were so closely observed.'

'Donald Astbury!' she chided him. 'You're a peer of the realm, and an eligible one at that. Of course people were watching you. So, before I give you my answer, I want to know whether it was true. Did you have a secret love?'

Donald tried to form an eloquent response, knowing it was essential he did so. 'There was someone whom I was close to, yes. But I promise you, Violet, it was all over a long time ago.'

'Are you sure?'

'Completely.' For the first time, Donald actually believed his own words.

'Well, I must say, I'm surprised at your proposal. I had an idea you weren't interested in me at all,' Violet confessed.

'Really?'

'Yes, I mean –' she blushed prettily – 'I think you may have realised a while back I was mighty interested in you.'

'Then the question is, are you still?'

'Why, Donald! How can you even doubt it? I feel I've done just about everything to show you in the past few weeks. You honestly haven't seen it?'

'To be truthful, I thought you'd fallen for our friend Harry Charlesworth.'

'No, you goose! I spent most of my time complaining to him about the fact that *you* didn't seem to notice me. When the whole of London knows how madly in love with you I am.'

'Are you really?' Donald asked in wonder.

'Of course, and I have been since the first moment I saw you walking up onto the terrace in your riding breeches!' She lowered her eyes coquettishly.

'So, does that mean you might consider becoming my wife?'

'Yes. In fact, I'd be awful happy to say yes right now.'

'Then I'm a very happy man too.' Donald pulled Violet to her feet and took her in his arms. 'So, if we are to consider ourselves formally engaged, may I kiss you?'

'I think you might, yes, but I do have to ask one thing: do I get a ring?'

'Violet –' Donald was aghast – 'I have it upstairs, I can go and get it now. I—'

Violet put a finger to Donald's lips. 'Hush, I was only teasing.'

Donald reached for her lips then, and they were soft and welcoming. He didn't feel the same urgent passion that he had for Anni, but he was gratified by her obvious eagerness. He broke away eventually and tipped Violet's chin so that he could look into her eyes. 'So, shall we tell everyone tomorrow that Lord Astbury has chosen his future "Lady"?'

'That would be wonderful. But I don't think they'll be surprised. We ladies presumed the reason you were so long over brandy and cigars tonight with Pa was because you were asking him for my hand. I've no doubt my parents will be pleased. My mother knows how I feel about you, and I gather from Pa's sudden desire to go to bed early tonight that he didn't pose any objections. And as long as Pa's happy, I think you've got yourself a deal.'

'Well, then, it looks like I have,' Donald said, smiling at her turn of phrase. He yawned suddenly. 'Forgive me, Violet, I feel completely exhausted. It's probably the tension of having to speak to your father. Shall we retire?' He offered her his hand and she slipped her slim, cool fingers into his. They walked from the drawing room into the main hall and stood together at the bottom of the stairs.

'I can hardly believe that this is to be my new home,' she said in wonder as she looked up at the vast dome above her. 'But I do think it could do with a lick of paint, don't you?' she asked as they walked slowly up the stairs.

'Most definitely.'

'And I'll bet there's no proper heating installed, and I'd guess it gets pretty cold here in the winter.'

'Again, you're right,' he said as they reached the top of the stairs. 'Goodnight, then, beautiful Violet.'

'Goodnight,' she said quietly, and then turned away to walk along the corridor to her bedroom.

Donald turned in the opposite direction to go to his. Once

inside, he sat down on the narrow bed and stared out of the window into the moonlight.

'Anni, wherever you are, please know I'll love you forever. Forgive me.'

Then he put his head in his hands and wept.

32

30 September

*V's 'folks', as she calls them, are about to return
to New York. Daddy Drumner has to get back
there for business reasons – presumably to count his
millions. Violet is staying on at Astbury to organise
the wedding with Mother. If I was hoping for a quiet
affair, I'm going to be disappointed. Anyone would
think it was a royal occasion from the numbers
V is determined to invite. Thank God Daddy
Drumner is coughing up the cost of it for his
little girl. Last night, he took me into the library
for a discussion . . .*

'So,' Ralph said as he poured himself a large brandy, sat down
in a chair and lit a cigar, 'it warms my heart to see my little girl
so radiant.'

'I will do everything in my power to see that she stays that
way, sir,' said Donald, sitting down opposite him.

'Now, let's get down to the detail – the matter of Violet's
fortune. It will come into her hands in six weeks' time, on her

twenty-first birthday. It's a serious amount of money, but I'm aware that a large chunk of it will be needed to pay off the estate's debts and restore the place she's going to make her future home.'

'Ralph, as I said to you that evening when I asked for Violet's hand, if you're uncomfortable with this scenario, I'm happy to tell Mr Kinghorn the estate is his. We can move into something much smaller.'

'And as you well know, young man, my daughter would be horrified at the thought,' Drumner countered. 'Let's cut to the chase: I'd like to know from you exactly how much. And you can add another fifty grand on top of that for the interior. You'll discover my daughter will only want the best. Can you do that for me, son?'

'I can certainly do what I can to give you a general idea,' Donald agreed.

'Well, just don't be shy. I'm a great believer in getting things right from the start, and I want Violet to have the best damned house in England. Whatever it takes, I can assure you there's enough to fund it. And then some,' Ralph added. 'Her investments have shot through the roof since the war. Violet is a very wealthy young woman. All I ask of you is that you make my little girl happy. If you don't, if there's any messing around – and you know what I mean by that – I won't be pleased. Understand me?'

'I do,' agreed Donald, thinking that Ralph Drumner certainly knew how to dispense with etiquette as well as emotions.

'As long as we're on the same page, I'm all for the marriage. It seems you have a project on your hands, and given I'll be the one writing the cheques as Violet's advisor, I suggest you start gathering quotes as soon as you can.'

'I will.'

As Donald began to investigate the costs of restoring the fabric of the building, Violet busied herself with the interior design. The house became awash with curtain fabric samples, and tradesmen arrived from London to offer her furniture in the modern style, colourful rugs, lampshades and new mattresses for all the beds, which she insisted on herself and Donald trying out.

'If we are to invite weekend houseguests, I simply can't have them sleeping on the ones here at the moment. They're probably crawling with bedbugs too.' Violet shuddered as she climbed off a mattress laid out on the drawing-room floor. She grabbed a sample of gold damask cloth and held it up to the window. 'Don't you think this would look darling in here? It would make the room so warm. Or –' she put it on top of her blonde tresses – 'shall I wear it as a veil instead?' She walked towards him and gave him a fond kiss on the cheek. 'It would just be swell to get the house looking the piece by the time all our friends arrive for the wedding.'

Donald knew that if anyone could get this house in order that quickly, it was Violet. Already, floorboards were up all over the place, with plumbers and electricians surveying what could be done to bring heat and modern lighting to the house, and painters gathered to plan for the enormous job of decorating the rooms once the basics had been done. Donald sent the quotes by post and telegram to Ralph as they came in, his eyes watering at the cost. So far, he had received no complaints.

Violet had already engaged an interior designer, Vincent Pleasance, whom one of her smart London friends had recommended. Personally, Donald couldn't bear Vincent, as he minced around the Hall extolling his vision of the new Astbury to Violet.

'Good grief,' said Maud at breakfast one morning when Violet was otherwise engaged with Vincent redesigning the master bedroom. 'Can't she see it's the emperor's new clothes? That ghastly little man will have you lying at night in a tart's boudoir if you're not careful, Donald.'

'I've told him not to touch my dressing room, Mother. I've said I like it just the way it is.'

'I should hope so too. Violet has also suggested that Vincent comes to cast his eye over the Dower House to "update" it for when I move in there after your marriage. Suffice to say, I've declined his help. It will do me very well just as it is.'

The wedding date had been set for early April 1920. Donald removed himself thankfully to London, leaving Violet in charge of organising the house and the wedding. She was tireless in her efforts to oversee the tiniest detail and Donald felt that the best thing to do was to let her get on with it.

At his club, he received numerous slaps on the back and bottles of champagne.

'Got yourself a good one there, old chap!'

'She'll sort you out well and truly, and the pile in Devon!'

'Absolute stunner, can't wait for the wedding, and I bet you can't either, eh?'

14 October

Went home to Devon last weekend to talk to the estate manager about the new equipment he needs. The house

*is in chaos with tradesmen and workers everywhere, and
V presides like a queen over everything. I do admire her,
though; her tenacity and refusal to take no for an answer
are so very un-British. Mind you, I do sometimes
wonder if she loves Astbury more than she loves me . . .*

The Drumners arrived back from New York for Christmas,
and Donald knew they were impressed with what their
daughter had achieved so far. Donald had declined to comment on the proposed rug for the drawing room. Fashioned
out of eighteen leopard skins, it was sewn together by a
famous Italian designer. Donald could not help but smile at his
mother's face as she surveyed it for the first time.

'What do you think, Mother?' Violet had taken to
addressing Maud thus.

'Well, it's not what I would have had in my day,' Maud
acknowledged with considerable grace.

'I think it's just gorgeous, honey,' said Sissy, sitting down on
the newly covered red Chesterfield. 'You've warmed the old
place up very well.'

'Do you like it, Donald?' Violet turned to her fiancé anxiously. 'Animal skin is just so in fashion right now.'

'I think it's . . . very striking,' he replied diplomatically.

The plan was for much of the structural work to be undertaken when Donald and Violet left for an extended honeymoon after their April wedding. First stop would be New York,
where Donald would be introduced to society. After that,
Violet had expressed a longing to go back to Europe, so they
were to take a house in Italy for the summer.

'Venice will be so romantic, just you and I,' Violet had said
happily, when she had made the suggestion.

Knowing Violet, Donald mused later, they almost certainly wouldn't be on their own for long. She'd already mentioned friends of hers who were staying nearby. Never one for the frantic social whirl, Donald only hoped that once they returned to Astbury after their honeymoon, Violet would settle down. But as a trail of friends from London came to stay for the weekend and the corridors rang with the sound of laughter and the gramophone played endlessly, he doubted it.

'We must employ some more servants, Donny,' Violet said one February morning as the final houseguest departed after a particularly raucous weekend. 'The ones we have simply can't cope.'

'Of course,' he replied, then took himself off for a hack across the moors on Glory. He sat in his favourite place by the brook and shivered in the cold morning air, wondering if he would ever have the courage to say no to any of Violet's requests. And indeed, given that she'd paid for everything, how could he?

Standing up and pacing because it was too cold out on the moor to sit still, Donald wondered what exactly *would* be left of the old Astbury once Violet had finished with it. Her current project was focusing on new artwork for the walls. This morning, she had expressed a dislike for the family portraits that ran up the stairs.

'They're so dull, honey! There's some wonderful work by modern artists that would really brighten the old place up. I'm just so in love with Picasso,' she said dreamily. 'I kind of gave Pa a hint that I adore him, so I'm hoping he might get one for us as a wedding present. Wouldn't that be swell?' she said as she hugged him.

He had buttoned his lip, deciding those kinds of arguments

were best undertaken once they were home from the honeymoon and the house was finished.

Donald kicked morosely at a frozen clod of wiry grass. During the past two weeks, he hadn't been sleeping very well, waking up in the middle of the night in a muck sweat, panicking about the future. All he held on to was the fact that the Astbury Estate would be secure for at least another couple of generations, even if he had to suffer it being filled with Violet's friends.

Donald sighed. In saving Astbury, he seemed to have sacrificed himself. Yet he knew there was nothing that could be done to stop it. The wheels had been set in motion, and like a runaway train, it was picking up speed as it hurtled forwards.

2 April

Tomorrow, I will marry V. The entire household is in a state of high excitement and nerves, with V racing around making sure everything from the flowers on the table in the ballroom to the exact style of her bridesmaids' hair is as perfect as she needs it to be. Yesterday, she threw a fit and sent back the Order of Service cards because the typeface was not to her liking. Sometimes I can only hope that I will be to her liking, too ...

Donald finished writing in his diary, then tucked it away on the shelf with his other books. He felt it had become his only form of self-expression – whom else could he talk to about his fears for the future? He had watched his mother's eyebrows rise time and again at what she saw as Violet's vulgar and ostentatious taste. But since she herself had initiated the process, which would finally lead her son to the altar in the family chapel, she could hardly complain.

Donald climbed into his single bed for the last time as a bachelor. Tomorrow night, he would be moving to their newly decorated master suite – complete with inter-connecting doors to a sitting room and bathroom – where he would begin to share a bed and a life with Violet.

He lay sleepless into the small hours, longing for Anni's calm, wise strength. And dusky, butterscotch skin. If only it was she whom he would be taking up the aisle tomorrow as his wife, and then to bed later . . .

Guilty with his sudden arousal at the thought, Donald turned over and tried to sleep.

For months afterwards, the wedding of Violet Drumner to Lord Donald Astbury was talked of in awed tones. The lucky guests who were present spoke in wonder of the abundant, beautiful flowers that filled the chapel, the sumptuous wedding breakfast and dancing in the Long Gallery to the sound of the Savoy Quartet, who had come all the way from London.

And, of course, the bride herself, stunning in hand-embroidered French lace, with a train nearly as long as the chapel aisle. *Tatler* awarded the wedding an unprecedented eight-page spread, with photos of the elite of both American and British society, a healthy gathering of politicians and glamorous stars of stage and screen.

The following morning over breakfast, Donald arrived downstairs and found the Drumners cooing over the photographs in all the national newspapers.

'It seems our little party caused quite a stir, son,' commented Ralph, beaming from ear to ear.

'Violet looks so wonderful in the photographs, and of course you look mighty handsome yourself, Donald. So,' Sissy said with a conspiratorial wink, 'how's my little girl this morning?'

'Very well indeed, I think. The maid has taken up a breakfast tray to her and I thought I'd leave her alone to give her a chance to get ready in peace.'

'Sensible boy,' murmured Ralph, 'you're learning the rules already.'

As the guests who had stayed overnight began to filter into the breakfast room, Donald made himself scarce and went up to his dressing room.

4 April

Well, here I am married to V. Everyone thrilled with the way the day went off, and I admit V did a wonderful job.

He paused, looking out of the window as he thought how to express his feelings in words.

And our first night together was fine. V looked a dream in her silk nightdress – preferred it to the mountain of lace she wore to marry me – and I think that all went off satisfactorily. Of course, not like it was with A, but then, I'm resigned to the fact that nothing ever could be. Henceforth, I'm a married man and will do my best to be a dutiful husband. V's a sweet girl and she deserves it. Have to pack now as we leave for America with Ma and Pa Drumner early tomorrow morning.

*

A month later, Selina was sitting in the drawing room of the London house, looking at the photographs of Donald and his new bride in *Tatler*.

Before the wedding, he had come to tell her that he had insisted to their mother that she, Henri and Eleanor were invited. And she had asked him whether he was happy.

'Happy enough,' he had replied, then swiftly changed the subject.

Selina was at the Belgrave Square house for the afternoon, organising the last bits and pieces that were to be taken to the new house in Kensington she shared with Henri. When Donald and Violet returned from their honeymoon, this would become their house alone, and a maid was upstairs packing the last remnants from her old bedroom.

Selina heard the bell ring but didn't move to answer it. Three minutes later, there was a knock on the drawing-room door and the housekeeper poked her head around it.

'Excuse me, Countess, but there is a – foreign person who wishes to see you. She came to the house yesterday saying she left something here a few months ago, but I sent her on her way.'

'Really? What is her name?'

'She says her name is Anahita.'

Selina's heart missed a beat. 'Right,' she said as she composed herself. 'Please show her in.'

She stood up as Anni walked into the drawing room. Selina saw immediately that she was agonisingly thin.

'Hello, Selina. I've come to collect my suitcase. I left it here before I went away.'

'Please, Anni,' said Selina, 'sit down. I'll send for some tea.'

'Thank you.'

She sat down, and once the maid had been dispatched, Selina said, 'Anni, what has happened to you? Where have you been? You look dreadful. Donald and I have been out of our minds with worry.'

'It's a long story. I fell ill when I was in France. I returned to England and was in hospital for many months.'

'Anni, why didn't you contact me? You know I would have helped.'

'Yes, Selina, I know and I thank you for it, but at the time I was too ill to know where I was. Some things happen – unexpectedly.' Anni sighed.

'I'm so sorry to hear of your illness.'

'Thank you. I'm regaining more of my strength as each day passes,' Anni said, smiling for the first time.

'Where are you living now?' Selina asked, understanding that whatever the truth of Anni's disappearance, she was guarded and reluctant to speak of it.

'I have a friend from my school days named Charlotte who lives up in Yorkshire. She very kindly offered me somewhere to live until I was recovered. Her family owns a house up on the Yorkshire moors and we – I live there. Soon, when I'm stronger, I hope to return to London and work as a nurse again.'

'You should have contacted one of us, at least,' said Selina as the maid reappeared with the tea.

'But, Selina, I sent a long letter from Paris telling Donald I'd be away for some time and to wait for me. I've sent more letters recently too. Did he not get them?'

'No, Anni, he didn't. In fact, he hasn't heard a single word from you for well over a year, since you docked in Calcutta.' Selina watched Anni pale and her long, thin fingers tighten their clutch on her teacup.

'How is Donald?' she asked.

'He's well, he's very well, he's . . . abroad at the moment for the summer,' Selina added, completely unprepared and unable to tell this sad, frail woman the truth.

'Oh, I see. Then I presume it will be more months before I see him.' She gave Selina a weak smile. 'Well, we've both waited this long; what's another few weeks?'

'Of course.' Selina was on the brink of tears at the desperation of the situation.

Anni took a tentative sip of her tea. 'So, where exactly is Donald?'

'He's currently in New York, and then I believe he'll go from there to Europe until the end of the summer.'

'I suppose he's sold Astbury and needed to get away?'

'No, Anni, Astbury has not been sold.'

'Really? Then I'm happy for him. I know it was causing him great sadness to think of selling it.'

'Yes. And you're lucky you've caught me today. I'm only here collecting the last of my things to move to the house that I now share with Henri in Kensington. We're expecting another child.'

'Selina!' Anni's eyes filled with pleasure. 'It seems your love, which was so difficult in the beginning, has had a happy conclusion.'

'Yes, it seems it has.'

As Anni sipped her tea, Selina came to a decision. It was not her place to tell this girl, who said she had written to ask

Donald to wait for her, that the man she loved had married someone else.

'Could you perhaps ask your maid to bring down my suitcase?' asked Anni. 'I believe Donald stored it for me in his bedroom.'

'Of course. The best thing is, I think, that you write down your address and I'll give it to Donald on his return. I'm sure he'll be in contact with you immediately, Anni dear.'

'Thank you.'

Selina rang for the maid to find the suitcase and searched for paper and a pencil in the bureau drawer. 'Now, Anni, tell me, honestly, do you need money?'

'No, thank you, I have enough,' she answered proudly.

Selina handed her the paper and pencil. 'Please write down your address, and I'm going to give you my new address in Kensington. While Donald's away, if there's anything you need, you must write to me. Do you promise?'

'Yes, but as I said, I hope to return to work very soon,' she replied as the maid brought in her suitcase. 'Do you have an address for Donald in New York? I'd like to write to him too. If he didn't receive my letter, he must be very worried.'

'Indeed he has been, but sadly, I don't have an address for him in New York; he's moving around a great deal,' lied Selina. 'Next time he telephones, I'll tell him you came by. He'll be extremely relieved to know that you're alive and well.'

Anni put her cup down on the table. And *Tatler* magazine, open at the photographs of the wedding, caught her eye. 'Is that Donald?' she said, bending forwards to take a closer look.

'Yes, at some social function –'

But it was too late. Anni had grasped the magazine in her hands.

Tatler magazine celebrates the wedding
of the year between Lord Donald Astbury
and Violet Rose Drumner . . .

Anni spent a few seconds surveying the pictures, then sat back abruptly in the chair, her eyes agonised. 'He's married?' she said, her throat closing, making it hard for her to breathe. 'He's married – I – why didn't you tell me? How could you not tell me!'

'Anni, I—'

'I can't believe he's married. I told him to wait . . .' Her head fell towards her hands, which she screwed into fists as she pummelled her forehead.

'Anni, please, Donald had heard nothing from you for months. Your friend Indira said you were returning straight to England from Paris. When you didn't come back, all he could think of was that you didn't want him any longer. Please, it's been fifteen months since you left for India. I'm so sorry, Anni, you deserve better than this,' Selina finished helplessly, all out of platitudes.

'I must leave now,' said Anni, staggering to her feet again. 'Goodbye.' She turned to walk to the drawing-room door.

'Anni, I promise you, he doesn't love her, I know he doesn't. It was you he loved, always!'

The drawing-room door slammed and Anni was gone.

21 *August*

*Well, here we are back at Astbury. Not that I'd recognise
it as my old home from the inside at all. The worker bees
have continued doing their job whilst we've been away
and I feel now that I'm staying in some form of luxury*

hotel as I walk into the drawing room or the dining room or along the corridors. It will take some getting used to, but I have to say that I'm impressed with V's organisation. New York was wonderful, and Violet's family and friends embraced me with open arms. No wonder she's so active – the energy in the city is unlike anything I've ever known. The pulse beats fast, twenty-four hours a day, and there's an urgency there that makes London feel positively pedantic and rather dull.

Europe was as wonderfully civilized as I remembered and Violet held parties and dinners every night to keep us amused. She is a wonder, and everyone adores her. Even Prince Henry, King George's young son, found time to enjoy her now-famous hospitality in Italy.

Happily, I'm growing fonder and fonder of her, for I find her willingness to learn and her zest for life so appealing, even if she makes me feel like an old man. Sometimes, I can hardly believe we're the same age. She's like an overactive child who also needs protecting and teaching, and at least I've found comfort in providing that for her. I'm yet to see her in a funk or a black mood. Whatever the problem is, she makes it her business to overcome it. Suffice to say, many of my fears that had surfaced before the wedding have been laid to rest. And, thank God, I truly believe the ghosts of the past are finally leaving me . . .

Donald sat in the library at his desk, opening the heap of post that had materialised for him over the past four months. Any request for money he now had the luxury of putting in a heap to give to Violet to pass on to her father. The room was sweltering – it was the first time he'd ever been tempted to open one of the old sash windows to let in some air. Violet had been testing the new central-heating system, and the smell of fresh paint permeated the air. Donald sank his shoes into the carpet, which was so thick he wondered if it should be mowed, and drank his coffee from a new Limoges china coffee cup. Everything in the house was designed to comfort, from the soft new mattresses on the beds to the new bathtubs with their glistening gold taps that always pumped out piping hot water, whatever time of day it was. Turning his attention back to the post, he recognised Selina's handwriting and opened her letter.

21 Pitt Street,
Kensington, London

15 August 1920

Dearest Donald,

I hope this letter finds you well on your return from your travels. Thank you for your postcards from all the marvellous places you've been lucky enough to visit. Perhaps when you're home you might find the time to visit me at our new house in Kensington. I'm sure it couldn't possibly be as grand as the newly renovated Astbury Hall, but I'd like to see you as soon as possible. I had a visit, you see, from someone we both know. Do give me a call and perhaps you could come up to town as soon as you can. You might include some other business that you need to attend to as well.

Best love, dear Donald, and Eleanor sends a kiss.
Selina

Donald reread the letter to make sure he hadn't mistaken the subtle inference, but knew he had not. He sat back in his chair and then, without further ado, picked up the newly installed telephone contraption on his desk, dialled the exchange and gave the woman Selina's number.

Two days later, Donald travelled to London and went straight to Selina's Kensington house.

'She came to the house in Belgrave Square? You saw her? How was she? Where's she been all this time? I—'

'Donald, please, I'll tell you,' said Selina, 'but first let's go into the drawing room where we can talk privately.'

'I apologise, Selina, but I haven't slept a wink for the past forty-eight hours, as you can imagine.' He sighed.

'I understand. As the sun's almost past the yard arm, how about a stiff gin?'

'Will I need one?'

'I certainly might.' Selina sighed and asked the butler to bring through a tray of drinks to the drawing room.

Having closed the door firmly behind them, Selina surveyed her brother. 'Firstly, I must say, Donald, that you look awfully well. Did you have a jolly time?' she asked as she sat down with difficulty and Donald noticed the bulge in her stomach.

'Yes, but, Selina! You're pregnant. How absolutely wonderful!' He walked over to his sister and threw his arms about her. 'Congratulations. When's it due?'

'In about two months, and to be honest, I wish it would hurry up. It's been a long, hot summer stuck in London. Henri refused to let us travel to France in case it harmed the baby.'

'May I say that you look absolutely radiant, Selina.'

'I'm terribly happy, yes. And I feel it completes the circle. It will be good for Henri and me to have a child of our own.'

'Of course. And this house is beautiful.'

'We moved here simply so that the children could at least have some space to run around in a garden when we're in London,' she explained. 'I've realised recently how lucky we were being brought up at Astbury with the moors all around us.'

The butler arrived to pour the drinks and Donald took a hefty swig of his gin. Once they were alone again, he could bear the suspense no longer. 'So, tell me, Selina, is she all right?'

'Well, she's certainly alive, but – oh dear, she looked dreadful, Donald. She was as thin as a rake. She told me that she'd been very ill in hospital.'

'Oh, God.' The blood froze in Donald's veins. 'Is she recovering?'

'The thing is, I don't know. I swear I didn't say anything to her about what had happened to you, but she saw the photos of your wedding in *Tatler*, which was lying open on the coffee table when she arrived. And then, I'm afraid, she left in rather a rush.' Selina bit her lip.

Donald put his head into his hands. 'What a dreadful way to discover the news. Did she say why she hadn't written?'

'She said she *had*, Donald, to tell you that she'd be away longer than she'd expected. And –' Selina's eyes filled with tears at the thought – 'to ask you to wait for her. I said that I thought you'd never received such a letter, as you'd certainly never mentioned it to me. Did you?'

'No, indeed.' Donald shook his head firmly. 'You know I would have told you. If I *had* received such a letter, I would have done as she'd asked. Do you know where she is now?'

'She wrote down her address for me before *Tatler* dropped the bombshell. I said I'd give it to you as soon as you were back from Europe.'

'Where's she living?'

Selina stood up and went to her writing desk. She removed a slip of paper and handed it to Donald. 'This is the address. She's somewhere up in Yorkshire staying with an old school friend.'

'What the hell is she doing up there? Anni knew if she needed help I'd be there for her. She *knew* how I loved her and that whatever she needed I—'

'Donald, please, forgive me, but I've spent every day since I saw her here three months ago asking myself the same questions.' Selina wrung her hands. 'I'm sure she had her reasons.'

'Well, of course, I must go and see her as soon as possible. Will you cover for me here?' he pleaded.

'Of course, but there's no certainty you'll still find her there. She may well have moved on by now.'

'At the very least, surely they'll be able to tell me where she's gone? My God, Selina, why on earth didn't I receive those letters?'

'I've thought about that too,' Selina said seeing the agony in her brother's eyes, 'and I fear that it might be my fault.'

'How on earth could it be your fault?' Donald asked her.

'Because I may have inadvertently mentioned to Mother, just before the awful row about Henri and I getting married, how you had met Anni again in France when the war ended. And that Anni had visited us at the house in Belgrave Square,' she added miserably.

At this, Donald sat down in his chair, understanding his sister's inference immediately. 'Right,' he said.

'Of course, I'm not sure, but given the fact that Mother knew how close the estate was to penury at the time, it may not have been in her interests to see you sell up her family home and marry an Indian girl.'

'Selina, are you saying Mother may have had Anni's letters to me intercepted?' asked Donald, aghast.

'Please, these are questions you'll have to ask her, if you dare. Certainly if they were addressed to you and postmarked India, or from anywhere abroad, she surely would have put two and two together? And then, eventually, when you believed Anni wasn't there any more, our dear Mama invited the wealthy and beautiful Violet Drumner to cure you of your broken heart and fill Astbury's coffers.'

'I can hardly believe she would be so manipulative.' Donald shook his head.

'Really? Well, if she did have Anni's letters intercepted, I would say her behaviour was true to form. I mean, Mother's life has always been very much about Mother, hasn't it? Sadly, Donald, I wouldn't put anything past her. At least it's made me determined to be a caring parent to my children. God knows how Daddy put up with her.' Selina shook her head. 'She's always been a cold fish.'

'If she has done this, Selina –' Donald clenched his fists in despair – 'I swear I may well be doing time soon for murder. Has the woman no heart?'

'Enough to keep her very much alive and kicking. To be fair to her, she's had to make a large sacrifice as well to save Astbury. I'm sure it's not been pleasant for her to watch your wife take over her beloved home. I heard endlessly at the wedding about the ghastly Schiaparelli rug made of eighteen leopard skins.'

'It is fairly vulgar.' Donald allowed himself a grimace. 'But listen, Selina, what on earth do I do?'

'I don't know, Donald. I doubt Anni will trouble you again now that she knows about your marriage. She has always had such pride.'

'Yes, and the truth is, even though I had so many reservations at the start about marrying Violet, we have been getting on awfully well in the past few weeks,' Donald admitted. 'I wouldn't want to hurt her. I swore the day I married her that I'd be a dutiful husband. I may not love her the way I loved Anni, but none of this is her fault.'

Selina reached her hand to his shoulder. 'I understand. Well, maybe you should let sleeping dogs lie.'

Donald looked up at her, his eyes full of sadness.

'I think we both know that I can't do that.'

33

1 September

*Still reeling from Selina telling me that A had visited her
in London. And worst of all, that she had written to me.
The fury I feel towards my mother if she did, as Selina
suggested, intercept her letters, knows no bounds. Until
I confront her I won't know for sure. That will have to
wait for now as the most important thing is to find A.
Even if she is no longer at the address she gave Selina,
I'm hoping they'll have a forwarding address for her.
Have told V I'm going to look at new machinery for
the farm. Hate lying to her, but no matter what it
takes I must find A . . .*

Donald pulled up his car alongside the Rectory in Oxenhope,
a pretty Yorkshire village nestled up on the moors. His heart
beat faster as he climbed out and walked towards the wooden
gate. He gazed up at the house, hardly daring to believe that
somewhere inside it might be the woman who had haunted his
dreams for the past nineteen months.

'Please God, you're still here,' he murmured under his breath.

Taking his courage in both hands, he rang the doorbell.

A maid opened it a few seconds later. 'May I help you?'

'Yes, I'm looking for Anahita Chavan. A friend told me that she was living here.'

'I'm sorry, I've never heard of that name, sir. It's the Reverend Brookner and his daughter in residence now. I've only been here two months, but I was led to believe that this house has always been his.'

'I see. Is either the reverend or his daughter at home?'

'The reverend is out in the parish, but Miss Brookner is in the garden.'

'Then, may I come in and see her?' He handed her his card.

The maid studied it, then stood aside so that Donald could enter. She led him into a dark drawing room. 'Please wait in here and I'll call for Miss Brookner.'

'Thank you.'

Donald waited despondently for Charlotte to appear. At last, a plain young woman with warm, intelligent eyes entered the room.

'Lord Astbury?' she asked, as she shut the door behind her. 'Or at least, I'm presuming that's who you are, if you've come in search of Anahita.'

'Yes,' he said, holding out his hand to shake hers. 'And you're Miss Brookner, Anni's friend?'

'Yes. Please do sit down.'

'Thank you. You know of course why I'm here?' Donald said, sitting down tensely in a chair.

'Yes, I suppose I do.' She looked at him, sadness in her brown eyes.

'Do you know where she is?'

'Yes, but I've been sworn to secrecy.'

'Is she well? My sister said she'd been very ill.'

'She was well enough last time I saw her.'

'She told my sister that you'd been most kind to her.'

'I did what I could to help her under the . . . difficult circumstances. But then my father returned from Africa two months ago and, given the situation, it was time for Anni to move on.'

'May I ask what situation you are referring to?' asked Donald.

'My father is a man of the cloth, Lord Astbury, and even though he has sympathy for poor souls who've found themselves in trouble, housing a woman in such circumstances under his roof would not have been approved of by his less open-minded parishioners. This is a small Yorkshire village, not London.' Charlotte paused, and then added, 'I must say, I'm surprised you're here.'

'Believe me, if I'd received the letters she apparently sent to me, I would have been here many months ago. Sadly,' Donald shrugged, 'I did not.'

'I can confirm she did write to you, Lord Astbury. I myself posted one letter to you when she was upstairs, too ill to move from her bed.'

'I can only beg you to believe that I speak the truth. I didn't receive a single letter from her for over a year.'

'If I may speak bluntly, after months of Anni receiving no reply, I'm afraid I rather gave up on you. And I told Anni that she must too. She refused, and that was when she decided to go to London to try to find you.'

'Yes.' Donald felt an edge of animosity underlying Charlotte's politeness.

'You were on your honeymoon, apparently,' she added darkly. 'Did you have a pleasant trip?'

'Yes, I— look here, Miss Brookner – Charlotte – I need you to tell me where Anni is, and at the very least I can go and explain that I wasn't ignoring her letters. I've been half out of my mind with worry. I had no idea whether she was alive or dead. I would never have agreed to marry another woman if I hadn't truly believed that Anni was lost to me.'

'She loved you more than anything and would never hear a word said against you. Even though I often told her that you deserved it.'

'I accept that you think I'm a cad and abandoned her—'

'No, Lord Astbury, I believed that, in the end, your social position would never allow you to entertain the thought of marrying an Indian woman,' she answered with candour.

'But surely Anni must have told you that I'd asked her to marry me before she left for India?'

'Yes, of course she did. But I was hardly surprised that, when it came to the reality of the situation, you changed your mind.'

'That simply isn't true!' he defended himself. 'If you must know, I'm almost certain that it was my mother who made sure I didn't receive any communication from Anni after she arrived in India. And I agree, it would not have suited *her* if I had married Anni. Or, in fact, if I had sold Astbury, which was what I had been planning to do.'

'So, a few months later, you married an American heiress?'

'Yes, but only after waiting more than a year without any word, and, at that point, I didn't care who I married if it couldn't be Anni.' Tears arrived unbidden in Donald's eyes. 'For God's sake, Miss Brookner, you have to believe me. I'm sorry, I . . .'

Seeing Donald's genuine emotion, Charlotte's attitude seemed to soften. She reached out a hand and tentatively patted his. 'If I am to trust what you tell me, then it is without doubt a tragic series of events. The sad thing is, I can't see now how it can ever be put right.'

'I beg you, tell me where she is, and then she and I can make that decision.'

'I swore I wouldn't—'

'You *must*!' Donald said insistently.

Finally, she nodded. 'I will tell you. I think that whether Anni wants to see you or not, you should at least have the chance to explain. Even if the past suffering can never be put right, it may help her to know why things happened as they did.'

'Thank you,' Donald breathed, relief washing over him as Charlotte stood up and went to a bureau in the corner of the room. She pulled out an address book and a piece of notepaper, and copied a few lines down onto it.

'She's living in Keighley, a mill town about forty-five minutes from here. I must admit I haven't visited her since she moved in. I've been rather preoccupied with caring for my father, who came back from Africa a virtual invalid.'

Donald was already on his feet. 'I can't thank you enough for seeing me and giving me this, Miss Brookner,' he said as he tucked the notepaper into his top pocket. 'I'll go and see Anni immediately.'

'And perhaps you'll let me know how she is?' she asked as she led him to the front door. 'I've no idea what her circumstances are. She's so proud, you see. I offered her money, but she refused to take it.'

'Yes, that sounds like Anni.' Donald sighed. 'Goodbye, Miss Brookner, and thank you again.'

Donald drove the short distance across the Yorkshire moors and shuddered as he approached the dark industrial mill town of Keighley. Parking his car, he wound his way through the labyrinth of narrow streets, the buildings on either side blackened with soot from the cotton factories. Filthy children sat outside on doorsteps, their feet bare, even though the September night was chilly.

Asking along the way for directions, he finally found himself in Lund Street and walked along it until he found the right number. He knocked on the door and eventually a haggard-looking woman with a baby clutched to her hip and a toddler holding on to her skirts opened it. She surveyed him with suspicion.

'You're not the new rent man, are you? I said to the last one t'would be paid on Friday. My old man's just lost his job at the mill, see.'

'I was told that Anahita Chavan lived at this address,' Donald explained. 'Perhaps I've got it wrong?'

'No, you 'aven't, Anni's our lodger, but don't you be telling the rent man. We're not allowed to sub-let, but with seven mouths to feed, needs must. You're a friend of hers, then?'

'Yes, my name is Donald. Is she in?'

'She hardly ever goes out, keeps herself to herself, does our Anni. Lovely girl, mind. You'd better come in,' the woman said, and Donald squeezed along the narrow hallway and into a tiny room which he saw served as a basic kitchen. 'Sit yourself down there, sir, and I'll go and call her.'

As the woman left, Donald saw a number of bright eyes staring at him with interest from the doorway.

'What's yer name, mister?' asked one of the children, a boy of about seven.

'Donald. What's yours?'

'I'm Tom,' said the boy, drawing closer. 'You speak dead posh, and your clothes are fine. Do you own a factory?'

'No, I don't own a factory.'

'When I grow up, I'm going to own a factory,' Tom pronounced, 'and then I'll be really rich, like you.'

A toddler had crawled into the room and, using Donald's trouser leg as a pulley, she tried to stand, her grubby hands leaving greasy marks behind them.

'Joanna, get off of the poor man!' said their mother as she re-entered the kitchen. 'Anni'll be down in a jiffy, and she says she'll see you in the front room. She didn't look too happy when I told her you were here, mind. Right now, follow me.'

'Thank you,' said Donald.

The woman took him back along the hallway and ushered him into the relative tranquillity of the parlour. As she closed the door, Donald shuddered at this dreadful place. What had Anni been reduced to since he'd last seen her?

The door opened and Anni stood there, her exotic beauty such a contrast to the dreadful drabness of her surroundings. The weight she'd lost made her cheekbones and her huge amber eyes stand out even more.

She shut the door behind her gracefully – as Donald remembered so vividly all her movements had been – and stood by it, not moving.

'Anni, I'm here.' Donald berated himself for stating the obvious at such an important moment, but he was at a loss to know what else to say.

'Yes,' she replied eventually. 'So you are.'

'I . . . are you well?'

'I'm well,' she said coldly. 'And you?'

'Yes, yes. Anni . . .' Donald sat down abruptly, feeling his legs would hold him up no longer. 'I don't know what to say.' He put his head in his hands.

'No, I don't suppose you do.'

'You have to believe that I didn't get a single one of your letters from the time you left the ship. I had no idea whether you were alive or dead. I even went to the hospital where you used to work and contacted Scotland Yard. I was desperate. In the end, I simply had to believe you no longer wanted me. And that maybe you had found somebody else in India.'

'So you married someone else?' she said in harsh, clipped tones, so unlike her usual gentle voice.

'Yes, I did,' he agreed despairingly. 'If I couldn't marry you, I didn't really care who it was. To be blunt, at least my wife's money could save Astbury.'

'I read in the magazine that your new wife is an heiress. I hope you're very happy together,' she said in the same emotionless tone.

'Of course I'm not happy!'

'You looked happy in the photographs.'

'Yes, I probably did,' Donald conceded. 'But everyone is told to smile for the cameras.'

There was a silence as Anni gazed anywhere but at him, and he simply drank her in. 'What have you come to say?'

'I've no idea!' Donald let out a strangled laugh. 'I wanted to explain that I'm sure it was my mother who intercepted the letters you sent to me.'

'Donald, even if I'd had no communication from you, I'd

have waited an eternity and never married someone else. But what does it matter now anyway?'

The distant coldness he felt from her was entirely new to him. He desperately wanted to throw his arms around her, search for the passionate, spirited woman she'd once been. 'Could we at least go somewhere else and talk?' he begged her. 'It's unbearable here.'

'You'll find there are no hotels where we can take tea in this area,' she replied with a hint of sarcasm in her voice. 'Besides, this is my home.'

'Anni, please, I know how you've suffered and what you must think of me, but I promise you that I've never stopped loving you or thinking about you for the past eighteen months.'

Anahita watched him impassively. 'Whatever has happened in the past, Donald, I'm here, and you're there, married to another.'

'Whatever my circumstances, my feelings for you remain unchanged. Please, this is me you're talking to,' he said urgently. 'You, more than anyone, know who I am.'

'I thought I did once, yes. But what's the point now?'

'The point is, my darling, that after all these dreadful months, I've found you, and we are sitting in the same room together talking. Can you not understand what that means to me?'

She didn't answer. There was a brief knock and then the door opened. Anni's landlady walked in, holding a screaming child in her arms.

'Sorry to disturb you, Anni, but he's giving off hell in the kitchen and none of us can hear or think.'

Donald watched as Anni took the child into her arms.

'Thank you,' she said to her landlady, who cast a further suspicious look at Donald, then at the baby, and left the room.

Donald was confused. 'Is that her baby?'

Anni surveyed him carefully, as if she was weighing something in her mind. Eventually she sighed. 'No, he is mine.'

Donald stared at the baby, his brain slowly computing the beautiful honey-brown skin, the shock of dark hair and the bright blue eyes staring at him inquisitively.

He found his voice. 'I . . . is he –?'

'Yes, Donald, this is Moh, your son.'

34

4 *September*

After that, using the health and welfare of my son as
leverage and brooking no refusal, I made A gather the
few possessions she had. Then I drove her and my son
away from the terrible house in which I'd found them.
We stayed in a hotel that first night before travelling
down south. I had little idea of where I was taking her.
I simply knew I could never leave her again. All of her
old fire seemed to have left her, as if she was empty
inside, as though nothing really mattered any longer.
On the long car journey, she barely spoke a word, and
only then to reply monosyllabically to my questions.

'Are you hungry?' Donald asked Anni as they drove through
the Derbyshire Dales.

'No. But I should change the baby's napkin.'

'Of course.' Donald pulled into a hotel on the outskirts of
Matlock and the three of them climbed out of the car. As he
waited in the restaurant for Anni to return, he asked if the
hotel possessed a telephone, for he needed to make a call. On

the long, silent journey, he had begun to formulate a plan. He would throw them all on the mercy of Selina, who, he was sure, for a time would be prepared to offer Anni and the child a room in her Kensington home. As a temporary measure, it was the best he could think of, and at least he knew that Anni wouldn't be able to disappear again if she was right under his sister's nose.

The waiter said that they did indeed have a telephone and Donald went off to use it. When he came back to the restaurant, Anni was sitting at the table, with the baby fast asleep in her arms.

'I've just spoken to Selina, and you'll stay there until I've sorted out something more permanent,' said Donald.

'I see,' Anni replied, giving no indication as to whether the arrangement suited her or not.

'I've ordered soup and sandwiches, will that be sufficient?'

'Thank you.'

Donald reached a hand across to her in desperation. 'Anni, please, I can't imagine what you've been through or how much you must hate me, but I'm here now, and I swear I'll never let you down again. You have to trust me, please, and believe that if I hadn't truly thought that you were lost to me forever, I would never have married Violet.'

Anni raised her eyes slowly to him. 'Do you love her?'

'I'm fond of her, yes,' he replied honestly. 'She's very sweet and very young somehow, even though she's older than you, and I wouldn't want to see her hurt, certainly. But no, I don't love her and I never have. It was, to all intents and purposes, an arranged marriage, just as you have in India.'

'She's very beautiful.'

'Yes, she is, but – for God's sake.' Donald shook his head

in frustration. 'I can't keep going over and over the reasons why. We all do things that we live to regret.'

Anni ate her soup in silence and then attempted a sandwich. The food seemed to revive her, brought some colour to her cheeks. Donald surmised that she was almost certainly malnourished.

They returned to the car, and both Anni and the baby fell asleep for the rest of the journey. Donald tenderly roused them when they arrived outside Selina's house in Kensington.

'We're here?' she asked.

'Yes. Shall I help you with the baby?'

'No!' A flash of fear passed across Anni's face. 'Does Selina know of the child? I didn't tell her when I saw her that time in London.'

'I told her, and she wasn't shocked,' Donald comforted her. 'She understands now why you disappeared.'

With the maid settling Anni and the baby into a bedroom upstairs, Donald drained a hefty gin with Selina in the drawing room.

'Oh, Donald, it really is all so tragic. I know only too well how Anni must have felt. She must have been terrified. And here's me with my little girl, safe and secure in a nursery and a new one on the way. The contrast couldn't be more stark, could it?' she sighed.

'No. Goodness, Selina, if you'd seen where Anni was living – it was a slum.'

'Well of course Anni and her baby can stay here temporarily, but what on earth will you do long term?' she asked. 'After all, that baby is your son and, until you and Violet have a child, technically could be your heir, but I dread to think what would happen if Violet should ever find out about him.'

'It's a bloody mess, the whole damned thing. But most importantly, I've found Anni. I love her, Selina. My only thought was to get her and our baby out of that hellhole. I haven't had time to really think about the ramifications. One of the solutions would be to install her in a house up here in town, visit her and my son whenever I was in London, but I don't want to treat Anni as though she were my mistress and I'm sure she wouldn't countenance it either.'

'Has she given an indication of what *she* wants?' asked Selina.

'She's hardly said a word,' he replied miserably. 'She's simply been surviving for the past few months. I'm sure it will take some time before she regains her strength, both mentally and physically.'

'Well, at least I can provide her with a warm bed, good food and a nursemaid who can take the baby from her to let her rest. Another little one in the nursery won't make any difference.' Selina smiled. 'After all, they are cousins.'

'And I only wish the world could know it.'

'Well, they can't, and that's that. None of this is poor Violet's doing and although I could never say that she and I will be close, I wouldn't want her to ever suffer the indignity of knowing her husband had a' – Selina refrained from saying the correct term – 'child by another woman.'

'You're right, of course,' said Donald, pouring himself another gin from the tray. 'My immediate plan is to go down to Devon and confront Mother. I must know for certain whether it was her who's put us all in this mess.'

'Will you tell her about the child?'

'Oh yes.' Donald smiled grimly. 'I can't think of a thing that would distress her more than to know she has a half-caste illegitimate grandson whom I could recognise as the heir to the Astbury Estate.'

'My God, Donald. The news might seriously finish her off!'

'I doubt it. Even though she acts as though she's eighty, we must remember our mother isn't even fifty yet,' Donald reminded her. 'She's as tough as old boots underneath all the drama and will probably outlive us all. This appalling situation, if we're both right, is down to her. I'm simply not frightened of her any longer.'

Anni professed she was too tired to join Selina and Donald downstairs for dinner that evening and the maid took her some supper up on a tray. Before he retired for the night, Donald went to her bedroom and knocked on the door.

'Who is it?'

'It's Donald. May I come in?'

Receiving no reply, he opened the door and found Anni nursing the baby in bed.

'My apologies,' she said, pulling Moh from her and covering herself.

'I don't mind,' said Donald. 'I think it's rather wonderful. Most women that I know of don't feed their babies themselves.'

'I had no choice, I couldn't afford the extra milk. But he's getting big now – he'll be a year old next month and I'm not enough to satisfy him. I think that's why he cried so often when we were in Keighley.'

'Oh, Anni,' Donald said with a sigh, 'may I come and sit down?'

'If you wish.'

Donald perched on the bed and looked at the baby, sated for now and sleeping in Anni's arms. 'May I hold him?'

'Of course,' Anni replied, and passed Moh over to him.

Donald could smell the warm, milky scent of his skin and the sweetness of the talcum powder the nursemaid had used after his bath. He looked down into his son's face and was overcome with such a wave of love, it brought tears to his eyes.

'I can hardly believe that we made him.'

'Every child is a miracle, whatever life they are born into,' Anni said.

'Anni, do you hate me?'

She paused before she answered him. 'I have wished to, Donald, many times. I may not like you much at present, but I've loved you since the day I first met you.'

'And now that I've found you? Do you trust me to take care of you and our son?'

'What choice do I have?' she asked him sadly.

The following day, Donald left Anni and Moh in the capable hands of Selina and the nursemaid and motored south to Astbury Hall. Immediately on arrival, he went straight to the Dower House where his mother now lived, on the edge of the estate.

'Is she in, Bessie?' he asked the startled maid as he marched into the house.

'I believe she's upstairs resting, My Lord.'

Donald took the stairs two at a time, then knocked on his mother's door.

'Come,' said a voice, and Donald entered Maud's bedroom to find her sitting in a chair by the fireplace reading a book.

'Donald, what on earth are you doing up here?' she said with a frown of displeasure.

'You and I must talk. Please put down your book, Mother.

There are some questions I want you to answer,' Donald replied, sitting down opposite her.

Startled by her son's vehemence, Maud did as she was told. 'What is it?' she asked him.

'I've recently discovered that a number of letters addressed to me went missing last year at Astbury Hall, and I have every reason to believe that you had a hand in making sure I didn't receive them.'

'Letters?'

Donald watched as his mother tried to feign ignorance. 'Yes, Mother, letters. Letters from India, Paris, and then Yorkshire, from a certain young lady whom you'd somehow discovered I was very fond of. Who, Mother, just for the record, I was and continue to be in love with.'

'I . . . really, Donald, we get so much post, letters from all over the world. Surely the postal service is at fault if they didn't arrive? I hardly think you can blame me if they've gone astray.'

'Oh, I think I can, Mother. And it would be perfectly easy for me to go to the servants at the Hall – who you might care to remember are under *my* employ these days – and ask them for the truth.'

Donald made to stand, but Maud hushed him immediately back down into the chair.

'Have you taken leave of your senses? The last thing we want is the servants talking about our private business,' she hissed.

'I can't say I care a damn.'

'Not even if it reached Violet's ears?'

'As well it might, given that I've finally found Anahita. She's currently staying with Selina in London until I decide what is best to do.' Donald had a dreadful urge to laugh at the horrified look on his mother's face.

'What exactly do you mean, what is best?' repeated Maud. 'Surely, you can't mean you'll tell Violet about this . . . liaison you had with that Indian girl?'

'I haven't decided yet, but unless you come clean and admit it was you who held her letters back, I might be very tempted to do so.'

'Good God, Donald! Are you completely mad? You'll bring this family to its knees. Violet would divorce you immediately, and then what would become of Astbury?'

'Do you think I care? That I've ever cared?' he shot back. 'You knew full well that I was prepared to sell it and had even found a buyer. That wouldn't have suited you though, would it, Mother? Admit it, before I go and tell Violet. Trust me –' he eyed her – 'I have absolutely nothing to lose. Selling Astbury was my plan in the first place. I'd be quite content to live a quiet life with the woman I love. And by the way,' Donald said, playing his trump card, 'Anni has recently given birth to our baby. Which means I have a son, and you a grandchild.'

Donald watched his mother crumple in front of him. But still he persisted. 'So, Mother, would you like me to go and tell my present wife all this? Can you imagine the scandal?'

'Stop it! Stop it! How can you be so cruel? I'm your mother!' she moaned.

'Yes, a mother who put her own needs and wants above those of her son. Anni is an aristocratic and educated Indian woman. Not some common little peasant I've dragged out of a brothel!'

'*Please!*'

'And it may interest you to know, too, that there are a

number of mixed-race marriages amongst society these days. But no, Mother, your prejudice wouldn't allow for your son to marry such a woman. You are, and always have been, cold, calculating and bigoted. I—'

'*Stop!* Enough!' Maud screamed, and abruptly burst into tears.

The sight of her crying brought Donald's tirade to a sudden halt. 'Look here, Mother, dry your eyes.' He awkwardly offered her a handkerchief from his pocket and she took it.

'You're right,' Maud finally choked out. 'I did hide those letters, or at least asked to have the post brought directly to me so that I could sift through it. But don't you see that I was only trying to protect you? You say that it's now accepted to marry someone such as her. I don't know, maybe you are right. But on top of that, you were also selling this estate. What would you have had then, with an Indian bride and no family seat?'

'I would have had love, Mother,' Donald said quietly. 'I would have been happy. But I can hardly expect you to understand that.'

She made no reply, appearing to be lost in her own thoughts.

'Thank you for admitting that you took her letters,' Donald said at last. 'Now I have to try and sort out the mess this situation has left me in.'

'What will you do?'

'Well, you'll be pleased to hear that I have no intention of hurting Violet. None of this is her fault.' Donald eyed his mother and she had the grace to blush. 'But equally, I'm not prepared to have the woman I love and the child she has borne me hidden away like a dirty secret, where I can't watch my son growing up. So I'm going to suggest to Anni that she and Moh come to live nearby. I will provide them with a home somewhere on the estate.'

'But, Donald, what if Violet discovers the truth?' asked Maud, horrified.

'There are only five people in the world who know. I can vouch that none of them will tell. This is the only way in which I'm prepared to live out the lie you fashioned for me.'

'You took the decision to marry Violet, Donald,' Maud countered. 'I didn't force you down the aisle.'

'No, Mother, you did not,' Donald said. 'But when all hope is lost, one hardly cares what the future holds. So, are we agreed?'

'As you wish,' she answered shakily, her eyes downcast.

'Good. Then I'll set about finding Anni a suitable home. And,' he said as he walked towards the door, 'perhaps one day you'd like to visit your grandson. He has your eyes.'

Astbury Hall,

July 2011

35

Rebecca awoke to find herself sitting upright, Donald's diary grasped in her hand. She had no idea when she had fallen asleep, but her dreams had again been disturbed and filled with the sound of strange high-pitched singing.

Flipping through the diary, she saw the entries stopped abruptly after September, which disappointed her because she wanted to know more, especially about Violet. Rebecca looked at her watch and saw that it was past nine o'clock in the morning.

She climbed out of bed to use the bathroom, washed her hands and stared at her face in the mirror. There was no doubt that Donald's description of Violet could just as easily describe her.

Rebecca shuddered suddenly. The sad thing was, from what she'd read, it wasn't Violet whom Donald had loved, but a beautiful, exotic Indian girl from another world. Rebecca wandered about the suite of rooms, touching Violet's possessions, smelling the now familiar scent of her perfume, unable to shake off her growing sense of the surreal. This had been Violet's bed, the one she had once shared with Donald. She was wearing Violet's clothes every day, re-enacting the world in which she had lived . . .

'Jesus.' Rebecca sank into a chair in the sitting room, wondering what twist of fate it was that had brought her here to Astbury. It was impossible to ignore the similarities between the two of them.

'Becks, are you in here?'

A familiar voice broke into her reverie. 'Yes,' she called, and a few seconds later, Jack burst through the door, followed by a red-faced Mrs Trevathan.

'Hi, honey,' he said, walking over to her.

'I'm sorry, Rebecca, I know you need your rest and I did try to tell Mr Heyward you didn't want to be disturbed.'

'Thank you, Mrs Trevathan,' Rebecca said calmly. 'Don't worry. I'm feeling better today.'

'All right, I was only doing as I was asked,' she said, turning round and shutting the door behind her.

'Thanks.' Jack collapsed into a chair and breathed a mock sigh of relief. 'Who the hell does she think she is anyway? Your mother? How dare she try and stop me from seeing my fiancée? Now, come here and give me a hug.'

Rebecca didn't move. She stared coldly at his bloodshot eyes and greasy, unkempt hair. He had obviously been out on another bender with James. 'Good night last night?'

'Yeah, it was fun.'

'I'm happy for you.'

Jack looked at her uncertainly, trying to work out what she meant. Eventually, realising she was being ironic, he went on the attack. 'Stop treating me like a child, Becks! That's half the problem with you,' he said, wagging his finger in her direction. 'Miss Squeaky Clean and Perfect who doesn't drink, never smokes, never does anything fun. Who thinks she's so above us mere mortals who do.'

'I didn't mean it like that, Jack,' she answered wearily. 'Listen. We really need to talk.'

'Oh Christ, here we go again – another lecture because I've been a bad boy. Well, get on with it then, Mommy, and smack me on my butt,' he said nastily.

'You've got a problem and you need to deal with it, Jack,' said Rebecca quietly. 'I'm only saying this because I care for you and I'm scared that if you don't stop it'll simply get worse.'

'And which problem would this be?'

'Don't be facetious, Jack. We both know you've been drinking too much, more or less since I met you, and you're doing coke all the time. You're an addict, Jack. And until you do something about it –' Rebecca steeled herself to say the words – 'I can't continue having a relationship with you.'

Jack threw back his head and laughed. 'Oh, Becks, you crack me up! Ever since you left to come to England, I've known that something was wrong. That maybe you'd fallen out of love with me, or perhaps there was someone else. And now, you sit here and pull the oldest trick in the book: you blame *me* and a problem that doesn't even exist as an excuse to break up with me. Oh yeah –' Jack nodded in mock wisdom – 'I can see it all.'

'Jack, I swear, the only problems I have with you are your drinking and drug habit. When you're sober and not on stuff, you're just the greatest and I love you. But when you're not, which is becoming more and more frequent, I simply can't deal with you. So, what I propose is that you go back to LA and do something about it. If you do, I'll be there every step of the way. But if you don't . . .' Rebecca let the words hang in the air.

'So this is an ultimatum?' Jack stood up in front of her, arms folded. 'Either I sort out a problem I don't have, or we're through. Is that it?'

'No, that's not it and you know it. Who else is going to tell you the truth?' she entreated him. 'Don't you understand that this is as difficult for me as it is for you? I don't want us to split up, Jack. I loved you from the first moment I met you. The only reason I haven't said yes to marrying you so far is because I can't cope with your problem.'

'So –' Jack started pacing round the room – 'you're asking me to go into rehab just to prove that I love you?'

'Oh, Jack, whichever way you want to phrase it, I can't go on like this any longer. I'm sick, I have a film to shoot and whatever happens in the future, I want you to get help. Maybe, when I'm back home, we can talk then and see where you are.'

'Jesus, Becks! Will you stop patronising me?' Jack sat down again heavily. 'As a matter of fact, there's a good chance I'll be shooting a film with that guy I met the other day. And my manager has called to tell me he's just received a couple of great scripts. So, even to please you, I may not be able to fit rehab into my schedule.'

'I'm happy some opportunities have come up for you, Jack,' she replied, exhausted now.

'Yeah, seems your guy isn't as washed up as you'd have him believe. And if I have been going a bit heavy on the booze, it's been out of boredom, nothing else. So –' Jack stared at her – 'you're serious? You want to call it quits?'

'No, I don't, but I feel like I haven't got a choice.'

'Okay!' Jack slapped his thighs and stood up. 'I'm not going to stand here and defend myself any longer. If that's what you want, that's what you can have.'

'I'm so sorry, Jack, I really am.' Rebecca's eyes filled with tears.

'Sure you are,' he sneered. 'But I think you should maybe ask yourself just why you're giving me such a hard time for doing nothing except enjoying a party. I'm not your piss-ass drunk mommy, Becks, and I don't deserve to be treated like her either. And if you think this will break me, then you just watch this space. Perhaps you'd be better with a preacher than you would with a red-blooded male. But hey, that's not my problem any more. So, I guess I'll say goodbye now.'

Rebecca felt as if she'd been slapped in the face by his dreadful words. She sat silently, unable to reply.

'Just one more thing,' Jack added, 'as I've been dumped and sent back home for being a bad boy, it's only fair to leave it to me to break the news to the media. I'll ask my manager to put out a short statement. Okay?'

'Yes, say whatever you want.'

'I will. And I hope you don't regret what you've done today. So long, Becks.'

Rebecca watched as the door slammed shut behind him. She shut her eyes and laid her head on the cool, silken fabric of the chair, reeling from Jack's cruel reference to her mother. And yes, she acknowledged, he was almost certainly right. What she'd been through as a child had sensitised her to any form of substance abuse.

However, that didn't make Jack's behaviour acceptable.

Tears pricked her eyes again as she realised the ramifications of what she'd just done and knew there would be no way back from here. Jack was used to women falling over themselves just to be close to him. She doubted he'd ever been dumped and would waste no time replacing her. When she saw future photographic evidence of it in the media, it would hurt like hell. But she had to accept that the Jack she'd once loved had disappeared.

'Are you all right, dear?'

Rebecca looked up and saw Mrs Trevathan standing by the door and she shrugged silently.

'It's none of my business, but I think you've done the right thing,' Mrs Trevathan said gently. 'As my mother always says, there are plenty more fish in the sea, especially for someone as lovely as you.'

'Thank you for saying that,' Rebecca whispered hoarsely. 'Could you possibly let me know when he's gone?'

'Of course I can, my love.' She smiled sympathetically at Rebecca and left the room.

Half an hour later, Mrs Trevathan arrived with tea and toast and told her that Jack had left the house.

'How are you feeling?'

'Shaky, I guess. I just hope I've done the right thing.'

'If it's any consolation, I was once married to a man like Jack. We lasted a year before I had to leave him. I'm not saying your Jack was the violent type like mine, but when they're looking down the neck of a bottle day after day, there's no telling what they might do.'

'No. Did you love your husband?'

'Of course I did.' She sighed sadly. 'At the beginning, anyway. But by the end, I couldn't stand the sight of him. Trust me, Rebecca, it might hurt now, but it's for the best, it really is.'

'Thank you, Mrs Trevathan,' Rebecca said gratefully.

'Well now, there're a number of people who'd like to come up and see you, but I've told them you're resting at the moment. Is that right, my love?'

'Yes, maybe I can see them later.'

'How's the headache?'

'Better today, thanks.'

'Well, you're still pale, although one way and another, I'm hardly surprised,' she clucked. 'I'll come back later and you can tell me whether you're up to seeing a few visitors.'

Exhausted, Rebecca slept for several hours and woke feeling a little better. She washed and dressed, then, feeling guilty that she'd kept everyone at bay, she asked Mrs Trevathan to send up Steve, who had understandably been asking to see her.

'Sorry to disturb you, sweetheart, I just wanted to see how you're feeling,' he said, as he walked into the sitting room.

'The headache is easing, so I'm sure I'll be okay to film tomorrow,' she assured him.

'That's good news, Rebecca. And I'm sure the stress of the past few days hasn't exactly helped you recover, either.'

'What do you mean?' Rebecca feigned innocence.

'Darling, this is a film set. None of us were blind to Jack's little problem. He asked me if I had any stuff the first time I met him.'

'Oh God, I'm sorry, Steve.'

'Don't be, it's hardly your fault. I saw him a few hours ago when he asked me to get a driver for him to take him to London. I'm not going to ask the state of play, but I gathered from the look on his face that all is not well on Planet Jack and Rebecca.'

'No,' Rebecca agreed, deciding the best thing was to come clean immediately. 'I told him it was curtains for us if he didn't stop using. But I'd prefer not to make it common knowledge.'

'Sadly, they've already guessed,' said Steve. 'You know how fast news travels on set. Anyway, Rebecca, the most important thing is you and your health. Hopefully, now Jack's gone, you can focus on getting better.'

'Yes, and I promise I'll be fine for tomorrow's shoot.'

'Well, we'll see. We've only scheduled in one scene for you late tomorrow afternoon. Keep your chin up, sweetheart,' he called as he left the room.

Half an hour later, there was another knock on the sitting-room door and Anthony came in. He stared at her for a moment, gave a sudden sigh of exasperation, then forced a smile.

'Just checking in,' he said gruffly. 'How are you feeling?'

'Better, I think,' Rebecca said. 'Thank you so much for letting me use this beautiful suite.'

'Well, I can think of no one more fitting to occupy it,' he said stiffly. 'I hear your young man has left?'

'Yes, and he won't be back.'

'I see.' He stood staring at her. 'I'm having dinner again tonight with our young Indian friend,' he commented eventually.

'Oh?' Rebecca replied, at a loss.

'Well, I hope you feel more chipper tomorrow.'

'I hope I will too. Thanks for checking on me.'

'Goodbye,' Anthony said, then turned and left the room.

When Anthony had gone, Rebecca luxuriated in the big bathtub. Having slept so late she now felt wide awake. When Mrs Trevathan appeared with tea and scones, she ate them hungrily.

'I really think I'm improving,' she told her.

'That's what I like to hear, dear.'

'Is Mr Malik around?' she asked.

'He went out earlier, but I believe he's somewhere about, yes. He's having dinner with His Lordship later.'

'If you see him, do you think you could ask him if he'd mind coming up to see me?'

'When I see him, I'll let him know,' Mrs Trevathan said as she left.

Twenty minutes later, there was a knock on the door.

'Come in,' Rebecca called.

'Hello, Rebecca, you wanted to see me?'

'Yes, Ari, come in. How did you get on at the local church?' she asked him.

'Well, I walked around the graveyard, but I couldn't find any sign of a headstone naming him Moh. Then I drove to Exeter to look him up on the main Births and Deaths Register, but again, nothing. So, I'm afraid, it's another dead end.'

'Isn't that odd?' Rebecca queried. 'Any death certificate that was issued would surely be on record?'

'I would have thought so, yes.'

'Ari, I found something yesterday in this suite and it's absolute proof that Anahita was here at Astbury.'

'Really? What is it?'

'Donald Astbury's diary. You probably already know quite a lot of what's in it, but it confirms that he loved your great-grandmother and that they did have a child together.'

'Rebecca, that's incredible! I'd love to read it,' Ari said eagerly.

'I think you might be shocked when you see the diary itself. I'll go and get it.' Rebecca went through to Donald's dressing room and took it from the bookshelf. 'There,' she said, handing it to him.

Ari studied the name on the spine and the insignia on the front. He opened it, saw the inscription and then the poem.

'Oh, my God,' he breathed, 'it's the poem I told you about only a couple of days ago.'

'I know, that's the reason I took it down from the shelf in the first place. It's like something was leading us to it.'

'Yes. You know, Rebecca, I've never given credence to my great-grandmother's hocus-pocus as I once called it, but now –' he studied the volume in his hands – 'one way or another, I'm beginning to change my mind. Do you think Anthony's read this?'

'I wouldn't think so,' said Rebecca. 'It's been masquerading as just another book on the shelf for all these years.'

'Can I borrow it tonight?'

'Well, it's not mine to say whether you can, is it?'

'No, but I don't think I'll run the risk of asking Anthony first.' Ari raised an eyebrow. 'Thank you, Rebecca.'

'And I need a favour in return, Ari.'

'Of course, what is it?'

'Well, I know this sounds ridiculous, but I'm really beginning to feel that there is some kind of link between me and Violet. It's messing with my head a bit.'

'I can certainly understand that,' Ari sympathised.

'So . . . I want to know how Violet died.'

'I see. Well –' Ari looked at his watch – 'I'm meant to be down at dinner with Anthony in twenty minutes. The best thing for me to do is to give you Anahita's story. She explains it all far better than I can.'

'Then would you go and get it now?' Rebecca asked him. 'I can make a start immediately.'

'Yes.' Ari stood up and left the room, the diary tucked under his arm. He was back a few minutes later holding the plastic file.

'I'm warning you, Rebecca, it doesn't make pretty reading, but I think you're right. You should know what happened to Violet.'

'Okay,' Rebecca agreed.

Once Ari had left, Rebecca curled up on the sofa, removed the pile of papers from the wallet and sifted through them to find where she had left off before . . .

Anahita

1920

36

When Donald told me where he intended us to live, I was shocked and disconcerted. The first question I asked him was what his mother would have to say about it.

'She'll have absolutely nothing to say, Anni,' Donald said firmly. 'She's created this situation through her own selfish actions. If it wasn't for her, you and I would now be married and raising our child together, and Astbury would have been sold.'

Although Donald tried to comfort me, a distinct feeling of unease remained. Maud Astbury had always disliked me, and I instinctively felt it was borne of more than racial prejudice. She knew I saw through her outer shell to the core of her selfish soul.

'But what if the servants talk?' I asked Donald. 'After all, they know who I am.'

'Yes, they do,' Donald had answered, 'but I've thought of that. We simply say that you were married whilst you were away in India, but sadly, your husband died and that you are now a widow. Perhaps it might be sensible to invent a new surname for the two of you?' He put his hand on mine. 'Will you come with me to Astbury, Anni? I wish you and our child to be near me. It may not be perfect, but it's the best I can do.'

I asked him if he would give me some time to think about his suggestion. There was much about it I didn't like. Living close to Donald and having to watch him with his new wife was not in any sense palatable to me.

Looking back now, I know I was extremely vulnerable. Yes, I'd survived, but only just. Back in Keighley, I'd simply sought to keep myself and you, dearest Moh, alive, having given up any thoughts for the future. I'd used all of the money from the rubies to pay my hospital bills, and to pay rent and buy food for us. Even though I wanted very much to reject Donald's support, the very moment he found me, I was facing destitution. I could no longer afford to refuse help.

I may have been happy to go to an early grave rather than betray my precious pride, but I could not cast you to that fate too. Providence had decreed that Donald had found us just in time, and despite the bile that rose to my throat every time I thought of us being hidden away by him, I knew that I simply had no choice but to accept Donald's solution, whatever it might be.

In the past week, as I'd sat in the pretty bedroom Selina had so generously provided for me, I could feel my strength returning. Good food and rest were beginning to restore me and my mind was clearing. At the very least, if I found the situation intolerable, I could see Donald's offer as providing a breathing space. And perhaps, once I was stronger, I'd be able to resume my nursing and gain our independence through that.

But could I bear the thought of Donald returning to his wife after he'd been with us? It was on this I pondered most of all. Our love had always been so complete; I struggled to imagine how it could survive with a third party in it.

Then, through Selina, who'd told her friend Minty I'd been

found, I received a letter from Indira, telling me that she was pregnant. She complained in her usual vociferous way about the morning sickness, and also about the unfriendliness of Varun's first wife, who held superiority over her in the palace, if not in her husband's heart.

That letter made me think about my own situation and wonder whether it was any different from Indira's. Both of the men we loved had wives who took technical precedence over us, even if, as Indira said, we had their hearts. If I'd married a prince of India, I would have had to share him with at least one wife. And although there was no ring on my finger from Donald, we were truly wedded in all the ways that mattered.

Once I began to look at it this way, I struggled with it less. The fact that Donald had married Violet because she was deemed socially suitable *and* brought a dowry that had secured the Astbury Estate was an arrangement identical to that of the marriage of any royal prince in my home country. If I thought of myself as Donald's second wife, rather than his mistress, the situation felt far more acceptable to me.

Besides, any lingering doubts were undermined by the simple fact that I loved your father.

'We will come to Devon with you,' I said to him finally.

'Oh, darling! I'm so glad you've agreed. I know it's not perfect, Anni, and I only wish I was taking you home to Astbury Hall. I have a cottage in mind which isn't inside the estate itself or in the village, but on the moors. It's isolated too, which, if I'm to come and visit you regularly, is going to be important.'

'I'm very happy to live in peace and solitude, especially as I have Moh to keep me company,' I agreed.

'Well, it's been empty for many years, so it will be a few

weeks before I can make it fit for human habitation. Are you content to stay here in Kensington whilst I do so?'

'If Selina is happy to accommodate us.'

'You know she adores you, and with her baby due soon and Henri still in France, I think it's good for her to have company. So, is that settled?'

'Yes, I believe it is,' I said.

Donald stayed with us for two more days, then said he must return for the weekend to Astbury Hall. His wife was giving a house-party to show off her new interiors, and he said he must be there. I did my best not to mind – this was only the first of many occasions I would have to endure if I were to be part of his life in the future. I waved him off with a pleasant smile, inwardly thinking of Indira and how she must grit her teeth and bow to her husband's first wife.

I remember the weeks while we waited for our new home to be renovated as being tranquil. You, thanks to the plentiful supply of wholesome food, a clean and warm nursery and a pair of less exhausted mother's arms around you, began to thrive. You put on pounds within a month and began to crawl, your now sturdy frame carrying you quickly across the nursery floor.

Selina's baby arrived without complication in October and I enjoyed being able to repay some of her kindness by caring for her and the child, whom Henri and she had named Fleur. Then, in early December, Donald drove us down to Devon. I could see he was excited at the prospect of my viewing our new home for the first time.

A rough track across the moors led us into a dip in which a cottage nestled cosily. Built of local stone, it was double-fronted and very pretty, reminding me a little of Charlotte's rectory in Oxenhope. The brook where Donald and I had talked together that summer long ago ran past in front of it.

Donald parked his Crossley at the back of the cottage, then shut the gate that sat in a high wooden fence behind us, just in case there were prying eyes. Taking me by the hand, he led us to the back door and opened it. We stepped inside a low-ceilinged kitchen, then along a narrow hallway into a snug, freshly painted sitting room with a fireplace.

Upstairs, in the tiny second bedroom that Donald had thoughtfully fashioned as a nursery, I laid you down in the cot for a rest. I then stepped into the larger bedroom, noticing the bright flower-sprigged curtains and the big brass double bed covered by a cheerful patchwork quilt.

'So, Anni, what do you think?' he asked eagerly.

'I think it's beautiful, Donald,' I replied, genuinely over-whelmed. After the claustrophobic squalor of Keighley, this was tantamount to heaven.

'I've had the window frames replaced and installed electric light and added a bathroom next to the scullery downstairs. *And* . . . this is for you.' He took a sheaf of papers out of his coat pocket and handed them to me.

I looked through them briefly, gleaning their meaning.

'What it says, my darling, is that I, Lord Donald Astbury, grant you a lifetime tenancy of this cottage. That means that no one can ever throw you out of here, no matter what happens to me. For as long as you need it, this is your home.'

Tears spontaneously filled my eyes. Ever since my father had died and Mother and I had moved to the zenana, I'd never had a real home of my own.

'Thank you, Donald.'

'Darling Anni, it's nothing really. You deserve so much more.'

He took me into his arms and hugged me, then began to kiss me. Maybe it was because of the relief of finally being in a safe place, of being cared for so thoughtfully, that I felt my body yielding to him. We fell as one onto the big, comfortable bed. Perhaps it was the length of time, or the many weeks of nearness to each other without physical contact, but our love-making felt even more passionate than it had before. We lay together afterwards, our arms wrapped tightly around each other, our son sleeping peacefully next door. I did my best to block from my mind the thought of him doing the same with his wife.

Ironically, he was the one to mention it. 'I remember now how it's supposed to be,' he said wistfully. 'I love you, Anni, so much you will never know.'

'And I love you, Donald.'

We slept then, and I knew that we both felt at peace for the first time since I'd left for India. Whatever pact with the devil we'd made to be here together and however morally wrong it was, nothing at that moment could have been more right.

Much later, as I fed you downstairs in the kitchen, Donald showed me how he had stocked the cupboards with food. 'And I have one last surprise for you. Come on, let's go outside.'

With a shawl wrapped tightly around you to keep out the bitter chill, we followed Donald outside. There was a stable next to the barn in the square courtyard and Donald opened the door and lit the lantern that hung on a nail.

'Here, girl, meet your new mistress.'

Donald fondled the nose of the mare. Her skin shone like

polished mahogany, and she had a white star on her forehead.

'I haven't named her yet, I thought you should do that, as she's going to be yours.'

I stroked the mare's soft nose and you, alert to a new plaything, reached out with your small hands to touch the horse, too.

'She's beautiful, Donald, thank you. I'll call her Sheba, as she looks like a queen.'

'Perfect. She's hardly the stallion you used to enjoy riding, but gentle enough for Moh to learn on when he's older. There's also a trap in the barn, so you can ride into the village when you need to.'

'It seems you've thought of everything,' I said as we hurried back inside and I put the kettle on the range to boil some water for a pot of tea. 'But you know the locals will notice I'm here immediately, especially if I'm to ride into the village in a pony and trap,' I pointed out.

'Yes, Anni, of course they'll recognise you. No doubt many of them will be very glad to see you. And remember, it would only seem natural, given your long association with our family, that we should offer you a home after the sad death of your husband,' he comforted me.

'What about Violet?' I questioned. 'What if she hears of me from the servants and suspects something?'

'I can promise you, the one thing I'm not worried about is Violet. She's currently the toast of the social scene, regarded as the most beautiful woman in London, if not England. You've never met a woman more secure or confident in her allure and position. I doubt she'd consider for a second that her husband would be carrying on with an Indian widow who lives on the moors.'

Donald noticed my sudden tension at his words.

'Sorry, darling.' He patted my hand. 'And as far as her relationship with our servants is concerned, they may as well be invisible for all the interest she takes in them and their personal lives. They simply perform a function and beyond that, she isn't involved. There's always plenty for them to do. She takes a bath twice a day. And the sheets on her bed are changed for fresh ones every single morning.'

'Like a queen,' I whispered, remembering how the Maharani had similar ways. But then again, everything in India was victim to the heat and the dust.

'Yes, and in America Violet *is* royalty, brought up with the best of everything. I believe she thinks that we English, me included, are rather grubby.' Donald smiled. 'What I'm trying to say is that it's Violet who's at the centre of Violet's world. I doubt she'll take any notice at all when I've told her of your arrival.'

'You'll tell her?'

'Of course. But she's currently wrapped up in arranging a big Christmas dance here. She's inviting all her smart friends from London. I'm sure she won't give you another thought once I've told her.'

'I hope you're right, Donald.' I shuddered involuntarily. 'None of this is her fault. We mustn't hurt her.'

'I know,' he said in agreement, glancing at his watch. 'And, sadly, dinner is in an hour and she'll be expecting me back from London. I'll come to check on you both tomorrow morning. Will you be all right here alone? It really is most awfully cosy. I wish with all my heart I could stay, but I can't.'

'We'll be fine,' I said, watching you grab the table leg and make a fruitless attempt to pull yourself upright.

'Moh will be talking soon, won't you, little chap?' Donald bent down and planted a gentle kiss on your forehead. 'Right, I'd better be off,' he said as he buttoned up his coat and headed towards the door. 'The good news is that I can drive across the moors from here to join the main road and then enter through the front gates of the estate. Alternatively, I can simply saddle up Glory and ride directly from the house across the moors in fifteen minutes. You'll become sick of the sight of me, I'm sure.'

'I doubt that,' I said as I planted a kiss on his lips. 'Thank you, Donald. I feel safe, for the first time in many, many months.'

He blew me a kiss in return, mouthed goodbye and was gone.

After I'd put you down in your cot to sleep, I wandered about my new home looking with delight at each nook and cranny that Donald had so lovingly fashioned for me. I lit the fire in the cosy sitting room and studied the books which stood on shelves to either side of the fireplace. Donald had chosen some of my favourite novels, and they were stories I knew I would read and reread over the evenings to come.

Over those first long winter months, when the moors became a desert of snow in which I was trapped and Donald struggled to make his way across them on Glory to bring food, milk and love, I read ferociously. Yet even though my life was solitary, I found myself experiencing a growing sense of inner peace. Perhaps the snow gave me a false sense of security; it cut me off from Astbury Hall and its unseen occupants, and I lived in a void, with only you and Donald for company.

In retrospect, I think those few months were exactly what I needed to heal my damaged soul; there had been times in that dreadful first year of your life when I'd almost lost hope. When I could no longer see, feel, hear or even *believe* in those things that had always guided me. When I'd wished for death more than I'd wanted life, and I'd truly understood for the first time what it was to be alone. Even though now days might pass without my seeing Donald, I knew for certain that I was loved.

I do remember Christmas being a difficult time. Donald was busy with the festivities at the Hall, where many of Violet's American relatives were arriving to celebrate with her, so I saw very little of him. On Christmas Eve, he appeared briefly with a hamper containing a turkey large enough to feed a family of twelve, and presents for both of us. On Christmas morning, I opened the gift for me which sat under our fir tree. It was a creamy string of pearls, with a loving message concealed inside the box. I put them on that Christmas morning of 1920, and they remain around my neck to this day.

As the snow began to thaw in early March, my life at the cottage by the brook began to change. Donald told me that Violet's mother was sick and she was returning to New York to stay with her.

'Hasn't she asked you to go with her?' I said as we sat in front of the fire in the sitting room, watching you attempt your first tottering steps.

'Of course,' said Donald, 'but I pointed out that if I am to run Astbury as a business like Daddy Drumner wishes me to, spring is a particularly bad time for me to leave the country because of the lambing season. And Violet didn't seem to mind when I said I must stay here.'

That spring, when Violet had left for America, was a singularly perfect time. Donald would arrange with Selina to pretend that he was staying with her in London. During those few days, he would drive over to us on the moors and hide his car at the back of the cottage, and we'd live together just like a normal family.

As the moors came to life around us, we three revelled in our tranquil, isolated world. The only sadness was that you could never be allowed to call your father 'Papa', and that Donald and I had to take great care not to make any fatal slip of the tongue in front of you. Inevitably, you found your own phrase for the man who became such a big part of your life.

'Mr Don, come!' you'd demand as you lifted your small arms to your father for a hug. Donald had begun to take you on the back of the pony, trotting you around the yard as you squealed in pleasure. He often brought small presents of sherbets for you and cuttings from colourful blooms taken from the grounds at Astbury for me to plant in my garden.

'Here –' he said one day, as he climbed down from Glory's gleaming back and handed me a tiny plant covered in thorns – 'I've brought you a rosebush. The Astbury gardener was replanting the beds and told me this one was a very unusual and exotic specimen called the Midnight Rose. I immediately thought of you.' He smiled as he kissed me. 'Shall we go and plant it? Maybe in the front garden?' he suggested.

After those terrible months doubting whether Donald loved me, I knew now with all my heart that he did. As I listened to him raging – against the poverty in which so many in England still lived, the unfairness of the fact that so much should be owned by so few, and how he couldn't change the world but could make a start by renovating some of his own workers' cottages on the estate – a new respect for him grew within me.

'David Lloyd George is doing his damnedest, but the fear

of change amongst politicians who are mostly gathered from the upper classes makes reforms difficult to push through.' Donald sighed as we sat together in the garden one evening.

'My father always said that to push a rock an inch in a lifetime was the same as throwing a hundred pebbles into the sea every day. Big change comes slowly, but it will come, Donald,' I assured him. 'You're unusual now, but many people will start to see the world like you.'

'My mother always saw me as odd, because I was friendly with one of the groomsmen's children when I was younger. I remember insisting he should come to eat with us at the Hall because he always seemed hungry. I used to steal food from the kitchen to give to him. I could never abide the class system and still can't.'

'I was wondering,' I said, changing the subject, 'whether I might come over to the Hall before your wife returns from America. I want to see if any of the medicinal herbs I planted in the kitchen garden are still alive. I'd like to take cuttings and start my own herb garden here.'

'Of course! Remember, Anni, the only secret is what *we* share, not your presence here at Astbury. There's absolutely no need for you to hide away now that spring is here. In fact, it would seem more natural if you didn't.' He reached across and stroked my cheek gently. 'As long as I remember never to reach for you in front of others.' He smiled, looking up at the kitchen clock. 'Right, time for me to get back there myself.' He sighed. 'Lambing starts at any moment.'

37

I drove us in the pony and trap up to the Hall a few days later and found that many of the herbs I'd planted in the sheltered corner of the kitchen garden had flourished. On my knees and trying to prevent you from tearing them from the ground with your eager hands, I heard a familiar voice behind me.

'Well, look who it is!'

'Mrs Thomas!' I smiled up at her as she came towards me with her basket, ready to collect the vegetables she'd need for dinner that night.

'I'd heard you were back here, Miss Anni. Tilly said she saw you in the village only last week, but I told her she was seeing things.'

'I've been here since the winter, but the snow was deep on the moors and I haven't been well,' I explained.

'I'd heard that too, and that your husband died. I'm sorry, my love. It must have been tough on you with a little one. But he's a fine young fellow,' said Mrs Thomas, fixing her gaze on you. You turned round, stared at Mrs Thomas, then waved at her sociably.

'Oooh, he's got blue eyes,' commented the cook. 'Bless my soul, I never knew Indians could have blue eyes!'

LUCINDA RILEY

'His father had blue eyes; some Indians do,' I replied, concealing my sudden wave of panic.

'Well, I wouldn't be knowing, would I? Anyway, he seems a lovely little chap and you're not to be a stranger here any more. Once you've finished outside, come into the kitchen and introduce your boy to the rest of the servants. They'll be very glad to see you, my love.'

'That's most kind of you, Mrs Thomas. I'll be up shortly.'

As she turned away, I looked down at you in trepidation and realised that your blue eyes were an instant betrayal of the secret your father and I kept.

In the kitchen, the servants clustered around both of us. After so many months of isolation, I felt gratified by their genuine warmth and friendliness. You were fed cake and chocolate until I had to refuse for fear you might be sick. I sat down at the kitchen table with a cup of tea as the servants plied me with questions. I answered them all as best I could, even inventing the name 'Jaival Prasad' for my imaginary dead husband.

'Well, I should think you might know already how things have changed up here at the Hall,' said Mrs Thomas, raising her eyebrows. 'Lord Donald married an American girl last year, and we've all had to learn Lady Violet's new ways.'

'Isn't that the truth,' said Tilly under her breath.

'Well, we'd all admit there have been some advantages that have come with the new lady of the house,' said Mrs Thomas. 'I got a new range' – she indicated it proudly – 'and a whole heap of new cooking pots. She said the old ones were unhygienic, and I said that no one had died yet at my table. But I'll admit to being glad of my fine, shiny ones now.'

'Do you like Lady Violet?' I asked, unable to resist.

'She's nice enough, I'd reckon,' said Mrs Thomas, 'for all the notice she takes of us down here. She didn't know the first thing about English food and what would be served in a house such as this, so I had to put her straight. Now she leaves it to me. What goes inside her body is not her particular interest. It's more what goes on *top* of it!' All the servants giggled at this.

'I never met a woman so vain,' said Tilly. 'Although, I was talking to a lady's maid who came down here and she said all the Yankees are the same. Lady Astbury had a whole wall of wardrobes built and they're already overflowing with clothes.'

'But she's very beautiful. I never saw someone so beautiful,' the scullery maid added shyly.

'That she is,' said Mrs Thomas, 'but wouldn't we all be, if we took the time she takes with her appearance and had the money spare to pretty ourselves up with all them dresses of hers?'

'Is she kind?' I persisted, feeling I'd heard nothing about what Violet the person was like, only how rich and beautiful.

'Kind enough,' replied Tilly. 'When I help her with her hair and into her gowns at night, she doesn't chat or gossip about anything except her clothes and jewels. I don't think she's ever asked me a question about my life.'

'I'd say we could've had worse,' said Mrs Thomas. 'At least she's not another battle-axe, like the one who's just moved to the Dower House. And at least the house is busy and full of young people, rather than dowagers in mourning. Astbury's come back to life since Lady Violet arrived and we must all be grateful for that.'

From that moment on, I was never short of company. You and I were invited constantly to the servants' cottages in the village to take tea or to join them at the local fete, the fair that arrived every few months on Astbury Green. I took care to make sure that it was us that visited *them*, pointing out that it was much more convenient as I had a pony and trap and it was a good three-mile walk from the village across the moors to my cottage. Even so, I lived in terror of a friend turning up unexpectedly while Donald was visiting me.

Word began to spread through the village that I was back in Astbury, and also about the herbal remedies that I'd begun to use again to help Mrs Thomas's arthritis, Tilly's bronchitis and even the butler's gout. The cuttings I'd taken from the kitchen garden and replanted in my own had taken well and were flourishing. Donald was building me a small greenhouse to protect them from winter frost and when I was out on the moors I came across many indigenous medicinal plants, which I also added to my growing collection.

Many afternoons that summer saw me trotting in the trap across the moors with you next to me, heading to the home of a villager whose child was sick with a fever. These people had no recourse to health care of any kind. The doctor charged a small fortune for a visit and most of them simply couldn't afford it. I didn't ask for any payment; the look on the face of a relieved mother was enough.

I also began to find my traditional nursing experience worked well with my knowledge of Ayurvedic herbs. I was able to spot when my remedies would be to no avail. And if the patient was too far gone for my help, I'd advise that the local hospital was the only course of action remaining.

In July, at a christening in the village, I met the local doctor again. I hadn't seen him since he'd arrived too late to deliver Selina's baby all those years ago.

'May I thank you, Mrs Prasad,' said Dr Trefusis, giving me a slight bow. 'You've made my workload less and the villagers are benefitting from your knowledge. Have you ever thought of resuming your career? A district nurse would be a blessing to everyone locally.'

'I have thought of it, but I have a son to care for and any proper employment would take up too much of my time whilst he's so young,' I told him. 'Also, I doubt the medical profession would approve of me using herbs from the land to help my patients.'

'No, you're probably right,' Dr Trefusis agreed. 'I'd be fascinated to learn more, however. Anything that gives the poor a free source of healing must be a positive thing. So carry on the good work.'

'My goodness, I hardly see you these days, in between your errands of mercy,' commented Donald in late August. Violet was due home any day, so Donald had 'gone to London' and was spending time with us at the cottage.

'It keeps me occupied and I like helping people,' I replied.

'I know you do,' he said as he spooned up the stew I'd prepared for us. 'It won't be so easy for you in the winter, though, will it?'

'Sheba's a strong pony and used to the moors now. I'm sure she'll cope if there's snow again this year.'

'Perhaps I should think about installing a telephone here,' mused Donald. 'That way at least I could contact you if there's a problem and the villagers could use the one in the post office if there's a patient who needs you urgently.'

'It's kind of you, Donald, but telephones are so expensive and I'd prefer not to take any more money from you.'

'Anni, darling, your upkeep comes to nothing material at all,' Donald said, trying to reassure me. 'Look here, if we were married, you wouldn't even question it. Which we are, my darling, in all but name. Besides, the fact that you're helping the local community is a wonderful thing, and I'm very proud of you. So installing a telephone is the least I can do to assist you.'

'All right,' I said with a sigh, 'thank you.'

'What you do is all in such contrast to my dear wife.' Donald sighed too. 'Violet does absolutely nothing to help anyone but herself. To be honest, I'm dreading her coming home from New York. We have only one more night together. It's really not very satisfactory, is it?'

'I'm grateful for what we've had, Donald,' I answered, although as I said the words my appetite suddenly vanished.

'It may be a few days before I'm able to get away,' Donald said, cautioning me, as he left for the Hall the following morning. 'Goodbye, my darling. Take care of yourself and our boy, won't you?'

'Yes,' I said, feeling tears spring to my eyes. Even though I'd see him soon, I knew he was returning to his other world and would be no longer solely mine.

Another winter began to draw in, and with the arrival of the cold weather the demands of my patients on my time became heavier. But I was glad of the distraction. I'd seen far less of Donald since Violet had been home. It would have seemed strange if he'd been absent from Astbury too often after spending six months apart from her. He dropped in as regularly as he could, often on his way to London for a party or a dance.

'Most of her friends are such arrogant, crashing bores, I can hardly bear it. But still,' he said with a sigh, 'I must do what is required of me.'

One mid-December evening, Donald arrived unexpectedly at the cottage. He looked haggard and drawn and stared at me with fear in his eyes.

'What is it?' I asked him, knowing immediately something was wrong.

'I have some news,' he said, sitting down heavily in a chair at the kitchen table.

'Is it bad news?' I asked as I put the kettle on the range to boil.

'I'd doubt anyone else would see it as such, but I worry that you might, Anni. And I wanted to tell you before anyone else did. You know what it's like around here; gossip, especially of this nature, spreads like wildfire. And I'm sure most of the servants are aware already.'

'Then tell me,' I entreated him, hardly daring to think what it might be.

Donald took a deep breath, then, unable to meet my eyes, looked down at his feet. 'Violet . . . is expecting a baby.'

'I see.' I understood then why he felt I was the only person who would not see the news as positive.

'Anni, in truth, do you mind?'

Of course I minded! Not about the forthcoming child but the intimate process it had taken to produce it. I shuddered involuntarily at the thought. However, I wanted to act with dignity in front of Donald. I'd known what the circumstances were when I'd first agreed to this.

'It's only natural that you and your wife would want to produce a family. And an heir to the estate,' I added, endeavouring to keep the bitterness from my voice. 'I'm hardly in a position to mind, am I?'

'Of course you are,' Donald said, suddenly angry. 'I mean

if the boot were on the other foot, and this were you telling me, I doubt I'd be able to cope with it at all.'

'I have no choice in the matter, I will cope with it,' I said firmly.

'And you should also know, Anni, that the process of making the child has been an act of duty, not of pleasure.'

I wanted to believe his words, and in fact, I had no doubt that he spoke the truth, but the thought of it still seared right to my soul.

'And the worst part is that already Violet is taking the pregnancy badly. She's cancelled all engagements for the next few weeks because she says she feels so ill, and has taken to her bed. This means, unfortunately, that for the foreseeable future, at least, her attention won't be otherwise engaged as it usually is. I'll have to spend much more time at home with her. I'm so very sorry, Anni.'

'We'll find our way through this, I'm sure. We have before, after all.'

'Yes, but it's just that, more and more, I feel the life I'm living with Violet at the Hall is a lie,' he said miserably.

'Well, there's nothing to be done, and we must both simply make the best of it.' I knew I was being short with him, but I was still trying to grapple with the ramifications of what he'd just told me. At present, I couldn't find it in me to be sympathetic.

'Yes.' He looked at me guiltily, understanding. 'Forgive me, darling, today of all days, it should be me comforting you. Sadly, I'd better be going. Dr Trefusis is coming to see Violet shortly.' Donald stood up and kissed me on the top of my head. 'I'll see you as soon as I can.'

38

Donald told me that Dr Trefusis had apparently pronounced Violet fit and well. He had given her charcoal for her sickness and told her to rest until it passed. The news was to be announced to the wider world when the pregnancy was over twelve weeks, although they had both told their parents.

'My mother has asked that I visit her at the Dower House this afternoon to discuss what she termed a "delicate matter", so I must leave,' Donald said apologetically when he came to visit us a few days later. 'God knows what it is she wants.'

After he'd left, I wondered what she wanted, too. I knew that Maud Astbury was my nemesis, the black crow on my shoulder, waiting for a chance to peck away at my little piece of happiness. When Donald arrived the following day, I could see from his face that her summons had been to do with me. I made tea for both of us and we took it into the sitting room to enjoy the warmth of the fire.

'So, what did she say?' I asked him.

'She told me there have been some rumours about my whereabouts locally. Apparently, I've been seen riding regularly across the moors.'

'Well, that's hardly a crime, is it?'

'In one particular direction,' Donald added pointedly.

'Oh, I see. By whom?'

'Apparently, the shepherd told his wife in the village, who told her friend Mrs Thomas, who told Bessie, my mother's maid, that he'd seen me on my horse in the vicinity of this cottage many times over the spring and summer months. Obviously I told her that in itself was not cause for rumour,' Donald added. 'After all, I've always ridden this way across the moors, stopping at the brook to give Glory a drink.'

I sat silently, listening to him.

'Mother made a big meal out of the fact that I'm lord of the estate, and every breath I take is analysed and gossiped about by the staff,' said Donald wearily. 'She said the reason she was bringing this to my attention now was because Violet is pregnant, and the doctor has indicated she's delicate. She said she wouldn't wish any of these rumours, no matter how spurious, to reach Violet's ears whilst she's carrying the heir to the Astbury Estate. She added that out of common decency, if nothing else, my visits across the moors to see you should cease immediately for the time being.'

'I see.'

'To be honest, Anni, she made me feel like a complete heel, saying it's bad enough that I'm carrying on a relationship under my wife's nose, but to continue doing so whilst Violet is with child is disgusting.'

'Well, on this occasion, however much it pains me, I believe your mother is right,' I said eventually. 'Violet knows nothing of all this. In fact, you could say that makes her more of a victim than either of us.'

'I know, Anni.' Donald hung his head in shame. 'She doesn't deserve any of it, especially not at the moment.'

'No, she doesn't. And whether or not your mother is using the pregnancy as a lever to achieve her goal and destroy us, we must both have compassion for Violet. Don't think I'm not racked with guilt every day about deceiving her too,' I added. 'We must both act with decency and integrity during this time. So you must stop coming to visit me.'

'But what will you do, Anni? How will you manage? More to the point, how will I?'

'Perhaps we could resort to writing letters to each other again.'

'Very funny.' Donald gave a mirthless chuckle.

'It's for the best.'

'But how can I keep away?'

'You simply must.'

He took my hand in his and kissed it tenderly. 'Right, it seems we have to say goodbye once more. But only temporarily, until the child is born.'

'The months will pass quickly, I'm sure,' I reassured him.

'My Moh will be almost three by the time I see him again,' Donald said wistfully.

We stood up and walked together to the kitchen door, then held each other close.

'I'll find ways of contacting you, my Anni, don't you worry. I love you.'

'Goodbye, Donald,' I whispered.

And after that conversation, I settled down to yet more time apart from the man I loved. But the fact that we were both in this pact together, equally intent on doing the right thing, made it a little easier. I was busy with you and my patients, and did my best to keep from dwelling on our enforced separation.

Christmas arrived and in the morning I found a basket on my doorstep containing another huge turkey, various treats and a present for myself and for you. In the evening, I joined the other villagers at the village hall for a Christmas party. It was wonderful to see your face light up at the garish decorations that had been strung around the room.

On New Year's Eve, Tilly and her sweet husband, Jim, invited us to their cottage. They had a child called Mabel, who was of a similar age to you.

'Happy New Year,' I whispered silently to Donald as the church bells rang in the New Year. Somehow, it made it even harder with his being so near and yet so far.

'Are you all right, Anni?' said Tilly, putting an arm around me. 'Thinking of your poor husband, no doubt.'

'Yes,' I replied.

'I'm sure there'll be someone for you one day, Anni. You're so beautiful and clever, I doubt you'll be alone for too long.'

At that moment, my heart cried out to tell my friend the truth of my situation, to confide in someone, but I knew I could not. I had no choice but to bear my secret alone.

As fate would have it, I was to see Donald far sooner than I imagined.

One crisp January night, as I was bathing you in the tub in the kitchen by the range, I heard the sound of a horse's hooves draw up in the courtyard. As no one ever came to visit me at night, I assumed it could only be Donald. He knocked politely and then opened the back door to the kitchen.

'What are you doing here? I thought we agreed—'

'We did, and I want you to know that I'm here with the full knowledge of my wife,' he said, still breathless from the ride across the moors.

'What on earth do you mean?'

'May I come in?' he asked me. 'Then I can explain.'

I stood aside to let him pass.

'Mr Don!'

Your eyes lit up as you saw your father and you splashed approvingly from the tub.

'Hello, little chap,' he said as his face broke into a smile and he kissed your soapy head. Then he turned to me. 'The thing is that unfortunately my wife's pregnancy sickness has not improved. It seems she finds it impossible to bear the smell of food, so she's not eating. Dr Trefusis isn't overly concerned, saying it will pass eventually, but Violet is utterly miserable.'

'Some women suffer terribly throughout their pregnancy,' I said tentatively, wondering why he was telling me all this.

'Which brings me to the reason I'm here. It seems that Violet has heard some talk from the servants about the miracles you perform with your special herbal remedies. And she's requested that you visit her to see if there's anything you can give her that might help with the sickness.'

I stared at him as if he had taken leave of his senses. 'You can't be serious!'

'Indeed I am, Anni. Your fame has spread, and the problem is now that it would seem very strange if you refused to look in on Lady Astbury herself when she's specifically requested your help. I know.' Donald shook his head and shrugged helplessly. 'The last thing I thought I'd be doing was coming here to see you on my wife's explicit instructions.'

'Oh, Donald, I . . .'

Perhaps it was the release of tension from weeks of not seeing him, or the irony of the situation we were now in, but I suddenly began to giggle. Finally, and with relief, Donald did the same, and you, my darling, gazed at your parents from your bathtub in astonishment.

'It's not funny really,' I said eventually, wiping my streaming eyes with the bath towel.

'No, it isn't,' Donald said, 'not at all. Oh, Anni, it's so wonderful to see you,' he said as he pulled me to him. 'Have you missed me as much as I've missed you?'

'More,' I said truthfully, loving the sensation of being once more in his embrace. 'So, Her Ladyship requests my presence,' I said as I left his arms to lift you out of the tub.

'She does indeed. I said I wasn't sure if you would be in, but I'd ride over and leave a message for you anyway. She'd like you to come at your earliest convenience. Perhaps tomorrow morning?'

'I shall have to consult my diary, of course,' I said, my eyes twinkling as I towelled you dry on my knee. 'But I'm sure I can squeeze your wife in somewhere.'

'Thank you, Anni,' he said gratefully. 'And truly, anything you can do would be appreciated. She's suffering terribly, poor thing, and making sure everyone knows it.'

'I'll ride over in the trap first thing tomorrow. Tell her to expect me around nine-thirty,' I said, as you slid off my knee and toddled over to your father, your arms raised towards him.

'Hug, Mr Don,' you demanded, and he pulled you up onto his knee.

'How he's grown in the space of just a few weeks,' he said, stroking your soft dark hair.

'Yes, he has. He's talking thirteen to the dozen now too. I'll ask Tilly to mind him whilst I come up to attend to your wife. As I'm sure you know, she's no longer working at the Hall.

Her husband, Jim, has just received a promotion to assistant postmaster.'

'Perfect, and whilst I'm here –' Donald dug in his pocket and pulled out some notes from his wallet. 'There, at least now I won't need to use Tilly's husband to deliver this to you in a letter.' He smiled.

'Thank you.' It was the moment I hated, but there was currently little I could do to change it.

'Mr Don, hortey?' you asked expectantly.

'Not today, little man,' said Donald regretfully, 'but I promise to take you riding on Sheba next time I visit. Now I must go.'

Your face dropped, and you toddled after Donald to the door. As I scooped you up into my arms to comfort you, I asked, 'Will you be there tomorrow with Violet?'

'I feel that in the best interests of all concerned, I should make myself scarce.'

'Yes,' I said in agreement.

When Donald had left, I put you to bed and sat by the fire mulling over his astonishing appearance and the reasons for it. Even though I'd laughed initially at the irony of the situation and made light of it with Donald, my senses sang a different emotional tune.

That night, as I tried to sleep, I heard the singing. It was distant, but it was there. And it warned me that danger was not far off.

The following day, once I'd deposited you at Tilly's cottage in the village, I drove the trap up to Astbury Hall. Entering the usual way through the lobby and into the kitchen, I was greeted with welcoming smiles.

'We're mighty glad to see you, Miss Anni,' said Mrs

Thomas. 'I said to Her Ladyship that if there was anyone who could help her, it had to be you. Do you think you can? 'Cause I'm running out of ideas to tempt her into eating something.'

'I hope I can, but I'll have to take a look at her first,' I said as Ariane, Violet's new French lady's maid, arrived in the kitchen to take me upstairs.

'Well, we're all keeping our fingers crossed. We're all getting right worried about her,' Mrs Thomas added.

'I promise to do my best,' I assured her as I left the kitchen and followed Ariane along the labyrinth of corridors that led to the main entrance hall. As she took me up the staircase, I was agog at the difference in the Hall, and saw that Violet had obviously got her way with the family portraits that led up the grand staircase. They had been replaced with striking works of modern art.

'Wait here, *s'il vous plaît*,' said the maid, leading me into a sumptuously furnished sitting room. 'I will let Her Ladyship know.'

I noticed that the temperature in the room was that of a furnace, so stiflingly hot, it reminded me of my days in India.

'Her Ladyship will see you now,' said Ariane, appearing at the bedroom door.

I followed her tentatively into the room and found it as stuffy as the sitting room next door. My immediate instinct was to open the large windows and let in some fresh air.

Lying in the four-poster, which was hung on either side with rich brocade drapes, lay a pale figure, dwarfed by the vast size of the bed.

'Hello, Your Ladyship.' I curtsied. 'My name is Anahita Prasad. I believe you sent for me.'

'Yes, I did, after hearing the servants talk of your wonderful healing remedies,' she said in her soft American voice. 'Please, come closer . . . Ariane, won't you pull up a chair for Mrs Prasad and she can sit down next to me?'

Ariane did so, and I sat down, properly studying the woman who was Donald's wife. She looked so young – barely older than a child herself. With her blonde hair, huge brown eyes and perfect bow-shaped lips set in her white, unblemished skin, she reminded me of a fragile porcelain doll. I could see immediately from her demeanour that she was weak, caused almost certainly by lack of nourishment.

'I'm very glad you're here, Mrs Prasad, even Dr Trefusis said it couldn't do any harm to see you.'

'It's my pleasure, Your Ladyship. I'm sure Dr Trefusis informed you that I have nursing training, as well as the Ayurvedic medicine I practise.'

'Either will do for me, if it'll make me feel better.' Violet sighed. 'I've been sick as a dog now for weeks.'

'Now, Your Ladyship, would you mind if I gave you a brief examination?'

'Go right ahead. I've been prodded and poked so much recently I lost all dignity long ago.'

I took time to check Violet's vital signs, surmising that her pulse was a little fast, although many women's were during pregnancy, but her temperature was normal and her heartbeat steady and regular. I felt the baby, who seemed to be small for the number of weeks, but was most definitely alive. Violet's skin was clammy to the touch, but I deduced that was probably more to do with the oppressive heat in the room rather than any medical condition. I then checked under her eyelids and found the tell-tale signs of anaemia.

Satisfied that I'd completed a thorough examination on

both traditional and holistic levels, I washed my hands in the basin on the stand, dried them and sat down.

Violet had remained silent and compliant throughout the examination, but now I could see that her eyes were expectant.

'Well, I believe I can help you, Your Ladyship.'

'Oh, thank the Lord! I've lain here for some days feeling like I was dying.'

'You're perfectly well, I promise you. Has Dr Trefusis mentioned anaemia to you?'

'No.' Violet shook her head. 'His prescription is simply chicken broth, which I loathe and detest. What's anaemia? Is it serious?'

'Not at all if caught in time and treated. It's simply the baby depleting your body's iron stores,' I explained. 'It makes you feel sleepy and lethargic, but it's very easy to put right, I promise you. Your Ladyship, have you ever heard of a drink called stout?'

'Isn't that something the navvies drink on the docks?' Violet curled her lips in disgust.

'Yes, but it's also very good for pregnant women because it contains a lot of iron. It's not particularly pleasant, but I promise you it will really help. I'll also ask Mrs Thomas to cook everything you eat in an iron pan. The food soaks up the iron and it's a natural way of getting the substance into your body.'

'But that's the whole problem,' Violet wailed, 'I simply can't eat! Even the smell of food makes me feel sick.'

'I think we can deal with that as well. I have some fresh ginger and I'll bring it over and ask Mrs Thomas to brew you up some tea from it. It's wonderful for settling a queasy stomach and will make you feel far less sick. For now, you must drink it at least three times a day.'

'Ginger?' Violet wrinkled her pretty nose. 'My, the medicines you're prescribing are making me feel worse!'

'They won't, I promise. And I'm also going to mix you up a herbal draught that will not only help the sickness, but will also give you more energy and perhaps bring back a little colour to your cheeks. I'll put the instructions onto the bottle. And no,' I said in agreement, 'that really won't taste very nice at all. The last thing is, Your Ladyship, that this room is simply too hot. You need to turn the heating down and have some fresh air in here. And also, a short walk every day in the garden to get some exercise will do neither you nor the baby any harm. Lying up here, miserable and alone, is certainly not helping you at all.'

'But it's so cold outside.' Violet shivered.

'I know,' I said, 'but you can wrap up warmly. And if you do everything I suggest, you'll soon feel like running around the garden like a spring lamb.'

'Are you sure?'

'Positive.'

'Okay.' She sighed, resigned. 'I suppose I have nothing to lose by trying it your way. None of these things are dangerous for the baby, are they?'

'If they were at all dangerous, Your Ladyship, I wouldn't give them to you.'

'No, of course not.' Violet blushed at her tactless remark.

'Now, I'm going to go downstairs and speak with Mrs Thomas. Together, we'll try to come up with something more tasty but equally as nutritious as chicken broth.'

'Well, that sure would be an improvement.' Violet shared a conspiratorial glance with me.

LUCINDA RILEY

'I'll come back and see you in a few days,' I said as I stood up. 'But if you need me before, then send for me.'

'Yes, and don't worry yourself about riding over to bring the medicines you wish me to take. I've troubled you enough and I know from the servants that you have a small child. I'll send someone to collect them from you this afternoon.'

'Thank you. I'm only too happy to be of some help.'

'Goodbye, Mrs Prasad.' Violet smiled at me as I walked towards the door. 'Leave the bill downstairs with the butler.'

'Oh no, I don't charge. My services are free. Good day, Your Ladyship.'

Downstairs in the kitchen, I wrote a list of instructions and explained them to Mrs Thomas.

'Well, if all these things you prescribe work, I'll be the King of England, but seeing as you've mended so many of us before, I'm prepared to trust you.'

'Thank you, Mrs Thomas. Now, I must go and collect my son from Tilly. He'll be wondering where I've got to.'

Donald himself rode over to the cottage that afternoon and I gave him the ginger and the herbal remedy I'd made up for Violet to boost her energy levels.

'You should see an improvement in the next few days, if she starts all these things immediately,' I advised him.

'Thank you, Anni,' he said as he tucked the ginger and the remedy into his coat pocket. 'I'll encourage Violet to do as you say. It's so awfully good of you to help her, under the circumstances.'

'She's a human being and she's suffering,' I said, as I ushered him to the door. 'Of course I want to do my best to help her.'

*

When I returned to the Hall a week later, I was taken upstairs, but this time, a fully dressed Violet greeted me in her sitting room.

'Mrs Prasad!' She stood up and walked over to me, then, to my embarrassment, embraced me. 'You are a miracle worker! Look at me!'

I did look at her and saw the pink tinge to her cheeks and a new vitality shining in her eyes. 'It seems you are much recovered.' I smiled.

'Yes! Although I still can't quite believe it. At first, having to drink all that disgusting stuff made me sure I was going to get sicker, but I didn't! And I've done as you said, every day, to the letter, and it's worked! Oh, Anni – may I call you Anni? All the servants seem to – how can I ever thank you?'

'Really, there's no need. I'm just happy that you're better.'

She gestured to me to sit down opposite her in a chair. 'Dr Trefusis came to see me yesterday and could hardly believe the change. Of course, I told him about you coming to visit and what a tonic you are,' Violet said, admiration and gratitude in her eyes. 'I cabled my mother yesterday in New York – she'd been so worried she was about to board the steamer and come over and visit me. But of course, she isn't well either, so I said that there was no need now and that I was feeling just fine. When she arrives for the birth, perhaps you'd be kind enough to take a look at her too, if she's not better by then?'

'I'd be glad to, if she wishes it, of course.'

'I'm even feeling as though I can face inviting some of my friends to come and stay with us again. Since I've been sick, the house has been empty.'

I felt gratified by the change in Violet and realised her

exuberance today was naturally part of who she was. I liked her for it.

'Well, I'm glad to tell you that you may come off the ginger tea. Take it only if you feel queasy. I've given Mrs Thomas some fresh mint leaves, which also help with nausea, and you may find more palatable. But I'm afraid you must continue with the stout.'

'Oh, I'm used to it now. Donny thinks it's a huge joke to watch me drink it,' she giggled. 'Oh, Miss Anni, he's just been so sweet, so concerned for me. I'd guess he wants to embrace you as much as I do!'

I held my facial muscles firmly in place at this remark and stood up.

'I must go, there's a baby in the village I have to visit urgently.'

'Of course.' Violet stood too. 'I do hope you can visit me often, and perhaps you'd be able to spare the time to come to one of my dinners.'

'Well –' I faltered – 'I couldn't, I'm afraid. I have a child and no one to leave him with.'

'Yes, Donny told me your husband died. I am so sorry. If your little boy is as good-looking as you, he must be a beautiful child. You have such an exotic quality, I'm green with envy!'

'Thank you . . . you are too kind. Now, I really must go.'

'Perhaps I could come visit you at your cottage and meet your little boy someday too?' she said as she followed me to the door like an eager puppy. 'I know so few people around here. All my crowd are in London.'

'I'm often out,' I said abruptly. 'Do telephone me first.'

'I will. Goodbye, Anni, and once again, thank you.'

39

'It seems I have my old wife back,' said Donald a couple of days later, when he dropped in on a further mission for Violet to present me with an enormous bouquet of flowers, chocolates and champagne. 'And you have a new admirer.' He grinned. 'I never thought in my wildest dreams that I'd be bringing gifts to you from my wife. Life is nothing if not ironic.'

'Yes, that is true,' I said, trying to stop you from getting your hands into the chocolates.

'You are just wonderful,' Donald said, giving me a hug. 'I can't exactly say your methods are traditional, but long may they reign.'

'They're certainly traditional in India, and all natural,' I countered.

'Well, you're incredibly clever, although I fear there is a downside to this,' commented Donald. 'Violet, with her newly returned energy, is racing around at top speed organising goodness knows who to come to stay at the house. She's obviously making up for lost time. And you know how I dislike her set. But, the good news is –' he pulled me onto his knee – 'that I've had a reason to visit you.'

He kissed me, and I put my arms around his neck.

'Yes, that is a very good thing. Although your wife did ask me if she could come to visit me here and meet Moh.'

'Really?' Donald frowned. 'What did you say?'

'I said to telephone me first because I was often out, but I can hardly stop her, can I?'

'No. Well, that's going to complicate things. I'm not at all comfortable with Violet knowing exactly where you live.'

'Do you think *I* am? But what can I do?'

'Nothing, I suppose. Although perhaps it's best to take that photograph of the three of us down from your bedside table. I mean, she might find that rather odd,' he quipped with an attempt at humour.

'Please, it isn't a joke. Violet's always eaten into my conscience from the start, but now, having to pretend I'm her friend . . .' I shuddered. 'It feels all too close for comfort. And besides, Donald, I like her. She's so sweet, and for all her money, I feel she's very vulnerable.'

'I know, Anni. Well, let's hope her attachment to you is temporary. As you seem to have been the only person who's been able to help her, she's currently clinging to the idea of you. You've become the fount of wisdom for all things to do with pregnancy,' he grinned. 'I think Dr Trefusis' nose is rather out of joint.'

'As a matter of fact, he telephoned me earlier and he's coming to visit me tomorrow,' I told him. 'He said he wanted to see my herb garden and learn more about what I put in my remedies.'

'Really? I'm surprised. I've always seen him as rather old-fashioned and narrow-minded.'

'Well, perhaps he is more receptive to new ideas than you thought.'

'I really do wonder whether you should start charging for all this help you give people,' said Donald. 'I wouldn't want to see you taken advantage of.'

'Perhaps, when Moh is older, I'll think more seriously about the future and take up medicine professionally again. But for now, I'm happy with the way things are.'

'Don't tire yourself out, will you, darling?' he said as he stroked my cheek gently. 'And don't let my wife bully you into doing anything you don't want. She can be very persistent.'

The following day, Dr Trefusis arrived at the cottage. I took him into my small greenhouse and he walked past the ledges full of different specimens, asking me questions about each of the herbs.

'It isn't just about the remedies themselves,' I explained. 'It's diagnosing who your patient is and which *dosha* – that is, whether she or he is a *pitta*, *vata* or *kapha*. This you discover through looking at the patient's physical shape and colouring, and also asking some simple questions to assess their emotional state and personality. Then you can fit exactly the right remedy to the patient. The remedies I use have been part of Indian culture for thousands of years. As well as using the fresh plants, I dry the leaves and store them in jars or grind them into a powder. The roots of them provide the most powerful remedies.'

'Fascinating, absolutely fascinating,' he murmured. 'So, what type is Lady Astbury?'

'She's a *vata* type, Doctor, which means she's small-boned, carries little fat and feels the cold very badly. She also has a

temperamental digestive system which is easily upset and probably accounts for her severe morning sickness.'

'I see. Well, would you mind if I took a few cuttings for
myself and tried to grow them? Perhaps you could teach me
how to mix some of the basic remedies? Something for a bad
chest, for example?'

'Yes, please take what you wish. Excuse me, I must attend
to my son. He'll have woken from his afternoon nap by now.'

'Of course,' Dr Trefusis said. 'I'll stay here and take the cuttings, then follow you inside.'

The doctor left, saying he'd return one day the following
week so that I could show him how to prepare a remedy. He
never appeared on my doorstep again.

Violet did appear, however, delighting in the cosiness of the
cottage and waxing lyrical about how quintessentially English
it was. When she met you for the first time, I held my breath,
waiting for a comment on your blue eyes that would give us all
away. But, thankfully, it never came.

'Oh, he's so handsome! And the image of you, Anni.'

You seemed to take to Violet immediately, although perhaps it was something to do with the toys and sweets she
lavished on you every time she came to visit us.

'Please,' I said to her on one afternoon, when Violet's chauffeur produced a gleaming red tricycle from the boot of the car,
which you proceeded to wheel ecstatically around the yard,
'you spoil him far too much.'

'Nonsense! In my book, no child can be spoilt enough,' said
Violet. 'Besides, Anni, I know you give your services for free
and have little income, so it's the least I can do.'

Over the following few weeks, many cold February afternoons would see Violet and me sitting together by the fire eating the buttered crumpets she'd brought with her.

'I'm far too fat now to go to London and it's so boring being cooped up in that house with only the servants and Donny for company,' she'd say. 'I'm so glad to have you to come and talk to.'

Despite the fact that I was always tense, knowing I must be on my guard, I listened to Violet, fascinated, as she spoke about her privileged life in America. She, too, was interested in hearing my stories about my childhood in India. And in truth, I found myself beguiled by her sweet, generous nature, and her naive certainty that everything in her life would always turn out just fine endeared her to me more and more. I began to actively look forward to our tête-à-têtes, as Violet's vitality brightened up many a long winter day. I would even go so far as to say that we became friends of a sort.

She didn't patronise me on any level; in fact, she said on more than one occasion that my royal connections by blood in India made her look positively common.

'Like everyone else in America, I'm simply where I am because my family has made a success in business. It's money that buys nobility in my homeland, not breeding. Of course,' she added wryly, 'Donny's ghastly mama will never let me forget where I come from. Have you met her?'

'Yes, she was living at the Hall when I stayed there years ago during my school holidays,' I replied.

'I know she constantly looks down her nose at everything I do.' Violet bit into her crumpet thoughtfully. 'However –' she smiled at me – 'she was perfectly content to see me spend my trust fund on restoring her family heap. I'm just so glad Donny insisted she move to the Dower House when we married. I don't think I could possibly stand living under the same roof as that woman.'

'She is a difficult character,' I said in agreement, choosing my words carefully.

'I'd go as far as to say she's an old witch!' Violet tittered at her own rudeness.

'Most mothers-in-law are. She's simply from a different era and finds it hard to adapt to a new one.'

'Oh, Anni, you're such a good soul. You're always so kind about everyone, yet you've suffered so much yourself. The servants talk of you as though you're a saint. I hope I can learn from you how to be a better person.'

I studied Violet at that moment and saw that she was genuinely eager to do as she'd just said, and I felt more acutely aware of my duplicitous life than ever before.

March came in, and, with it, the frosts disappeared and yellow gorse covered the moors, spreading like a golden carpet in front of the cottage. Donald would pop round on an occasional errand for Violet and complain, only half joking, that his wife was seeing more of me than he was. I'd also begun to notice that when he was negative about her, I would find myself coming to her defence. In fact, as April arrived, I began to believe that I liked his wife more than he did.

When Violet had been an unknown person, seen by me only through Donald's eyes, the situation had been easier to deal with. But as my fondness for her grew, I began to question just how long the three of us could sustain the eternal and monstrously deceitful triangle we were embroiled in.

One morning, I received a letter from Indira, forwarded to me from London by Selina.

Patna Palace
Patna
India

29 March 1922

Anni, my dearest, oldest friend,

*How are you? WHERE are you? I'm at least glad to
hear that you're no longer lost, as Selina thought you
were when I saw her in France. Why haven't you
written to me???*

Please write and tell me everything very soon.

*As for me, Varun is in Europe, and I'm stuck in the
zenana with the dreaded Number One wife. Dearest
Anni, I beg you to take a trip over here and see both me
and my beautiful baby. He is a boy and we have named
him Kunwar. This pleases me so much as Number One
wife has only had two girls, which means our precious
son will be the Crown Prince when Varun becomes
Maharaja on his father's death. Varun has promised
to come and collect me in June when the baby is old
enough to travel and we will take a house in the South
of France. Perhaps you might be able to join us there
too?*

I miss you, darling Anni. Please write very soon,
Indy xxx

In truth, I hadn't written because I wasn't sure what to say.
Indira and her husband moved in similar circles to the Astburys and discretion was simply not part of her make-up.

As I penned a bland letter back to her saying as little about myself and my circumstances as I could and asking after her, I was struck low by the fact that I couldn't even be honest with my oldest friend. My entire existence was currently a web of deceit; more and more the fundamental *wrongness* of it hung over me like a black cloud. Whichever way I looked at it, I realised that our deception, which had the potential to wound another human being to the core, was removing all the intrinsic goodness from the love that had begun it.

Now every time someone thanked me for my help in treating them or a relative and spoke at length about my kindness and generosity, I only felt the guilt cutting deeper and deeper into my soul. For I was not the person they thought they saw – not a poor widow who gave up her time and skills so generously to the community, whom everyone liked and trusted. I was a kept woman, a mistress, who had borne her lover an illegitimate child and continued to conduct a relationship with him right under his wife's nose. That same wife who now believed that I was her friend . . .

'What is it, Anni?' Donald asked one clear spring afternoon. Violet was napping at the Hall and he'd taken the opportunity to surreptitiously ride over and see us. 'I know something's bothering you.'

'Yes, it is. I hate myself!' With that, I burst into tears.

Donald immediately took me into his arms. 'Anni, really, I'm sure that once the baby is born, Violet will resume her old life and have lots to keep her amused. She'll almost certainly want to go to New York to show the baby off to the relatives, and of course, she loves the winter season in London. I hate to say it, but she'll almost certainly forget all about you.'

His platitudes fell on me like ineffectual raindrops in a

drought, not touching my inner core which was so in need of redemption. I watched him leave, not knowing how to explain to him that what he was talking about were practicalities – arrangements that would remove Violet physically from my sight but wouldn't begin to touch the complex and painful emotions in my heart.

That night, after I'd put you to bed, I contemplated leaving Devon for the first time. Perhaps it would be for the best if we moved away. I could live openly as the person I really was and have a clear conscience. As I climbed the stairs to bed that night, I honestly wasn't sure which fate was worse, but I knew that the deception was eating me from the inside out.

As I tossed and turned later in bed, I remembered that Violet had begged me to be by her side during the birth of her child. 'My sister-in-law, Selina, said you were just wonderful when she gave birth,' she had said. The least I owed her was to do as she asked. But once the child was born, I knew I must come to a real decision about our future.

To make matters worse, the singing was becoming louder each day, warning me of danger and a death not far away. I only hoped it was simply a reflection of my own despairing state of mind and tried to ignore it.

The final few weeks of Violet's pregnancy coincided with the burning July heatwave, and Violet begged me to visit her at the Hall almost every day. We would sit in the cool orangery, where she had installed electric ceiling fans.

'My goodness,' she said looking down at herself, 'I'm the size of a house these days. It's terribly hard for me to sleep, especially in this heat.'

'Not much longer now,' I said, trying to comfort her.

'You reckon? I feel like I might be pregnant forever. You'll have to help me slim down afterwards to what I used to be. I doubt I'll be able to get into a single gown of mine ever again,' she complained.

'Of course, the best thing to do in order to regain your shape, and also for the baby, is to feed it yourself. Would you consider doing that?'

'Oh my!' said Violet with an expression of disgust. 'That's the kind of thing the natives do out in Africa.' She shuddered.

'I fed Moh myself,' I said affably, and I saw her blush.

'Anni, I didn't mean to imply anything by that. I mean, you're from a different culture, I—'

'Really, Violet,' I said, patting her knee, 'I understand.'

A few days later, I'd noticed Violet's ankles were swollen and she'd recently been complaining of a headache. I suggested she now rest with her legs raised to try to stop the swelling.

'Her Ladyship is really most uncomfortable,' said Dr Trefusis after he visited her one morning and Violet had insisted I wait in her sitting room. 'I always think August babies are the worst, although I suppose it's like this where you come from all the year round.'

I ignored the comment. 'She's been complaining of the headaches for the past few days. Does this concern you, Doctor?'

'Not unduly,' he said as he packed his stethoscope into his bag. 'I palpated the baby and listened to its heartbeat, which is strong and robust. Her Ladyship still has three weeks to go. Let's hope the baby doesn't delay its entrance into the world any longer than that. Perhaps you could give her one of your remedies to hasten the process?' he suggested.

'At this stage, I wouldn't want to interfere with nature. Babies come when they're ready,' I replied firmly.

'I thought everything you used *was* natural,' said Dr Trefusis pointedly. 'Anyway, I shall look in again tomorrow morning to check on Her Ladyship.'

'Of course.'

He smiled at me and left the room. I went in to see Violet, who reached out for my hand. 'Anni, this headache's really bad and I feel sick. Can you give me anything?'

I looked down at her and saw how pale she was. Suddenly the singing began strong and loud in my ears. I brushed it away determinedly, not wishing to acknowledge it.

'I'll have your maid bring you cold cloths, and perhaps there may be something I can give you for the nausea. Please, try to rest now, and see if it eases.'

'Would you stay a while with me? I feel real dreadful, Anni.'

'Of course, I'll sit here until you're asleep.'

Finally, when Violet had fallen into a restless sleep, I released my hand from hers and made my way down the stairs. Donald greeted me at the bottom of them.

'How is she?'

'She isn't feeling at all well today,' I told him. 'She's asleep now, and I'm going to go home and see what I have to help her.'

'The doctor says it's nothing to worry about. But are you worried, Anni?'

As he helped me into my trap, I did not tell Donald that I'd seen similar symptoms before and they did not bode well.

Having collected some fresh mint leaves and mixed up a remedy of fennel seeds, cumin and coriander for Violet's swollen ankles, I returned to Tilly's house in the village to ask her to mind you and even gave her a change of clothes in case I was detained longer.

'Is Her Ladyship ill?' Tilly asked me.

'She's not feeling well today.'

'She's always been fragile, that one,' she commented. 'You stay with her as long as you need to, Anni. I can always put Moh to bed here in the cot with Mabel.'

'Thank you.'

Violet was further distressed when I arrived, saying she could no longer stand the pain in her head and that she still felt nauseous.

'Please, drink this,' I said as I forced the mint tea down her throat. I placed a napkin scented with lavender on her forehead and checked her temperature, which was normal, then felt her pulse, which was racing. If she didn't settle in the next hour, I would send for Dr Trefusis. Eventually, she calmed, and I sat by her bedside as she slept peacefully for two or three hours. At some point, there was a knock on the door and I saw Donald peer round it.

'How is she?'

'She's sleeping. We'll see how she is when she wakes.'

'Yes, of course.' He smiled at me in such a sweet and grateful way that my eyes filled with tears. I couldn't imagine how it was for him to watch his wife and his lover together.

'Please, call me if there's anything either of you needs.'

'I will, thank you.'

Violet awoke just before midnight, and I noticed her colour had changed. She clutched her stomach suddenly and gave a yowl of pain.

I uncovered her immediately and asked her to point to where the pain was coming from.

'It's . . . it's like a tight band, stretching right across my belly –' She couldn't continue as another pain ripped through her.

'Violet, I believe you're in labour!'

'My head . . . my head,' she moaned.

'Is it still hurting?' I asked as I looked down at her and felt her forehead. She was burning with fever.

'Terribly, it's—' As the violent contraction continued, she couldn't speak.

'There's no need to be scared,' I told her firmly as I rang the bell by her bed to alert her maid. 'What you must do now is follow your body. It knows exactly what to do and you must listen to it.'

'So glad . . . you're here . . .'

'I'm going to call now for Dr Trefusis. He would want to know that you've gone into labour and be here with you.'

'Don't leave me!' she said, reaching out for my hand and grasping it tightly.

'Violet, I'll be gone for only a few minutes, I promise,' I said as I wrenched my hand away and flew down the darkened stairs to try to find someone who could raise the alarm. The singing was continuing in my head and I was not happy with Violet's current condition. Not happy at all.

There was no one to be found downstairs, so I ran through Violet's suite and knocked loudly on Donald's dressing-room door.

'Anni, what is it?' he asked me as he emerged in his pyjamas.

'Violet's in labour, and I want you to call Dr Trefusis immediately. She's running a temperature and says she still has the headache. I think she should be removed to hospital as soon as possible. Something isn't right,' I added. 'I've called for her maid, but she hasn't arrived. Can you rouse her and tell her to bring boiled water, cold flannels and clean towels whilst we wait for Dr Trefusis to arrive?'

'Of course, but the doctor still has no telephone, so I must send one of the grooms to fetch him.'

I nodded and disappeared back into Violet's bedroom.

Since I'd been gone, she'd been sick all over the covers and was groaning unnaturally. The baby was coming fast – too fast – and again the singing rang in my ears.

I stripped the covers from her and propped her up into a more comfortable position, whispering soothing words, trying to calm her.

'Ariane, go and find His Lordship and bring him here at once,' I said, panic rising within me at Violet's high fever. Everything, instinctual and medical, told me that she was in danger.

Donald appeared almost immediately. 'My God!' he uttered, shocked at the sight of his wife.

'If Dr Trefusis doesn't arrive in the next half an hour, you must take her in your car to the hospital. We can't afford to wait any longer.'

'I'll go downstairs and have it brought round to the front anyway,' he agreed and ran from the room.

Twenty minutes later, I ordered Ariane to wake Mrs Thomas and get her to make a sugar-water drink, partly because I couldn't stand the girl hovering, horrified yet intrigued, behind me.

Suddenly, Violet went still and her eyes opened. She stared at me.

'Something's wrong, isn't it?'

'No, nothing's wrong, I promise, the baby wants to be in this world very fast, faster than she should come, and you must be very brave and help her.'

'Her?' Violet smiled suddenly. 'It's a girl?'

My comment had been instinctive, but I nodded then with complete certainty. And I knew it was important to tell her.

'Yes, Violet, I believe it is.'

Her eyes closed, and after that, she swam in and out of consciousness as Dr Trefusis finally arrived. Another twenty minutes later, Violet and Donald Astbury's baby girl made her entrance into the world. As I looked at her, I saw she was tiny and wondered if she'd survive. But it was her mother who took our attention. Blood was pouring out of her, and although Dr Trefusis and I worked for the next two hours to do everything we could, the bleeding would not abate.

'My God,' said Donald as he sat by a motionless Violet, stroking her hair. 'Is there nothing we can do? Surely, we should take her to the hospital!'

'Lord Astbury,' said Dr Trefusis, 'your wife is too sick to be moved.'

'But we can't just stand here and watch her bleed to death, for God's sake!'

Dr Trefusis glanced at me in despair and gave a slight shake of his head.

'I'm so very sorry, Lord Astbury, but there's nothing more we can do to save her. I think that perhaps you will want to say goodbye.'

I watched Donald then, as he laid his head on Violet's chest and began to sob.

Knowing it could not be my place to comfort him, I picked

up the tiny baby, who'd been placed in a bassinet and virtually forgotten as we'd attempted to save her mother's life.

'I'll take the baby and feed and wash her,' I whispered to him.

He gave a slight nod and I left the room.

At six o'clock the following morning, Lady Violet Astbury was pronounced dead by Dr Trefusis. She never woke to see her daughter.

40

The village of Astbury went into mourning. The tragic death of Lady Violet cast a pall which hung like a heavy fog over the whole estate. I lay low at the cottage, tormenting myself with thoughts of that day. I'd known during the final hours of her life that there was something terribly wrong. I tried to comfort myself by remembering that the doctor himself had been satisfied that she was not in danger, but nonetheless I couldn't forget Violet's eyes, so trusting, so full of the belief that I could help her. And at the last, because I hadn't followed my instincts, I had failed her in the most grievous way possible.

I hadn't seen Donald since the day of her death. He, too, had trusted me with his wife's care, as had the whole village. They had believed so utterly in me. The fact that my telephone didn't ring as it usually did with requests to visit the sick said everything I needed to know. In some immutable way, I knew that I was being blamed. Yes, I could cure lumbago, gout, a common cold . . . but when it had really mattered, I had failed them.

Even though, in my heart of hearts, I knew that Violet's condition had been beyond human help – after all, the eminent Dr Trefusis had been with me as we tried to save her life – I could not help but torment myself with her death.

And, of course, Donald was now a widower . . .

This thought of him as a free man, which in any other circumstances would have given me pleasure, somehow made everything even more unbearable.

Did Donald blame me?

If he didn't, then why on earth hadn't he called, or ridden over the moors to see me? My affection for Violet had been open and genuine and I'd expressed it to him on a number of occasions. Surely, he didn't think . . . ?

A few days after Violet's death, I had a visitor. From my bedroom window I saw Maud Astbury climb out of the car and walk carefully up the narrow path to my front door. Putting you in your cot with toys to keep you occupied, I took a deep breath and went downstairs to answer her knock.

'Hello, Lady Astbury,' I said.

'May I come in?'

'Yes.' She followed me along the hall and into the sitting room. 'Won't you sit down? May I get you some tea?' I asked her as she stood uncomfortably in the centre of the room.

'No, thank you, this isn't a social call, as you might well imagine.'

'No,' I agreed with a sad sigh. 'How can I help you?'

'I've come to ask you not to attend Lady Violet's funeral next week. Under the circumstances, I feel it would be entirely inappropriate if you did so.'

'I see.'

'Surely you must too?'

'If you're referring to my relationship with your son, then yes, I can see it would be wrong for me to attend his wife's funeral. However, with regards to Lady Violet herself, she was my friend and I did all I could to help her the night she died,' I answered as calmly as I could.

'*Help* her? Is that what you call it?'

'Yes, Lady Violet was suffering from a life-threatening condition called eclampsia. Even if she'd been taken to hospital, it's doubtful she could have been saved. In my opinion, at least.'

'I hardly think that your limited medical experience and the subsequent death of one of your so-called patients gives you the right to have one,' Maud sniffed. 'Be that as it may, Miss Chavan, it's not my task to judge you. I leave that to others. What are you going to do now?' she asked me bluntly.

'I haven't given it a moment's thought,' I lied. 'I'm still grieving for Lady Violet. May I ask what will become of the baby now her mother is no longer on the earth?'

'I will, of course, move back into the Hall and help Donald to oversee her upbringing. It is nothing more than my duty. Donald has insisted the child be named Daisy, which was apparently Violet's choice.'

I could tell from Maud's expression that she didn't approve. I also knew she wasn't here to pass on mere detail or pleasantries.

'Your Ladyship, may I ask the real reason that you're here?'

'You may. I wish you to leave Astbury immediately. You've done enough damage already, and for the sake of my son and his newborn child, you must see you have no alternative.'

'As you had none when you intercepted my letters to Donald?' I retorted.

'I was doing what was necessary to protect my family. Others may be taken in by your sweet and caring countenance, but, Miss Chavan, when I first met you, I saw you immediately for what you are.'

'And what am I?' I whispered, feeling my whole body beginning to shake with anger and tension.

'Nothing more than a common Indian slut. Don't think I haven't seen your sort before, because I have, oh yes.' Maud wagged her finger aggressively at me. 'When I was living in India, I saw the devil inside that woman my husband kept hidden from me. He'd sneak off for his sordid little trysts to the hovel she lived in when she left our employ as a maid. And he thought I didn't know! I saw the tears in his eyes when we left India. They were all for her.'

I saw the disgust and fury burning in her eyes. And I began to understand her hatred of me.

'Like father, like son, eh?' Maud managed a hollow chuckle. 'You even look a little like her. I thought it on that first day you arrived here all those years ago. But then, all Indian peasants look the same, don't they? And obviously, your type holds an unfathomable allure for the Astbury men. Miss Chavan, you and I are both women, and we understand how susceptible men are to the sins of the flesh. It is we who must make their decisions for them. Surely, if you love Donald as you profess to, you will see your involvement in Lady Violet's death makes your further presence at Astbury untenable for him?'

'Your Ladyship, I was not responsible for Lady Violet's sad passing. I did everything I possibly could to help save her.'

'You may think that, my dear, but it's common knowledge you were with her at the time. Tongues will wag. Do you really think there can now be any future for you and Donald after what's happened? You must see that any continuing liaison with him is not only fruitless, but would also destroy his reputation in society?'

'I shall have to ask Donald what he thinks. There hasn't been an appropriate moment to discuss the future.'

'That is because there is no future.'

Finally, I was forced to play my trump card. 'And what about our son, Moh? Does he not exist either? Forgive me if I'm wrong, but I could make him heir to the Astbury Estate.'

At this, Maud threw back her head and laughed. 'Miss Chavan, do you know how many illegitimate children have been fathered out of wedlock by men in a similar position to Donald? My dear, your son was born on the wrong side of the blanket and will never inherit Astbury.'

I looked at her, and suddenly realised exactly what it was she was so frightened of.

'You're right, of course. Unless we marry in the future, as we'd originally planned to do three years ago.'

I stood there watching her horrified expression and knew my instinct had been right.

'My son would never marry you,' she said, not looking at me.

'Well, Donald's certainly asked me once before. So perhaps he will again,' I added, and saw her cringe. I was the cruel one now, but I'd suffered so much at this woman's hands for nothing more than being, in her eyes, the wrong colour and nationality. 'I'll certainly let you know once we've discussed our future plans, Your Ladyship. Now, I can hear my son crying upstairs and I wish to go to him. Will that be all?'

'Is it money you want? I'm sure I can make some available to you if you'll leave immediately.'

'Donald has always looked after me very well, and I'm sure he'll continue to do so. Lady Astbury, I must ask you to leave.'

I walked behind her to the door and opened it for her when we reached it.

'Then what is it you want?' She stared at me intently.

'Nothing, except for your son to be happy,' I answered.

She misinterpreted my meaning, and I saw the desperation in her eyes. 'You will destroy him if you stay; you know that, don't you?'

I didn't reply as she left my cottage and walked back to her car and waiting chauffeur. Closing the door and feeling suddenly breathless, I ran upstairs to take you from your cot and hold you close. I knew that what Maud had said was right, but I was not going to give her the pleasure of letting her into my future plans.

I'd already decided in the long, lonely hours since Violet's death that there was no hope left for Donald and me. When Violet drew her last breath, she'd also signalled the end of the two of us. However strong our love was, and from whichever angle I looked at it, nothing could surmount the guilt we would both feel for the rest of our lives.

Maud was right about the dreadful inferences that could and would be drawn from my involvement in Violet's last hours. Even my friends who knew and loved me at Astbury would not be able to condone any relationship I had with Donald in the future. Some might even believe that I'd cooked up some Machiavellian plan.

'Moh,' I said, sighing into your hair that dreadful afternoon, 'I really believe there is no hope.'

Over the next few days, I began to make plans. I had some money saved from the housekeeping allowance Donald had given me over the past year. If I sold the pearls he'd given me for Christmas, I reckoned the amount I would receive might buy us a third-class passage to India. I still had my one large ruby buried under the pavilion at the palace in Cooch Behar. If the two of us could reach it, then it would provide enough money to put a roof over our heads until I'd worked out how I could earn a living.

During those long, silent nights, I wrote to Donald time and again, trying to explain why we were leaving. I tore up each attempt because they seemed so imperfect. And perhaps, I thought to myself, it was best to say nothing at all. If he loved me and knew me as I believed he did, he would understand everything.

Violet's funeral was held three interminable weeks after her death to allow her parents to arrive and for them to make the appropriate arrangements. My heart went out to them – they'd set sail from New York to be there just after the birth of their grandchild, only to be told halfway across the Atlantic that their beloved daughter was already dead. It was Tilly who told me when I met her in the village shop the day after the funeral. She invited us both back to her cottage for a cup of tea.

'Oh, Miss Anni,' she said as I broke down in front of her, the solitude of time alone with my thoughts proving too much, 'please don't cry. I know you did your best.'

'I know you do, and I thank you for it. But the villagers and servants blame me.'

'Oh, you mustn't take any notice of them. Nothing sets them alight more than gossip. It'll all die down and they'll be back to you when their small one has a cold or a cough and they need you, don't you worry.'

'But there has been gossip about me?'

'Well, everyone knows you were there and, of course, the doctor's got to blame someone, hasn't he?'

'What do you mean?'

'Well, those who watched you care for Her Ladyship that night know how you helped her. But the doctor wouldn't like to admit it was him who was to blame for not seeing earlier that Her Ladyship was in trouble.'

I could feel my heart turning to lead as she spoke the words. Was I to be the doctor's scapegoat?

'Anyway, it'll all die down now she's been laid to rest. The world moves on and there'll be other things to gossip about.' Tilly patted my hand comfortingly. 'Don't you worry about it, Miss Anni. We who know you realise there was nothing more you could have done to save her.'

I looked up at her, honesty blazing from my eyes. 'No, there really wasn't.'

My dear child, I'm about to relate to you the last time I saw Donald, your father, and what happened to me after that. I will do my best to give you the bare facts of what transpired, but forgive me if my retelling of this terrible time distresses you.

A week after Violet's funeral had taken place, Donald appeared on my doorstep. He looked dreadful. Neither of us knew what to say, but you, Moh, not knowing anything of what had happened, asked for your usual cuddle and climbed up on his knee. I made him tea and we sat together silently in the kitchen.

'Do you blame me?' I remember asking.

'You said she would be all right, that day . . .'

'I said that if her headache didn't improve, we should call the doctor. And it seemed to, for a while at least. Please remember, Donald, you came in to see us and she was sleeping?' I entreated him.

'Yes, yes,' he replied, but I could tell he was lost in grief – or guilt; I wasn't sure which. 'I'm sorry I haven't been to see you.'

'I understand.'

'Oh, Anni, what have we done? I . . .'

I took him into my arms, and he cried like a baby. I understood every nuance of what he was feeling, because I was feeling it too. Even if we were both innocent of blame in Violet's death, actual fact was immaterial. We both *felt* culpable and that was all that mattered.

I put you to bed soon after, not wishing you to see your beloved Mr Don so distressed. Then I went downstairs and suggested he eat the soup I'd prepared earlier.

'You look as though you've had nothing in you for weeks,' I said as I stirred it.

'Probably not.' Then he paused with the spoon halfway to his mouth. 'It doesn't have any strange herbs in it, does it?'

'Donald, please believe me, everything I gave Violet was innocuous. Nothing I wouldn't give my own son, or you . . .' my voice trailed off.

'No, sorry, that was a rotten joke,' he agreed. 'Forgive me.'

When he had finished the soup, he seemed somewhat revived.

'Do you have any brandy?'

'I believe I do.' He followed me into the sitting room and I went to the cupboard and pulled out the bottle he'd left in one of my Christmas hampers. I uncorked it and poured a measure into a glass. I watched him take a large gulp and then another, until the glass was drained.

'I feel better now.' He looked at me properly for the first time and reached out his hands towards me. 'Forgive me, Anni. You don't deserve this from me, and I feel like a wretch for my behaviour. The gossip, you know. I admit it's got to me.'

'Yes, I can see,' I answered sadly.

'Of course you did everything you could to help her, I saw you. Come here.' He opened his arms to me and I went into them, needing so terribly to feel his touch and warmth and belief. 'Forgive me,' he said again, as he began to kiss me. 'I love you, and my guilt for loving you' – his hands were all over me – 'has eaten into my rational mind. I love you, Anni, I love you, I love you . . .'

Before that night, I had only known Donald as a gentle and considerate lover. But that evening, he took me there on the floor of the sitting room, and as he shouted my name, I could feel his frustration, guilt and anguish pouring into me.

Afterwards, we lay together on the floor.

'So sorry,' he whispered. 'I'm not quite myself.'

'None of us are,' I comforted him.

'Can I stay here tonight, Anni?'

'Of course you can,' I said gently.

I lay in his arms that night, wanting to tell him that you and I would be leaving Astbury in the next few days. But I knew that if I did, he would try to stop me and my resolve would not be strong enough to resist the force of my love for him. I watched him sleep, and as I did so, I heard the singing again, warning me of death. It was loud, which meant it was very close. Confused, I convinced myself that it was due to the fact that in the next few days Donald would be far away from me, lost to me forever. Our love must be at an end.

At dawn, he rose, dressed and said he needed to get back before the servants noticed his absence. I followed him downstairs to see him out. He held me with such tenderness then, hard against his chest, and I felt his heart beating against mine for the last time.

'Goodbye, Donald,' I said, tracing his beloved face with my fingertips, determined to imprint every detail of it onto my memory.

'I love you, Anni, please always remember that.' He tipped my face up to his. 'Always remember that.'

I watched him leave, stemming my urge to run after him. My heart broke as he rode away across the moors, but I had to find the strength to love him enough to let him go.

I spent the next day numbly packing our clothes and few precious objects into a suitcase. I had decided we would travel to London and I would take rooms at a boarding house while I took my pearls to Hatton Garden and organised our passage back to India from Southampton.

The following morning, there was a harsh rap on my front door. I opened it and two policemen stood on my doorstep.

'Are you Mrs Anahita Prasad?'

'I am,' I answered cordially. 'Can I help you?'

'You are under arrest for causing the death of Lady Violet Astbury. You do not have to say anything but it may harm your defence if you do not mention, when questioned, something which you may later rely on in court. Anything you do say may be given in evidence, do you understand? We'd now like you to accompany us to the police station.'

41

I stared at the officers as if they'd taken leave of their senses. I was so shocked that I couldn't find the words to use, so I stood dumbly, unable to reply.

'Come on, Mrs Prasad.' One of the officers reached out a hand to grab my arm and pull me out of the front door. 'Let's not make any trouble.'

His aggressive manner finally made me find my voice. 'My baby's upstairs sleeping in his cot. I must go and get him.'

'No need to worry about that. Someone will be along to collect him later.'

'No!' I shouted, struggling out of his grasp. 'I can't leave him here alone. I have to get him now!'

The grip on my arm tightened as I fought to free myself. The second officer immediately took hold of my other arm and forced me out through the front door. Then they bundled me into the back of the car and drove me away from you.

My memories from then on are vague. Perhaps, like anybody would, I've blocked much of it from my mind. But on that dreadful journey from the moors, I believe I saw Donald on Glory just before we passed through Astbury village. I turned back towards him and, with all my might, I screamed out your name to him, before a rough male hand was placed across my mouth.

I do remember vividly, though, that the singing continued loud and strong in my ears, but I put it down to my own terrible distress.

Once I'd been formally charged, I was eventually driven to Holloway Prison in London, the kind of place one can only imagine in a nightmare. Mostly I remember the cold and the wet of the rainwater that poured in through the iron grille in the wall of my cell, and the perpetual sounds of souls in mental and physical torment all around me. In the first few days, all I could think of was you and where you were, and I, too, joined the cacophony and screamed your name over and over. I entreated anyone who entered my cell to find out. The thought of you alone and abandoned in the cottage on the moors haunted every second of my existence.

I don't know how long it was before I received my first visitor; perhaps, in reality, only a few days had passed, but it seemed an eternity to a mother who'd been wrenched from her child and had no idea of his whereabouts.

When Selina entered the dark visitors' room looking like an angel of mercy, I fell to my knees and wept, my arms encircling her ankles.

'Thank the gods, thank the gods you're here! My son, Selina, I don't know what they've done with Moh!'

I was forcefully pulled away from her by a warder and placed back on the chair with a warning that if I moved to touch her physically again, my arms would be bound behind it.

'Oh, Anni . . . I . . .'

I could see that Selina was crying, too.

'I'm so, so sorry,' she said.

'Please, don't worry about me, I just need you to find my son,' I said as my voice broke in despair.

'Anni, oh dear, oh dear . . .'

I remember feeling hysteria rise within me, and I knew I must try to control myself to make her understand. 'Selina, please, do you know where he is? He might still be there at the cottage by the brook. I think I saw Donald when they were driving me away in the car, but he may not have heard me shouting to him. Please, Selina, go and make sure Moh's still not there. He'll be so hungry, and frightened . . .' I broke down again and sobbed, my head in my hands.

'Forgive me, Anni, Henri and I were travelling in Europe. We only arrived back at the château in France a few days ago, and I received both telegrams. Of course, I left to come to England immediately. I'm still in shock. What a tragedy. Such a terrible tragedy . . . I can hardly believe it.'

'Please believe me, Selina, I didn't murder Violet. Nothing could have saved her. Dr Trefusis was there and he knew it too. I didn't give her anything that could possibly have harmed her.'

'I'm sure that you did all that you could, Anni,' said Selina.

'I did, I swear, I did. And Donald? How is he?'

'Oh, Anni, they really haven't told you anything, have they?'

'Told me what? I haven't seen a soul since I arrived in this terrible place.'

Selina put her fingers to her temple. 'Then I must. Anni, I'm so very sorry, but Donald must have ridden back to the cottage to get Moh. And I . . . good God, how can I begin to tell you this?'

'Selina please,' I entreated her. 'Whatever it is, just say it.'

'Anni, no one knows what happened, but Donald and Moh were found together by the brook. We can only believe Glory stumbled and threw them off. When they were eventually discovered, Donald was already . . . gone. He'd hit his head on a jagged rock and they believe he died instantly. And Moh –' Selina tried to compose herself to say the words. 'They think that when he was thrown off Glory, he tumbled down into the brook. And . . . drowned.'

I stared at her as if she was insane. 'You're telling me that my son is dead? And Donald too? Tell me you are lying, Selina, for God's sake, tell me . . . tell me . . .'

'No, Anni. I'm so terribly, terribly sorry. I—'

A deep guttural wail echoed around the walls as I toppled off the chair to the floor. I saw Selina's horrified face, as one of the warders picked me up and dragged me from the room and half-carried me stumbling along the passage, then down the steps, before throwing me into my cell.

'You can come out when you've calmed down,' he said as he slammed the door. The sound of wailing continued endlessly in my ears, and it took me some time before I realised that I was the source of it.

After that, time passed as the hysteria eventually left me, and instead, I became catatonic. I remember that occasionally I was taken to the visitors' room where strange shadowy figures would try to talk to me and explain what was happening, but I could not be reached. I disappeared deep inside myself into a void of nothingness. I simply did not exist, for if I did, I knew the pain I'd feel would overwhelm me. The strangers talked about the charges I was facing and how I must begin to defend myself, or it was likely I would hang. That if I didn't start to respond, they'd have to send me to an asylum until the trial.

My son, perhaps you might think your mother terribly weak for not speaking up for herself. But the news of your own and your father's death broke me completely. I lay there, in my cell, only praying for death to come soon so that I could join you both.

'Get up! There's someone here to see you.'

I recall one of the warders looking down at me, curled up on my bunk. I shook my head listlessly.

He sat me upright, then dipped a filthy rag, which was all I had to wash with, into a bowl of water and wiped my face. 'Can't have anyone saying we don't take care of our prisoners here,' he said as he lifted me to a standing position and then dragged me like a puppet out of the room.

'Now, none of that screaming caper in front of your visitor this time,' he ordered me.

He dumped me on the chair in the visitors' room and I hung my head to my chest, too weak to hold it upright and not in the least bit interested in who my visitor might be. When this new ordeal was over, I could return to the solitude of my void.

I heard someone entering the room and a familiar scent pervaded my nose, although I couldn't place where I knew it from.

'Anni? Anni, look at me.'

The voice, too, I recognised, but I supposed it was a dream and still I didn't raise my head.

554

'It's me, Anni, Indira. Please tell me you know who I am.'

A voice inside my head was chuckling at the ridiculous thought of Indira being here in this dreadful place. I knew it was my mind playing cruel tricks on me yet again, for everything about my dearest friend brought back memories of warmth, safety and happiness.

'Anni,' the voice entreated me for a third time, 'please look at me.'

'It's not really you,' I whispered to myself as I pulled at the thin cotton covering my knees with my fingers, 'just a trick, just a trick . . .'

I heard the sound of footsteps walking towards me and then a pair of warm hands taking mine.

'Anni, open your eyes now! You're not dreaming, I swear, I really am here. And please hurry up, or I'll really start to believe you're as mad as they've told me you are.'

Finally, I screwed up my courage to do as the voice had asked and steeled myself for the fact that when I did, she wouldn't be there.

'Hello, Anni. See? I really am here.'

Indira was crouching in front of me, her eyes full of concern.

'Yes, it's me! Please tell me you know who I am, Anni.'

I nodded, still unable to speak.

'Well, thank goodness for that.'

And, as her arms reached round me to hug me, I finally began to believe that she was real.

'Oh, Anni, what a state you've been brought to,' Indira whispered as she drew back and looked at me, tears in her eyes. 'But I'm here now and you don't need to worry about anything any longer.'

'Who told you?' I whispered as I managed to find my voice.

'Selina. We saw each other in France just before she received the terrible news. She then telephoned me there in desperation a week or so ago to beg me and my family for help. Jolly good job she caught me, as we were just about to sail home to India. So, here I am.'

'How long –' I licked my dry lips to form the words. 'How long have I been here?'

'About three weeks, I think. Anyway, we can talk about everything once we've got you out of here.'

'No, Indy.' I shook my head sadly. 'They won't let me out. I've been accused of the murder of Violet Astbury. I think they will hang me soon, but I don't mind. Moh . . . my son, is dead. Donald too. I really don't want to live.'

She stared at me sternly. 'Anahita Chavan, do you not remember me saying those very words to you a few years ago when you travelled back to India to help me?'

'Yes.'

'Well, I'm here to do the same for you, my dearest friend.'

'No, Indy. It's different. Moh has gone, and Donald. I wish to die, really. Leave me be.'

'Yes, I agree it's all the most dreadful mess. But, Anni, I've known you since you were a little girl. I've seen how you've given strength to others, including me, and now you have to find that for *yourself*. You can do it, I know you can.'

'Indy, thank you,' I replied, weary now, 'but you can't do anything. I'll receive a death sentence at the trial, I'm sure.'

'Anni, there's not going to be a trial. The charges have been dropped. I'm here to take you home.'

I stared at her, not understanding. 'But I can't go back to the cottage by the brook, surely they won't let me?'

'No, Anni, I'm taking you home. To your real home. We're going back to India.'

Again, my memories of my release from Holloway and my arrival at Indira's family home in Knightsbridge where I'd stayed as a child are vague. More than anything, I remember the sudden wonderful softness that surrounded me – gentle hands, feather pillows and voices talking to me in whispers. There were no more screams of agony, just silence. I think I must have slept constantly – nature's way of healing the body and mind.

I do remember that every time I awoke, Indira would be there next to me, sitting in a chair beside the bed. Tenderly, she would insist that I open my mouth so she could spoon-feed me broth, and it was her own hands that washed and tended to the dreadful sores, caused by weeks of filth, that covered my frail body. Often, as she cared for me, she would reminisce on funny incidents from our past, asking if I remembered when she'd slept with Pretty in the elephant enclosure before we left for boarding school in England, or the night we'd deceived Miss Reid on the ship and she'd changed into the peach chiffon dress and won her prince's heart.

I didn't respond, but I did listen.

Looking back, I know for certain that it was Indira and the love she showed me then that saved me. And finally, I knew I couldn't hide any longer in my veil of sleep and that I must find the strength to return to the living.

'Anni, I think you're getting better,' Indira said to me one morning as I took the soup spoon from her, having announced that I could manage to feed myself.

'Yes, I think I am,' I agreed.

'Thank goodness for that. To be truthful, there have been moments when I truly wondered whether you would. I was beginning to doubt my skills as a nurse.' She grinned. 'Caring for others has never been my strong point.'

'Indy –' my eyes misted over – 'you've been wonderful. If it hadn't been for you . . .' I left the words hanging in the air.

'Never mind all that. I know you're still weak, Anni, but I'd like to book our passage back to India as soon as possible. I don't trust that evil Astbury woman not to try something else.'

'What do you mean?' I asked as terror clutched at my heart. I hadn't asked, nor had I yet been told, the details of my release.

'Oh, don't worry about her.' Indira waved away the problem airily. 'The point is that I just want to get you home. When you're up to it, I'll tell you the whole story.'

'Yes,' I answered, knowing that at present I was not. 'Does your mother know I'm here with you?' I asked.

'Of course she does! She's the one who managed to gain your freedom.'

'So she's forgiven me?'

'Oh, Anni, of course she has. And me too, which is rather important. The minute she had a grandchild, she couldn't resist coming to see him. She writes every day, sends her love and says she'll see you soon. Now, Anni, let's see if you can stand and perhaps take a little walk to the bathroom.'

For the following few days, my strong young body began to heal fast, and physically, I knew I was finally well. I agreed that Indira should book our passage to India as soon as possible. But still, I was unsure of my mental and emotional capacity and shied away from asking the questions I knew I must hear the answers to before I left England.

One afternoon, Indira arrived in my room to tell me I had a visitor.

'It's Selina, Anni, and I think you should see her before we leave.'

Fear filled my heart, and I could feel the blood draining from my face. Indira took my hand. 'I'll be with you all the time, I promise. Really, Anni, we leave in two days' time and you must speak with her.'

I nodded in resignation, and five minutes later, Indira and I walked down the stairs to the drawing room.

'Anni.' Selina stood up and walked over to me, her face as drawn and pale as my own. 'How are you?' she said, as she reached for my hand and clasped it in hers.

'I'm better, thank you.'

'Thank goodness! I was distraught when I saw you in that terrible place.'

'I can only apologise for causing so much trouble,' I replied sadly.

'Anni, don't you ever dare to blame yourself for what has taken place,' Selina said with unusual vehemence. 'This whole terrible tragedy is the work of one person alone. Come –' she took me by the arm – 'please, sit down.'

We sat together on the Chesterfield sofa, my hands still clasped in Selina's. Indira sat opposite us in a chair like a protective mother tiger watchfully guarding her fragile cub.

'Thank you for helping me, Selina.'

'Well, you mustn't thank me. It's Indira and her family who were the miracle workers.'

'Selina, please tell me you know that I did not try to murder Violet. She was my friend, I cared for her and at the end, even though I knew it was hopeless, I did everything I could for her.'

'Of *course* I know that, dearest Anni. You have a heart that's only full of goodness. Anyway, let me start from the beginning. It'll make everything easier to explain. When I eventually received the two telegrams in France that told me of both Violet's and my brother's deaths, I came home to Astbury immediately. It was only then I heard of your arrest on a charge for murder. I knew there was only one person who could possibly be responsible for it. So I went to see her.'

'You are referring to your mother?' I questioned.

'Yes. Of course she told me that she'd had absolutely nothing to do with it and insisted it was Dr Trefusis who first voiced his doubts as to the remedies you'd given Violet both during her pregnancy and on the day she died. By that time, Violet's parents had arrived for her funeral and Dr Trefusis discussed his concerns with them. Understandably, they wished to blame someone, so both they and my mother told Dr Trefusis he should go to the police with his suspicions.'

'And yet he knew he was culpable himself,' Indira interjected. 'After all, he was the doctor in charge.'

'The two of them had many reasons to want to see you out of the way, Anni,' said Selina, sighing. 'Dr Trefusis was using you as his scapegoat, and my mother – well, we all know why she wanted rid of you.'

'She came to see me a few days after Violet died,' I mused. 'She was terrified that now Violet was gone, Donald might go ahead and marry me as he'd originally planned.'

'And if he'd lived, he may well have done so,' Selina said, trying to comfort me. 'He loved you so very much.'

'And I him . . .' My voice trailed off and I felt the panic begin to rise inside me at the thought of what I had lost. I knew I must steady myself to continue without becoming hysterical.

'Selina, I must tell you that before your mother came to visit, I'd already decided I must leave Astbury forever. I understood that neither of us could ever have recovered from Violet's death. But how could they find any proof that I had poisoned her?'

'Anni, do you remember Dr Trefusis visiting you once to take cuttings of the plants and herbs you grew?'

'Why yes. He said he was interested in discovering more about their medicinal properties.'

'Sadly,' said Selina, 'the good doctor took some cuttings not only of innocuous herbs, but also specimens that are apparently renowned to be dangerous, especially in pregnancy. And he took these to the police as evidence. One was Penny Royal, a species of mint that has been proved to be harmful to a pregnant woman. On that day of Violet's death, you brought her a remedy you had made yourself for her swelling ankles and fed her mint tea to stop her nausea.'

'Oh my God.' My hand went over my mouth and my eyes involuntarily filled with tears. 'Yes I did, but not Penny Royal! Just ordinary, plain mint leaves, which also grow in my garden. Selina, I have studied Ayurvedic medicine since I could walk. Penny Royal can normally be drunk in a tea safely in small amounts. It grows wild in Devon and is very good for treating colds and influenza. But of *course* I'm aware of how dangerous it can be to a pregnant woman. It can cause premature birth, fits, bleeding . . .' My voice trailed off as I realised how well it all fitted.

'Anni, please, try not to upset yourself. We all know you'd do nothing to harm anyone,' said Indira, trying to comfort me.

'And to make matters worse,' Selina continued, 'Dr Trefusis was able to produce a paper written by an eminent professor in America. It gives specific details on the damaging effects of Penny Royal to pregnant women. Dr Trefusis also produced a sample of Black Cohosh root, another herb considered dangerous in pregnancy. One of the kitchen staff said you'd given her a tea of it to drink recently.'

'Yes, because it's very good for rheumatism!' I could feel my heart pounding.

'So, the police went to your cottage and saw that indeed you did cultivate these and other herbs in your greenhouse and garden,' said Selina.

'But surely even with the cuttings from my garden, there could be no proof I had actually given them to Violet?'

'Dearest Anni, please try not to be naive,' Indira shook her head in exasperation. 'Really, nothing more was needed. Maud Astbury reigns like a queen locally and holds the authorities in the palm of her hand. Violet was dead, and if Maud decided she wanted someone charged with her murder, the local police would see to it immediately, no matter how limited the evidence.'

'Yes.' I sighed helplessly. 'I suppose I can see that. So how were the charges dropped?'

'I immediately went to confront my mother and begged her to convince the police to drop the charges. She wouldn't hear of it; she said it was out of her hands and that justice must be done.' Selina grimaced. 'Anni, I must tell you that I lost control that day. I'm afraid I said exactly what I'd wanted to say to her for years; that she was a bitter, bigoted, selfish woman and that as far as I was concerned, she was dead in my eyes, just like my poor brother. I told her I'd never come to Astbury again as long as she was alive.'

'So that was when Selina contacted me.' Indira took up the

story. 'And, thankfully, my mother is much more intelligent and has friends in far higher places than Maud,' she explained with a glint of triumph in her eyes. 'I believe it only took one telephone call to make sure the charges were dropped. The only stipulation was that you must return to India and never go back to England again.'

'I see. What about the Drumners? Do they still believe I murdered their daughter?'

'I think they have enough troubles of their own,' said Selina. 'Sissy is not at all well, but even so, they insisted their granddaughter should return to New York to live with them. My mother, of course, refused, saying that Daisy must remain at Astbury Hall under her care, as she was the legal heiress. They returned to New York ready to launch all kinds of court battles to win custody of their granddaughter.'

'So that poor little baby might be brought up by Maud?' I said in horror.

'Almost certainly,' said Selina. 'After all, baby Daisy is a British citizen and even the Drumners' vast resources are unlikely to help them win custody of her. I begged Mother that dreadful day to give Daisy to me so that I could bring her up in my nursery with her cousins, but, of course, she wouldn't hear of it. She has already moved back to Astbury Hall, once more in control of her kingdom, with free rein to fashion the next generation in her own form. I haven't seen her so full of energy in years,' Selina said bitterly.

The three of us sat in silence, and I felt sick to my stomach. Maud Astbury had destroyed one generation and now had been handed the power to destroy another.

'I always thought she was mad as a hatter,' said Indira with a smile, ever eager to lighten a dark atmosphere.

'You may be joking, but I think you might be right,' said Selina. 'It was there in my mother's eyes when we were talking. Something that looked like actual madness.'

'She is the devil incarnate,' I muttered, shuddering. 'I do apologise, Selina,' I said quickly.

'Please, say what you wish,' she comforted me. 'I can assure you that I feel exactly the same. So much so that Henri and I have decided that we'll move to France with the children permanently. I don't even wish to be in the same country as her.'

'Witches can't cross running water at least,' I said with a glimmer of a smile.

Selina glanced at the clock on the mantelpiece. 'I'm so sorry, but I must leave now. I beg you, Anni, keep in touch with me. If you have an opportunity, please come and visit us in France. Where will you both be heading once you reach India?'

'My parents' palace in Cooch Behar to begin with,' replied Indira. 'Ma is desperate to see poor Anni, and it means I don't have to return to the zenana at my husband's palace for a while longer.' She gave Selina her cheeky grin.

We stood up and Selina wrapped her arms around me. 'I'm so terribly, terribly sorry for the pain you've suffered. I'm sure that, wherever he is, Donald and your little one are looking down at you and loving you.'

'Thank you, Selina, for everything,' I whispered. As she walked towards the door, I knew I had to ask the question that had been assiduously avoided by all of us since she had arrived.

'Selina, where is my son buried?'

She stopped at the door, took a breath and turned round. 'I asked the same question when I arrived back at Astbury.

Anni, the villagers and servants are unaware of Moh's death. They have been told he went with you when you were arrested. My mother obviously didn't want it known that Donald had died riding over to the cottage to rescue his own son. The only other person who knows the truth is Dr Trefusis, who told me that Moh had been discreetly laid to rest in a corner of the parish church in the village. When I subsequently visited, there was fresh earth on a grave, but the priest told me that when he performed the burial and enquired whether a headstone was needed, Dr Trefusis said it wasn't required. The vicar was told the child had died at birth and had no name. I'm so sorry, Anni,' she said, her eyes full of tears.

'Even in death, his existence had to be a secret,' I whispered.

'I know it's no consolation, but he's buried in a very tranquil spot, Anni. I placed some beautiful roses on his grave for you. I know you're of a different religion, but I hope that was right. I . . . there are no words to describe how terrible this must be for you, Anni. I'm so very sorry.'

I felt for her then, desperately stumbling over the words in order not to hurt me further. She was a mother too.

'Thank you, Selina. What you did was perfect.'

'I've also given Indira a copy of Moh's death certificate signed by Dr Trefusis,' she added. 'Goodbye, Anni, take care.'

As she left, I saw the concern on Indira's face. I knew she was fearful that facing the reality of my dead child might break me again. After all, it was the first time I'd mentioned the subject.

'I'm going upstairs to rest,' I said to her.

'Anni, are you all right?'

'Yes,' I reassured her and left the drawing room.

Looking back, as I climbed the stairs and entered the peaceful sanctuary of the bedroom where Indira had nursed me back to life, I realised that I was indeed calm.

But why?

As we left England's shores two days later, and the terror and pain of the past few weeks began to drop gradually away from my befuddled brain, I realised.

I knew then that I'd heard the singing for Donald on that last night we spent together. But never for you, Moh. On that last morning, just before the police arrived, when I'd laid you down in your cot for your nap and kissed you on your forehead as I always did, I'd neither felt nor heard anything.

Every night when I stood on deck and asked those above for guidance, I listened for the voices that would assail my senses when someone had passed over, just as they had done for both Violet and Donald, yet I could hear nothing for you.

Just before we docked, Indira – who had taken my new-found calm as acceptance – handed me two envelopes one evening before dinner.

'Open that one first,' she said encouragingly, pointing to the smaller one.

I did so, and inside my fingers recognised the cool, silky texture of the pearls Donald had given to me.

'They were with your clothes when we left the prison, but I thought it might upset you too much to see them. Can I help you with the clasp?' said Indira as I pulled them out of the envelope.

'Thank you.' Feeling their weight around my neck once more comforted me, and my fingertips reached to touch them as they had done so many times before.

Indira indicated the other envelope. 'In there is a photograph of you and Moh. And also his death certificate, Anni. I thought you'd want to keep it.'

I paused for a moment before I answered. I smiled to myself. 'Thank you, Indy. But I don't need his death certificate.'

'I understand,' she said sympathetically.

'Because my son isn't dead. I know he still lives.'

Astbury Hall,

July 2011

42

Rebecca laid down the pages and glanced at the clock by her bed. It was past midnight. She stared out into the dimly lit room, feeling her heart still pumping fast with adrenaline.

Violet Astbury had given birth to a child exactly where she, Rebecca, was lying now. Violet had been a perfectly healthy woman in her twenties, who had complained of headaches and nausea, and had subsequently died.

'Stop it!' Rebecca whispered to herself as she felt her panic rising. 'Violet died in childbirth!' She stood up and paced the bedroom, talking to herself to try to calm down. 'You're not pregnant, for God's sake, Rebecca . . .'

But then she remembered the doctor asking her if she could be, and that she was still waiting to hear the results of her tests. She burst into tears of fear and frustration. Even if her imagination *was* running away with her, one thing was for sure; she couldn't stay in this room which was so full of Violet and her tragedy a minute longer. Shivering with panic, Rebecca decided she would go in search of Ari.

She tiptoed out of the suite and walked along the shadowy corridors, knocking softly then opening each of the doors as silently as she could, trying to survey the darkened interiors.

They seemed to all be empty along her corridor, so she walked across the landing, past the main staircase, and began quietly opening doors on the other side of it.

Then a sudden, familiar sound assailed her ears. It was very faint, coming from some distance, but it was the same high-pitched singing she'd heard in her dreams. Terrified now, but knowing she had to confront whoever it was making the strange sound which Anahita had described as a warning of death, Rebecca began to walk towards it.

She halted in the dark corridor. The singing was emanating from behind the door she now stood in front of. Using every ounce of her courage, her fingertips touched the doorknob and she turned it silently, then pushed it forwards a couple of centimetres.

Rebecca peeped through the crack and into the room. A soft light glowed inside, and to her left she could make out a figure sitting in front of a mirror. Opening the door wider, Rebecca could see the figure was sitting at a dressing table, brushing her long, blonde hair, singing to herself as she did so. Even from this distance, she could smell the summery scent of the perfume that had pervaded her bedroom at night – Violet's perfume. Rebecca pushed the door a little further to try to see the woman's face in the mirror, and the singing stopped abruptly. Something had alerted the woman to her presence.

As her head began to turn towards the door, Rebecca fled away along the corridor, her breath coming in short, sharp bursts. Almost back in the sanctuary of her room, a figure stepped suddenly out of the darkness and caught her as she ran.

Rebecca screamed out loud as the arms gripped hers and pulled her through the door and into her bedroom.

'Hush! It's me, Ari,' he said as she continued to struggle out of his arms, gulping for air and moaning from shock. 'Rebecca, what on earth has happened? What's frightened you? Please, try to calm down,' he said as she leaned her hands on the bed and bent forwards trying to slow her breathing.

'Ari, please, you have to get me out of here . . . I think I'm being poisoned, like Violet, and I just saw a strange woman sitting in a bedroom, brushing her hair and singing. I –' Rebecca took some more gulps of air to enable her to continue. 'I don't know whether she's alive or a ghost, but I saw her, Ari, I swear. And I know she's been to my room when I've been sleeping . . . oh God . . . Violet died in here!' Rebecca collapsed onto the floor. 'Ari, you have to get me out of here, now, tonight! I'm so frightened, I'm so frightened,' she whimpered.

Tentatively, Ari knelt down next to her.

'Rebecca, I understand you've just had a shock, that you're still unwell and perhaps have a fever, which can produce all sorts of hallucinations and—'

'No! I *saw* her with my own eyes and heard her with my own ears. Please, Ari,' she begged, 'you've got to believe me. I'm not going mad. That woman was real!'

'Okay,' Ari said, 'I believe you. So, let's think about this rationally. This is an enormous house, with goodness knows how many bedrooms, and it may be that Anthony has a guest staying with him. I mean, he wouldn't necessarily tell us, would he?'

'Yes, but I've felt her and heard her before,' Rebecca said insistently, 'and sometimes at night in here, I can smell the perfume that she wears – that *Violet* used to wear. If there is another woman in this house, she's been here for some time. But why wouldn't we have seen her, and why has she been into my bedroom at night? I know she has, Ari. I've been so ill in the past week, these terrible headaches I've had, and nausea, just like Violet. I swear, someone is trying to kill me. I just want to get out of here!'

'Rebecca –' Ari watched her shoulders heave with fear and emotion – 'I completely understand that, having read Anahita's story this evening, you'd find some of the comparisons between you and Violet strange. But there's absolutely no logical way that your presence here could have been engineered by someone who meant you harm. The fact that you've been sick hasn't helped, but I think you're letting your imagination run riot. Please, Rebecca, trust me. What I'm telling you makes sense.'

'I don't care what makes sense, Ari, I want to leave this house,' she sobbed, 'and I want to leave it *now*.'

'I hear you, Rebecca, but you know all the hotels around here will be closed for the night. It's almost one o'clock in the morning. I'm sure you can move tomorrow.'

'My God,' Rebecca groaned, 'I don't even have a lock on my door, anybody could walk in and—'

'Rebecca,' Ari said patiently, 'do you feel safe with me? I mean, do you trust me?'

She considered this. 'I guess tonight I don't know whom to trust.'

'Well, what I'm going to suggest is that I stay next door in the sitting room for the rest of the night. What you need more than anything else is some sleep.'

'Jesus Christ, if another person tells me that, I think I really will go insane,' Rebecca said with a sigh.

'Even if they're right?' Ari smiled at her. 'Shall I help you up?'

'No, I can manage,' she said as she hauled herself shakily to standing and walked towards the bed. 'And yes, I'd be grateful if you'd sleep on the sofa next door.'

'My pleasure. Goodnight, Rebecca.'

'Thank you. Sorry if you think I'm behaving like a wimp.'

'That's okay. It's understandable.'

'Ari?'

'Yes?' He paused by the door and smiled at her.

'Tomorrow, I want to ask you some questions about your great-grandmother's story.'

'Of course, but for now, Rebecca, get some sleep.'

Rebecca woke with a start the following morning, feeling disoriented. Remembering what had happened last night, she climbed out of bed immediately, ran to the sitting room and saw that it was empty. Leaving the bedroom, she ventured out into the corridor and walked along it.

Standing at the top of the main staircase were Mrs Trevathan and Ari. They were chatting together in low voices, and both turned at the sight of her.

'Morning, sleepyhead,' said Ari. 'It's past noon.'

'Oh my God! I'm due on set this afternoon and I have to pack my stuff and move out of here and—'

'Rebecca, please calm down, my love,' said Mrs Trevathan, with Ari following behind her. 'Ari has told me who you saw last night and, I promise, there's a very simple explanation. Come on now, let's go back to your room.'

'Really, Rebecca,' said Ari comfortingly, 'there is.'

'Well, I for one would like to hear it. I know what I saw and I'm not crazy,' she added defensively as they stepped back inside her bedroom. She sat on the end of the bed, her arms folded. 'Okay, who was that woman? And why has she been in my room sometimes at night when I've been sleeping? Because she has, Mrs Trevathan, I know she has!'

'Yes, dear, I believe you,' said Mrs Trevathan. 'The woman you saw last night is my mother, Mabel. She worked here as His Lordship's nanny, taking care of him from the time he was a newborn baby.'

'Your mother? But why is she here?'

'Please, Rebecca, let me explain. My father died twenty years ago and after Mum retired from the Hall, she lived quite happily on her own in the village. But a couple of years ago, she started to take a few falls, and her mind began to wander. She is ninety-one, after all.'

'Of course,' Rebecca said.

'So I told His Lordship I felt I had no choice but to leave his employment and go back to the village to take care of her. Well, he came up with a solution. He offered to turn two of the attic rooms into a comfortable flat for her. At first, it worked well, and I could take care of her as well as His Lordship, but in the past year, my mum's health has deteriorated. His Lordship then had the kindness to employ a full-time live-in nurse for her. I think you may have seen her in the kitchen on the day you arrived, dear.'

'Yes,' acknowledged Rebecca, 'I did, and outside once, too. She was pushing an old lady in a wheelchair. I thought they were extras on the film, to be honest.'

'Well, that was my mum. The problem is, Rebecca, sometimes her mind wanders, and so does she. Especially at night, when her nurse is sleeping. The room you saw her in last night was the room she used to occupy when it was His Lordship's nursery. It's not the first time I've found her in there. So, dear, does that make you feel any better?'

'But I'm sure the woman I saw last night wasn't an old lady.' Rebecca frowned. 'I didn't see her from the front, but she had long, blonde hair and she was singing to herself whilst she brushed it,' she said.

'My mother certainly has long hair,' said Mrs Trevathan, 'but I'd call it more white than blonde. I'm so sorry you've had some frights over the past few weeks, but I swear there are no ghosts in this house, nor anyone trying to harm you. Just an innocent old lady who sometimes gets confused about where she is.'

'I guess I just got upset reading the story about Violet Astbury that Ari gave me,' Rebecca admitted. 'She had bad headaches, just like I've had, and after she died, they thought she'd been poisoned.'

'Rebecca was very overwrought last night,' said Ari. 'She doesn't think anyone is trying to poison her, do you, Rebecca?'

'No, of course not,' she said hastily, understanding his expression.

'I see,' said Mrs Trevathan. 'Well, why don't you stay here and keep Rebecca company whilst I go and sort out a break-fast tray for her? I suggest scrambled eggs on toast. And I'm sure you can ask Mr Malik to taste it first, dear, just in case you're worried,' Mrs Trevathan retorted as she left the room.

'Oh dear,' Rebecca said. 'I've really upset her.'

'I'm sure she'll get over it,' said Ari, unable to prevent a grin. 'Now, the next question is, given that Mrs Trevathan has given you a very plausible explanation, are you happy to stay on here, or do you want me to ask Steve to find you a hotel?'

'I don't know. I suppose I did overreact a little last night.'

'Okay, well, let me know as soon as possible. If need be, I'll do what some of my ancestors used to when they were in service to the Brits and lie flat out on the floor outside your bedroom door guarding you.'

'Ari, don't tease me! But my God, the tragedy I read about last night,' she sighed. 'What a dreadful woman that Maud Astbury was. And she was the one who brought up poor Daisy, Anthony's mother. No wonder Anthony's kind of weird.'

'Well, I was thinking that for a great family and an estate to survive for four hundred years, I'm sure those at the head had to be ruthless. Maud Astbury could see the end of the line and was prepared to do whatever was necessary to save it.'

'But she didn't, did she? Unless Anthony has kids, the line stops with him anyway.'

'Yes, you're right, it does. I read Donald's diary last night, by the way, which was how I was still awake so late and heard you creeping around in the corridor outside. I was in the bathroom when you knocked on my bedroom door,' he explained. 'The diary filled in some blanks for me too, so thank you.'

'Do you think we should give the diary to Anthony?'

'To be honest, I had dinner with him last night and if anything, I feel he's shut himself off even further. I'm not sure what good it would do. It's obvious he doesn't want to know. And I understand that.'

'So do I,' she said with feeling.

'Rebecca, can I ask you something? Now that you've read the story, do you think Moh did die that day by drowning in the brook?'

Rebecca took a deep breath before answering. 'I'm not sure how to answer that. I mean, there's no proof either way, is there?'

'No, but after all my lack of faith in Anahita's story, my instinct now tells me he didn't,' Ari said quietly. 'I'm desperate to find out the truth before I leave.'

'Well, you do realise, don't you, that Tilly, Anahita's friend from the village, was Mrs Trevathan's grandmother? Which means her ninety-year-old mother, who apparently gave me such a fright last night, played with Moh when she was a baby.'

'Yes, of course, you're right! She'd almost certainly have been too young to remember anything, but you never know. Maybe I'll pay her a visit later on.'

'I'm sure Mrs Trevathan knows more than she lets on, too,' said Rebecca.

'Perhaps, but she's far too loyal to Lord Anthony and the Astburys to ever say a word. Still, I do think you're safe here, Rebecca. I'd hate you to leave here believing in ghosts, or that you're the reincarnated spirit of Violet Astbury.'

'Okay, lecture over.' She gave him a short smile of resignation. 'It does all seem rather crazy in the bright light of day.'

'Good. Now, if you'll excuse me, I have a few things to do, unless you want me to stay and taste your food?'

'Ari!'

'Only joking. See you later.'

Rebecca dutifully ate up every mouthful of the food Mrs Trevathan served her even though she wasn't at all hungry, or much of a fan of scrambled eggs. When Steve came to visit her after lunch, she pronounced herself well enough to shoot her scene later that afternoon, even though she was still suffering from the headache.

When she appeared on set, she received many hugs of welcome from the cast and crew. She wasn't sure whether the warmth of their greeting was because they all knew her relationship with Jack was over or because she'd been unwell.

Robert came over to speak to her privately before the cameras rolled.

'Darling, you're a trouper, and we thank you. I'll try and get this scene done as quickly as possible and then I want you straight back upstairs to rest. You've got a heavy schedule tomorrow.'

James gave her the biggest hug of all as they waited to begin their scene. 'Sorry to hear about Jack,' he said. 'Is it really curtains?'

'Unless he sorts himself out, definitely.'

'I'm feeling rather guilty about my role in his fall from your favour. I was hardly an unwilling victim during our nights out on the tiles in Ashburton together.'

'How was the waitress?' Rebecca asked acerbically.

James blushed and she knew she'd scored a bullseye.

At that moment, Robert shouted, 'Action!'

'As a matter of fact, I can't remember her terribly well,' James replied after Robert had professed himself satisfied with the take. 'I'm not trying to put the blame on Jack, because I was easily led, but that boy certainly knows how to party.' Rebecca was saved from having to reply by Robert calling 'Action!' again.

After about half an hour of stop-and-start filming, Robert indicated they had a take and Rebecca fled to Wardrobe. As she exited ten minutes later, Mrs Trevathan called to her. 'Rebecca, I'm glad I caught you. His Lordship wondered if you were up to having dinner with him tonight. He said he hasn't seen you for a few days.'

'Yes, of course,' she said, feeling guilty for having neglected her host.

'Good, I'm sure it will cheer him up. He's not been himself recently.' Mrs Trevathan frowned anxiously.

'Is he sick?'

'No, dear, not really. What with the film crew here, then all this talk of his grandparents with the arrival of Mr Malik, it's all been a bit much for him. Oh, by the way, Dr Trefusis telephoned to say he'd be round with the results of your tests tomorrow.'

'Thanks, Mrs Trevathan, I'll see you later.'

As she made her way upstairs, the name 'Trefusis' jangled in her brain, until she made the connection with the doctor from Anahita's manuscript. There seemed to be no end to the blurring of past and present in this place . . .

Having rested for an hour, she awoke feeling a little better and took a bath. At seven o'clock, as she was deciding what to wear for dinner, there was a knock on her door. She opened it and saw Ari.

'Hi, come in.'

'How are you feeling?' he asked.

'I'm okay. I'm having dinner with Anthony tonight.' Rebecca raised an eyebrow. 'To be honest, I could do without it.'

'The good news is that he never makes it beyond ninethirty, so at least you won't be on for a late night.'

'I feel bad about the uproar with Jack, so it'll give me a chance to explain and apologise. Are you joining us?' Rebecca looked hopeful.

'No, I wasn't asked, actually,' said Ari.

'Oh, by the way,' remembered Rebecca, 'I realised today that the doctor who came to see me the other day must be related to the one who was in league with Maud Astbury. They share the same surname, anyway – Dr Trefusis.'

'Really?' said Ari. 'That's another possible line of enquiry for me – so, thanks. Right, I'll leave you to it. Have a good evening with Anthony and if by any chance you need me, my room is just down there on the right.'

'I'm sure I'll be fine. Steve told me the film crew are shooting out in the park until at least midnight tonight. They've fallen behind, due to a difficult horse forgetting his lines. At least it wasn't me causing the problem today,' Rebecca replied, with the ghost of a smile.

'Okay, see you later.' As Ari left the room, Rebecca looked at her watch and saw that it was time to get ready for dinner with Anthony.

Twenty minutes later, she entered the dining room and was surprised to see Anthony wearing what looked like a new tweed jacket. His hair was washed and combed neatly and he was freshly shaved.

'Good evening, Rebecca.' He offered her one of his rare smiles. 'Do come and sit down.'

'Thank you.'

'Mrs Trevathan tells me you're still not feeling yourself, so I've taken her recommendation and we're having fish. Nothing too heavy for a delicate stomach.'

'That's kind of you, Anthony,' she said as she sat down.

'And may I say, you look absolutely charming tonight.'

'Thank you,' said Rebecca, a little puzzled by Anthony's none-too-subtle efforts to please.

'So, are you fully recovered from the drama of having to send your young man packing?'

'I'm feeling better about it, yes. It wasn't something I wanted to do, but, sadly, he left me with little choice.'

'Well, if one has fallen out of love, then one must do the right thing.'

'Well, it wasn't quite as straightforward as that, but, yes, I'm feeling okay about it.'

'Let's raise a glass to calmer waters and a return to normality,' Anthony interjected, proffering the wine bottle.

'Really, I'll stick to water tonight,' Rebecca insisted as she covered her glass.

Mrs Trevathan entered and began to serve the fish.

'This looks very healthy,' Anthony commented. 'You Americans love fish, don't you? I know Violet had it sent in fresh from Lynmouth when she was here. We British tend to be more carnivorous.'

'Most Americans enjoy a good steak too,' Rebecca replied.

'So,' said Anthony, picking up his knife and fork, 'only one more week, and I presume you'll be on your way back to the Big Apple?'

'More or less, yes, although there are a couple days of post-production stuff in London. I guess it's going to be strange being back in New York. I'll miss the peace and quiet of Astbury Hall.'

'Will you?'

'Yes, it's been wonderful here, Anthony. I can't thank you enough for your generous hospitality and kindness towards me.'

'No need for thanks, it's been a delight having you.'

They ate in silence for a while.

'Well, that was extremely good,' Anthony said as he finished and wiped his lips on a napkin.

'It was,' Rebecca agreed.

'My dear Rebecca, are you absolutely positive that you're not related to my grandmother Violet?' Anthony asked suddenly. 'Because I really do feel that you were somehow sent here to Astbury for a reason.'

'As sure as I can be. I guess it's just coincidence.' She smiled at him, trying to ease the sudden tension she felt as he put his knife and fork together and stared at her intently.

'Well, I don't believe it is.'

Rebecca watched Anthony's hands as they drew together, the long fingers interlocking as they clenched and unclenched. 'The thing is, Rebecca, I . . .'

'Anthony, what is it?' she asked, knowing he was desperate to say something.

'Forgive me if the timing may not be appropriate, but I thought I must speak to you before you begin to think about leaving. I . . . well, from the first moment I saw you, I knew you'd been sent to me. You, the living, breathing image of my American grandmother, Violet. Rebecca, do you believe in reincarnation?'

'I've never really thought about it, to be truthful,' she replied nervously, dreading where this conversation appeared to be heading.

'Well, I do,' Anthony said. 'My mother always said I was like Violet when I was a young boy, and indeed, I did look very like her. But you, coming here from America, so young and so beautiful, just like she was.' Anthony reached for Rebecca's hand suddenly and grasped it tightly. 'Don't you see it was meant to be?'

'What was meant to be?' Rebecca asked, confused, and uncomfortable with the grip on her hand.

'You and I, of course! Donald and Violet, who both died so tragically young and were unable to take the Astbury Estate into the future. But now, together, I'm sure that we can.'

'I—'

'I know that this is a shock to you,' Anthony continued urgently, tripping over his words, 'but of course, as a gentleman, whilst you were engaged to another man, I couldn't make my feelings towards you clear. But now he's gone, it's as if fate has decreed it. Our path lies clear before us. Don't you see, Rebecca?' he urged her.

'Anthony, I – I really don't know what to say.' Rebecca looked to the door for the normally ubiquitous Mrs Trevathan to arrive to clear the dishes and break the tension.

'I've told Mrs Trevathan that we're to be left alone to talk until I call for her,' said Anthony, following her eye-line and reading her thoughts. 'So don't be afraid that we'll be interrupted. The reason I've told you this tonight is because I knew you'd need a few days to think about it.' Anthony reached into his pocket and brought out a worn leather box. 'Rebecca Bradley, I would like to ask you to do me the honour of becoming my wife.'

Rebecca watched as he opened it to reveal a magnificent sapphire and diamond engagement ring.

'This was the ring Donald gave to Violet when he proposed. It sat on her finger from that moment until the day she died. It's only right that it should now sit on yours. Give me your hand, Rebecca, and let us see if it fits.'

He reached for her hand and, in a daze, she watched as Anthony slid the ring onto her finger. It fitted perfectly.

'There!' Anthony smiled in pleasure. 'It's back where it was always meant to be.'

Rebecca gazed down at the ring, which glinted as it caught the light from the overhead chandelier.

'So, what do you say, Rebecca?' Anthony asked her eagerly. 'Will you think about it?'

Rebecca knew she must choose her words carefully. 'Forgive me, Anthony. I'm very flattered by your offer, but as you said, up until yesterday I was engaged to another man. I don't think I'm able to move on from that just yet. And besides, I hardly know you – nor you me.'

'I understand you might need time to think but, Rebecca, we've spent many hours together since you arrived, and I took you into my home when you needed sanctuary. I'm in no doubt that you're the woman I've been waiting for all my life. Just think how we could rebuild Astbury together! Your presence here has lifted the atmosphere, just as Violet's did in her time. With you by my side as the new Lady Astbury, I'd have the strength and belief to restore this house to its former glory for the future generation we'll produce together. Violet, please say yes,' he said, pressing her.

'Anthony, my name is Rebecca,' she replied firmly.

'I apologise.' He smiled gently at her. 'Understandably, it's an easy mistake for me to make.'

'Yes, but—'

'Come here.' Anthony lurched across the table, gripped her by the shoulders and pulled her towards him. Before she could stop him, his lips were upon hers, violently and aggressively forcing them open to kiss her. She struggled to free herself, but the iron grip on her shoulders was too powerful. Suddenly he pulled away and released her. Rebecca rushed to stand up and began to make for the door, but as she did so, he grasped her hand and pulled her to a halt.

'Please accept my apology, I was suddenly overwhelmed. You are so beautiful,' he added, looking sheepish. 'Forgive me for losing control.'

She turned to face him and pulled her hand away from his. He let it go without any resistance, his eyes full of desperation, his shoulders suddenly slack. She felt a mixture of sympathy and disgust. Slowly, her right hand moved towards her left and she pulled off Violet's ring and handed it to him. 'I'm so sorry, Anthony, but I can't marry you. I think it's best if I leave the house as soon as possible,' she added. 'Thank you for your hospitality over the past few weeks. Goodbye.' Rebecca turned away and walked quickly towards the door.

'Please, don't go, Violet, don't leave me—'

She was out of the dining room, racing up the stairs towards the sanctuary of her bedroom. Reaching it, she sank into a chair, panting heavily.

She knew now, without a doubt, she must leave Astbury immediately. Anthony, the poor, deluded man, genuinely believed she was Violet. In a daze, she threw her possessions into her suitcase, wondering how she could leave the house without Anthony trying to stop her. First, she would see whether Ari was in his room, and if not, she knew that the film crew were somewhere in the park on the night shoot.

She tentatively opened the door and peered out along the corridor. It seemed to be deserted, so she knocked on Ari's bedroom door and, when there was no response, opened it to find it empty. Not wanting to spend another second in the house, she hurried back past the main staircase and towards the back stairs that would take her down to the kitchen and out of Astbury. Almost tripping down the narrow steps as she bumped her case behind her, she flung open the door to the empty kitchen. Racing through the lobby, she breathed a sigh of relief as she stepped out into the courtyard at the side of the house and weaved her way between the lorries used to store the camera equipment.

Night had fallen, and it was very dark, with no moon to light the sky. Hiding behind the hedge that edged one side of the courtyard, Rebecca paused to get her breath and to listen for any sounds that would guide her to where the film crew were shooting. There was only silence. Racking her brain to remember which scene it had been – something to do with the horse – Rebecca deduced they must be somewhere near the front drive. Making her way as quietly as she could across the gravel, she headed towards the front of the house, sticking close to the shrubbery to give her protection from prying eyes. As she rounded the side of the house and walked onto the park that flanked the drive on either side, Rebecca could see she'd made a mistake. From here, the bright lights used on a night shoot were now just visible from the moors beyond the back garden.

Stowing her case in a bush – she could collect it later, for now it was slowing her down – Rebecca began to retrace her footsteps, zigzagging around to the back of the house, then along the shadowy edge of the walled garden. Beyond the tall yew hedge that separated the garden from the moors, she would be able to follow the lights towards the crew and safety. She doubled her speed towards them. Arriving at the hedge, she walked through the opening and there, not three hundred yards away, saw the film set.

'Thank God,' she breathed in relief, and stopped for a few seconds to catch her breath and garner the energy to run the final few hundred yards across the open moor.

There was a sudden rustle behind her. Rebecca began to turn, but before she could see who it was, a cloth was placed tightly across her mouth and nose. As she struggled to breathe, a strong smell permeated her nostrils and she immediately felt dizzy.

A few seconds later, Rebecca lost consciousness.

43

It took some hunting to find the staircase that led up to the Astbury Hall attics, but eventually Ari emerged into a dark, narrow corridor. Walking along the labyrinth of corridors, he wondered in which room Anahita had spent her first summer here.

The sound of a television alerted Ari to the area of the attic that was currently occupied and he tapped on the door. A few seconds later it was opened by a woman in a nurse's uniform.

'May I help you?' she asked suspiciously.

'Yes, I was wondering if I could speak to Mrs Trevathan's mother. I believe she lives up here.'

'She does, but may I enquire what it's about?'

'I'm currently staying here at the Hall and doing some research on the Astbury family history. I know she used to work here and I was wondering if she could help me with a couple of things.'

'I see.' The nurse hesitated.

'Who is it, Vicky dear?' said a voice with a thick Devon accent from inside the room.

'A gentleman who wants to speak to you about when you worked here, Mabel,' the nurse called to her.

'Then ask him in,' said the voice.

The nurse made room for Ari to pass. He entered a cosy, overheated sitting room and saw an old lady in a chair in front of a television with the sound turned up to maximum. Her white hair was fastened in a coil at the nape of her neck and Ari noticed she had the same inquisitive green eyes as her daughter.

'Hello,' she said, 'and who might you be?'

'My name is Ari Malik. Your daughter told me you lived up here. I've been staying as a guest of Lord Astbury here at the Hall.'

'Oh yes, I think Brenda, my daughter, mentioned you to me, although she didn't tell me to expect a visitor,' the old woman said. 'Never mind. I've seen you in the garden from my window. Turn that off, Vicky, I can't hear myself think,' she ordered the nurse. 'So, dear, what is it you want to ask me?'

'May I sit down?' Ari asked.

'Of course. And my name is Mabel Smerden, by the way.'

'Well, it's a pleasure to meet you, Mrs Smerden, and thank you for letting me talk to you. I've come to Astbury because I've discovered that an ancestor of my family spent the first three years of his life here on the estate. His name was Moh Prasad and I believe that Anahita, his mother, was a close friend of Tilly, who was your mother. And that you actually played with Moh as a young child yourself.'

As he spoke, Mabel's smile abruptly disappeared and she sank back into her chair. 'My mother is dead, and I don't remember anything.'

'Probably not, no,' Ari replied gently, sensing her unease, 'but anything you could remember, even if it's just a tiny detail, might help me in my search for what happened to him. I was wondering, for example, whether there was ever a photo taken of Moh. I know he spent time with you at your cottage when your mother minded him.'

The woman sniffed. 'There might be a photo, perhaps,' she said, 'somewhere in my mother's bits and pieces.'

'I'd love to see it,' Ari replied.

'Vicky?' she ordered the nurse imperiously. 'Get that old cardboard box out from under my bed.'

The nurse did as she was told and arrived back in the room carrying it.

'Give it to Mr Malik, Vicky. You might find one or two in there of your relative. There's a few of me when I was a baby, anyway.'

'Thank you.' Ari opened the box and saw the black and white remnants of another era. The more recent ones, showing many images of Mrs Trevathan as a child, were on the top. Sifting carefully through, Ari murmured in fascination as the quality and content of the photos went back in time. He felt he was viewing a potted version of the huge changes that had taken place over the past hundred years. And there, near the bottom, was a photo of a woman who was unmistakably his great-grandmother Anahita, alongside a woman who must have been Tilly. They sat stiffly on chairs arranged outside a stone cottage, each bouncing babies – Mabel and Moh – on their knees. Ari stared at Donald and Anahita's son. He was cherubic, as all young babies are, his dark hair and huge eyes showing a strong resemblance to his mother. There were other photographs too, of Anahita with Moh at a Christmas gathering. Studying her, he saw she'd been a real beauty.

'You've found one, then?' asked Mabel.

'Yes. They look so happy,' Ari said as he reached over to show her.

'They do. You can keep that, if you'd like. I've no need of it.'

'Thank you,' he said, 'this means more to me than you can possibly imagine.'

'Would you like a drink, my love? I normally have a cocoa at around this time. It's not often I have visitors these days.'

'A cup of tea would be very welcome.'

'Righto, Vicky'll put the kettle on, won't you, dear?'

When the nurse had left the room, Ari said, 'I know you were a baby when all this happened, Mabel, but did your mother ever discuss the details of how Moh died? I know he took a fall from a horse near the cottage on the moor where he lived with his mother.'

'You know about that?' Mabel eyed him with amazement. 'How?'

'Just before she died, Anahita entrusted me with the story of her life. She was told by Lady Selina that Donald had come to collect Moh from the cottage just after she was arrested, and that father and son had both died together after Donald's horse bucked them off. Moh drowned in the brook, apparently.'

'I . . . oh dear . . .' Mabel's eyes filled with sudden tears. 'Mr Malik, you do realise you're opening up a whole can of worms, don't you?' she said as the nurse returned with the drinks. 'Thank you.' Mabel pulled herself together as she took her cocoa from Vicky. 'Why don't you take yourself off to your room whilst I speak with Mr Malik?' she said to the nurse.

'Call me if you need me,' Vicky said, and left the room.

'Mabel, you do know exactly what I'm talking about, don't you?'

'Yes, sadly I do,' she replied after a pause. 'They had to tell his poor mum something, didn't they? Otherwise she wouldn't have rested until she found him. No mother would have.'

'The sad truth is, Mabel, that Anahita never did rest. Even though she was handed Moh's death certificate before she arrived back in India, she refused to believe he'd died with Donald that day.'

Mabel stared off into the distance, then sighed heavily. 'That woman,' she breathed eventually, 'would stop at nothing to get what she wanted.'

'You mean Lady Maud?'

'I do, dear, I do. For all her time spent in that chapel, she had precious little of the Lord inside her, that is the truth,' muttered Mabel. 'I saw it with my own eyes when I was taken on by Daisy to care for poor Anthony when he was a baby. We all suffered at her hands.'

'Yes, it would seem so, from what I'm discovering,' Ari agreed grimly. 'Anahita's story gives me a very clear picture of who Maud Astbury was.'

'Well, I can tell you she didn't mellow with age,' Mabel said. 'With Donald and Violet gone, Lady Maud had free rein to bring up their child however she chose. That poor little girl, growing up all alone in this great big house. Daisy was forced to pray in that chapel three or four times a day, and was told by her grandmother that all men were evil. No wonder Daisy made such a mess of bringing up her own son – Lord Anthony, that is,' Mabel said. 'I was taken on as his nursemaid and then had to stand by and watch it all without being able to say a word. That poor boy –' she sighed – 'he really didn't know whether he was coming or going the way Daisy treated him. And all this trouble goes back to one evil woman, who managed to destroy her own family and excused her behaviour by saying it was what her God would have wanted. The devil would have been more like it,' she muttered darkly.

'Mabel,' said Ari, knowing he had to tread carefully, 'you didn't seem surprised when I mentioned Moh had died with Donald by the brook that day. If the village and servants were told Moh had left with Anahita when she was arrested, how did you know the truth?'

'I don't,' Mabel said, shrugging uncomfortably, 'it was just gossip and hearsay as I grew up. You know what servants are like.'

'Well, I'm here to tell you that Moh was *not* taken with Anahita that morning. She wasn't allowed to take him with her when the police came to get her, and she never saw him again after that. But I think you know this already,' he said quietly.

'I said I don't know anything for certain,' she repeated.

'Mabel –' Ari tried a last throw of the dice – 'I leave for India in just a few days. I'm never going to return to Astbury Hall. It was my great-grandmother's last wish for me to find out the truth about her lost son. I've come up against a brick wall time and again. Anthony doesn't want to talk, even if he *does* know anything, and—'

'His Lordship knows nothing!' she interrupted vehemently. 'Of course he doesn't, and don't you go upsetting him, Mr Malik. He's delicate, he is, and my daughter has enough of a time with him already, as it is.'

'I won't, of course, but you're my last hope. Please, Mabel, if you do know what really happened to Moh that day, I beg you to tell me. I swear I won't breathe a word, but I think after what Anahita suffered at the Astbury family's hands, it's only right if you do. Mabel, did Moh meet his death by the brook that day, or was Anahita right for all those years and he lived on?'

The old lady sat, her eyes flickering nervously, and Ari knew she was remembering.

'No, little Moh didn't die that day,' she sighed eventually, 'but God strike you down if you breathe a word to another soul. Brenda knows nothing of this, nor His Lordship, you understand?'

'I do,' said Ari, feeling suddenly choked with emotion that finally he knew Anahita's instinct had been right for all those years. 'Thank you, Mabel,' he said quietly.

'There, there, my love,' Mabel said, trying to comfort him, 'you have to understand that it was only on my mum's – Tilly's – deathbed that I heard any of this. She wanted to confess to someone, you see. She'd been keeping the secret for all of her life and felt she'd betrayed her friend Anahita. But what else could she have done? If she'd breathed a word of what my dad had seen, they'd have been out of the cottage and a livelihood without so much as a by-your-leave.'

'What your father saw?' Ari asked, now completely confused.

'Yes. And maybe it's fate my old mum *did* tell me, and now you've come looking for Moh. So, my heart says I should tell you what my dad saw that day at the brook. He was the assistant postmaster, you see . . .'

The Cottage by the Brook,

August 1922

44

Jim Fenton cycled across the moors, enjoying the warmth of the midday sun on his back. On days like this he felt his job delivering the post was the best in the world, but in winter when the snow came, it was a different kettle of fish. He especially liked it on the rare occasions he had to deliver to Miss Anni, who would sometimes come to the front door when he arrived and they'd have a chat over a brew. He didn't normally take up offers of hospitality, but her cottage was so isolated that no one was likely to find him slacking for fifteen minutes or so.

And besides, Jim felt sorry for her, living out here with only her little boy for company. Tilly often said she thought Anni should move into the village for a bit more society, but Anni seemed perfectly content to stay exactly where she was.

He heard the unusual sound of a car engine humming behind him and looked back along the rough track. Motors were a rare sight crossing the moors and as it passed him he saw that it was a police car. He wondered where it was headed. There was only one cottage around here and that was Miss Anni's. Sure enough, when he arrived a few minutes later, he saw the car was parked in front of the cottage.

Then he heard the sound of raised voices from inside. Just

as he was leaning his bicycle against the fence, the front door opened and he watched in shock as two men man-handled a screaming Miss Anni out of the cottage.

'I can't leave my boy! Please let me take him with me! He'll be so frightened – I can't leave him by himself, *please* . . .'

Instinctively, Jim ducked out of sight behind the high fence as Anni was bundled into the back of the car, screaming hysterically. He heard the engine turn over and the car reversed then drove off at top speed back towards the village. He didn't really understand what he had just seen and heard, but the one thing he did know was that little Moh was apparently in the cottage alone.

Peering out from behind the fence, Jim saw the car disappearing over the horizon in a cloud of dust. He spotted the back door to the cottage and ran towards it, then pushed it open. He saw something simmering on the range and a basket of wet laundry on the kitchen table. Whatever had just taken place, Miss Anni definitely had not been expecting to leave in a hurry. Removing the pan from the range and shutting off the heat, he walked through the kitchen door and along the narrow hallway beyond to check the sitting room for Moh. It was empty, so he climbed the stairs and poked his head into a small room. There in the cot lay Moh, still sleeping peacefully, undisturbed by the rumpus that had occurred below.

Jim decided the best thing would be to use Miss Anni's telephone and tell Doreen on the exchange at the village post office to run down the street and ask Tilly to telephone him here. She would know what he should do, but he didn't feel comfortable leaving the poor child alone. Jim headed down the stairs towards the table in the hall where the telephone stood. He had only got halfway when he heard the sound of another car pulling up in front of the cottage. Not able to see who it was, and realising he had no real reason to be inside the house as Miss Anni wasn't here, Jim turned tail and ran back up the stairs and went into the bedroom at the front of the cottage to see who the new visitor was.

His heart missed a beat when he saw Lady Maud Astbury herself emerge from the car, accompanied by Dr Trefusis. Lady Maud marched up the garden path towards the front door and Jim, now terrified of being discovered, knelt down and wriggled beneath the big brass bedstead. He heard the front door open and close, and the sound of low voices downstairs.

'The child must be upstairs sleeping. Go and get him, will you?'

Jim heard the heavy tread of the doctor climbing the stairs and held his breath as the door to the bedroom he was hiding in opened. He glimpsed a large pair of shiny black shoes, which paused for a few seconds a couple of feet away from him before disappearing out again onto the landing.

'He's here, Lady Astbury. Shall I pack a few belongings for him? He'll need a change of clothes and some napkins for the journey,' Jim heard the doctor call from the other bedroom.

'Collect whatever you need, but be quick about it,' he listened to Lady Maud answer irritably from the bottom of the stairs.

Jim heard the sound of the doctor moving about in the room next door and then a loud cry from Moh, before footsteps descended back down the stairs.

'Hush now, child,' he heard the doctor say, trying to soothe Moh, who was rightly complaining at having been woken so abruptly by a stranger. 'I should take some bottles for him, Your Ladyship. I'm sure the mother has some in the kitchen.'

LUCINDA RILEY

'If you must, but I hardly think the child is likely to starve on the way to London,' Lady Maud replied. 'Please, hurry up!'

Jim's heart was now pounding in his chest. Perhaps they were taking the child to London, to Miss Anni? Taught from birth never to question the ways of the gentry, Jim remained hidden, listening.

'Are we finally ready?' Maud said a few minutes later.

'Yes, Lady Astbury.'

'Good. Now, you will drop me at the Dower House and then proceed on to London with the child.'

'Yes, Your Ladyship. It's a reputable establishment and they take excellent care of the children there.'

'And you will, of course, tell them that the child has been abandoned and that you have no idea where he's from or what his parentage might be.'

'Of course, Your Ladyship,' replied the doctor as Jim heard them open the front door and shut it behind them.

Jim let out the breath he was unaware he had been holding as he had struggled to catch every word the two of them had been saying.

He heard the car engine turn over, followed by the sound of it struggling to turn round on the rough grass outside.

Crawling out from under the bed, he chanced a surreptitious glance out of the window and as he did so, he saw a figure on horseback racing towards the cottage.

Crouching down, his face half-hidden by the curtains, Jim had a bird's-eye view and could hear every word as the window was ajar to let in fresh air.

The figure who flung himself off the horse was Lord Donald Astbury. As the car prepared to move off, he placed himself in front of it to stop its progress.

602

'Where's Anni, Mother?' he asked as he wrenched open the car's passenger door. 'And where are you taking Moh? What the hell is going on here?'

Donald reached inside the car, grabbed Moh from his mother's lap and took him into his own arms. By this time the boy was hysterical, but when he looked at the person who was now holding him, his face broke into a smile. 'Mr Don!' he cooed with glee.

'Yes, yes, it's Mr Don, Moh. I'm here, and I'll look after you, as soon as I've worked out what on earth is happening!'

By this time, Lady Maud had stepped out of the car and Donald turned to face her. 'I've just seen Anni being driven through the village in the back of a police car. She was weeping hysterically, and she screamed Moh's name to me. Where were you taking my son?'

'Donald, I heard what had happened to Miss Chavan, so I came immediately to collect the child with Dr Trefusis to take him with me and care for him until we knew the outcome.'

'Really, Mother? Well, then, Moh can come back with his father to the Hall on horseback, can't you, little chap?' Donald remounted his horse, taking Moh astride with him.

'Are you out of your senses?' Maud screamed suddenly. 'You cannot take that . . . *bastard* back to Astbury Hall. For God's sake, Donald, see sense! Your wife has just died and your lover has been arrested for her murder and taken away by the police an hour ago! Surely you must understand what this means? All trace of your association with that Indian woman and . . . *that*,' she indicated her grandson, 'must end. If any whisper of it gets out, you will be disgraced! And the Astbury name will be trampled in the mud.'

Donald was staring at her in disbelief. 'Anni has been

arrested for Violet's murder? How? Why? It's totally ridiculous – it's obscene!'

'Donald, for once in your life, stop being blinded by lust. Dr Trefusis found some dangerous herbs growing in her greenhouse. He already had his suspicions, so he handed them over to the police and subsequently she has been charged. Sadly, Donald, the matter is now completely out of my hands.'

'No, it isn't, but I'm sure it started there, Mother,' he said, in a voice cold with hatred. 'So before I go and try to free the mother of my child from prison, just where *were* you thinking of taking my son? Perhaps you had a thought to do away with Moh completely? I really wouldn't put it past you.'

'Don't be ridiculous! Dr Trefusis has told me he knows of a very good orphanage in London where they take cases such as this.'

'"Cases such as this"? Good God, Mother!' Donald exploded as he looked down on her. 'I truly think you're mad. But it seems I've arrived just in the nick of time. Now, if you'll excuse me, I'll take my boy back to Astbury Hall.'

'No!' shouted Maud as Donald tapped Glory's flanks in preparation to move off. 'I can't let you take the child.' She sprang out to position herself in front of the horse. 'Give that child to me!'

'Mother, I suggest you move out of the way, because if you don't, I will simply ride over you and it will be no less than you deserve!'

Jim, still crouching by the window, watched the stand-off between mother and son in fascinated horror.

'Doctor, move your car and stop him,' ordered Maud.

'For the last time, get out of the way!'

Glory's hooves were dancing nervously as the woman in

front of her refused to move. Donald tried to steer the horse to the right, but as he did so, Dr Trefusis swerved the car round to block their path. Glory gave a whinny of terror and reared up to her full height, bucking off her master with Moh still grasped in his arms.

There was a dreadful thud as Donald, unable to use his hands to break his fall, landed on a jagged rock protruding from the ground nearby. Father and son lay motionless together, Moh's head still resting on his father's arm.

Dr Trefusis leapt out of the car and immediately went to tend to them as Maud watched him, frozen.

'Your Ladyship, I can barely feel a pulse. Lord Astbury must have hit his head on the rock as he fell. There's blood seeping from his ear. We must get him into the car and to a hospital as soon as possible.'

'What about the child?' asked Maud. 'Is he alive?'

As if Moh wished to prove it, he stirred suddenly and let out a yell of pain.

'He must go to a hospital too. I've no idea what injuries he's suffered internally.'

'Don't be a fool, man! That child should never have been born, and you'll take him to London now as planned.'

'Your Ladyship, I beg you, there's no time to lose. We must drive Lord Astbury to a hospital immediately!' Dr Trefusis repeated.

'You will do as I say. Now, pick up the child and we'll go.'

'I don't understand . . .' Jim could see the agony on the doctor's face. 'You'll leave your son here alone? Lady Astbury, he may well die if he isn't attended to immediately.'

'Come on, man! Get that child.'

Reluctantly, Dr Trefusis picked up a tearful, shocked Moh

in his arms and rested him on the back seat of the car as Lady Maud climbed into the front. They set off at top speed, away from the cottage.

Jim, too horrified to move from the window, stared down at Donald's prone body, his horse standing sentinel over him a few yards away.

'My God,' Jim breathed, turning around slowly in the bedroom, his limbs sluggish with shock. He then saw the photograph of Moh, Anni and Donald by the bed. If he needed any further proof of what he'd already heard, this was it. Lifting the photograph from where it stood on a table next to the bed, Jim hurried down the stairs and outside to see if he could help Donald.

'Your Lordship, Your Lordship, can you hear me?' Jim said urgently as he crouched down next to him, wishing he knew something about first aid. Donald stirred suddenly and opened his eyes. 'That's it, Your Lordship, keep awake until help comes. For God's sake, sir, just keep awake!' Jim begged him.

Donald stared up at Jim. A sudden smile appeared on his lips.

'Anni,' he murmured. Then he closed his eyes for the last time.

Astbury Hall,
July 2011

45

As Mabel's story came to its end, Ari found his eyes were wet with tears.

He looked across at Mabel, who was staring out of the window watching the approaching dusk.

'It's . . . shocking beyond all comprehension,' Ari said, clearing his throat, 'that a mother could leave a son to die out there alone on the moors. It truly beggars belief.'

'Indeed it does,' Mabel agreed. 'My mum told me that when Dad came home after it happened, telling her that Lord Astbury had died in his arms and Moh had been stolen away, she thought he'd been on the bottle.'

'Do you think Maud wanted her son to die?'

'My dad said it took over two hours for help to turn up. Of course, when it did, my dad made himself scarce. It wouldn't have done for anyone to know that he'd seen anything. Lady Maud probably would have done away with him too. What a terrible tale it is,' Maud shuddered. 'It haunted both my parents for the rest of their lives.'

'I'm sure it did, Mabel. What a secret to have to carry. Do you have any idea where the doctor took Moh?'

'Only that Dad thought Moh had been taken to an orphanage in London.'

'I'm amazed Maud didn't drown him in the brook there and then,' said Ari.

'My dad always reckoned she would have done if the doctor hadn't been there.'

'For all the use he was,' Ari said with a sigh.

'Mr Malik, you must understand that in those days the local gentry held those who served them in the palms of their hands. No one would dare to refuse their orders. Dr Trefusis had no choice but to do what was asked of him. He knew she'd ruin him one way or the other if he didn't.'

'It was him that signed the death certificate Selina Astbury gave to Indira to give to Anahita,' said Ari. 'That surely must have been a criminal offence?'

'But who was there to know he wasn't telling the truth?' said Mabel. 'Except my poor old dad. After that, even when I was grown, my mum refused to work up at the Hall ever again and I never knew why. They'd have moved away completely if they could have done, but in those days, it was easier said than done.'

A knock on the door frame made them both look up. 'Excuse me for interrupting, but it's getting late and I don't want you tiring yourself out, Mabel,' the nurse said, pushing a wheelchair through the door. 'Perhaps you can carry on your chat tomorrow, Mr Malik?'

'Yes,' said Mabel, as the nurse helped her gently into the chair. 'Although I can't think there is much more to say, except please remember your promise to keep what I've told you to yourself.'

'Of course. I really can't thank you enough for telling me, Mabel,' Ari replied.

'Well, it was the right thing to do. I feel at least one wrong has been righted. Goodnight, Mr Malik, pop up and say goodbye before you leave and perhaps we can talk of happier times.'

'I will.' Ari stood up and was walking towards the door when a thought struck him. 'Can you walk at all, Mabel?'

'Not these days, no. My blessed arthritis has done for my legs. The only way for me to get anywhere is in my chair. Sometimes, Lord Anthony will carry me downstairs so that Vicky can take me around the garden and I can get some fresh air. That kind to me, he is.' She smiled. 'But my grey cells are still functioning, aren't they, Vicky, dear?'

'They certainly are, Mabel.' Vicky smiled at her. 'She misses nothing, this one.'

'I have no trouble believing that. Well, goodnight,' he said as he shut the door behind him.

Ari made his way downstairs, his head full of the new information he'd gleaned. He was still filled with a sensation of euphoria at the thought of Anahita being right all along. Although, who knew what had become of Moh once he had left Devon?

He suddenly thought of someone who might . . .

The other thing that was troubling him was Mrs Trevathan's very definite presumption that it would have been Mabel whom Rebecca had seen in the bedroom last night. Mabel herself had just told him she couldn't walk, so how on earth could she manage to wander the Hall in the depths of the night? And as for describing her as partly senile, Ari knew he'd not met an elderly woman since Anahita who was clearly as compos mentis as Mabel was. Mrs Trevathan was obviously lying. The question was, why?

*

Rebecca was dreaming, dreaming again of the singing, of the smell of the flowery perfume, of running away from Astbury and all the dangers it presented . . .

With a jolt, she awoke, opened her eyes and found her vision was blurred. She moved a hand to rub her eyes to try to clear them, but her arms seemed to be stuck fast behind her back and she longed to release them because they ached. The scent was strong, as strong as it had ever been, and in the dim light, the woman she'd seen before was here again.

I'm dreaming, she thought, *I'm asleep and I'll wake up and then she will be gone.*

Some time later, Rebecca's senses told her she *was* awake and she forced her eyes open. Thankfully, her vision had cleared and this time she could see the back of the woman she had seen the night before, sitting at her dressing table brushing her hair. She bent her neck and saw her own knees. She was sitting on a high-backed chair, and, as she tested out parts of her body, she found her arms were tied behind her and her ankles were strapped together beneath her. Still woozy, and with a headache that made the others she'd suffered from recently feel like a walk in the park, Rebecca struggled to collect her thoughts and find out where she was. Tilting her head slowly upwards, immediately, her instincts told her this was not her bedroom at Astbury Hall.

Rebecca closed her eyes. Slowly, her drugged brain released information: Anthony's marriage proposal, his sudden aggressive kiss, her flight from Astbury Hall in search of the film crew on the moors, the cloth going over her face and then – blackness.

She tentatively opened her eyes again and studied the woman. She breathed deeply, knowing that the more oxygen she inhaled, the faster her brain would clear from whatever drug she'd been given. Whoever it was that was sitting at the dressing table in front of her was certainly not a frail old lady of over ninety. From the back, her frame was broad and sturdy.

Rebecca studied her own legs, and saw that they were no longer covered in jeans, but in the soft silk fabric of a skirt that skimmed her ankles. Surreptitiously moving her eye-line up the front of her body, she saw the same material covered her upper torso too.

She was wearing a dress. Which meant that whoever this woman was, she had undressed her.

A shudder of terror ran down Rebecca's spine.

I will die, just like Violet, I know I will . . .

She closed her eyes, her head and heart pounding. An instinctive deep breath escaped her, despite her efforts to stifle any sound.

'I know you're awake. I can see your eyelids twitching.' There was a sudden, tinkling laugh. 'Open them and show me their beauty. You won't come to any harm, I promise. My name is Alice, by the way. Just like in *Alice in Wonderland*.'

With every ounce of mental strength she possessed, Rebecca did as she'd been asked and saw that Alice had turned round to face her. She caught her breath in horror, for this was not a woman, but a ghoulish parody of femininity. The long, blonde hair framed a face caked in badly applied make-up. Blue eyelids, false eyelashes covered in mascara, black liner around the entire eye. Bright red lipstick melted into the small cracks of ageing skin, and vivid circles of pink blusher glowed on each cheek.

'There we are,' said Alice smiling at her. 'See?' She patted her hair. 'Am I so scary?'

Rebecca persuaded her mouth to shape a 'no'.

'Well, I do apologise for having to take such measures to keep you with me. It really wouldn't have been right for you to have left. I hope you see that. You're my new friend.'

Instinct told Rebecca she must simply agree with everything Alice said whilst she tried to understand what was happening and get her bearings.

'You poor thing, you look awfully pale, so I shall go downstairs and make you a nice cup of tea.'

Rebecca nodded again.

'Do answer me, my dear. Mummy always said it was rude not to.'

'Yes please,' Rebecca managed to say.

'Good-oh.' Alice stood up, and Rebecca realised how tall she was. From her lowly viewpoint, the woman towered above her. Her eyes followed Alice as she walked from the room, and saw that she wore an old-fashioned silk dress, not dissimilar to the one Rebecca herself had also been dressed in. As Rebecca wrenched her head round as far as it would go to watch her leave, she saw enormous feet wedged into a pair of silk shoes.

'Oh God, oh God . . .' she breathed, begging her sluggish brain to make sense of what she'd just seen. Finally, having the freedom to turn her head, she looked around and saw she was in an unfamiliar bedroom. The old-fashioned brass bedstead had a patchwork quilt upon it and the closed curtains were sprigged with faded flowers. The dressing table was heaped with cosmetics lying on its marble surface. A bottle of the same perfume that had been in Violet's room stood open.

Think, Rebecca, think . . .

She let out a sob of despair. She didn't understand what was wanted from her.

And *who* was Alice?

She heard the heavy tread of footsteps approaching and turned her head back to where it had been.

'Here we are, I've made you a nice cup of tea. I'll untie you and then you can drink it yourself,' Alice said as she put down two cups of tea on the dressing table, slopping most of the contents out as she did so. She came towards Rebecca, moving behind her to free her wrists and then walked round the chair and bent down to untie her ankles. 'I do hope I didn't hurt you; it was only so that you didn't fall off the chair whilst you were sleeping. I used a silk scarf so your wrists wouldn't chafe. There we go, that's better now, isn't it?'

And as Alice turned her eyes up towards her for a response, Rebecca realised exactly who she was.

Talk of the devil, Ari thought, as Mrs Trevathan appeared along the bedroom corridor and looked at him anxiously.

'Have you seen Rebecca?' she asked him.

'I thought she was having dinner with Lord Anthony.'

'She was, but then she disappeared. I've checked her room and it seems she's left, because all her belongings have gone, as has her suitcase.'

'Really?' Ari frowned. 'Perhaps she finally decided she wanted to move to a hotel. I wouldn't blame her, given the fright she had last night.'

'Yes, that occurred to me too,' said Mrs Trevathan, 'but I thought she might have asked you to take her.'

'Well, surely the person to ask is Lord Anthony himself? After all, he was the one having dinner with her.'

'Yes, but normally after dinner he takes himself off to his bedroom and I don't like to disturb him.'

Ari could see Mrs Trevathan looked nervous. 'Well, perhaps on this occasion, you can make an exception? If you show me where his bedroom is, I'll go and ask him.'

'I'm sure that won't be necessary,' she answered. 'Perhaps first I should telephone Steve, the production manager, to see if he's heard anything from her. He should be back at the hotel by now.'

'Good idea.' Ari nodded.

He watched her walk downstairs to the telephone in Anthony's study. He went into Rebecca's room and saw that it was indeed deserted; all of her things were gone. He left the room and followed Mrs Trevathan downstairs to see if there was any news from Steve, but her frown told him immediately there wasn't.

'He hasn't heard a dicky bird, I'm afraid,' she said.

'If you could hand me a telephone directory, I'll call the local hotels and see if she has arranged a room for herself,' said Ari.

Fifteen minutes later, Ari had drawn a blank on any establishment within twenty miles. Steve had called to say he'd had the same idea and result.

Ari paced up and down the small study. If Rebecca *had* decided to leave, he was sure she would have left him a message in his room, or, at the very least, told Mrs Trevathan. She was simply too polite to walk out. And besides, who had driven her? Steve had said Graham hadn't heard from her either. Unless she'd called a taxi herself.

'Any news?' Mrs Trevathan asked as she came back into the study.

'No. It seems Rebecca has disappeared into thin air. I'm

now seriously concerned, and I'm afraid that it's time to ask Lord Anthony. He was, after all, the last person to see her.'

'He told me he didn't want to be disturbed during dinner,' said Mrs Trevathan suddenly, as if she was remembering.

'Really? Isn't that unusual?'

'I –' Mrs Trevathan sighed. 'One never knows what's going on in His Lordship's head.'

'Where's his bedroom?' said Ari, marching from the study and heading for the stairs. 'Because if you don't tell me, I'll batter down every last door in this godforsaken mausoleum until I find him.'

'All right, all right,' said Mrs Trevathan, close to tears. 'I'll take you to him.'

Walking along the corridor on the other side of the main staircase from the one he and Rebecca occupied, Mrs Trevathan passed a number of doors and paused outside one towards the end of it.

'This is his suite,' she indicated. 'Now, please wait along the corridor whilst I knock. I don't want him to see you here if he opens the door. He really doesn't like being disturbed by strangers at night and it's more than my job's worth to do so.'

Ari took a few steps backwards. Satisfied, Mrs Trevathan gave a rap on the door.

'Your Lordship? Sorry to disturb you, but I need to speak with you urgently,' she said loudly.

There was no reply.

'He may be asleep,' said Mrs Trevathan, glancing apprehensively at Ari. 'I'll try again.' She did so, but still got no response.

'You'll have to go in and wake him up,' ordered Ari.

He watched the fear on Mrs Trevathan's face as she paused.

617

'He really doesn't like anyone entering his room without his permission.'

'For God's sake, tell him it's an emergency! And if you won't, I will.' Ari took a step towards the door and instantly Mrs Trevathan opened it herself.

'Wait there,' she said as she disappeared inside and closed the door behind her.

A few seconds later, she emerged. 'He's not in his room.'

Ari stared at her, not convinced.

'Listen, young man, I'm as worried about Rebecca's disappearance as you are, and I am telling you now His Lordship isn't in there. Although it's not unusual for him to take himself off on night walks.'

'And where would he usually take himself?'

'Oh, just around the estate.'

'Mrs Trevathan!' Ari's patience finally ran out. 'It's well past midnight now and Rebecca is still missing. Now Anthony is apparently missing too. I'm worried enough to call the police right now.'

Mrs Trevathan looked at him in horror. 'Please! Don't do that. I'm sure she's fine. Perhaps she went with His Lordship . . .' Her voice trailed off.

'I realise your loyalties are divided, but we're both aware you know more than you're saying. I saw your mother earlier, the woman you convinced me wandered the house at night. She told me herself that she can't get about without a wheelchair. It wasn't her that Rebecca saw the other night, was it? You were lying, Mrs Trevathan. So, you have precisely thirty seconds to tell me where I can find Lord Anthony before I call the police!'

Ari walked swiftly along the landing and down the main

staircase, and marched back into the study. Mrs Trevathan hurried to catch up with him and entered the room panting with exertion. She watched as Ari lifted the receiver, his fingers paused above the dial. There was a stand-off for a few seconds before Mrs Trevathan capitulated.

'Stop, please . . .' Her voice trailed off as she collapsed in tears into a chair. 'I knew that upsetting his routine would be bad for him. As long as he has peace and quiet and privacy, we can cope between us. It's all this disruption that's done it, I should have seen it coming.'

'Look, just tell me where they might be and I'm sure we can sort all this out without involving the police.'

Mrs Trevathan gave a final breath of surrender.

'We'll need to take your car.'

46

As she went through the ritual of drinking tea with Alice, a thousand thoughts ran through Rebecca's mind. She made the polite responses Alice seemed to require to keep her happy, and Rebecca's slowly awakening mind began to mull over the past few weeks and slot the answers into place.

'Isn't this fun? We're having a tea party together!'

'Yes.'

'Mummy simply worshipped you, you know, Violet,' Alice said. 'She kept your suite of rooms pristine, she made sure the servants dusted them every day, had fresh linen put on your bed, flowers in all the vases. Of course, you were dead, but she always said I'd meet you one day. I think she meant in heaven, but here you are on earth! Isn't that just lovely?'

'Yes,' Rebecca answered obediently.

'Of course, whilst you weren't here, whilst you were up there, Mummy liked to pretend that *I* was Violet.' Alice stroked her hair. 'Mummy always said I was the spitting image of you when I was a child. She grew my hair long and I wore it in pretty silk ribbons. She used to buy me the most beautiful dresses, sent from Harrods, just like this one I'm wearing now.'

'It's very beautiful,' Rebecca said, having learned fast that Alice liked flattery.

'Thank you. It's so nice to sit here and have a pleasant conversation with another young lady. Mummy was never keen on boys – or men, for that matter. Nasty, aggressive, smelly things, she always said. Much better to be a girl. I remember her telling me they were only useful for one thing, and I think we both know what that is, my dear.' Alice tittered and a genuine blush came to her cheeks.

'I'm sure your mother was right,' said Rebecca. The more Alice said, the more Rebecca was starting to understand.

'You know, I was so lonely as a child. Mummy didn't let me have any other little girls over to play, so I had no friends. I wish you could have been here then.' Alice mused sadly. 'We do get on well, don't we? We're so similar, aren't we?'

'Yes,' said Rebecca, 'and I'm so sorry you were lonely.'

'Well, as a matter of fact, I made up an imaginary friend called Amy. We used to talk for hours, although I knew she wasn't real. But now I have you. I want you to stay with me forever. You won't leave me, will you?' Tears suddenly filled Alice's eyes.

'No, of course I won't.'

'My mother left me, you see, and then I was completely alone. And do you know, I really don't think she liked me very much. She was always shouting at me. I –'

Rebecca watched as Alice began to cry, the tears sending rivulets of black mascara down her cheeks.

'Can I get you a handkerchief?' Rebecca offered, grasping a reason to rise from the chair.

'Thank you, you are so very sweet,' Alice replied gratefully. 'They're just over there, in the drawer by the bed.'

Rebecca realised it was now or never. She stood up and headed as fast as she could for the bedroom door, threw it opened and stumbled down the narrow staircase. She reached the front door and turned the handle desperately, but it was stuck fast.

'Where are you going? Come back!'

As Rebecca turned back down the hallway towards the rear of the cottage, praying there was another way out, she heard Alice thumping down the stairs behind her.

'Help!' Rebecca shrieked in terror as she found herself in the kitchen. Banging the door shut in Alice's face, she groped around in the pitch-black trying to find a back door. She could hear Alice was in the room with her now, stumbling over furniture.

'Where are you, Violet? Please, I don't like this game. I'm afraid of the dark . . .'

Unable to find a way out, Rebecca backed into a corner and slid down the wall as she heard Alice coming towards her.

'There you are!' The huge hands pulled Rebecca to a standing position. 'I don't like this game. Why don't you come back upstairs with me and we can play dressing up?'

'Please . . . let me go,' Rebecca moaned as Alice dragged her clumsily across the kitchen. Then she heard a door open from somewhere in the room.

'Now, come along, dear, stop being naughty and let your friend go,' said a familiar, gentle voice. 'I know you're only playing, but really, Mummy won't be happy at all with you if she hears about this, will she?'

There was a pause before the hands holding her let go. Rebecca slumped to the floor like a discarded rag doll.

'Mr Malik, can you switch the light on, please? These two naughty children have been playing "murder in the dark".'

Suddenly, the room was illuminated and, dazed, Rebecca saw Mrs Trevathan and Ari standing in the kitchen.

'I'm sorry, Brenda,' said Alice, 'I've been a naughty girl, haven't I?'

'You have a bit, yes, but if you're good and come quietly with me, I promise not to tell Mummy. Come on now, dear.' Mrs Trevathan held out her hand. 'It's time for your new friend to go home.'

'But I don't want her to go. Please, Brenda, can't she stay? I . . .'

Rebecca and Ari watched as Alice's bottom lip wobbled and she began to weep.

'If you're a good girl, perhaps your new friend can come back and play tomorrow.'

'Please, can she? I'm so lonely all by myself, so lonely . . .'

'I know, dear, but it's very late. Now,' she said pointedly to Ari, 'I'm going to take this child upstairs and get her ready for bed. Why don't you take your little girl home with you and maybe they can play together another time. All right?'

Ari, who was staring in shock at the creature holding Mrs Trevathan's hand, nodded mutely.

'Goodnight, then, and thank you for coming,' said Mrs Trevathan firmly.

As Ari pulled Rebecca to her feet and half carried her out of the back door to his car, they could hear Mrs Trevathan's voice continuing to talk calmly. He placed Rebecca gently in the passenger seat.

'Are you hurt?' he asked as he climbed behind the wheel and started the engine. 'Should I take you straight to hospital?'

'Just get me away from here,' she moaned. 'And from that terrible – *thing*.'

'Did he hurt you, Rebecca? Really, even though I promised Mrs Trevathan I wouldn't call the police if she told me where he'd taken you, what I've just seen goes beyond that.'

'I'm not hurt, honestly. Just get me away from here!' Rebecca repeated with a sob.

'Okay,' he said. 'Don't worry, sweetheart, I'm taking you somewhere safe.'

As he drove across the moors, Ari picked up his cellphone and called Steve.

'Rebecca's with me. I won't go into detail, but I need to take her to a hotel and I'd like you to telephone the doctor she saw the other day and have him come and check her over.'

'Is she hurt?'

'I don't think so, no, but she definitely needs to be looked at.'

'Right, well, bring her here to my hotel in Ashburton and I'll contact reception immediately. I'm sure they can find her a room. If not, she can have mine.'

'And get the doctor there as soon as you can.'

Steve gave Ari the address and he set his satnav to the post-code.

When they arrived at the hotel, Ari was grateful that Steve had managed to procure a suite for Rebecca. He had left a message with reception telling Ari to contact him if there was anything more he could do.

Rebecca let Ari steer her towards the lift and then along a corridor to her rooms.

'I don't have anything with me,' Rebecca said, sighing wearily as Ari helped her up onto the bed.

'Where's your suitcase?' he asked.

'In a bush somewhere in Astbury's grounds.' She gave him a weak smile.

'Never mind. I'll go and collect it tomorrow. There's nothing you need urgently, is there?'

Before she could reply, they heard a knock on the door, and Ari went to answer it.

'Good evening,' said Dr Trefusis, 'or should I say, good morning? I'm sorry it's taken a while for me to get here, I was with another patient. How is she?'

'From what I can see,' said Ari, 'she's physically unharmed but very shaken. Can I explain what happened?'

'No need for that,' the doctor said quietly. 'The patient I've just been attending to is Lord Astbury. Mrs Trevathan sent for me.'

'I see. Where is he now?'

'Still at the cottage on the moors. I've given him a heavy sedative, which means he'll sleep soundly until I organise things for him in the morning. Mrs Trevathan is watching over him. The chances are he'll wake up tomorrow and remember nothing of what happened tonight. Anyway, let me see how Miss Bradley is.'

'Of course. I'll give you some privacy.' Ari tactfully withdrew from the room as Dr Trefusis walked over to Rebecca.

'I hear you've had a bit of a time tonight,' he said gently as he sat down on the edge of the bed and took her limp hand in his to feel her pulse. 'Did he harm you?'

'No.' Rebecca was so exhausted, she could barely string a sentence together. 'But he put a cloth over my face that smelt strong and I lost consciousness, then I woke up in some house. I still don't know where it was.'

'I'm pretty sure he used chloroform, which is what surgeons used years ago to knock a patient out. It's harmless, with no long-term side-effects. Mrs Trevathan thinks he probably found it in the medical cupboard in the pantry. I dread to think how old it is. She's handed me the bottle and I'll have its contents analysed tomorrow just to make sure.'

'I thought –' Rebecca licked her dry lips – 'that I'd never get away from him.'

'I'm sure you did, Miss Bradley. It's been a terrible shock for you. All I can do is reassure you and say that I've known about Lord Astbury's condition ever since I took over the medical practice from my father. And it's extremely doubtful that, however upset and confused he was tonight, he would have hurt you.'

'He thought I was his grandmother Violet,' murmured Rebecca.

'Yes, Mrs Trevathan did tell me that.'

'Oh my God! He doesn't know where I am, does he? He won't come after me, will he?' She gripped his forearm as terror appeared in her eyes.

'You're perfectly safe, Rebecca, trust me. He has no idea where you are, and he's so heavily under sedation at present that he doesn't know where he is either. Now, I'm not going to make you relive what happened tonight, but let's have a look at you.'

As the doctor prodded and poked her, checking her vital signs, Rebecca lay still. There were so many questions she wanted to ask him, but her muddled, exhausted brain couldn't find the energy to voice the words.

'How's the headache?' he asked as he listened to her heart.

'Terrible just now.'

'Well, the chloroform Lord Astbury used won't have done it any favours. As a matter of fact, I was going to come by and see you tomorrow morning, because I think I've discovered what's been making you feel so ill.'

'Really?'

'Yes. And I can at least reassure you on that count; there's absolutely nothing to worry about,' he smiled.

'Am I pregnant?'

'No, Rebecca, you're not. In fact, all the tests came back negative. Anyway, I'll explain my theory tomorrow. For now –' Dr Trefusis reached into his bag and pulled out a couple of tablets – 'I suggest you take these. They're a light sedative, which will calm you down and help you sleep.'

'What's wrong with Anthony? Why was he dressed up like a little girl? He called himself Alice. I—'

'It's a very long story, Miss Bradley, and one which I'd be happy to explain at length tomorrow, when you've had some rest. But for now, my prescription for you is to tell you that you're physically fine, very safe here and the best thing you can do is sleep.' Dr Trefusis stood up. 'I'll tell the young man outside he can come back in now. Goodnight.'

Outside, Ari was pacing up and down. 'How is she?'

'As you said, unharmed but very frightened. And I don't blame her.'

'I saw him in his – costume, and even I was terrified,' admitted Ari. 'I know Rebecca won't feel safe until he's under lock and key. Surely we should be calling the police after what has happened to her tonight? After all, he abducted her.'

'If that's what Miss Bradley decides she wants, then yes, she should call them,' Dr Trefusis agreed. 'But I'd like to talk to her before she does so. I'll be back to see her early tomorrow morning. Goodnight.'

Ari watched the doctor leave and re-entered the suite. He perched on the edge of the bed and took Rebecca's hand in his. 'How are you?'

'Okay,' she mouthed, her eyes closed.

'Are you comfortable with me staying in here with you tonight? I can sleep on the sofa in the sitting room next door again.'

'No!' Her hand gripped his and she opened her eyes. 'Please don't leave me alone. Please stay in here, Ari.'

'Of course, if that's what you'd prefer.'

'Yes, thank you,' she said and her grip relaxed. 'So many questions,' she said, sighing.

'I know,' he said, trying to comfort her, 'but they're not for now. Please, Rebecca, try to get some sleep,' he said as he walked to the chair in the corner of the room.

'Ari?' she asked shyly.

'Yes?'

'Would you come and hold me? Then I'll know it if you leave.'

'Yes, but do you mind if I climb onto the bed next to you? It might be easier than trying it from here.' He grinned at her.

'Of course.'

Ari climbed onto the bed and Rebecca turned over and snuggled into his arms like a child.

'Thank you for being here,' she murmured wearily.

'That's okay. Sleep well, Rebecca,' he whispered.

As a pale but calm Rebecca sat nursing a cup of coffee in her suite the next morning, Dr Trefusis spoke to her.

'Lord Astbury was diagnosed as a schizophrenic when he was in his mid-thirties. He had a breakdown after his mother died and exhibited similar behaviour to what you saw last night. Hardly surprising he lost the plot – his mother, Daisy, controlled him completely, hardly letting him out of her sight for his entire life. Anyway, he was taken into the local psychiatric hospital, where he spent almost a year being stabilised with drugs and constant therapy. No one knows exactly what triggers this condition, whether it's nature or nurture, but certainly, given Lord Astbury's difficult childhood, I'm sure that had an effect.'

'He talked to me when he was –' Rebecca swallowed – 'dressed up. He said his mother bought him beautiful dresses from Harrods. Surely, that can't be true?'

'Sadly, it's perfectly true. Lord Astbury's mother, Daisy, had been brought up by her grandmother to believe that all men were evil. So, when she herself was forced to marry and produce an heir to the estate, and that heir turned out to be a boy, she refused to accept it,' Dr Trefusis explained. 'You can ask Mrs Trevathan, or in fact, her mother, Mabel, who have both known him all of his life. She put ribbons in Lord Astbury's long hair and he wore dresses every day of his childhood.'

'Oh my God, that poor child,' Rebecca said. 'You know, thinking about it, I saw a photograph in his study of a little girl who looked just like Anthony. I thought it was his sister, but it must have been him. What about his father?' she asked. 'Didn't he have something to say about it?'

'From what my own father said, who took over from his father and was Daisy's doctor at the time, Lord Astbury's father was an absentee husband and parent. The marriage had been no more than a pragmatic arrangement in the first place.

However much Maud Astbury loathed men, she accepted one was needed for her granddaughter to produce an heir. The man she chose for Daisy turned out to be a renowned drunkard and he spent most of his time in London, frittering away the estate's money. He died there when Lord Astbury was very young.'

'Yes, Anthony told me that once. So it was just Maud, Daisy and Anthony at the Hall as he grew up?'

'Yes, and then Maud died, which should have helped, but by then the damage was done.' Dr Trefusis shook his head slowly. 'Daisy refused to send Anthony away to school, and instead had him tutored by a collection of female governesses. Her obsession with Violet, her beautiful but dead mother, didn't end either. Lord Astbury was brought up to idolise her.'

'Yup, I got that much,' said Rebecca, irony in her voice.

'Anyway, when he was deemed stable enough to be returned into the community after his breakdown, he came home to Astbury under the care of Mrs Trevathan, who had worked at the Hall as housekeeper for years and understood him. I swear, Miss Bradley, that woman is a saint. She's dedicated most of her life to his care.' Dr Trefusis sighed. 'And as long as all was calm and nothing disrupted the tranquillity and privacy of Astbury Hall, Lord Astbury could function perfectly well. He loved pottering around his beloved garden, which was therapy in itself. The drugs he took every day stabilised him so at least he could have a modicum of normality. He would occasionally disappear off to the cottage on the moors to enjoy what Mrs Trevathan rather euphemistically called "playing house" and "dressing up". We both felt it was better if he indulged his alter-ego somewhere isolated where he wouldn't be seen. I checked up on him regularly, of course, as did his psychiatrist, and Mrs Trevathan would contact me if there was any cause for concern. He went for a number of years without having a relapse.'

'I see,' said Rebecca.

'But earlier this year, he decided to let the film company use the Hall. Money is tight at Astbury and he needed to pay some bills. Mrs Trevathan was against it from the start. She knew him well enough to know he almost certainly couldn't cope, but what could she do?'

'Nothing, I suppose.' Rebecca shrugged.

'Then, of course, you arrived. And immediately, Anthony saw a likeness to his dead grandmother, Violet, whom he'd been brought up to believe by his mother was the perfect woman, and the woman his alter-ego is modelled on.'

'The first time Anthony met me in my ordinary clothes, he didn't react at all,' mused Rebecca. 'It was only when he saw me with my hair dyed blonde in my 1920s costume that he told me I was like her.'

'Yes, I'm sure he felt he was seeing a ghost. And at the same time – and I'm partly surmising here, because I haven't yet read the psychiatrist's report – he was also having a normal *masculine* reaction to you as a woman. And this sent him into total confusion. Both personalities were in conflict with each other, both destabilised. As the main, male part of Anthony fell in love with you, the "little girl" didn't understand what Violet was doing back, because you were supposed to be dead. Do you see, Miss Bradley?'

'Yes,' Rebecca said slowly, 'sadly I do. And everything you've said fits in with what he told me last night. You know, I also saw him dressed up the other night at the Hall. Mrs Trevathan swore it was her elderly mother I'd seen, but of course, it wasn't. And I'd heard him singing before too, in a weird high-pitched voice. I'm also pretty sure he came into my bedroom at night,' Rebecca added with a shudder. 'I smelt the perfume.'

'I do apologise, Miss Bradley. I know Mrs Trevathan feels very guilty about letting it get so far without taking action. Normally, Lord Astbury's alter-ego doesn't make an appearance at the Hall itself. And to be fair to Mrs Trevathan,' he added, 'she was only trying to protect him.'

'Well, she certainly knew the day after I'd seen Anthony in the bedroom. It completely freaked me out. She lied to me, Doctor,' Rebecca reiterated.

'I know, Miss Bradley, but do try and forgive her. She was trying to protect Lord Astbury, because she knew that if he *were* having a relapse, he'd end up back in the psychiatric hospital. And he hated it there.'

'I do understand, but all this doesn't let Anthony, or whoever he thought he was last night, off the hook for drugging me, kidnapping me and then tying me up in some cottage in the middle of nowhere!' Rebecca put her hand to her brow. 'I'm trying to listen to the reasons why I should just drop this, but I genuinely thought I might die last night!'

'I'm sure you were terrified, Miss Bradley. I'm so very sorry. I feel responsible too, as I should have also seen the warning signs sooner,' Dr Trefusis said guiltily. 'You'll be relieved to know that, as of now, Lord Astbury is under lock and key at a secure psychiatric hospital, which will give him the help he requires. As to whether you bring in the police, that decision must be up to you. Although, the chances are, if you did press charges, Lord Astbury would only end up exactly where he is now. Besides,' he reminded her, 'you'd both have to endure dreadful media coverage.'

'I'm aware of that,' Rebecca said. 'How long will he be in the hospital for?'

'Until his psychiatrist believes he's once again stable. Given his current state, I would say that could be many months, if not years, away. Sadly, he may never be well enough to leave.'

'You know, I always felt there was something childlike about Anthony, even when he was himself. I felt like I wanted to protect him somehow . . .' Rebecca found her eyes suddenly filling with tears. 'He was such a gentle man, but the horror I saw him become last night – my God, I can't describe how awful it was.'

'Miss Bradley, for your own sake and his too, please try to remember Lord Astbury as the kind, highly intelligent man you knew, not the freak of nature you saw last night. Given what he suffered as a child, he deserves our pity. He never really stood a chance of a normal existence. And you can certainly rest assured he won't be causing anyone a problem for a very long time.'

'I understand that. And I do feel desperately sorry for him,' she agreed.

'Now before I forget, I want to discuss the possible cause of your headaches.' Dr Trefusis dug in his Gladstone bag for his papers. 'As I said to you last night, your blood tests all came back negative. However, I did notice slightly higher adrenaline levels than normal in one of them. Tell me, Miss Bradley, do you suffer from hay fever?'

'Why yes.' Rebecca was surprised. 'I get it very badly in the States. I noticed my eyes were itchy and Mrs Trevathan said that it was a reaction to the ragwort, or ragweed, as I'd know it, which grows nearby here.'

'Right, next question: have you by any chance been drinking chamomile tea?'

'Yes, Mrs Trevathan made me some regularly; she said it was good for relaxing. I've been drinking two or three cups of it a day.'

'Then I think we may have the cause of the problem,' Dr Trefusis said, relieved. 'Ragwort and chamomile are from the same plant family, and an allergic reaction to the two taken concurrently can occasionally create an adverse reaction in the bloodstream – especially if the tea is freshly made from an indigenous local species. And cause symptoms like the ones you've described. Severe headaches and constant nausea being the most common ones. I would surmise this is what's been the cause of your problem, Miss Bradley. So,' Dr Trefusis said, his eyes twinkling, 'next time I see Mrs Trevathan I'll tell her that, unwittingly, she *was* poisoning you!' He closed his bag and smiled at her. 'Stay off the chamomile tea from now on and let's see if those symptoms of yours abate. Now, I've left you more sedatives in case you need them, and if you have any further problems, of course I'd be glad to come and see you.'

'Thank you for all your assistance, Doctor,' she said as he walked towards the door. 'I'll have a think about what to do with the Anthony situation.'

'Of course. Goodbye now.'

Dr Trefusis made his way to the lift and took it down to the lobby.

'How is she?' asked Ari, who had been pacing back and forth, waiting for the doctor's return.

'Doing remarkably well under the circumstances,' he commented. 'She may look fragile, but she's a tough young lady.'

'I think she's been incredible so far,' Ari said. 'Before you go, Doctor, there is just one other matter which I'd very much like to discuss with you.'

'Concerning what?'

Dr Trefusis listened as Ari began to explain.

Ari made sure Rebecca had eaten lunch and then suggested she take a rest. An hour later, there was a knock at the door and Ari went to open it.

'How is she?' James Waugh asked. 'May I come in?'

'Of course you can,' Rebecca called, smiling as she entered the sitting room.

'Oh good!' James bounded into the room and came to hug her.

'Rebecca, if you've got company, would it be okay if I pop out for an hour or so?' Ari asked her.

'Yes, that's fine,' she agreed.

'I won't be long,' he said, 'and I'll retrieve your suitcase from the Hall on the way back.'

'Thanks, Ari.'

'You've obviously got him where you want him, darling,' James commented when Ari had left. 'Anyway, do tell all. You can imagine the film set is awash with gossip about what exactly happened to you last night. I've heard stories about you being dragged off to some godforsaken cottage on the moors by Lord Astbury.'

'Who told you that?' said Rebecca, horrified.

'Who knows where the story came from originally, but I'm sure it's been blown out of all proportion. Has it?'

As Dr Trefusis had rightly pointed out, the last thing Rebecca needed was for the story to hit the newspapers. It was the kind that would stick; she would be asked about it forevermore on chat shows. All she wanted to do was forget about it and move on.

'He asked me to marry him and didn't take it well when I refused,' Rebecca said briefly, with a hint of irony in her voice.

'My goodness,' said James, sitting down on the bed and stealing some grapes from the fruit bowl. 'Bees round the proverbial honey pot with men and you! And what about the handsome Indian who's playing your protector? Is he another one of your suitors?'

'Ari's been wonderful,' said Rebecca defensively. 'But he's just a friend.'

'If you say so,' James said with a smirk. 'Anyway, darling, it's good to see you looking more like your old self.'

'Yes, I've told Steve that I should be fine to continue shooting tomorrow.'

'Well, I don't mind the delay in the slightest. As all the scenes I have left are with you, I've had a pleasant few days off.'

'With the waitress to keep you company?'

'Touché!' James grinned. 'She's stalking me now, following me around the hotel. I think she wants to have my babies. Sadly, that's not in my life plan just at the moment. Well, I'll leave you to it, but if you fancy a light supper later, I'd be more than happy to keep you company.'

'Thanks, James, but I think I'll stay put in here and have an early night,' said Rebecca.

His eyes narrowed as he looked at her. 'So, where am I currently in the queue for your affections? I must be going up the ranks as you slowly dispatch them.'

Rebecca gave him a friendly punch on his arm. 'You're a player, James. I know you're not serious.'

'No, probably not,' he agreed. 'But I do hope we'll keep in touch when you go back Stateside. Seriously, Rebecca, I've really enjoyed your company. It's been fun. Robert's said there's been a real chemistry on-screen between us. You never know, we could become the next Olivier and Leigh, or Brad and Angie! Anyway, I'm off to see if my pet waitress will serve me a nice cream tea downstairs.' James kissed her warmly and stood up. 'See you later, darling.'

When Ari arrived at Dr Trefusis' house, he followed him back to the kitchen.

'Do you fancy a cup of tea? I'm just about to put the kettle on.'

'Thanks.'

'As you asked, I've sifted through all my grandfather's patient records for 1922 and haven't found any details on the death of a child by the name of Moh Chavan or Prasad, on or around the dates you gave me.'

'Well,' Ari said with a sigh, 'I'm hardly surprised, to be honest.'

'I'm a little confused about what happened to your relative. You said a death certificate was issued for him?' the doctor asked as he pulled out two mugs from a cupboard.

'Yes.' Ari reached into the plastic file and pulled out the certificate. 'You can see it was signed by your grandfather. But I've looked on all the parish and public records for this area and there seems to be no record of it anywhere.'

'How odd.' Dr Trefusis leaned over Ari's shoulder to study the certificate. 'Yes, that's my grandfather's signature, but by law he'd have had to send the duplicate to be officially registered.'

'I've checked every public record online too, and there's not a trace. Of course,' he said, 'his mother never believed Moh did die that day.'

'Really?' Dr Trefusis was obviously surprised. 'So, did he?'

'No. Mabel Smerden was able to confirm he didn't die. She's sure that Moh was taken to an orphanage somewhere in London that day.'

'By whom?' said Dr Trefusis, sitting down opposite him.

'I'm sorry to say, by your grandfather.'

Ari was waiting for a defensive reaction and was surprised when the doctor only lowered his eyes.

'Sadly, it doesn't surprise me. I'm not sure of the circumstances surrounding your relative's birth, but I can confirm that my grandfather aided a number of young women who found themselves in trouble. When the babies were born, he'd remove them discreetly to a number of church-run orphanages. You do understand, Mr Malik, that the world was a very different place in those days.'

'I'm certainly beginning to, yes.'

'My grandfather wasn't a bad man,' the doctor said. 'He did what he could to help. In fact, I can help you with the names of the orphanages my grandfather used. Goodness knows whether any of them are still open today, but it's worth a try. Wait here.'

Dr Trefusis stood up and was back a few moments later with a slim leather book. 'This was my grandfather's medical contacts book, containing addresses and numbers of local hospitals, names of surgeons and the like. At the back are the addresses of three orphanages. Only one of them is in London. Shall I write down the details of it for you?'

'Thank you, although, as you say, who knows if it's still open?' Ari sighed. 'Also, I have no idea whether Moh retained his birth name or not, although I can be accurate as to the day he would have been taken there. It was the day Donald Astbury died.'

'Really? Well, you can check online, I'm sure,' Dr Trefusis suggested. 'And if you don't have any luck, please feel free to contact me and I'll see what else I can do to help. I must admit I'm now intrigued to hear more of the story.'

'Mabel Smerden is the one to ask, although she swore me to secrecy. Anyway, I mustn't take up any more of your time,' Ari said as he stood up. 'I'll let you know if I find out what happened to him.'

'Please do that. By the way, how is that delightful patient of mine doing?'

'Extremely well, thanks,' said Ari as Dr Trefusis walked with him to the front door.

'I must admit to being very taken by her. I'm hardly surprised Lord Astbury was too. You're a very lucky man, Mr Malik.' The doctor smiled at him. 'Goodnight.'

On his way back to Ashburton, Ari turned in to the Astbury Hall drive, parked his car in the courtyard and went off in search of Rebecca's suitcase. It took him quite a time to locate the bush where Rebecca had dumped it, but when he did, he stowed it in the back of his car. Then he went inside the Hall and made his way up to the attics to say goodbye to Mabel Smerden.

She smiled when she saw him. 'Have you got time for a cup of tea, my love?' she asked him.

'No, Mrs Smerden, sadly I haven't. But I just wanted to say goodbye. I leave for London tomorrow and I saw Dr Trefusis this afternoon. He gave me the name of an orphanage in London, so I'm going to investigate it whilst I'm there.'

'Good for you, and do let me know if you find out what happened to him, won't you?'

'I will, and thank you for trusting me.'

'I'm glad for all of us that the truth has finally come out. My mum, Tilly, thought Anahita was a wonderful woman.'

'She was,' Ari said proudly.

'Oh, and by the way, I looked this out for you.' Mabel reached for a photo in a frame on the table beside her and handed it to Ari. 'It's the photo of the late Lord Astbury, Anahita and Moh that my dad took from the cottage by the brook.'

Ari gazed in wonder at the three people in the photograph. Their story was part of him now; he felt it in his bones. 'Thank you, Mabel, I will treasure this all my life. Goodbye.'

Ari walked downstairs to retrieve his own possessions from his room. He studied Donald's diary, before putting it in his holdall with the photograph. Anthony certainly wouldn't have need of it now and it was his family history too.

Taking his holdall down to the main entrance hall, he paused for a few seconds under the great dome, thinking of Anahita and all that she had suffered at the hands of the Astburys. He was still wondering why it had been him whom Anahita had trusted to discover the story.

And then he heard it, soft at first, so soft he simply wondered whether his ears were ringing. But then, as the singing gained in strength, a pure, perfect sound that seemed to swell upwards towards the vast dome above him, he was filled with a strange but beautiful euphoria.

Ari found tears in his eyes as he stood looking up, finally understanding everything, knowing then that Anahita had passed on far more than just her story to him.

47

That evening, Ari and Rebecca ate supper together in her suite.

'You're amazing,' he said as he poured her a small glass of wine. 'If I'd had to go through what you did last night, I'd have been a wreck, I'm sure.'

'Well,' Rebecca shrugged, 'I suppose I kind of understand weird behaviour. Even though my mother wasn't schizophrenic like Anthony, when she drank she could behave aggressively. So I'm used to the strange side of human nature. It's you who's the hero, Ari, refusing to take no for an answer and insisting Mrs Trevathan told you where he'd taken me. Thank God!' She shuddered.

'No wonder Anthony didn't want me investigating the cottage by the brook. He told me it was derelict when I asked him about it. Of course, the big question is whether you *are* related to Violet.'

'As I don't know who my father is, I'll probably never be able to find out. But you know what?' said Rebecca, 'I don't want to. The past is gone. I want to concentrate on the future now.'

'You're right, Rebecca, there's no point dwelling on the

past, as you said. I have to follow your lead, be strong and get on with my future, whatever that is.' Ari sighed.

'Well, I'll do my best to anyway. I admit that I cried buckets when I saw a photo of Jack with his new girlfriend in the newspaper they delivered to the room. Now that really hurt.' Rebecca stood up, walked to the sofa and reached underneath it, sheepishly producing a newspaper. 'It says, "*It's over! Jack bins Becks for his new love!*" I suppose I wasn't expecting anything less than I got,' she said in resignation.

'I'm sorry, Rebecca.'

'Don't be. It's for the best, really. I knew there'd be no going back once I told him to clean up his act. His pride wouldn't have been able to deal with it.'

'And are the media circling like vultures to get your side of the story?'

'Apparently so. My agent called me while you were out. At least they don't know I'm staying here for now anyway. But someone is sure to spill the beans – they always do.'

'God, Rebecca, your life isn't exactly easy, is it?'

'My agent wants me to put out a statement, and you know what? I've refused. I'm fed up of playing the game. Who gives a damn what other people think! I know what happened and that's all that matters. I'm so tired of it all.' Rebecca shook her head. 'You won't believe this, given the last twenty-four hours, but I'm actually sort of missing the peace and quiet of Astbury Hall. No one could get to me there with this kind of shit. I'm on a merry-go-round where my life is served up as public fodder and I just don't want it any more.'

'I understand,' said Ari.

'In fact, I'm dreading going back into it.'

'Speaking of going back, I have to tell you that I need to

leave tomorrow morning. I've got some things I must do in London before I fly home to India at the end of the week.'

'Do you really have to? I mean, I understand, of course.'

'You'll be safe now, I'm sure of that. Anthony is taken care of, you're here at the hotel with the film crew all around you and in a couple of days' time you'll be leaving yourself.'

'Yes, I will. So is tonight goodbye?'

'I suppose it is, yes.'

'Well, all I can say is thank you for everything you've done to help me over the past few days. I'll never forget it.'

'Or me, I hope.' Ari smiled at her.

'No, I couldn't forget you,' she said quietly. 'You know, a few days ago, I'd really convinced myself that I was related to Violet, somehow . . . And maybe I am, but there's no chance of me ever finding out.'

Ari looked at her and said, 'Why, can you not ask your parents?'

'No, my mother is dead and I have no idea who my father was. Anyway, as much as I hate to say it, I've got a busy day back on set tomorrow and I need to prepare. And I'm sure you have packing to do yourself,' she added.

'Okay. I'll leave you to it.'

They both stood up.

'Well,' she said, smiling brightly, 'I guess this is it.'

'Yes.'

They walked to the door in silence.

'Well, goodnight, and take care of yourself,' he said.

'I will.' Suddenly, Rebecca felt tearful. 'I'll walk with you to the elevator,' she said.

They left the room side by side and made their way to

the lift. He pushed the call button. Neither spoke as the lift arrived.

'Well, goodbye, Ari,' she said as he stepped inside and the doors began to close.

He pressed the button to halt the doors. 'Rebecca?'

'Yes, Ari?' she asked, her eyes downcast.

'Look at me.'

Rebecca looked up towards him and he read the emotion in her eyes. It mirrored his own.

'I want to say something before I go. We've both got a journey to finish over the next few days, and I have to return to India. But, I think we should meet again soon. Do you agree?'

The lift doors began to close again. This time, Rebecca put her finger on the button to stop the doors closing.

'Yes,' she said.

'I want to say also, that if you ever decide to come to India, please let me know.'

'I will.'

'Promise?'

'Promise.'

The doors began to close and Ari disappeared from view.

When she returned to Astbury Hall the following day to shoot her scenes, Rebecca felt a flutter of nerves.

'Try not to worry, Rebecca, we're all here to protect you from any amorous suitors lurking down darkened corridors,' said Steve comfortingly as he accompanied her into Make-up. 'Only one more day to go.'

'I'll be fine,' she answered, embarrassed that some version

of her story seemed to have already become known to the cast and crew.

Luckily, most of the filming was taking place outside and Rebecca was chauffeured back to the hotel the minute it was over.

Back at the hotel, Rebecca realised that now she was no longer staying at Astbury Hall, she couldn't wait to leave Devon. She felt claustrophobic in her suite, albeit the largest in the hotel, and she longed for the wide-open spaces she'd grown used to.

'God help me when I get back to New York,' she brooded, thinking of her apartment on the high floor of a gleaming steel tower, where she'd be trapped by the paparazzi as soon as she returned to the city.

But it wasn't just the sprawling gardens and wild, sweeping moors of Astbury she would be missing, she acknowledged. And it wasn't Jack, either. An emptiness she found difficult to describe had descended on her in the past twenty-four hours. Simply put, it was as if some part of her had disappeared, and there was a dull ache in place of it. Just now, she refused to acknowledge exactly what that might be.

On the final day of the shoot, once the director had called it a wrap, the cast and crew stood on the terrace in the glorious evening sunshine and drank champagne.

'Are you sorry it's over, Becks?' asked James.

'In many ways, yes. It's been an amazing experience. I think I've grown as a person, as well as an actress.'

'Indeed you have,' said Robert, putting his arm around her. 'Wonderful job, darling, really wonderful. Expect awards aplenty next year.'

'Thank you, Robert. I hope I didn't let you down.'

'Not at all, darling, not at all. And I hope we can work together again very soon.'

Rebecca glanced across the terrace and saw Mrs Trevathan serving the champagne. Rebecca had avoided speaking to her in the past two days, unwilling to confront what had taken place. But now she knew she must go and say her farewells. Whatever had happened, Mrs Trevathan had been very kind to her.

As the film crew began to pack up for the last time, Rebecca stepped inside the drawing room and went in search of her. She found her in the kitchen, washing up glasses.

'Hello,' she said shyly. 'I've just come to say goodbye.'

Rebecca watched Mrs Trevathan dry her hands on her apron and turn round to look at her, an expression of anguish on her face. 'Rebecca, I'm so sorry for what happened to you. I hold myself entirely responsible. I was the one person who should have seen where all this was heading.'

'Please don't blame yourself, Mrs Trevathan, I certainly don't. I think that you've been amazing caring for Anthony for all these years.'

'Well, we do what we must for those we love.' She sighed. 'Anyway, I hope you won't remember your time at Astbury as all bad.'

'Of course I won't. Putting what happened a few days ago aside, I loved being here. And what about you?' Rebecca asked her. 'What will you do with Anthony no longer living here at the Hall for a while?'

'The Astbury Estate is in the hands of the trustees now, dear. They'll have to decide what they think is best for the place. Even if they decide they're going to sell it, that'll take a while.'

'The trustees can do that? I thought it was only Anthony who could make that decision.'

'Yes, but sadly, His Lordship will be declared as not of sound mind. I was going to write to you, dear, because I've been to see him every day in hospital and he wants you to know how very sorry he is that he scared you. The trouble was that he fell in love with you, and that made him so confused, the poor thing.'

'I know, Dr Trefusis explained it to me. I'm so sorry.'

'No need for you to be sorry. You can't help being who you are, dear, nor the effect you had on him. Anyway, if you ever wanted to write to him, I know he'd appreciate your forgiveness. It might help him.'

'Yes, I will.' Rebecca watched Mrs Trevathan's face brighten at her acquiescence. 'So he's a little better, you say?'

'Well, it's early days, dear. I find it a bit difficult going to visit him; he cries a lot, you see, and asks to come home because he doesn't understand yet where he is. He's very confused, poor lamb. I can only hope they can stabilise him soon. That's why it would be wonderful if you wrote. He has no one else, you see, except me.'

'I will, I promise. But right now, I'd better be going. I'm leaving for London straight from here.'

'I bet you'll be glad to get back to your real life in New York.'

'Not just now, to be honest,' Rebecca admitted. 'I'll miss you, Mrs Trevathan, really.'

'Oh, stop it, dear, do! You'll make *me* all weepy. Just lovely, you are, dear, lovely. Now, come here and give me a hug.'

Mrs Trevathan opened her arms, and Rebecca went into them.

'Quite a time we've had here since you've arrived,' Mrs

Trevathan sighed as she released Rebecca. 'Are you going to see that young Indian chap again?'

'I don't know.'

'Well, it's none of my business, but I thought you fit together well. And better for you in the long term than some fly-by-night actor,' she added and the two of them were silent for a moment at the memory of Jack.

'Maybe.' Rebecca nodded.

'Well now, you go off and make me proud of you.'

'I'll try, I promise, and if ever, if *ever*,' Rebecca reiterated, 'you wanted to come across to New York and visit me, you know there'd be a place for you at my apartment for as long as you wanted.'

'Thank you, dear. But I think we both know I can never leave His Lordship, not even for a few days. You write to me as well, do you hear? And tell me what you're up to.'

'I will, I promise, Mrs Trevathan.'

'Oh, I've just remembered. I was going to ask you if perhaps you'd like to take this with you as a keepsake of your time here.'

Rebecca watched as Mrs Trevathan reached across the sink to the window ledge and retrieved the rose which Anthony had cut for her in the Astbury gardens.

'Can you believe it continued to bloom since I first put it up in your room all those weeks ago?' said Mrs Trevathan. 'Then after you left a few days ago, the first petal dropped off. But it's such a beautiful colour. Perhaps you could press it and keep it in a book? It might help you remember His Lordship as he was.'

'Yes,' said Rebecca, taking the rose. She understood why Mrs Trevathan wanted her to have it. She put it to her nose and inhaled the still-strong scent. 'Goodbye, Mrs Trevathan.'

'Goodbye, dear.'

Rebecca left the kitchen and walked across the main entrance hall. She paused under the great dome, remembering the first time she'd seen Anthony standing by the door.

'Goodbye,' she whispered into the silence.

48

Ari looked out of the window onto the leafy green of the city garden that surrounded the Victorian house. He could hear the chatter of children's voices playing outside.

'The registrar, Miss Kent, will see you now,' said the receptionist.

'Thank you,' said Ari, standing up and following the woman along a narrow corridor, the very particular smell of overcooked food reminding him of his own school days in England. He was ushered into a small, cluttered office, where an immaculate, tiny woman in her sixties sat behind a desk.

'Good afternoon, Mr Malik. I must tell you this is most irregular. You're meant to go through the process of contacting an official adoption agency, who will then contact us with details of your ancestor.'

'Do forgive me, Miss Kent, but for a number of reasons – the first one being that I'm not sure of the name he would have been given – and secondly, because I leave for India tomorrow, I've thrown myself on your mercy.'

'I see. May I ask how long ago it was that you believe your relative was brought in to the orphanage?'

'I believe it was eighty-nine years ago. In 1922, on the twenty-second of August.'

'Well, at least that is precise,' Miss Kent said. 'How old would he have been?'

'About three. He was of mixed race, an Anglo-Indian. And he had blue eyes. I believe he was probably brought here by a Dr Trefusis, although whether he'd have used his true surname either, I've no idea.'

'It seems you're very well informed, Mr Malik. Although I should warn you that it was rare for a child of that age, especially of mixed blood, to be accepted here. Forgive me for using a blunt analogy, but, a little like puppies, newborn babies were easier to re-home than older children. And finding families has always been the goal of this home for the children in our care. It was a cruel world back then, Mr Malik.'

Ari realised this woman called a spade a spade. 'The family was wealthy, so perhaps there was money offered?'

'Perhaps.'

Ari watched Miss Kent's keen eyes appraising him, as she weighed the unusual situation in her mind.

'Well, despite the fact that you've chosen to circumnavigate the system, Mr Malik, I'm pleased to tell you that our particular institution is allowed to release archived details to relatives after eighty years. You understand, of course, that this is because we assume the person in question is already dead and therefore won't be threatened by such personal information being passed on. Other places specify ninety or even one hundred and ten years before these kinds of records can be released. We're all living so much longer these days, you see.'

'Suffice to say, the relative I'm searching for is almost

certainly dead, although whether he died in infancy, or only ten years ago, is another question I currently can't answer.'

'Well, why don't we start with the date you've given me and see what the archives hold?' Miss Kent picked up the telephone and asked for the relevant ledger. A few moments later, a young woman appeared with a large leather-bound book.

'Thank you, Heather. Right, now let's see.'

Ari watched in an agony of suspense as she turned the pages to find the correct date. He knew that if this was a blind alley, he had nowhere else to go.

'Right, here we are, August the twenty-second . . .'

He waited with baited breath as she read what was written, grateful at least that there must be something noted down on the pages.

'Now, a baby boy was brought to the home at ten o'clock that evening by a Dr Smith. The child was a foundling, apparently, and had been dumped on the good doctor's doorstep.'

'Hardly,' muttered Ari.

'Mr Malik –' Miss Kent eyed him over her glasses – 'I can assure you that this was quite normal behaviour for desperate women. It was either the vicar or the doctor of the parish that usually received the little bundle of joy to be disposed of. And they did their utmost to help.'

'Of course.'

'And you're right.' Miss Kent turned her attention back to the ledger. 'The child was not named. He's described here as "of Eurasian appearance with blue eyes. Healthy, seems well nourished and approximately three years old. No distinguishing marks. Donation made."' Miss Kent looked over her glasses at Ari. 'Sound like him?'

LUCINDA RILEY

'Yes.' Ari felt a wave of emotion but did his best to control it.

'Don't blub just yet, Mr Malik,' said Miss Kent with a hint of a smile, 'there's more to come.'

'Did they name him?'

'They did.'

'And . . . ?'

'They called him Noah. Don't ask me why, perhaps there was a flood in London that day. Children here have been named for less and I think it's a rather distinctive name.'

'Yes, it is. What about his surname?'

'Adams. A good biblical name too. And do you know, that rings rather a large bell . . .'

'Noah Adams,' Ari repeated to himself. 'Did he stay here for long?'

'Patience, Mr Malik, I'm just checking something.'

Miss Kent had risen and moved towards a filing cabinet. She pulled out a folder and studied it. Then she turned to him, seemingly moved herself.

'Goodness,' she exclaimed.

'What is it?'

'It seems he became the esteemed trustee and member of our board whom I knew as Dr N. Adams.'

'You knew him?'

'Yes, I did. He was a wonderful man. He did so much for the home in terms of raising money and improving conditions for the children. He retired in his late seventies due to ill health and died a few years later. He was an institution here, I can tell you.'

Ari dug in his plastic wallet for the envelope Anahita had

654

sent from her solicitor and took out its contents. 'Do you by any chance know the exact date of his death?'

Miss Kent went back to the file and pulled out a photo-copy of an obituary. 'Here, this was in *The Times*. We kept it because it mentions he was a trustee of ours.'

Ari took it and read the date of Noah Adams's death. Then he compared it to the date Anahita had written down ten years ago in her weak, spidery writing just before she herself had died.

'Oh, my God.'

The dates were identical.

'Are you all right, Mr Malik? You seem shaken.'

'I am, forgive me.'

'Well, the good news is that you now have everything you need in order to learn more about his life, courtesy of *The Times*. How very strange,' mused Miss Kent as she walked to the photocopier. 'I knew that Dr Adams was here as a child himself but I never had reason to investigate further. I was extremely fond of him – we all were. There.' Miss Kent handed Ari the photocopy of the obituary.

'Thank you.' Ari looked down at the black-and-white photograph of an attractive, elderly man. And there was not a doubt left in his mind that he was staring at the features of his *own* bloodline. Still dazed, he tried to collect himself to think what more he could ask Miss Kent to fill in the blanks that the obituary wouldn't tell him. 'He was a kind man?'

'Oh yes. He used to visit the children once a week on a Wednesday and bring them cakes as a treat. They'd have tea together and he listened to them, Mr Malik, rather than talk-ing at them. And because we're a private institution and not government-run, Dr Adams did all he could to fundraise and improve facilities here. He also sponsored and encouraged the brighter children to take up places at university as he had himself. He was an inspiration to them.'

'My great-grandmother never believed her son had died, as she'd been told. Do you by any chance know if Dr Adams ever tried to find his real mother?'

'I don't, Mr Malik, and unfortunately, the person who could perhaps have told you – his wife, Samantha – also died a few years ago.'

'Did they have children?'

'Sadly, no. Dr Adams used to say that the children here were his family. In fact, on his wife's death, we discovered the two of them had bequeathed everything they had to the home. It's kept us going, Mr Malik, I can tell you.'

'Were they happily married?'

'I believe it was a real love match, and they certainly seemed devoted to each other when they visited. But you can read the details in the obituary.'

'Of course. Thank you, Miss Kent, for all your help. I really mustn't take up any more of your time.'

'Not at all. I'm only glad I could be of some assistance. Here's my card with my email on it. If you think of any further questions, don't hesitate to contact me.'

'I won't.' Ari tucked the card into his wallet, then stood up. 'Goodbye, Miss Kent.'

Having made a donation himself, Ari walked out of the building into the bright light of the July afternoon. There was a playground to one side, where a couple of young children were sitting in a sandpit with buckets and spades. Ari heard their cries of pleasure, saw the well-tended gardens and the immaculate paintwork on the old house.

This was Moh's legacy, he thought, as he found a bench and sat down in the sunshine to read the obituary. Anahita would have been so very proud of her son, who had obviously inherited his mother's gift for medicine and his father's philanthropic nature.

Dr Noah Adams MB, BCh (Oxon), FRCOG, OBE

24 February 2001

The eminent obstetric surgeon Dr Noah Adams grew up in the Randall Home for Foundlings in Walthamstow, East London. Despite a less than easy childhood, Dr Adams won a scholarship to Oxford to study medicine. His time there was interrupted by the Second World War and he joined the medical corps, in which he served in France and later in East Africa. Returning to Oxford to complete his degree, he married Samantha Marshall, a British nurse he had met whilst out in France. Dr Adams moved to London and worked at St Thomas' Hospital, subsequently completing the necessary exams to be admitted to the Royal College of Surgeons. His speciality was obstetrics and the care of pregnant women in particular. He was a pioneer in the study and causes of pre-eclampsia, a life-threatening condition which can result in death to mothers and their unborn babies. Dr Adams wrote many eminent papers on the subject and on maternal health in general. Dr Adams was a trustee and on the board of governors of the children's home in which he had grown up, and was a tireless campaigner for orphaned children. He subsequently received an OBE from the Queen for his charitable work and research into obstetrics. Dr Adams leaves behind his widow, Samantha.

Ari only realised he was crying when he saw damp patches were blurring the photocopied words. Wiping his eyes, he sat in the sunshine watching the young children playing happily.

He took Moh Chavan's death certificate out of the plastic wallet, then tore it up and let the pieces flutter to the ground around him.

'I found him, Anahita,' he whispered as he looked upwards.

49

'I said I'm taking a break, Victor,' Rebecca repeated to her manager. 'And I won't be back for at least six months, maybe even a year.' *Maybe never*, she thought to herself.

'But, Becks! You're as hot as hell right now. I get that you need a break, but couldn't you come back home and maybe plan this for a year or so's time from now?'

'No. I'm leaving tomorrow,' replied Rebecca firmly.

'Well, personally, I think you're crazy. The media will assume it's because your heart is broken over Jack, and share those thoughts with the world.'

'Let them. You know what, Victor? I really don't give a damn.'

There was silence on the other end of the line. 'I just don't understand, Becks. All these years we've worked together planning your career, picking the right films. We get you to this point and then you say you're off! Hey, you're not pregnant, are you?'

'No, Victor, I'm not pregnant,' said Rebecca, wanting this conversation to be over. 'As I said, I just need a break.'

'Okay, so where are you going?'

'I'm not going to tell you. I get that you don't understand, but there's absolutely nothing you can say to change my mind. So I suggest we end this conversation. If you'd pay me whatever comes in to my checking account in the next few months, I'd be grateful.'

'Yeah, and it might be the last you'll receive as an actress if you go through with this scheme of yours. You know as well as I do how soon the phone can stop ringing and you're yesterday's news.'

'Goodbye, Victor, and really, thanks for everything.'

Rebecca put down the receiver and flopped back onto the bed in relief. Maybe she *was* crazy, but for the first time in her life, she didn't want to please anyone else. She needed to spend some time learning about the world and her place in it. She wasn't a commodity to be bought and sold, she was a human being. And if her career faltered in the time she was going to be away, then so be it.

As Marion Devereaux had said to her that day, it was knowing *herself* and gaining life experience which would truly improve her skills. She wasn't likely to see any of that living in her rarefied, privileged world playing make-believe women who always got a happy ending, being treated like a princess. She stared around her Claridge's hotel suite and smiled wryly, knowing there'd be none of this where she was going tomorrow.

She had left a couple of messages for Ari earlier, asking him to call her, but so far he hadn't. His silence hurt more than she cared to admit, but whether or not he was part of the deal, she wasn't going to change her mind. She knew that men and their demands had played far too big a role in her life so far. It was time she gained some respect for her own opinions and intelligence, rather than simply her beauty. Maybe then she could begin to form an honest and healthy relationship with someone else.

So, whether Ari Malik returned her message or not, tomorrow morning she was on a plane to India.

Ari arrived back at his hotel, had a quick bite to eat in the restaurant, then went up to his room. He collapsed fully clothed onto his bed, exhausted from the tension and emotion of the past few days. He woke at six the following morning, realising he had to leave immediately if he was to catch his flight. Throwing everything into his holdall, he checked out and hailed a taxi to take him to the airport. He looked at his cellphone, saw it was out of battery and cursed himself for falling asleep last night before he'd put it on charge. He would have liked to have said goodbye to Rebecca, reminded her how much he'd love to see her again, but now he'd have to wait until he was back home to do so.

Standing in the business class queue, Ari considered what he would be returning to. And it wasn't palatable. His grand but soulless apartment, followed by a day at the office catching up, did not appeal to him in the slightest. In fact, in the past twenty-four hours he'd been thinking he might sell the business and have done with it. He wanted to do something that felt worthwhile, like Anahita and Dr Adams had, not just earn himself financial security.

Maybe he would go straight to visit his mother, tell her what he'd discovered in England and ask for her advice. And, of course, he'd give Donald's diary to Muna, his grandmother. He'd asked Mrs Trevathan if he could borrow it for a while to show to her and she'd agreed.

'Well, His Lordship won't be missing it in the next few weeks,' she'd replied, sadly.

Receiving his boarding pass, he glanced at the queue in economy, thinking that at least his hard work had provided him with a few luxuries. As he did so, he spotted a girl in the queue with a rucksack on her back, dressed in a T-shirt, a pair of cut-off jeans and flip-flops. Her dark hair was pulled back into a short ponytail under a baseball cap and she wore no make-up. She looked vaguely familiar but he couldn't place her.

He was about to turn away when the faint sound of the singing he'd last heard at Astbury gently caressed his ears. He looked again more closely, and this time he did a double take as he watched the girl take slow steps towards the check-in counter.

Walking towards her, his face broke into a smile because he knew as he got closer it was her. He reached over the barrier separating business from economy and tapped her on the shoulder.

She turned round in surprise.

'Hello, what are you doing here?' he asked. 'I nearly didn't recognise you with your dark hair and cap. And may I say –' he smiled – 'that you now look absolutely nothing like Violet.'

'No.' She shrugged. 'I've realised that the whole thing was smoke and mirrors.' She looked at him and frowned. 'Didn't you get the message to call me?'

'No, I have no battery on my cellphone. So, what are you doing here?' he asked her.

'As you can see, I'm going to India.' She grinned at him and they both giggled.

'In economy?'

'Yup,' she said firmly. 'I want to do it properly.'

'I understand,' he said, nodding, 'but do you think that, on this one occasion, I might be able to persuade you to join me in Club? Remember, I am a native, and it would be sad if I weren't able to spend the next nine hours helping you work out where you should be looking in order to go and discover yourself, don't you think?'

She thought for a moment or two, then said, 'I do, yes.'

'And perhaps I could come along too for some of it? Continue in my role as your spiritual guide and protector? India can be a pretty dangerous place for a young lady alone, you know.'

'Really? As dangerous as Astbury?' She gave him an ironic smile.

'I seriously doubt it. Well, Rebecca, will you join me?' He reached his hand across the barrier and she took it. They stood there for a few seconds, smiling at each other.

'Yes,' she replied.

'Here, let me take that,' Ari said as he released her hand, slipped the rucksack gently off her shoulders and hauled it over the barrier. 'You next,' he said.

He stood there, waiting for her as she ducked under the barrier that had separated them.

'Hello.' He grinned.

'Hello.'

And then he took her into his arms.

Epilogue

India, 1957

Anahita

So, my story draws to a close, my child. All that remains is to tell you what happened when I returned to India. The Maharani welcomed me back into her arms as if I had never been away. The last ruby I discovered still safe in its hiding place under the pavilion, and I knew that beneath its dull, mud-covered exterior lay the key to my future freedom and independence.

Indira was desperate for me to accompany her back to her palace and take up my old role as her companion, travelling back and forth with her to Europe, but I declined her offer.

For you see, my Moh, I had been given a last gift by your father before he died. Only the heavens can explain how the tiny speck of life implanted inside me on the last night we spent together managed to weather the storms of my imprisonment, grief and subsequent illness, but survive it did. When I arrived back in Cooch Behar, it was confirmed by my old friend Zeena, the wise woman, that I was four months pregnant.

This time, there was no terror, only peace. Even though my heart broke over your loss, whether orchestrated by mere

667

physical absence or death, I felt that at least there was a flowering of new life from the ashes of tragedy.

Indira returned to her own palace, husband and child soon after our arrival, but I stayed in Cooch Behar. A strange, sleepy calm descended upon me as I grew fatter, like a brood mare in a field full of new-mown hay.

Your sister, Muna, was born on the fifth of June, 1923, with Zeena in attendance. And my new baby proved to be as relaxed and peaceful as her entry into this world had been. I wondered sometimes, as I nursed her in my arms in the small hours and looked down upon her, whether she had inherited my gift. But it transpired as she grew up that she had not. However, I know that, somewhere along the line, one of her children, or her children's children, will inherit it. And that I'll recognise it immediately when the time comes.

When Muna was five years old, I felt I must at last begin to form my own life, follow my dreams and move away from the protective shield of the palace.

Due mostly to my old matron at The Royal Hospital forwarding my nursing records from the time of the First World War, and a glowing reference from her, I was offered a placement at a local hospital and I began the official training necessary to become a nurse. Of course, my dream was always to become a doctor, but in 1928 in India, this was very rare for a woman.

But I made the most of my situation, and as India began to change, so did my opportunities. I became vociferous in my support of Gandhi, especially on the subject of women's rights. My dear son, it might be true to say that I began to gather myself rather a reputation.

As I write this, we are ten years into independence from

the British. The country still struggles to find its true identity, to believe it is capable of making decisions for itself after so many years of them being forced upon us. But I do believe we will get there. I'm currently, with the backing of Indira and her mother, setting up the first women's hospital of its kind in India. With the help of royal connections, we are consulting with some eminent obstetricians from all over the world.

One in particular, a doctor from England, has been most helpful to me. Dr Noah Adams works in St Thomas' Hospital on the women's wards themselves, and has therefore been of vital practical help, as I struggle to put the nuts and bolts of patient care into place. I hope that, one day, when our hospital is completed, he will have time to visit me here.

My dearest Moh, I have come to the end of my story. If you are alive, as I've always believed you are, I wish you happiness, peace and contentment. And I can only pray that, if not in our lifetime, we will meet again when we pass over.

My child, always know that you were truly loved.

Your devoted mother,

Anahita x

Acknowledgements

I'd like to thank my publishers around the world, especially Peter Borland at Atria Books, who inspired me to have the confidence to take on such a daunting challenge as *The Midnight Rose*. I hope I've met it. A special thank you to Catherine Richards at Pan Macmillan, who so patiently collated the manuscript, Jeremy Trevathan, Almuth Andreae and Georg Reuchlein, Judith Curr, Jorid Mathiassen and Knut Gorvell, Fernando and Milla Baracchini, Annalisa Lottini and Donatella Minuto. Without their friendship, encouragement and support, my books wouldn't be reaching their audience.

There are many people who helped me with my research, including Raj Chahal, Dr Preema Vig, Rachel Jaspar at Coram, Line Prasad, Pallavi Narayan, Mark at 'All Experts', Radhika Artlotto, Greg and his staff at the Dhara Dhevi Hotel, Chiang Mai, for giving me not only the peace I needed to write Anahita's story, but also a short course in Ayurvedic medicine.

My wonderful PA, Olivia Riley (who says family can't work together successfully?), my fantastic friends and cheerleaders: Jacquelyn Heslop, Susan Boyd and Rita Kalagate, my mother, Janet, and my sister, Georgia. And of course, my husband Stephen and my children: Harry, Isabella, Leonora and Kit. All of whom make the hard work worthwhile.

And lastly, all the wonderful new friends and readers I've made as I've travelled around the world, whose enthusiasm and support inspire me to keep writing.

Bibliography

The Midnight Rose is a work of fiction set against a historical background. The sources I've used to research the time period and detail on my characters' lives are listed below:

Lionel D. Barnett, *Hindu Gods and Heroes: Studies in the History of the Religion of India* (Crest Publishing, 1995)

Deepak Chopra, *The Complete Book of Ayurvedic Home Remedies* (Piatkus Books, 1999)

Gayatri Devi, *A Princess Remembers: The Memoirs of the Maharani of Jaipur* (Rupa Publications, 1995)

E. M. Forster, *A Passage to India* (Penguin Publishing, 1995)

Rudyard Kipling, *Rewards and Fairies* (Folio Society, 1999)

Lucy Moore, *Maharanis: The Lives and Times of Three Generations of Indian Princesses* (Penguin, 2004)

Ruth Prawer Jhabvala, *Heat and Dust* (Abacus, 2011)

Trevor Royle, *Last Days of the Raj* (Michael Joseph Ltd, 1989)

Paul Scott, *The Raj Quartet* (Arrow; New Edn, 1996)

Amy Stewart, *Wicked Plants* (Algonquin Books, 2010)